...Even If It Meant
Forsaking Her Last
Chance At
Happiness

CANDACE CAMP

RAIN LILY

HarperPaperbacks
A Division of HarperCollinsPublishers

This is a work of fiction. The characters, incidents, and dialogues are products of the author's imagination and are not to be construed as real. Any resemblance to actual events or persons, living or dead, is entirely coincidental.

HarperPaperbacks *A Division of* HarperCollins*Publishers*
10 East 53rd Street, New York, N.Y. 10022

Copyright © 1993 by Candace Camp
All rights reserved. No part of this book may be used or reproduced in any manner whatsoever without written permission of the publisher, except in the case of brief quotations embodied in critical articles and reviews. For information address HarperCollins*Publishers*,
10 East 53rd Street, New York, N.Y. 10022.

Cover illustration by Roger Kastel

First printing: July 1993

Printed in the United States of America

HarperPaperbacks, HarperMonogram, and colophon are trademarks of HarperCollins*Publishers*

10 9 8 7 6 5 4 3 2 1

1

Maggie hadn't realized a storm was brewing until a thunderclap shattered the evening still. Startled, she jumped, and the brush she was pulling through her hair knocked painfully against her scalp. She laid down the brush and went to the window, pushing aside the curtain to look out. Menacing gray clouds had massed in the sky, obliterating the stars. Thunder rolled again, and lightning flashed, briefly illuminating the farmyard below.

It promised to be a hard spring Arkansas deluge. She'd better look in on the boys. Willy hated thunderstorms. She wrapped her robe around her, picked up the oil lamp, and crossed the landing to the bedroom opposite hers.

Holding her lamp up, she opened the door softly and peered inside. Will was curled up on his side in his narrow bed, and Maggie breathed a sigh of relief that he was sleeping through the disturbance.

Across the room, Ty was still awake, sitting up in bed, a book open in his hands and tilted to catch the meager light from the lamp burning low on the night table. At her entrance he glanced up and grinned sheepishly, knowing what she was thinking: *You're going to ruin your eyes reading in that light!*

Maggie had to smile back at him. She and her son could communicate without saying a word. They had always been close, alike not only in looks, with the same thick dark brown hair and wide gray eyes, but also in temperament. As a child, Maggie, too, had had a lively curiosity, though she had never been as serious as Ty. But, then, she had never had Ty's reasons to be.

The boy slipped off his bed and crossed the room to her, noiseless in his stockinged feet. "He's been asleep awhile now," he whispered, gesturing toward Will. "I think he'll be fine."

Maggie nodded. "I'm going downstairs to make sure all the windows are closed."

"I'll be here if he wakes up," Ty assured her.

"I know." She smiled at him again. She would have liked to lean over and plant a kiss on his forehead, but he was getting big enough that things like that embarrassed him. He was eleven now and already starting to be all arms and legs, his voice nearly baritone, yet sometimes sliding up into a squeak, startling them both. His tenuous maturity made Maggie's heart ache with both pride and regret. With a slight catch in her throat, she turned from her son and headed for the stairs.

The wooden risers were steep, and she descended carefully in the dim light from her lamp. Once downstairs, she began making the rounds of the windows and doors, hoping everything was closed tightly. She couldn't afford water damage to any of the curtains or furniture; they were all older than Ty and had to last many years yet.

Maggie had never been a spendthrift, but since the War she had learned to stretch every cent to the limit, and then some. The seemingly endless conflict, as well as the punishing Reconstruction measures imposed on the South, had all but crippled the rural economy on which she and most of her fellow Arkansans relied. With most of the men off fighting, commerce had ground to a standstill, and it had been a struggle even to raise enough crops to feed the women and children who remained on the land. Maggie couldn't remember the last time she had had a new dress, let alone funds for something as frivolous as more stately tables or chairs.

It was raining harder now, and she could hear the wind frantically whipping through the trees. Lightning flared, and in its brief flash she could see bushes tossing and the rain coming down in hard, slanting sheets. She hurried into the kitchen and saw to her dismay that the window above the dry sink stood open a couple of inches. Setting her lamp on the counter, she leaned over the sink to tug down the window sash. At that moment another lightning bolt lit the sky, and in the eerie white glare she was sure she spotted the dark silhouette of a man skulking across the farmyard toward the barn.

Her heart began to slam in her chest, and for an instant she couldn't breathe, couldn't think. But the panic lasted only for a moment. Maggie had been on her own for a long time now, and she was used to handling whatever came up. She ran to the back door and made sure the lock was turned before she went to the gun cabinet in the hallway beyond the kitchen.

With only slightly trembling hands she pulled out the rifle and loaded it. Then she returned to the kitchen window. She peered out into the yard again, but she could make out little except the vague outline of the barn and the wind-tortured cherry tree nearby.

Staring out into the black night, she hesitated, pondering what, precisely, to do. How could she simply stand here in the kitchen, rifle in hand, waiting for the trespasser to break into the house? Struggling against the twin demons of anxiety and anger at her seeming helplessness, she realized such passivity went against her grain. Especially when the safety of her family might be at stake. Besides, maybe the stranger was after her livestock. Why, he could be out there stealing her family's last remaining livelihood out from under her right now!

Anger won the day, surging hotly through Maggie's veins. She had struggled to keep a mule, a cow, and a goat on the farm, not to mention a few hogs and her precious chickens. And the cow had finally calved only a week ago! No shiftless stranger was going to come in here and make off with any of her prized possessions under cover of a stormy night.

A mulish expression came over her face at the very thought and she jettisoned her remaining fear and ran back into the hall. "Ty!" she called in a loud whisper. "Ty!"

She quickly jerked the shotgun from its notch in the gun rack, hurriedly broke it, and shoved in shells.

Her son appeared at the top of the stairs, looking down at her in puzzlement. "What? Ma! What are you doing?"

"Come down here. I need you."

He was beside her in an instant, his eyes round with excited curiosity. "What's the matter? Why'd you get out the guns?"

"There's a stranger in our barn. I saw him run there a minute ago." Wasting no more words, she thrust the shotgun at her son. "You take this and sit here at the table. I'm going out to the barn."

"I'm coming with you."

"No, you're not." About to give him a stern motherly look, she quickly rethought her strategy. She couldn't tell him that she didn't want him to get hurt; that would only raise all his burgeoning male hackles. "I need you here more than out there. In case I don't get him. In case he comes for the house. Somebody's got to be here to protect the house and Willy." She gazed at him solemnly. "Will you do that for me, Ty?"

Straightening his narrow shoulders, Ty nodded and gripped the shotgun manfully. "All right."

"Lock the door after me, and don't let anybody in except me."

He grimaced. "Ma . . ."

"All right. I know—you know what to do." Maggie spared another smile for her son, thinking, not for the first time, how lucky she was to have him. "Sometimes I can't help talking like a mother."

Maggie strode into the kitchen, with Ty trailing after her, and took down the lantern from the hook by the door. She hesitated about carrying it. The man might see her coming. Worse, she would make an easy target in the circle of light. On the other hand, trying to confront someone hiding in the dark barn would be almost impossible, and she didn't relish the thought of his pouncing out of the shadows at her. All in all, she decided, she had no choice but to take the lantern.

She lit the wick and turned for one last glance at her son. His face was taut, and he clenched the shotgun with both hands. She gave him what she hoped was a reassuring smile and opened the back door, stepping out into the ominous, blustery night.

The wind tore at her as she ran across the yard, whipping at her robe, and the rain viciously pelted her face and body. But Maggie ignored the discomfort, her thoughts on coming face to face with the unknown man lurking, doubtless with evil intent, in her barn.

When she reached the heavy barn door, she grasped the rain-slick handle and fought the wind to pry it open wide enough to slip inside.

Although she had known there was an intruder, it was still jolting to see this stranger, who stood facing away from her, in the flesh, there in the safety of her homeplace.

Evidently the noise of the storm had covered any sound of her approach, even the rasping of the barn door, but the man whirled now at the gust of cold, wet air and the sudden light.

He squinted, then froze as his eyes fell on the rifle she held. He didn't speak, just stared at her.

Carefully Maggie set the lantern down on the floor, never taking her eyes off him. He wasn't an extraordinarily big man, but then, Maggie was tall, like all the Tyrrells. His hair was dark and plastered against his head, and the air was redolent with the scent of his wet wool clothing. He didn't appear to be carrying a weapon; still, he was a stranger, and Maggie wasn't about to relax her guard. The times were troubled, and she had learned to be careful.

"Get your hands up," she told him crisply. "And come into the light where I can see you. Slowly."

He stepped forward, raising his hands as he did. "I'm not armed." His voice was smooth and cultured, Southern but not like that of someone from around here.

"Well, then," Maggie replied icily, "it's best you remember that I *am*." She raised the gun slightly for emphasis.

The stranger was inside the ring of light now, and Maggie could see that his features were as even and smooth as his voice—and gave as little away. Despite his matted hair, he was the most handsome man she had ever seen, saved from perfection only by a mouth that was a trifle too wide and bracketed by deep lines of experience. His expression was cool but wary, the look of a man who had seen much and was surprised by very little.

Still, despite the stubble on his chin and the shabbiness of his clothes, something about his stance and tone bespoke a gentleman. Whatever he might be, Maggie sensed he meant her family no harm, and she relaxed fractionally.

At that moment he jumped forward, his hand closing around the barrel of her gun and wrenching it aside. As

Maggie grasped futilely for the rifle, a shot rang out, deafening in the cavernous barn. Maggie gasped. The man frowned at her and dangled the rifle harmlessly at arm's length.

"Lord, lady, is that the way you greet strangers around here? You could have blown my head off!"

"Well, I saw no call to impress a trespasser with my hospitality!" Maggie spat. Her heart was pounding with fright, yet she realized he had not turned the rifle on her, and the combination of confusion and fear boiled over into anger. "Who are you? What are you doing in my barn?" she demanded.

He looked at her expressionlessly for a moment. Then, confusing her even more, he chuckled and shook his head. "I'll say one thing for you, lady—you've got grit."

He calmly unloaded the rifle and thrust the weapon back at her. "In case you haven't noticed," he commented dryly, "it's a little damp outside. I came in here to get out of the rain, that's all. I assure you, I have no designs on you or your property."

Maggie automatically gripped the rifle, set it butt down on the ground, and gazed at him consideringly. He didn't exactly *look* dangerous. Unless one believed, as her Granny Weatherly had always maintained, that all handsome men were dangerous. He looked merely wet, cold, and mighty irritated.

An involuntary shiver ran through him, and Maggie felt a pang of sympathy for his plight. No matter how disturbing his intrusion had proven, she could hardly send him back out into the driving rain. It was another mile and a half into town, and, besides, no one in Pine Creek was any more likely to take him in than she was.

For several years now, there had been men like this one roaming the roads, some heading through Arkansas on their way to Texas to seek a new beginning, others simply rootless and wandering, their lives upended by the long and bitter struggle between North and South.

Maggie knew well enough how war could wreck a person; it had hurt her own family deeply.

Obviously this man was one of its victims. His shabby shirt was the old butternut of a Confederate soldier's uniform. A bedroll lay beside his discarded jacket and hat. He had obviously spent more than one night under the stars recently. Maybe he had lost his home, or even his loved ones. Or perhaps he was simply among the human flotsam and jetsam cast astray by the turbulent tides of war's upheaval—one of those who, after four years of fighting, could no longer bear to stay in one place and till the fields of home.

Maggie thought about her own brother, Hunter, and hoped that some woman out west somewhere might give him shelter and a bite to eat if he was in need. She sighed. "All right. I reckon you can spend the night in the barn."

"Thank you." He nodded at her shortly, and Maggie wasn't sure whether he was being sarcastic.

"Mama?" The barn door scraped open.

Maggie whirled. "Tyrrell Malcolm Whitcomb! What are you doing out here? I told you to stay inside!"

"I thought I heard a shot," Ty replied. "I had to make sure you were all right."

Maggie grimaced. Even if Ty preferred to think it was the other way around, she didn't like this stranger knowing she had a child to protect.

Maggie glanced at the man. While he didn't seem to harbor dangerous motives right now, as the night went on, he might start thinking about the fact that she and a child alone in the house would be awfully easy pickin's for a grown man intent on robbery. After all, among the South's vagrants were those who were just plain too shiftless to work. Or those whose minds had been warped by the carnage they'd participated in until they didn't know right from wrong anymore. Some of them were even outlaws, or renegade Union soldiers.

He saw her glance, and he returned it evenly. "I'm

just looking for a dry pile of hay to lie down on tonight. Nothing else."

"Good. I hope you'll remember that I have more bullets for this rifle inside the house."

"Yes, ma'am, I'll do that."

He hardly seemed bothered by her threat. If anything, he looked vaguely amused, Maggie noticed. She glanced down at herself. Heavens! No wonder the man looked amused. He was probably having difficulty not guffawing aloud at the picture she presented! Her robe, its sash pulled free by the wind, had fallen open, revealing the long white night rail underneath. She must look like a slattern, especially with her thick hair hanging loose and wind-tossed about her shoulders. She was clutching an empty rifle, which she hadn't even been able to keep him from taking away from her. And next to her was her protector, an eleven-year-old boy wearing an old red flannel nightgown he'd outgrown long ago, his skinny legs sticking out beneath it.

A blush heating her cheeks, Maggie scowled up at the man and wrapped her robe around her, belting it tightly. The amusement in his eyes only seemed to increase at her attempt to gather her dignity about her.

Well, let him laugh at her if he wanted, Maggie thought. After all, *he* was the one wandering the roads, a beggar, while *she* had managed to salvage home and family from the ravages of war and its bitter, punishing aftermath.

"Come on, Ty, we're going in now," she said, taking her son's hand.

"But wait!" Ty tugged his hand away. "Who is this man? What's he doing here?"

"He got caught in the rain, so he's going to spend the night in our barn." Maggie let contempt stain her voice. Laugh at her, would he?

"My name is Reid Prescott," the man interjected, and he held out his hand to Ty. "I don't mean you or your family any harm."

Placated by the way the stranger spoke to him, man to man, Ty gladly shook his hand. "How do you do? I'm Tyrrell Whitcomb."

"Pleased to meet you." Prescott nodded at him gravely.

Lightning flashed and thunder boomed simultaneously, so loud and startling that all three of them flinched and glanced toward the open barn door.

"Willy!" Maggie said and glanced at Ty. If anything would wake Will up, that would, and he would be scared, especially if they weren't in the house. "Come on, honey, let's get back inside."

Ty nodded and quickly headed out the door. Maggie hesitated, then turned back toward Reid Prescott. "I—if you want the lantern, I can leave it."

He shrugged his indifference, but Maggie saw him shiver again, though he tried to hide it by folding his arms tightly against his chest. And suddenly she couldn't hold on to her earlier irritation. This Reid Prescott was wet and cold and doubtless hungry as well; he was simply too proud to ask for help.

Maggie understood pride. It was something she and her family—indeed, most of the folks she knew—had held on to long after everything else was gone. If there was one thing that stubborn Arkansans had in common, it was that they were too proud to admit defeat. Maggie hung the lantern on a hook and hurried after Ty.

By the time they reached the house, both of them were wet through.

"You be sure and change, now," she told her son.

Ty's reply was cut off by a wail from upstairs. "Ty! Ma!"

"We're right here, Willy!" Maggie called back, her heart clenching.

Ty was already off, dashing through the kitchen and taking the steps two at a time. "We're coming!"

Maggie followed more slowly. It unnerved her to see

Willy scared, as he was in thunderstorms; somehow it was worse than all his other childish ways.

The first time they'd had a storm after she'd brought him home, she had hardly been able to bear staying with him, holding his hand as he quivered at the thunder, his eyes closed and his face screwed up in terror, whimpers of fear escaping his lips. She had wanted to drop his clinging hand and run crying from the room, to race to her bed and hide her head under the covers like a child herself. How could this man be Will? Will, whom she'd seen calmly squeeze off a shot at a bobcat leaping toward him from the branch of a tree. Will, who had always been her hero.

Will, who was her husband.

Maggie had grown somewhat used to it over time, had learned to accept him as he was. She was more mother to him now than wife. She had even reverted to calling him Willy, his childhood nickname. Still, it was hard to watch the big, strong man she had married tremble with fear at the sound of a storm, pain and confusion stamping his face.

Maggie stepped into the boys' room. Will was huddled on his bed, his arms locked around his bent legs, his head tucked down on his knees, and he was shuddering. Ty was beside him, murmuring comforting words and stroking his back. But much as Willy loved and revered Ty, Maggie knew that right now what he needed was a mother's comfort.

"I'm here, sweetheart," she told him and sat down on the bed beside him.

Immediately he curled up against her, laying his head upon her chest. "Noise. All that bad noise."

"I know, sweetheart." Maggie curved one arm around his broad shoulders, and with the other hand she smoothed his hair. "But it's all right now. I'm here, and so is Ty. Nothing's going to happen to you."

"I don't like it."

"It's only thunder, just a storm," Maggie crooned.

She suspected that the noise upset Will because it reminded him of cannon fire. His company had lost half its men in the battle in which he himself had been wounded, one arm, shoulder, and side torn open by rifle fire. Those wounds had healed. It was the shrapnel from an exploding cannonball that had done the permanent damage, slicing into his head, leaving a deep furrow across his skull, and lodging pieces of metal inside that could not be removed. It was that that had turned him into a child again, who looked upon his son as an older brother and his wife as a mother.

"It won't hurt you. I promise." Maggie continued to soothe him, her hand rhythmically stroking his thick blond hair, and gradually Will's trembling began to subside, until at last he was resting quietly in her arms.

Finally he pulled away then and smiled up at her blearily, worn out by his fear. "I'm sleepy."

"I'm sure you are. It's late, and you should be asleep." She fixed her eyes on her son as she added, "You and Ty both."

"Ah, Ma . . ."

"Now, Ty, you know it's far past your bedtime."

"But I wanted to talk to you. You know, about . . ." He trailed off and glanced uncertainly toward Will.

"I know," Maggie stuck in quickly. She, too, was unsure whether they should mention the stranger in front of Will right now. Likely he would be nothing more than curious and excited about their nocturnal visitor. On the other hand, the presence of a stranger nearby might make him nervous and frightened again. "We'll talk tomorrow morning. Everything's fine for now, I'm sure."

"All right," Ty agreed reluctantly. "But don't you think . . . well, it's awful cold and wet out."

Maggie had been thinking the same thing. She couldn't help remembering the way Reid Prescott had shivered. And everything he owned was wet clear through. It was positively uncharitable to leave him out there in that condition. He needed dry things to put on, a towel and blanket at the very least.

Still, she might be taking a foolish risk going back out to the barn. If nothing else, she might wake up tomorrow to find that he had made off with the blanket and clothes. Or, if he had been thinking about what easy prey she was, she might find herself hit over the head and left in the barn while he ransacked the house —or worse.

Yet whatever the possibility of danger, it went against all her instincts to turn away from someone who needed help.

"You're right," she told Ty now, glancing over at Will. His eyes were closed, and his chest was already rising and falling in the even rhythm of sleep. "I'll take some dry things down to Mr. Prescott. But, you stay here and get to sleep. Morning's going to come awfully early tomorrow, and you still have to deliver your eggs, no matter how much excitement we had here tonight."

"Yes, ma'am."

Maggie gathered up some clothes of Will's, as well as a towel and blanket. On her way through the kitchen, she paused, then dished up a bowl of red beans left over from supper and added a hunk of cornbread. The food might be cold, but she was willing to bet the drifter would be glad of anything to fill his stomach. If times were rough for those who lived on the land, as her family did, it must be desperate for men who had no home or work.

The rain had stopped, and Maggie walked quickly across the yard, sidestepping mud puddles. She reached the barn door and opened it, then stopped abruptly, her mouth dropping open.

Reid Prescott was standing not ten feet away from her in the lantern light, spreading his sodden clothing out over the side of the stall. And he wasn't wearing a stitch!

Maggie gasped, and Prescott whirled around.

That only made matters worse. Maggie blushed to the roots of her hair. "Oh! Oh, my—" Words failed her. Belatedly, she thought to turn around so that she wasn't looking at him.

Behind her she heard Prescott let out a string of soft curses as he quickly strode around the side of the stall.

"I—I'm sorry." Maggie's face felt as hot as fire. "I—I should have knocked. I didn't think—I mean—"

She broke off abruptly and dropped the bundle she was carrying onto the nearest bale of hay. With trembling hands she lowered the bowl of food to a tack box, then turned and bolted out the door. And she didn't stop running until she reached the sanctuary of her house.

Reid towelled himself dry as quickly as he could, pulled on the clothes the woman had left for him, and wrapped the blanket around him. Finally, for the first time all evening, he began to feel warm. His most immediate need taken care of, he turned to the food on the tack box. The cold beans and cornbread were like manna to him; it had been over a day since he'd had a meal. Sitting on a bale of hay with the blanket draped around him, he wolfed down the food. When he was finished, he set aside the bowl with a sigh and leaned back against the stall, luxuriating in the pure, sensual pleasure of being warm, dry, and full. He couldn't remember the last time he had felt this content. The only thing lacking to make it perfect was a fire, he thought—and maybe a woman beside him.

Not just any woman, though, he realized, but his fiery, gun-toting benefactress.

He smiled, remembering her shocked expression when she'd caught him buck naked. He, too, had been startled, but he could see the humorous aspects of it.

Then another aspect of the oddly intimate situation crossed his mind. A sexual aspect.

Smiling no longer, Reid closed his eyes as heat flickered through his loins. Damn. That was the last thing he'd been expecting tonight—to meet a woman who aroused his interest, either mentally or physically. It had been so long since anything, anyone, had.

But this woman . . . well, this woman was hard to ignore.

He remembered the way she had charged into the barn earlier, her rain-spattered robe hanging open around her, the white cotton gown beneath clinging damply to the curves of her body—and a rifle in her hands, aimed straight at him.

Damn, but she had courage. It had taken plenty of it for a female to come out in the middle of the night to confront a trespasser. For all she had known, he could have been a thief or a murderer, not just a cold, wet traveler seeking shelter from the storm. Even with a gun, it had been a risky thing for her to do.

And, damn, but she was beautiful, too. Color high in her cheeks, those pale eyes flashing under thick, intriguing eyebrows, her rich brown hair curling wildly over her shoulders. The kind of hair a man could sink his hands into . . .

Despite her exotic, untamed appearance, though, she had been remarkably calm and cool, composed even after he'd taken the rifle away from her. The only thing that had really upset her was when the boy came into the barn. Still, once she had judged that their intruder meant her and her son no harm, she had been kind, too, bringing out food, clothes, and bedding. There were plenty who would figure they had been more than generous just to give him shelter.

Reid wondered about her. Obviously the boy was hers. They were as alike as two peas in a pod, and Tyrrell had called her mama. It was equally apparent that there was no man around the house, else he, not his wife and son, would have come out to confront the stranger.

Had the woman's husband died in the War? If so, that meant she had been on her own since at least 'sixty-five, struggling these past four years to survive and raise her child. It was hard for anyone nowadays, let alone a widow with a little boy. That made her generosity even greater.

It also meant she was alone in her bed inside the house. Again Reid was faintly surprised at the heat that arose within him at the thought. Somewhere in the midst of too much carnage that intensity of desire had disappeared, along with most of his other emotions, and the occasional stirrings he had felt since had been merely dull animal urgings, readily satisfied or easily ignored. The sharp, sustained quickening of blood he was experiencing now was altogether different, and he wasn't entirely sure he liked it. There was something to be said for numbness; he had been living in its safety for a long time now.

He forced his thoughts back to the widow woman's generosity and wondered how he might pay her back tomorrow. He could paint a fence or chop some wood. On the other hand, he should probably be gone by sunup. That was the way he was used to living, and it was better all the way around. If you got involved with people, even a little, they might start expecting things of you. And Reid knew he was not a man who had anything to give anyone.

Still, he could do a few chores before he left, and in that way he would work off his obligation to this woman for her kindness. Then he could forget all about her and her child. That would be best. Safest.

2

Maggie awakened the next morning with a slight sore throat. It was no surprise, she told herself, given that she had been running around in the rain last night. She wasn't one to coddle herself, however, so she got out of bed, dressed, and went downstairs to begin her chores.

Dawn was just beginning to glimmer on the horizon when she left the house, a shawl wrapped around her against the early-morning chill and a basket over her arm. She walked straight to the henhouse, not even glancing toward the barn. She was hopeful that Reid Prescott was already gone. After their late-night encounter, she wasn't sure she could look him in the eye without blushing remembering what he had looked like without any clothes on. She didn't think she could endure having a man—especially this man—know that she was thinking about something like that!

In the dim warmth of the chicken coop, she set about collecting the eggs, carefully placing them in her basket, cooing and clucking at her hens in praise for what they had produced. It was a good number this morning; after accommodating her usual customers, she would still have some left over.

Upon returning to the house, she counted out how many Ty would take into Pine Creek to sell and set the others aside for their own breakfast. Then, after securing an apron over her dress, she laid a fire in the stove, lit the kindling, and started the breakfast preparations.

As if on cue, Ty came in through the back door carrying a pail of milk. Offering a cheery good-morning, he carefully poured some of the foamy white liquid into a pitcher.

"Did you see our visitor?" Maggie asked in what she hoped was a casual voice.

"Mr. Prescott? Sure. He was in the barn, dead asleep. I think I woke him up, but he said it was all right. He fetched some water from the cistern, and he was shaving when I left."

"I see." She focused her attention on the coffee she was brewing. "You guess he's about to leave?"

Ty shrugged, his forehead wrinkled. "Do you think he'd go before breakfast? I told him we'd be having breakfast right after I did my egg route."

Maggie inwardly winced but said nothing. She couldn't very well chastise her son for showing kindness to the stranger, no matter how awkward a position it put her into.

She watched indulgently as Ty sidled over to the cornbread pan on the counter, fished under its cloth covering, and triumphantly filched a golden square. A moment after taking a hefty bite, he poured a glass of milk from the pitcher and drank half of it down in one gulp.

"Ty, don't bolt your food," she reminded him automatically.

"Yes, Ma."

"And don't talk with your mouth full."

He nodded exaggeratedly, then made a show of

swallowing. "I hope you have enough eggs today. Mrs. Kendall was all in a tizzy yesterday because I only had one left to sell her and she usually takes three."

"I know. I'm sorry. I put in two extra for her. Don't charge her for them."

"Ma . . ." Her son shot her an exasperated look.

"Well?" She gazed back at him, her hands planted on her hips. "Ty, we have to keep our customers happy. We can't have Alice Kendall telling everybody in town that we don't fill our orders."

"Even though she bought on credit for two months last fall? She still hasn't paid us back the whole amount."

"I realize that, dear, but times are so hard. Mrs. Kendall has only her daughter to help her, and, Heaven knows, Callie and her family aren't doing all that well themselves. She'll make it up sometime, I'm sure."

Ty shook his head, but he smiled at her fondly. "I don't think you'll ever make us rich."

Maggie grinned. "You're right about that." She put her arm around her son's shoulders and squeezed him, bending down to plant a kiss on top of his head. "But we don't need to be rich, do we? We get by. We're luckier than most because we've got family. And your uncle Gideon helps us out every bit he can. Besides, I'd rather not have money than press every last penny out of others who don't have enough, either."

"I know." For once Ty didn't slip out of her embrace with a look of boyish embarrassment. "I'm glad of it, I guess."

Loud footsteps thudded on the stairs, and Will burst into the room, frowning. "Ty!" As soon as he saw the boy, his worried expression changed to a beaming smile. "How come you didn't wake me up? I reckoned you'd left!"

"I'm about to leave now, if you want to come."

Will nodded vigorously. "Sure. Can I pull the wagon?"

"Some," Ty replied cautiously. "As long as you don't run with it like you did the other day."

Will's face clouded over. "I won't. I swear. I didn't mean to break any eggs." After a moment's thought, he offered, "I'll pull you coming back!"

Ty grinned, looking more like a child than usual. "All right! Come on." He picked up the basket of eggs and started for the back door. "Bye, Ma."

"Bye, Ma," Will echoed, turning to wave at her.

"Good-bye, honey." Her voice wobbled a little. For a moment she thought of the way Will used to turn back and wink at her as he left the house. His smile had always been a bit devilish, and he had called her Mags.

But since he'd come back, he never winked. He never called her Mags. He hadn't called her anything at first, for he hadn't even recognized her. After a time he had taken to calling her Ma, as Tyrrell did. And Maggie had realized that her loving husband, the man she had watched leave for war, was gone forever.

Even his face had changed. Although the features were the same, it was as if they'd been wiped clean of character, leaving the blank, open, innocent countenance of a child.

When she'd first brought him home in 'sixty-five, Will was so ravaged that she had set up a bed for him on the ground floor. After he had gotten well enough to move upstairs, he had instinctively gone to Ty's room. It seemed never to have occurred to him that his place was in the bedroom he had once shared with Maggie. It was as if all the adult male in him had been destroyed by the metal that had pierced his brain. Whenever he touched her or kissed her, it was in a purely asexual way. He seemed so much a child that Maggie could not even imagine having sex with him again; the thought of it made her a little queasy. It would be like taking a boy to bed, unnatural and revolting.

It had been four years now, and Maggie supposed she had finally gotten used to the way things were.

Most of the time she thought of Will as another son, younger and less bright than Ty. She didn't know why this morning she had suddenly thought of him as he had once been. Was it the presence of the stranger in their barn, reminding her that Will had once been grown and male like him?

There was a knock on the back door, and Maggie jumped, startled out of her disquieting reverie.

It had to be Reid Prescott himself. She hesitated, and the knock came again, louder this time. Bracing herself, Maggie went to the door and opened it, trying to school her face into impassivity. But as soon as she saw the man, heat began to rise in her cheeks.

"Mr. Prescott."

"Mrs. Whitcomb." He seemed unaffected by the embarrassment that assailed her. He had shaved, and possibly trimmed his hair, too, Maggie noted. Will's clothes fit him, even hung a trifle loosely. He was, all in all, perhaps even better looking than she had realized last night. His hair, medium brown, glinted with bronze highlights in the morning sun, and his eyes were a light hazel flecked with gold.

Maggie quickly looked away. "Ty's gone into town to sell the eggs and milk. I'll be fixing breakfast as soon as he gets back. It won't be long. You're welcome to stay, or I could pack you something if you're wanting to leave," she said in a rush, hoping the hint was not too heavy-handed but simultaneously wishing he would heed it.

He didn't. "I reckoned you might have some chores I could do," he said, slightly stiff, aloof, as if he always held something back from the world even as he offered his services.

"You needn't bother." Maggie remained tense, even though nothing in the man's manner hinted at her inadvertent impropriety of the night before.

"You did me a kindness," he replied. "I'm obliged to return it. I don't like to be beholden."

"Oh." Maggie could understand that; she liked to pull her own weight, also. But there was something cold and hard in Prescott's tone, as though accepting her simple kindness was somehow distasteful, compromising his very soul. "Well," she mused, "I reckon I could use some more firewood."

She gestured toward the old tree stump they used for a chopping block. Her brother Gideon had cut down a dead tree a couple of weeks ago and hauled it back there. Ty had sawed off many of the smaller boughs and chopped them up for the stove, but the thicker limbs had been slow work for him.

"The ax is hanging on the wall in the barn," she explained.

He nodded. "Anything else?"

Maggie glanced around. So many things needed doing, the problem was picking out which was the most necessary. She couldn't expect the man to work all day long just for a night's shelter in the barn. "Well, let's see . . . one of the fence slats on the hog pen split; it needs to be replaced. All big Maisie has to do is ram it, and it'll break clear through."

"All right." He continued to look at her.

"That ought to be plenty, don't you think?"

He nodded and walked off toward the barn.

Reid Prescott wasn't exactly the friendliest of people, Maggie decided. Even by way of thanking her for her help last night, he seemed more eager to rid himself of an onerous debt than anything else.

Again oddly disquieted by the man, Maggie went back to her breakfast preparations. Her sore throat hadn't subsided as she'd hoped it would once she was up and moving about; instead, she was beginning to have a headache, too. She grimaced, praying she wouldn't come down sick; she had too much work to do, and there wasn't a doctor for miles around.

Soon the rhythmic sound of the ax cleaving wood came from across the yard. It was somehow pleasant to hear, and after a moment Maggie realized that the sound was different from when Ty was out there chopping the wood. He didn't have the long swing of an adult, nor the smooth rhythm of years of practice. Gideon chopped that way, and Will had, too. Maggie wondered why she had never noticed the contrast before.

She fried spicy circles of sausage in her large iron skillet and made gravy with the fat. She buttered thick slices of bread and toasted them in the oven. Finally everything was ready except for the eggs, and she didn't dare cook them before the boys got home; they got done too quickly and might be stone cold by the time Ty and Willy straggled in.

They weren't usually late—Ty was a responsible boy —but sometimes customers slowed them down or Willy went off on a lark, requiring Ty's attention and leaving Maggie torn between irritation and worry. Whatever the reason, today was one of the times they were tardy. Maggie puttered about, sipping at a cup of coffee and wondering what was keeping them. The sound of chopping ceased, and a few moments later Mr. Prescott appeared at the back door, a load of cut wood in his arms. Maggie hurried to open the door for him, and he piled the logs into the nearly empty bin beside the stove. He left, then came back with another armful, this time filling the woodbox to the top.

He straightened up, slapping stray pieces of bark from his sleeves. Maggie smiled at him apologetically. "I'm afraid the boys haven't gotten back yet. But would you like for me to scramble your eggs now?"

"The boys?" he questioned. He had seen only one child last night.

Just then Ty's wagon rattled across the rocky drive.

"Ah, there they are." Maggie set the skillet to reheat and began cracking the eggs into a bowl. "You might as well sit. I'll have breakfast on the table in a minute."

"Mind if I clean up some?" he asked. At her nod, he strode to the washstand and poured water into the basin. As he scrubbed his hands with the strong lye soap, the back door flew open, and Ty clomped in, swinging the empty egg basket. "Whew! Sorry we're late. Hello, Mr. Prescott. Ma."

"Hello, Ty." Drying his hands, Reid turned toward the boy. Then his gaze flew to the door, where Will, his head down, was slowly walking in. Reid froze, his face registering surprise.

"Willy got scared by the Covermans' dog again," Ty told his mother by way of explanation for Will's sad look.

Maggie groaned sympathetically as she took the iron spider from the fire and set it aside. She went to Will. "I'm sorry that happened, sweetheart," she murmured to him. She ran a hand over his hair and turned his face up so she could look into his eyes. "But you're all right now, aren't you," she assured him.

It was obvious that Will had been crying. His eyes were red, and he looked both frightened and ashamed. "I don't like that dog!" he declared emphatically, pathos in the downward curve of his mouth. "He's got no feathers."

"Feathers?" That astounded even Maggie, and she stared at him blankly.

"He means fur, Ma," Ty explained. He glanced toward Reid, and a flush of embarrassment stained his cheeks. "You know, the Covermans' dog is short-haired."

"Oh. That's right." Quickly Maggie went up on tiptoe and hugged Will, giving comfort even as she struggled to hide a smile at his unique description. "You know, sweetheart, some dogs simply don't have a lot of hair like Blackie did," she explained, referring to the barnyard mutt they'd once had. "That doesn't mean they're bad or mean."

"But he's big. And he's got lots of teeth."

"Willy climbed up the Covermans' oak tree, and I had the hardest time getting him to come down," Ty went on disgustedly, setting the basket down on the counter with a thud. "Finally Mrs. Coverman had to come out and whistle the dog up to the porch and hold on to him."

"It turned out all right in the end then, didn't it?" Maggie gently pointed out. "No harm done. Now, you two must be starved. Ready for some breakfast?"

Ty nodded, and Will brightened. "Wash our hands, Ty," he told the boy.

Will delighted in routines and in remembering them. He turned now toward the washstand but stopped short when he saw the stranger standing there. He gazed at Reid with wide, innocent eyes. There was no real surprise on his face; things happened without logic or consequence all the time in Will's world.

"Who's he?" Will asked, pointing at Mr. Prescott.

Maggie shot a glance at the man. To his credit, he was neither staring at Will with open-mouthed horror nor averting his eyes as many people did. He was simply looking at Will with the same sort of reserved detachment he had shown earlier to Maggie.

"I'm Reid Prescott." He stepped forward and held out his hand to Will.

Will grinned. It wasn't often that people shook his hand, and he took a small boy's pleasure in the honor.

"I'm Will." He walked up to Reid and pumped his hand enthusiastically.

"Will Whitcomb," Maggie added. "My husband."

Prescott's eyes widened, but he made no comment on the incongruity of the situation.

Maggie silently blessed the man and went back to the stove to dish up the scrambled eggs. She wished more people had his kind of tact. It amazed her how often folks would bluntly ask her what was wrong with Will—and right in front of him, too, as if he wasn't there or had no feelings.

Finally they were all settled at the table, but Maggie found she couldn't eat much. It hurt to swallow, and she felt rather ill-at-ease around the newcomer to this domestic scene. For so long she had been the only adult, and what guests they did have were usually her brother Gideon or her mother or her brother Shelby's widow, Tess—family, not strangers.

Ty and Will seemed to have no such reservations about company at the meal; they were both obviously quite taken with Reid Prescott.

Ty immediately began to ply him with questions. "Where you from, Mr. Prescott?"

A slight, almost rusty smile touched the man's lips, making Maggie suspect that he wasn't used to doing it.

"A little bit of everywhere," he replied.

Will looked puzzled and turned toward Ty. "What's that mean?"

"It means he's been a lot of places," Ty explained importantly.

"I've never been anywhere," Will assured their visitor gravely. He paused and frowned uncertainly. "Least, not that I can remember."

"Neither have I," Ty admitted. He looked hopefully at Mr. Prescott. "Have you been to Texas?"

"Yes."

Ty brightened. "Really? My uncle's in Texas. I mean, one of my uncles. Hunter Tyrrell."

"You know Hunter?" Will piped.

Will's words startled another rusty smile out of the man. "No, I'm afraid I've never met him."

"Oh." Will's face fell.

"Texas is a big place, Willy," Maggie told him gently. "There are too many people there for Mr. Prescott to have met them all."

"I wish you had," Will told Prescott. "I like Hunter. I wish he hadn't gone to Texas."

"He'll be back someday," Maggie said with more confidence than she felt. Her brother was one of those who had not been able to settle down after the War. Like Mr. Prescott, she presumed.

Hunter had been listed as one of the conflict's early casualties, reported dead after the First Battle of Manassas back in July of 'sixty-one. Not until several tear-filled months later had they learned that he had not been killed but injured and taken prisoner by the Yankees routed at Bull Run. At the end of the War, released from the Union prison, he had finally come home, only to learn that his fiancée, beautiful Linette Sanders, had married another—and that only a few weeks after he had been reported killed.

Hunter had left Pine Creek almost immediately, and he had been roaming the West ever since. He had tried returning once, but after a week he was gone again, his last letter from somewhere in Texas.

"But where were you born?" Ty asked Prescott, pressing his original question.

For a moment Maggie thought the man wasn't going to answer. Then, as if against his will, he bit out, "Savannah."

"Oh. Georgia," Ty said, looking knowledgeable. "We have cousins there, don't we, Ma?"

"Yes, dear. Second cousins. But I doubt Mr. Prescott's interested in hearing about that. I also imagine he's a little tired of answering all your questions, so why don't you let him eat in peace for a while?"

Ty looked deflated. "I'm sorry, Mr. Prescott."

"It's all right," he said, but Maggie noticed that he didn't volunteer any more information about himself, and not long after he stood to leave the table. "I'll just finish up the chores, and I'll be gone."

"What?" Ty exclaimed.

Will looked crestfallen. "Aren't you going to stay?" he asked.

"No."

Prescott's green-brown eyes slid from Ty to Will, and his mouth tightened.

"Where are you going?"

Prescott shrugged. "Somewhere. Anywhere."

Ty stared at him. "But why are you traveling, if you don't know where you're going?"

He shrugged again. "I guess I'm what you'd call a wanderer."

"Since the War?" Maggie guessed.

He looked at her without expression. "Yes. Since the War."

"But don't you want to go home?" Ty pressed.

"I . . . have no home to go to."

"No home?" Will asked, a frown once again creasing his forehead at so awful a thought. "Don't you have a ma or pa?"

"They're both dead, I'm afraid."

"You could stay here," Will offered, brightening. "This could be your home."

Prescott's eyebrows arched nearly to his honey-brown hair. "Well . . . thank you, Will, that's kind of you. But I . . . I've gotten used to not being hemmed in, I guess."

He looked at the three people staring at him with patent disbelief. Obviously, they could not conceive of living so rootlessly. Clearly, he and this family were as far apart as the moon and earth. He turned and walked toward the back door.

"Can we go with you?" Ty asked, following him. "I mean, doing the chores."

Prescott hesitated.

"Don't plague the man, boys," Maggie said quickly, instinctively trying to spare him their inquisitive, talkative company.

"Oh, Ma . . ." Ty complained, disappointment etching his young face.

Mr. Prescott surprised her. "I don't mind," he said. "They can show me what needs doing."

Ty and Will grinned and happily followed him out to the farmyard.

Shaking her head, Maggie turned back to her work. But the cleaning up proved slow going. She felt astonishingly tired, and her neck was stiff, her head and throat now beginning to throb. Still, she forced herself to wash the dishes, then turned to her Wednesday chores. First she dragged her braided rugs to the clothesline in the side yard and beat the dust out of them, then left them to air.

Usually the task gave her pleasure, for she was especially proud of her rugs. The large one from the parlor had been her grandmother's and had come out here from Georgia with her. The two smaller ones from the bedrooms were from her own hope chest, made by her and her mother in those halcyon days just before she and Will were married. Maggie had never been happier than in those months of her engagement, flushed with excitement and love, innocently unknowing of a world where war or deprivation or wounded husbands existed.

But today, as she moved through the house, sweeping and mopping the floors, Maggie was nearly bowed down from fatigue. Pausing to catch her breath, she gazed out the window into the yard to see what the boys were up to. They stuck like glue to Mr. Prescott's side as he replaced the split slat in the pigsty. Then they all slopped the hogs and turned the cow and calf and mule out into the pen. Maggie wondered if Ty had convinced the poor man to help him muck out the animals' stalls and pitch down their hay, his least favorite tasks.

Mr. Prescott was staying far longer than she had expected, Maggie realized. It was getting close to time for the noon meal.

She had put on a pot of blackeyed peas, seasoned with a slab of salt pork, to simmer while she worked. Now she returned to the kitchen to put a few sweet potatoes into the oven to bake. Then, to her amazement, she simply sat down at the table to rest until it was time to put a fresh batch of cornbread in to bake and to call the boys and Mr. Prescott in to eat.

No one answered her summons, so she stepped off

the back porch and walked across the yard to check the barn. No sign of them. She headed for the animal pen beyond, and there she found all three missing males, Ty and Will intently watching Mr. Prescott as he cleaned caked mud and pebbles from the mule's iron shoes. Crouched beside the animal, which was safely tied to a fencepost, he turned at her approach and peered up at her, shading his eyes from the sun.

"Mrs. Whitcomb," he acknowledged.

"Hi, Ma," Ty and Will said in unison.

"It's time for dinner," Maggie informed them. "The cornbread will be ready in just a few minutes."

"You got any honey?" Will asked hopefully.

Maggie smiled at him. "Yes, I do. But it's our very last jar, so that means you boys will have to go hunting for some again soon."

Ty grinned, and Will, after a glance at Ty to make sure what he thought about the gentle command, grinned, too. Mr. Prescott released the mule's hoof and stood up, stretching.

"It looks like you've been doing more than we agreed on," Maggie observed.

"A lot of things needed doing," he said simply.

"Yes, but you needn't do them all just to thank me for letting you sleep in the barn."

"You fed me, too," he pointed out. "Gave me dry clothes. Seems like adequate repayment."

"Well . . . thank you. That's very generous of you. As long as Ty hasn't talked you into doing *too* much. Maggie cut a suspicious glance at her son. "For instance, *his* chores—like cleaning out the stalls."

"I helped!" Ty protested.

Prescott shrugged. "I didn't mind. I reckon he carries a pretty heavy load for a boy his age."

Maggie stiffened. "I'm afraid we haven't much choice. Since the War . . . well, Will can't do everything."

Will spoke up. "I'm strong. Stronger than Ty."

"I know you are, dear. But no one can do everything." Maggie spoke to him soothingly, laying a hand on his arm. He was right, of course. His strength was that of a man, and though his fingers were clumsy on any sort of small work, he could be counted on to lift and carry, to do the heavy things, as long as they weren't complicated and someone told him exactly what to do.

"I can do what Ty tells me," he went on.

"You help a lot," Maggie agreed. The only problem was that his attention was inclined to wander, and one always had to watch him to make sure he didn't stop what he was doing to go off after a butterfly or some other diversion. When something required both strength and skill, he was hopeless, and he seemed unable to learn anything remotely complex.

Will looked satisfied that he had made his point and subsided into silence.

"You know, you're awful quick to fire up, Mrs. Whitcomb," Reid observed. He crossed his arms and looked at her. "When I said Ty carried a heavy load, I wasn't criticizing you or your household. I was simply saying that I was glad to be of help. Or can't you allow anybody to help you out? Maybe it only works the other way around?"

"Don't be ridiculous." Irritation flashed through her. Her head was pounding and her throat ached, and this man had the nerve to act as if she was somehow at fault because she hadn't wanted him to go out of his way for them.

"I wasn't aware that I was."

Maggie narrowed her eyes. She felt like lashing out at him, but she couldn't think what she would say. That he was pompous and irritating? After he'd just done a half dozen badly needed chores for her?

"The bread's going to burn. I have to get back," was all she said, and she whipped around, heading for the house. "Coming?" she called over her shoulder. Ty and

Prescott followed her, with Will trailing along behind them.

Dinner was a largely silent affair. Even Ty was uncharacteristically quiet. But toward the end of the meal he blurted out, "Maybe Mr. Prescott could stay on! We got lots of things around here he could do."

Maggie's head snapped up. "Oh, no, I'm sure Mr. Prescott has other places he needs to go, things he needs to do."

"But you don't have to go anywhere right away, do you, Mr. Prescott?" Ty pursued the matter doggedly. "I mean, you could live here for a while, like you did last night."

Ty's words fed Will's excitement. "You're going to live with us?" His face wreathed in a smile, Will leaned across the table, looking intently into the other man's eyes.

"Now, Ty, Willy, it's . . . it's not as simple as that," Maggie protested. "I'm sorry, Mr. Prescott, they don't mean to press you, I'm sure. They simply like you."

"But why not?" Ty asked, frowning. "Why couldn't he stay? You said yourself the other day that you can't get everything done. You said we mustn't depend on Uncle Gideon to always—"

"I know, dear, I know. There *are* lots of things that need to be done, and I'm sure it would be wonderful to have Mr. Prescott stay here and do them. But you don't understand. A person gets paid for working like that, and we just don't have that kind of money." Her cheeks flushed in embarrassment.

"I don't stay anywhere long," Reid said flatly. He looked at Ty, and his expression softened a little. "I'm sorry, Ty. That's just the way it is. I'll get this work done and stay in your barn one more night if your mama allows, but then I'll be leaving in the morning."

Maggie nodded her thanks at Mr. Prescott, then looked at her son sadly. He needed a man around the house. Not just Will, but someone who thought and spoke and behaved like a man, who could talk to Ty adult to child, explain and teach and help. He needed a father, which Will could never be for him again. Her brother Gideon tried, bless him, but their principal contact with him was only once a week over Sunday dinner with the family. It was a most unfortunate situation, but no passing stranger could give Ty what he needed.

Disappointment stamped Ty's face, and he looked back down at his plate.

Maggie got up and began to clear the table.

3

As the day went on, Maggie felt worse. She began to cough and sneeze, and by suppertime she knew she had caught the grippe. She dished up dinner, but, too listless, she herself ate little.

"Ma, are you all right?" Ty asked uncertainly partway through the meal.

"I have a slight touch of the grippe," Maggie told him. "Nothing serious." She smiled at Will, who was frowning in concern. "I'm sure I'll feel much better by morning."

"I'll help with the dishes," Will offered.

Maggie smiled. "Thank you, dear. That's sweet of you." Inwardly she groaned, for with Will's help the chore would take her twice as long. But she wouldn't hurt his feelings for the world.

Reid Prescott said nothing. He looked at her consideringly for a moment, and Maggie thought he was about to speak, but then he looked away, his mouth firmly shut.

After the dishes, Maggie wearily climbed the stairs to

her room. She was so tired that she lay down on top of the covers, fully dressed, intending only to rest for a moment before she got ready for bed. The next thing she knew, however, she opened her eyes to utter darkness.

She felt strangely hot, and the counterpane beneath her was damp from her sweat. She sat up slowly, for the bedstead seemed oddly unsteady. The room tilted a little, then righted itself. The curtains were still open, and she could see the night sky, the stars shining brightly. Disoriented, she realized that she was still dressed. She pulled one foot up and began to unfasten her shoe. It was a tiring task, and when she had finished, she fell back against her pillow. Disrobing was too much trouble; she would just sleep in her day clothes.

Maggie passed the rest of the night in fitful sleep, dreaming strange, vivid dreams, and early the next morning, she awoke shivering, thinking that she had never been so cold in her life. Frantically she pulled the covers up around her, and slowly she grew warmer, but before she knew it, she was far too hot again. She peeled off the covers and loosened the dress she had worn since yesterday. She knew she needed to get up and fix breakfast soon, or the boys would begin to worry.

Finally she managed to pull herself out of bed, but it was difficult to think straight. Her head was aching, and her eyes felt sandy. She put on her shoes, but the effort it took seemed enormous. She knew she would need all her energy to cook some food, but after that, she promised herself she would return to her bed and rest.

Stubbornly refusing to give in to her queasy stomach or pounding head, she went downstairs, hanging on to the rail because she felt peculiarly weak. When she reached the kitchen, she sank into a chair gratefully and leaned her head on the table.

That was the way Ty, Will, and Reid Prescott found her.

"Ma?" Ty's voice spiraled upward with fear. "Ma, are you all right?" He raced to her side, while Will shrank nervously in the doorway, staring at her.

Maggie raised her head and looked at them, blinking in confusion. "Oh, I'm sorry. I—I must have fallen asleep."

"Ma, your face is all red."

"I'm a little warm," she admitted.

Now Mr. Prescott approached, and he placed a hand on her forehead. His palm felt deliciously cool, and Maggie leaned into it.

"You're burning up." He tilted her chin up to look into her face. "You have a fever. You should be in bed."

"Somebody's got to get breakfast," Maggie said mulishly, and she stood up.

It was a mistake. The room whirled around her, and she felt her legs give way beneath her.

"Ma!"

"Damn!" Reid grabbed Maggie as she fainted. Her head lolled back, and the sloppy bun her hair was done in came loose, spilling curls every which way. Reid scooped her up into his arms and turned to Ty. "Where's her bed?"

"Upstairs. I'll show you." Ty's eyes were round with fear, his face white, and he fairly ran up the stairs to lead the way.

Maggie Whitcomb felt light in his arms, Reid realized, almost fragile despite her robust appearance. It must be her spirit that made her seem larger and stronger. But right now, out cold, with her head against his shoulder, she didn't seem strong at all, only very vulnerable.

Ty led him into his mother's room. Reid glanced around, taking in the disheveled bed linens and an open window.

"Close that window," he ordered, "then turn down the bed."

Ty hurried to do so, and Reid slid Maggie gently onto the mattress, pulling the covers up around her. He poured water into the washbasin and dampened a facerag. Then he came back to the bedside and draped the cool cloth over Maggie's forehead.

Ty had retreated to the foot of the bedstead, regarding his mother uncertainly, and Reid noticed that Will would come no farther than the doorway, his large face frightened, his mouth trembling.

"Is she going to die?" the boy-man asked, his voice quavering.

"No," Reid said brusquely, looking down at Will's wife. Her rich brown hair was spread over the pillow, riotously curling. High color stained her ivory complexion, and her dark lashes cast shadowy crescents against her cheeks. In other circumstances, it might have made a sensual, seductive picture, Reid couldn't help noting.

He promptly clamped down on the unwarranted surge of lust. "She won't die," he said sternly, as if his voice alone could command her fate. Evidently the tone of authority was somewhat reassuring, for both Ty and Will relaxed a fraction. "She has a fever," he went on, "and she needs to lie here and rest, so you two will have to take care of yourselves today."

"We can do that." Ty drew himself up straighter. "I can gather the eggs. And we can have some of the cornbread from last night for breakfast."

"Good plan." Reid removed the cloth, now warm from the woman's heated brow, dipped it back into the water, and wrung it out. He knew that the quickest way to reduce her fever would be to strip off her clothes and bathe her entire body with cool water, but that simple procedure seemed far too . . . intimate. He settled on unbuttoning the collar of her dress to sponge her throat and upper chest.

Maggie's eyelids fluttered, then opened, and she stared blankly around the room. "What—?"

"You fainted. You're sick. You need to stay in bed," Reid said more harshly than he had intended.

"Mr. Prescott carried you up here," Ty added excitedly, reassured now that his mother was conscious again.

Maggie attempted to wet her parched lips, and Reid poured her a glass of water from the china pitcher. Putting his hand behind her neck, he raised her up so she could drink.

"Take small sips," he said gruffly as she began to gulp it down.

"But I'm so thirsty."

"That's because you're running a fever. But you don't need to make yourself sicker. That's why you're going to stay put, sleep, and sip more water whenever you wake up."

"I can't stay in bed," Maggie said fretfully, pushing away the counterpane as if to rise. "I have to fix breakfast."

"I'll take care of breakfast," Reid heard himself say.

"But—" Panic welled inside Maggie at the thought of being helpless and sick in bed. "The boys—somebody has to look after the boys."

"Oh, Ma . . ." Ty put in scornfully, pride pushing away his earlier fear. "I can take care of myself."

Visions of disasters tumbled through Maggie's fevered imagination. What if one of the boys burned himself at the stove, or cut himself with a knife? What if—

Reid saw the panic in her eyes, and he shook his head. "Don't worry. I'll—" He hesitated, then went on. "I'll stay and see to them."

"Would you?" Maggie touched his arm gratefully. He might be a stranger, but at least he was an adult. She felt too awful and weak to think beyond that. "Thank you," she said, tears of gratitude in her eyes.

Reid drew back, and the concern he had shown a

moment earlier was replaced by his usual cool reserve. "Sleep," he repeated. "I'll come back and check on you later."

Maggie nodded weakly, already slipping back toward blessed oblivion.

Reid herded the others downstairs to the kitchen. Nervously glancing around the cozy but suddenly intimidating domestic haven, he finally admitted, "Frankly, I don't have the slightest idea what to do."

A taut silence followed. Then Ty chuckled, and Will's frown left his forehead, the big, friendly smile returning. And, while a moment before Reid had been feeling uncomfortably cornered, now the tension was gone.

"You have to light the stove first," Will offered helpfully.

Reid smiled. "That I can probably manage. Then, if you'll help me locate a skillet, I might even prove passable at scrambling eggs."

"I'll have to go milk the cow and slop the hogs," Ty said, "but then I can gather the eggs."

"Maybe Will and I could do that, if Will will show me the chicken coop," Reid suggested as he fired up the stove.

"Sure." Will's face lit up at the notion of being helpful—and at the prospect of actually showing a grown-up where to go and what to do. He strode to a cabinet and pulled out a large basket. "This is what Ma puts the eggs in."

He looped it over his arm importantly and soon led Reid out the door and across the yard to the henhouse. They had to stoop to enter the dim coop pungent with the odor of straw and chickens, and as they confronted a row of bright-eyed hens, Will, looking uncomfortable, handed Reid the basket.

"You'd better pick the eggs," he said in a hushed voice. "Sometimes I break them."

Arching his eyebrows, Reid cautiously approached

the nearest hen. From childhood he remembered watching their kitchen servant Eulalie gather the eggs some mornings, but he had rarely been allowed to help. Like Will, he, too, had "sometimes broken" them.

Will saw him hesitate. "You have to stick your hand in and under. Like this." He thrust his large fingers awkwardly between the hen and her nesting box. The chicken let out a loud squawk and flew out of the box with a great flurry of ruffled feathers. Abashed, Will glanced at Reid, but the surprised look on the other man's face made him laugh and checked his embarrassment. "Ma's a lot better at this than me," he confided.

"I'm sure she's a lot better than both of us," Reid grumbled good-naturedly as he reached into the box and took out the brown speckled egg the hen had left behind. Then, imitating Will, he slid his hand down beside the next chicken and managed to find an egg and bring it out successfully. Beaming with inordinate pleasure, he turned toward Will, triumphantly holding up the egg. Will grinned and managed to duplicate the maneuver at the next box, and together they finished gathering the eggs without breaking a single one.

As they were walking back toward the house, Will turned toward Reid. "I like you," he said candidly.

Reid didn't know quite how to answer. The other man's openness was startling. He gazed at the big blond farmer, noting the large scar that started on Will's forehead and curved into his thick hair. Had a war injury caused his brain damage? he wondered.

For the first time in years, Reid found himself wishing for some of his old books. Simple, lumbering Will piqued his curiosity, as did his intelligent, responsible son, who acted much more the father in the relationship.

Then there was Maggie Whitcomb herself, of course. She was pretty to look at, the kind of woman he found his eyes straying to again and again. She didn't have a typical sort of beauty; there were no giggles or frills to her. But strength of character shone out of her eyes and lit up her face with a life and beauty few ladies had. He liked how she looked when she talked to Will, kind and patient, with a quiet, sad sort of love in her gaze. He liked it when she laughed, her strong white teeth flashing, her soft gray eyes twinkling with humor. She was a strong, brave woman.

She had to be to get along on a farm like this with only a boy and a man with a boy's mind to help her. There must have been times when she had wondered where their next meal was coming from, times when she had been scared to death. Yet obviously she had struggled through it all—and done a damn fine job of raising her son, as well.

Suddenly Reid remembered how fragile she had felt in his arms when he'd carried her up the stairs, how panicky she had looked at the thought of being too sick to take care of her "boys," and an odd kind of feeling pumped through his chest. Fortunately, Will interrupted his unwelcome thoughts.

"I like you a lot," Will continued happily. "I like you better than anybody—'cept Ma and Ty," he added hastily. "I like you better than Ginny or Tess. Or Gideon."

"Who are they?"

"Ginny's a . . . cousin, and her ma, Tess, is Ma's . . . sister. No, that's not right. She's something like that. Gideon's Ma's brother. He lives on the big farm. But he comes by to see us sometimes."

Of course. Maggie had relatives living nearby, Reid thought. He was off the hook. He could go to them and tell them she was sick and let one of them come to take care of her household.

"Gideon used to be my friend," Will continued. "That's what Ma says." He frowned. "But I'm not sure. I don't think he likes me."

"Has he said so?" Reid asked carefully.

"No." Will's face screwed up in frustration at his inability to express his inchoate feelings. "It's just . . .

sometimes he looks at me real . . . sad-like." Will heaved a sigh. "I don't know. He's . . . he's . . ." He tightened his body all over in imitation. Then he shrugged. "Ma says it's because he used to know me. She says it's because he remembers me." He cast a puzzled look at Reid. "Do you understand?"

"I think so. Sometimes we miss . . . what we used to know."

Will shook his head mournfully. "I don't understand." Then his sad mood fled, and he looked curiously at Reid. "Do you like me, too?"

Reid surprised himself by grinning. "Yeah. I like you, Will."

Will's teeth flashed in a proud smile. Impulsively he wrapped his arms around Reid, giving him a big bear hug.

Reid was startled. For a moment he stood stiffly. It felt so strange to be hugged, especially by a grown man. Yet the childlike, spontaneous affection stirred up a strange welter of emotions inside him as well—an ache akin to loneliness, an oddly nostalgic yearning. He returned Will's hug awkwardly, relieved that he would soon be on his way, putting a safe distance between himself and this family that evoked such confounding, unwanted feelings in him. Once back at the house, however, Reid's resolve weakened at the sight of Ty and Will's hopeful, hungry faces. He did his best at making breakfast, warming up cornbread from the night before and scrambling a sticky mess of eggs. It wasn't anything to compare with Maggie's cooking, but at least it filled them up.

After breakfast, Ty and Will hurried off to sell the extra eggs and milk in Pine Creek, and Reid realized he hadn't yet asked Ty how to contact the family's relatives. Well, he'd find out later. For now, he'd better get upstairs to check on Maggie.

She was sleeping fitfully when he entered the room, and her eyes fluttered open as he stooped to bathe her face and neck with a cool cloth. Hushing her protests, he gave her some more water to drink, once again helping her to sit up. When she lay back down, she fell asleep almost immediately, but he thought with relief that she looked slightly less flushed.

Strangely restless and edgy, Reid headed back downstairs and out to the farmyard in search of something to busy himself with until help could arrive. He was no farmer, and he wasn't even sure what needed to be done, but he reckoned he was skillful enough with a hammer to be able to make some minor repairs around the place. There was no point sitting around doing nothing.

So he went to work, shoring up a sagging stretch of fence and straightening a badly listing gate. Just as he was thinking it was time to check on Maggie Whitcomb again, he heard the rattle of Ty's wagon returning.

"Mrs. Diggs sent some broth," Ty called. "When I told her Ma was sick, she insisted I bring some of this chicken broth home to her," he explained as he reached Reid's side.

"Good," Reid said with a strange mix of relief and regret that now Maggie's son could tend to her immediate needs. "Why don't you take her up a small bowl and see if you can get her to eat a little of it."

"All right. Then I'll start my studying. Ma'll have my hide if I don't."

Will went into the house with Ty, but after a while he came wandering back out, bored with watching Ty read, and he joined Reid where he was repairing a stall in the barn. Will remained Reid's shadow for the rest of the morning, following him everywhere he went, happy to help when he could and equally content to sit and watch when he couldn't.

Late in the morning, Reid went into the house and warmed up a pot of beans for dinner, grateful Maggie had leftovers from the meals yesterday. Ty brought in a sausage from the smokehouse, and Reid, his skillet skills rapidly improving, fried it to produce a meal that was, at least, edible and filling.

As they ate, Reid gestured at the large book on the counter. When he and Will came in to fix lunch, Ty had been reading it at the table.

"You're studying English history, Ty?"

Ty nodded but remembered to swallow before speaking. "Ma makes me study whatever she and her brothers studied when they were in school. Sometimes it's hard because we don't have the right books or Ma can't remember what she learned. That's Uncle Gideon's book—he loaned it to me."

"So you don't go to school?"

"There's no teacher in Pine Creek anymore. He went off to fight, and he didn't come back. And now the town can't afford to hire a new schoolmaster, so we just have to learn on our own."

"You seem to be doing a pretty good job of it."

Ty shrugged. "I guess. But Ma doesn't have much time to teach me, and she never got past the sixth grade. Grandma and Grandpa didn't think too much schooling was right for a girl. But I like learning," he confessed with a little smile. "Course, sometimes there are things I can't understand. And I know there must be lots and lots I'm missing."

Reid recalled his own early education at the small schoolhouse near his home, followed by the private academy for young men, then his years at William and Mary. "Perhaps I could help you," he said without thinking.

"Do you think so?" Ty brightened. "See, where I'm confused is the Tudors and Stuarts. I don't understand why Mary, Queen of Scots, was a threat to Elizabeth. How could she take the throne? And then her son got it when Elizabeth died, right?"

"That's right. It's not direct descent. Since Elizabeth had no children, you have to go back up the line, first to

her brothers and sisters—all dead, no descendants—
then to her father's siblings, and then—''

"Wait," Ty interrupted. "Maybe you could show
me." He eagerly jumped up, grabbed the heavy tome
from the counter, and opened it to a genealogical chart
of British royalty.

"All right. Look . . ." And Reid traced the chart
with his forefinger to illustrate the line of descent and
how it had led to Mary, Queen of Scots.

"I see, but why would they want to put Mary on the
throne while Elizabeth was still alive?"

Reid then proceeded to explain the position of English Catholics and the Protestant Reformation, marvel-
ling that the boy's intellectual curiosity was every bit as
avid as if they had been discussing the great Confederate generals. The excitement shining in Ty's eyes reminded Reid of his own youthful thirst for knowledge
and the subsequent hunger to put that knowledge to
good use in adulthood.

The latter thought brought him back to the present
with an unpleasant start, and he realized that over an
hour had passed in their impromptu lesson.

"Well, I'll be." He turned to Ty. "Look at how late
it's gotten. We'd better check on your mother."

"Oh, dear." Guiltily Ty got up and hurried upstairs,
while Reid began to clean up the dishes from their meal.

Ty soon returned with a report. "I don't think she's
any worse. She drank some more water, but she said
she wasn't hungry."

"It's the fever. We'll try some broth again later."

"Mr. Prescott . . ."

"Yes?" Reid looked up from the soapy tub of dishes.

"Do you think we could talk some more? I have lots
more questions, and not just about history, either. I'm
having trouble with arithmetic, and Ma's no good with
numbers unless it's eggs, and Uncle Gideon hasn't come
to visit us lately."

Uncle Gideon. There was Reid's chance to discharge

his duties to Maggie Whitcomb's family. But then, he reasoned, why disrupt another household when he was already here?

"Sure. I don't mind talking some more," Reid found himself saying to Ty.

So Ty brought in his other books and sat at the table consulting Reid as he finished the kitchen chores.

When he was through, Reid decided he could no longer put off checking on Maggie himself.

She was awake this time, her eyes bright and her cheeks flushed, but it seemed to him that she was a little cooler. Though still awkward with the intimate task, he was able to get her sitting upright and feed her a few spoonfuls of broth before she refused any more.

"How's Willy?" she asked in a small, tired voice.

"He's fine. You needn't worry yourself about him."

Maggie looked up at him questioningly, and, despite her fever, Reid could feel the intensity of her gaze. It was as if she could probe his very soul with those wide, honest gray eyes, and Reid didn't think he'd ever want to have to lie to this woman.

What she saw in his face must have satisfied her because she nodded and said quietly, "Thank you."

"For what?"

"For everything. Staying here. Trying to help me get better. Looking after the boys."

"I don't mind." Strangely enough, he found that he didn't. "It's been . . . refreshing."

She seemed to want to say more but apparently was too exhausted to do so. As if against her will, her eyes closed and she drifted off to sleep.

Reid stood watching her for a moment longer, again experiencing an odd tugging sensation inside, where he thought he'd long since ceased to feel anything. To distract himself, he considered her medical status. He thought of malaria and scarlet fever, but she didn't have the cyclical chills of malaria nor the telltale rash of scarlet fever. Pneumonia worried him more than anything else. But with luck and proper care, they could probably ward it off.

He tromped downstairs and went outside to work, leaving Ty in the house with Maggie. Will looked pleased to see him and tagged along after him, asking his usual blunt questions. Though it was a topic he tended to be closemouthed about, Reid found himself chatting freely about Savannah and New Orleans and the other places he had roamed since war's end.

Ty had come out to join them after his studies, and the threesome completed the farmyard chores and then prepared for supper, another hardscrabble affair constructed from the last of Maggie's leftovers.

"Tell you what," Reid suggested to Ty and Will. "If your ma's feeling well enough tomorrow to leave her alone for a while, we can go fishing. One thing I know how to do is clean a fish and fry it."

"I know how to make squirrel stew," Ty offered. "Uncle Hunter taught me."

"Well, we'll be able to have a regular feast, won't we?" Reid smiled even as he stood to tackle the thankless task of washing up the dishes.

Before he retired to the barn for the night, he went upstairs to look in on Maggie. She was more flushed than she had been that afternoon, and her skin was hot to the touch. Damn. Her temperature was higher. Reid made to bathe her face and wrists with a cool cloth, then decided there was nothing for it but to unfasten her clothes and bathe her chest as well. He noticed that his hands trembled as he loosened her collar and placed dampened cloths over her throat and the uppermost swell of her breasts.

He sat down in the rocker beside the bed. Maggie was tossing and turning, muttering unintelligibly. He waited, reapplying the cool, wet cloth to her brow every few minutes, urging her in her lucid moments to sip a little water. She sweat profusely, and her thick hair was damp and curling about her face.

Just as Reid became dreadfully certain she was heading into pneumonia, she stopped tossing, and her moans and mutterings ended. Reid leaned over and cautiously laid his hand upon her forehead. She was cooler —her fever had broken! Relief swept through him, and he sagged back in the chair. She would make it now.

Reid was right. By the next morning, Maggie's fever was gone. She sat up in bed and drank some of the chicken broth Reid and Ty served her. Will, as usual, loitered in the hall, seemingly frightened at seeing Maggie in bed.

Reid took Will downstairs to help him with breakfast, leaving Ty beside his mother.

"Reid's taking us down to the pond to fish," the boy told her. "He said he would if you were better. Do you think you can stay by yourself all morning?"

"Oh, yes, I'm feeling much better. My sore throat's gone, and I feel mostly tired and achy. All I'll do is sleep, I'm sure."

"I could stay here if you needed me . . ." Ty said.

Maggie smiled and shook her head. "You're sweet, but there's no need."

"I like Reid—"

"Mr. Prescott," Maggie automatically corrected.

"But he told me I could call him Reid."

Maggie raised her eyebrows but wasted no energy protesting further.

"He helped me study yesterday," Ty bubbled. "He knows a lot! More than Uncle Gideon, I think. He could tell me all kinds of things—about plants and history and mathematics!" Ty suddenly looked wistful. "I wish he could stay here all the time. I could learn a lot from him."

Once again Maggie wondered what a well-educated man was doing roaming the countryside. Surely he could get a job; surely he couldn't be content with a hand-to-mouth existence. She frowned, wondering about Reid Prescott.

At her negative expression, Ty looked disappointed. "I thought maybe . . . maybe he could stay on a while longer, maybe help me with my lessons, too."

"But how would we pay him?" Maggie protested as she had before, startled at the tingle of excitement she herself felt at her son's suggestion.

"He told us yesterday that sometimes he's worked for just food and a place to stay. Maybe he could do that here. I bet you're a better cook than folks are at some of the other places he's stayed."

Maggie looked doubtful. She could see how much Ty wanted the man to stay, and right now, weak as she was, the idea of having someone to help out around the place was absolutely heavenly. There were so many things that needed doing; she was barely able to scrape by, and her brother could help only so much. After all, Gideon had his own farm to look after, and he helped Tess out, too.

Yet somehow Maggie was reluctant to ask Reid Prescott to stay. She hated to ask favors of anyone, and there was something about the man that made her feel especially unsettled, uncertain.

"He's . . . not like us, honey," she told Ty slowly. "You know, the other day he said he didn't want to stay put. He likes to travel."

"You won't know unless you ask." Ty leaned closer in entreaty. "Please, Ma? Will really likes him, too. Reid hasn't gotten mad at him or anything. He talks to him and lets him hang around while he works. Will thinks Reid hung the moon."

"Let me think about it," Maggie hedged, too weak to argue just then.

"All right. But promise you'll *really* think about it."

Her son knew her too well, Maggie thought not for the first time. "All right, I promise." And her words sent Ty happily scampering from the room.

*   *   *

By the next morning, Maggie felt well enough to dress and come downstairs to the kitchen.

There she found Reid Prescott lighting the stove. The egg basket already sat full on the table.

"Mrs. Whitcomb! Are you sure you're feeling well enough to get up?" He came over to her, frowning a little.

"I'm fine, I assure you. I simply can't stay in bed being lazy another day."

"It's hardly lazy to recuperate," he pointed out.

"I can't continue to let everybody else do my work."

He shrugged and glanced around. "Well . . . I guess that leaves me free to go."

Was that reluctance she heard in his voice? Maggie wondered. No, just wishful thinking on her part, she decided, since she knew she had to honor her promise to Ty. As he started to turn away, she blurted, "Mr. Prescott—"

He pivoted and looked at her questioningly.

"Do you . . . that is . . . I was wondering if you would consider staying on. I mean, we could use another pair of hands around the place, and Ty told me how you helped him with his studies. I—I couldn't pay you, at least not yet, but I could give you room and board. We could fix up a better place in the barn," she rushed on. "Would you consider it?"

An odd look crossed his face. "I . . . That's a very kind offer, ma'am, but . . ."

Maggie nodded quickly, embarrassed now at having asked him when he'd already said, days ago, that he was eager to move on. "That's all right. I understand."

"Well, I, uh, I'd better go out to the barn and get my things together. I'll need to say good-bye to Will and Ty."

"We all appreciate your help. The boys have both become very fond of you over the past few days." Maggie almost thought she saw him blush but decided she was wrong when he rapidly replied.

"I like them, too. It's . . . nothing to do with them. I just like to keep traveling."

Maggie nodded uncomfortably, and he began to amble to the door, his eyes down as if he were studying something on the floor. Maggie reached for the skillet and set it on the stove.

Reid Prescott had reached the door and was staring out. Maggie followed his gaze and saw Ty and Will walking up from the barn, each carrying a pail of milk. She looked back at him but could read nothing in his face.

Finally, almost as if the words were being pulled from him, he said, "You know . . . I guess I could, uh, stay on a while longer. Till I get some of the things around the yard caught up."

Maggie went still. Unaccountably, she could feel a smile spreading within her, but she struggled to keep it off her face. "Why, thank you, Mr. Prescott. That's very kind of you. I—the boys would like that, I'm sure."

4

Saturday morning, as Maggie was doing her chores after breakfast, she heard the sound of a wagon rolling into the yard. She smiled, guessing who it was, and washed the flour from her hands. Just as she reached the back door to greet her visitors, it opened and Josephine Tyrrell came bustling in.

Maggie's mother was a trifle plumper than she had been when she was young, and a streak of white now ran through the dark brown hair as thick and curly as her daughter's. Jo, as she was known to her friends, was still a striking woman, however. Maggie had inherited her strong, even features, and she knew that when she looked at her mother, she was seeing herself in thirty years.

"Hello, honey," Jo greeted her daughter warmly, reaching out to hug her.

"Hello, Mama."

Maggie's brother entered the door behind their mother. "Hello, Sis."

"Gideon!"

Though Maggie was tall for a woman, she had to go on tiptoe to hug her brother. At nearly six and a half feet, Gideon was the biggest of the Tyrrell men, none of whom could be considered small, and his shoulders were proportionately broad. His arms and chest were heavy with muscle, and his wide, thick hands were callused from years of working a plow. His wheat-colored hair, lightened by almost constant exposure to the sun, was tousled, as it usually was, because of his habit of running his fingers through it. In startling contrast to his deeply tanned face, his eyes were a pale, clear blue.

Thirty-five now, Gideon was the oldest of the Tyrrell children, and time and weather and care had worn creases into his stalwart face. Their father had died not long before the War began, and Gideon had assumed the responsibilities of head of the family without complaint. He had never married and had continued to live on and work the family farm, leaving it only to fight in the War between the States. Unlike Shelby and Hunter, he had not been one of those who rushed into the fray but had gone only after long and careful thought. Gideon rarely did anything impulsively.

Footsteps thundered down the stairs, and Ty and Will came rushing into the room. "Gran! Uncle Gideon!"

Jo reached out to pull her grandson into her arms. "Ty! How are you, honey? Goodness, I think you've grown since I saw you last."

"Ah, Gran . . ." But Ty's grin was proud.

"And Will." Jo hugged him, too. She, it seemed, had had the least trouble adjusting to the new Will, perhaps because he had grown up alongside her Gideon. Both his parents having died when he was young, Will had been raised by a rather strict maiden aunt, and, always eager to escape from her quiet solemnity, he had spent a great deal of time at the more rambunctious Tyrrell household. As a result, it was easy for Jo to revert to treating him like the child she had known then.

Will returned her hug, hard. "Hello, Gran. I love you."

"I love you, too, dear." Jo kissed him on the cheek.

Gideon reached out and ruffled Ty's hair playfully. Two years ago, Ty would have run at his uncle full tilt and thrown his arms around him, but he was getting too old and self-conscious to do that any longer.

"Hey, Ty. Will." Gideon clapped Will on the back a little awkwardly.

"Well, what brings you all here today?" Maggie asked as the family naturally grouped itself around the big kitchen table. "Going into town?"

"Yes. I need to buy some sugar and flour. Do you want to come? Gideon's going over to Tess's to fix her fence," Jo said. Tess was her son Shelby's widow, and all the Tyrrells tried to help her out. It was difficult, especially in these bad times, for a woman to make it alone. "The last time I was there, I noticed it was sagging in the back."

"I see." Maggie glanced toward her brother. For a time after Shelby died, she had hoped that something might develop between Gideon and Tess. They were both such good people, deserving of happiness, yet each lived a relatively lonely life. But Gideon and Tess remained only friends, and Maggie had finally decided that they were simply too different to take to each other in a romantic way. Gideon was quiet, almost shy, a practical, hardworking man, whereas Tess was bubbly, sparkling, talkative, always ready to laugh and a favorite at parties and balls.

"Please, Ma!" Ty wheedled. "Can we go to town, too?"

"May we," Maggie corrected automatically. "Oh, I suppose so. It might be fun to get out a little."

"Good." Jo smiled, then sent a searching look at her daughter. "I also had to stop by to make sure you were all right. When you didn't come to church or dinner Sunday, I was afraid something was wrong."

"I had a fever for a day or two," Maggie admitted, "but I'm fine now."

"Are you sure?" Jo took hold of Maggie's chin and studied her face. "You look a mite peaked."

"Ma, it was only a cold."

"Well, why didn't you send Ty to fetch me? I'd have come taken care of you and the boys."

"There was no need," Maggie demurred.

"Reid was here," Ty offered from behind them.

Maggie stiffened.

"What did you say, dear? Something about reeds?"

Ty chuckled. "Not *reeds,* Gran, *Reid.*" "Reid Prescott took care of us when Mama was sick. That's why she didn't send for you."

"Who's Reid Prescott?" Jo turned to her daughter, puzzled. "Maggie, what is he talking about?"

"Reid's come to live with us!" Will burst out, grinning from ear to ear, proud to impart the information.

"What?" Both Jo and Gideon stared at Maggie.

"Mr. Prescott is our new hired hand," Maggie explained quickly.

"Hired hand! You've hired a man to work for you?" A frown darkened Gideon's brow.

"Well . . . yes. That is, well, I don't know if you can call it hiring someone if you don't pay a salary, but Mr. Prescott agreed to stay for a while and work in return for room and board."

Jo looked shocked. "He's living here with you?"

"Well, not in the house, Ma! There's that room in the barn, and we put a bed and chest in it for him. He's staying there."

"But, Maggie, you know that if you needed some work done, I'd have come over to do it for you," Gideon protested.

"I know, and you're a dear. But I hate being an extra burden to you. You have so much to do on the homeplace. Why, you're so hard-pressed, you're having to let a lot of land lie fallow. On top of that, you try to help both Tess and me, repairing things and plowing our vegetable gardens and all. It's too much for you."

"No, it's not. I'm glad to help," Gideon replied earnestly. "I don't want you to have to rely on some stranger."

"Yes, who is this man?" Jo put in, raising the question dearest to the heart of a Southern mother. "Is he from Pine Creek?"

"No, Ma, he's from Savannah."

"What's he doing way out here?"

"I—well, he travels a lot, I think."

"A vagabond," Jo interpreted. "Margaret Anne Tyrrell Whitcomb, just what do you think you're doing, hiring a complete stranger, a drifter? And you all alone on this place! What were you thinking of?"

"I was thinking of all the things that need to be done around the farm," Maggie retorted.

Jo Tyrrell fixed her daughter with a stern look, one Maggie had seen many times before. "There's no need to be rude."

Maggie sighed. "I'm sorry, Ma. I didn't mean to be. But I am a grown woman, able to make a simple decision without having my mother and big brother interrogate me about it."

"Ah, Maggie . . ." Gideon, always soft-hearted where his younger sister was concerned, looked distressed. "It's not like that. You know Ma and I think you're perfectly capable of handling things."

"We're simply concerned about your safety," Jo interjected. "And I see no reason to apologize for that. I've been a grown woman for many, many years now, and I'm pleased to think that you and Gideon are still concerned about me."

"And what about when Uncle John is concerned about you? Or when Aunt Cecy insisted you come into town to live with her family while Gideon was away fighting?"

Jo quirked an eyebrow at her daughter, her lips

tightening. "That's different. They're interfering busy-bodies. John still thinks of me as the little girl who used to tag around after him, and Cecy always has tried to run the whole family."

Maggie folded her arms across her chest and stared pointedly at her mother. Gideon quickly smothered a chuckle and swiveled so that his back was to Jo.

"Oh, stop laughing," Jo said crossly, rapping Gideon's arm. Then she chuckled herself, shaking her head. "All right, all right, I admit it. I *am* sticking my nose into your business. But you're my only daughter, and I don't know what a mother's supposed to do if she can't be concerned about her only daughter."

Jo looked so woebegone that Maggie had to laugh. She doubted that Josephine Tyrrell, the strongest woman she knew, was ever at a loss for what to do—about her only daughter or anything else. Similar in temperament—self-reliant, protective of those they loved, quick to flare up and just as quick to cool down—she and Jo had been at odds many times over the years, but they never remained angry at each other for long. It was easy to forgive her mother's meddling, since she knew it was done only out of love.

"You know," Gideon said thoughtfully, "it might be a good idea if I went out and had a little talk with this man while you all are getting ready to go."

"Honestly, Gideon!" Maggie frowned at him in exasperation. "I'm not a schoolgirl you have to defend from the class bully."

"You're my sister," he retorted unarguably. "And he ought to know that there's somebody around who's watching out for you."

Maggie groaned, but she knew it was pointless to argue. Most of the time Gideon was sweet and fairly tractable, but when the safety of his family was in question, there was no stopping him. "Oh, all right," she said grumpily. "Just don't scare him away. It's ever so much easier having someone around to take care of things."

"What do you take me for, an ogre?" Gideon grumbled as he rose from the table and started toward the back door.

"I'll take you out and introduce you, Uncle Gideon," Ty offered, jumping up after him.

"Oh, no, you won't, young man. You and Willy are going straight upstairs to wash your hands and put on decent shirts."

"Oh, Ma . . ."

Maggie fixed him with a look. "I'm not having you going into town looking like a ragamuffin."

Ty grimaced, but he and Will obeyed Maggie, glumly clumping out of the room and up the stairs.

Gideon quickly made his escape from the house. Much as he loved his nephew, he would just as soon not have him around while he talked to this hired hand. He didn't plan to get rough with the man—unless he had to, of course—but it would be easier to talk man-to-man with him if they were alone.

He found Reid Prescott in the barn, oiling the mule's harness. The man looked up at the sound of footsteps, and his eyebrows rose in surprise.

"I hear Maggie's taken you on to work this place," Gideon said abruptly, never one to waste time in small talk.

"That's true. Who are you?"

"I'm Maggie's brother, that's who. And I want to know your plans."

"My plans?" Reid shrugged. "Didn't Mrs. Whitcomb tell you she hired me to do some odd jobs around the place and teach Ty for a few hours a day?"

"How long do you intend to stay?"

Reid's eyes narrowed. "Exactly what's your point here?"

"I reckon you might have thought my sister was a woman alone when you came upon this place. That she was helpless, unprotected. I just wanted to let you know she's not."

Reid arched an eyebrow. "Is everybody around here this suspicious when you meet a stranger, or is it just your family? Frankly, when I came here, I didn't think much about who lived here or what they were like. The only thing I was interested in was getting out of a storm. Then Mrs. Whitcomb showed up, toting a rifle. The last thing I thought her was helpless."

Gideon struggled to keep his lips from quirking into a grin. That sounded like Maggie, all right. No doubt she was right in saying that she didn't need anyone looking after her. Besides, this man seemed like a decent enough sort, and Gideon was impatient to get to Tess's. However, that very fact made him feel guilty, so he frowned and went on, "Just remember, if you have any thoughts about stealing from her, or hurting her in any way, I'll know about it. And if I found you'd hurt her, I'd track you down and kill you," he said evenly.

"Very admirable, I'm sure," Prescott commented dryly. "But I can assure you, I intend no harm to either Mrs. Whitcomb or her family. I plan to work here for a few weeks, maybe, and then I'll be gone."

"All right." Gideon gazed at the man, then nodded and walked away, satisfied for the moment that his sister was safe.

Now he could go see Tess. His heart speeded up at the thought, though he quickly, guiltily, tried to tamp down his excitement. The last thing in the world he wanted was for his family to know his feelings for his dead brother's widow.

When Shelby had married her, Gideon had thought Tess Caldwell pretty and flirtatious but little else. He was glad that his brother was happy with her, but she wasn't the sort of woman he ever would have imagined for himself. But over the years Gideon had discovered that there was much more to Tess than he had suspected. She had handled Shelby's death and the other disasters that had befallen her during the War with strength and maturity. And, somewhere along the way, Gideon had fallen in love with her.

Not all at once. But gradually he had found himself looking forward to the Sundays Tess brought Ginny to the farm, or when he had a chore to do at her house. He thought about her, worried about her, wondered if she had enough food or if she was well, if her roof was leaking in the rain or if she was sweltering in the summer heat.

Then his thoughts had started to stray from brotherly concern to more intimate ideas, ideas that made him feel restless and guilty. He had been calling on a widow woman on the other side of Pine Creek after he came back from the War, but he couldn't sustain any interest in her, and he finally stopped seeing her. When his mother had questioned him about it, he had shrugged and conceded that there wasn't anything wrong with her, exactly. She just hadn't been . . . right.

Finally he had admitted to himself that no woman would be right because she would not be Tess.

But it seemed wrong, sinful, to covet his brother's wife, even if Shelby *was* dead. Though technically free to love Tess, even to marry her, Gideon didn't feel free. It seemed to him as if he were desecrating his brother's memory; he even worried that deep down inside somewhere maybe he had wanted Shelby to die so that he could have his woman.

Yet he had loved Shelby dearly. Only a year apart in age, they had been constant companions all their lives. Shelby had held a special place in Gideon's heart that even his best friend, Will Whitcomb, hadn't broached. But whenever he thought of Shelby now, Gideon suffered the taint of his secret desire for his brother's wife. Surely it was wrong. In a Tyrrell's mind, possibly the worst sin was disloyalty to a member of the family.

Still, whatever guilt he felt, however impossible his

dreams might be, Gideon could not keep from wanting to see Tess every chance he could.

So now he hustled his family out of Maggie's kitchen and into the wagon and drove his team as fast as he could. It was only a mile and a half into town, but the trip seemed much longer to his eager heart. When they reached Main Street, he dropped the women and the boys off in front of the general store and drove the three blocks to Tess's. Quickly he tied the mules to the hitching post and started up the walkway toward her door.

The Caldwell house was a grand, lavish affair, the most beautiful mansion in all Pine Creek. Tess's father, owner of a huge cotton plantation outside of town, had been the wealthiest man in the county before he died. George Caldwell had built the house in town for his adored wife, who hated the lonely life in the country, and his extravagant love for her showed in every line of the lovely home, a stately white two-story structure fronted by a porch that ran its full width, boasting six majestic columns to brace the graceful balcony above.

As Gideon walked up the path, a little blond dynamo came tearing out the front door and threw herself at him, trusting him to catch her. "Uncle Gideon!"

Gideon grinned and wrapped his arms around her in a bear hug, bending his head to nuzzle her pale, fine hair. Her small-boned body felt so precious in his arms that it made his eyes sting. Whenever he was with his niece, he experienced the bittersweet ache of love and loss. Ginny was as dear to him as if she were his own, but whenever he looked into her face, he saw the shadow of Shelby in her determined chin and laughing eyes.

"What is this?" he asked with good humor. "Are you a little girl or an Arkansas wildcat?"

"A wildcat," Ginny replied promptly, showing her pearly little teeth in a smile as wide as Gideon's own. "That's what Grandmama Caldwell says."

Tess, who had followed her daughter out the front

door at a more sedate pace, groaned softly at the child's statement. "Ginny . . ."

Ginny looked up at her innocently. "Well, it's true, Mama. She does."

"Yes, but I doubt she would want you to repeat it," Tess admonished.

Ginny heaved a great sigh. "That's 'cause Grandmama always wants me to be a lady. I like it better at the farm. Can I come live with you, Uncle Gideon?"

A flush stained Gideon's cheeks, and he glanced at Tess awkwardly, then away. "Well, now, you know I'd love to have you, pumpkin, but I reckon it'd make your mama pretty sad for you to leave."

"We could both come," Ginny offered reasonably.

"Ginny, hush up now. Stop badgering your uncle Gideon," Tess said, smiling and coming down the steps to greet him. "Just pay her no attention, Gideon. How are you?" She put out her hand to shake his, smiling. "I didn't expect to see you today."

Gideon took her small hand in his and gazed down into her face. He was sure that he was grinning idiotically, but he couldn't help it. Tess was so lovely that it was all he could do not to babble out his love for her.

Blond and slight of build, Tess was a pretty, vivacious woman. She had strawberries-and-cream skin and big blue eyes, and had it not been for the vibrance of her personality, she would have looked like a porcelain doll. Deep dimples marked her cheeks whenever she smiled, which was often, and her eyes sparkled with life and humor.

The pampered daughter of a wealthy Southern aristocrat, she had known nothing but ease before the War. But her father, a staunch Confederate, had invested heavily in now-worthless Confederate money and bonds. And because they had been unable to ship out cotton through the Union-controlled port of New Orleans, his plantation had had to lie fallow for nearly the whole War. In the end, the Caldwells' finances had been as much in ashes as the Confederacy itself. With both her father and Shelby dead and most of the slaves gone, Tess and her mother had been forced to sell the plantation at only a fraction of its value to a carpetbagger from the North. They were reduced to only one house servant now, an old woman who had nowhere else to go.

Tess had not fallen to pieces at the cataclysmic changes in her life. Instead, she had determinedly taken up the burden of running the big house, including doing much of the cleaning and cooking, even hauling water from the cistern and growing her own vegetables. Tess had surprised everyone, even herself, by doing so. Despite her delicate appearance, she had stamina, and after a miserable period of learning and adjustment to hard physical demands, she had found she could keep the house and her family's lives running fairly smoothly. And she had never lost her sense of humor or her cheerful outlook.

Standing there looking at her, Gideon was so overwhelmed with love for her that for a moment he couldn't even remember why he had come. "Oh . . . I . . . well, Mother said your fence needed fixing."

Tess chuckled. "And here I thought she hadn't noticed. I tried to push the boards back into place so it wasn't so obvious."

Gideon grinned. "It's hard to hide anything from Jo Tyrrell. Believe me, I've tried."

"I'll just bet you have." There was a flirtatious lilt to her voice, and Gideon wished he could convince himself it was meant for him. But he knew that that was simply Tess's manner of speaking with everyone, man, woman, or child.

"Mama's letting me make cookies!" Ginny stuck in, bored at being ignored.

"Cookies! Is that so?" Gideon grinned at her. "Well, I certainly hope you intend to save a few for me."

"I didn't know you were coming!" she protested. "But I will. You can have all you want."

"Mmm . . . and fresh out of the oven, too. I can hardly wait." He sniffed exaggeratedly. "I think I smell them already."

Ginny giggled. "We just put them in, silly!" She took Gideon's hand and pulled him into the house and down the hallway into the kitchen.

"I hope you don't mind sitting in here," Tess said. "I have to wait for Ginny's cookies to bake."

"Heavens, no. We're family, after all." Gideon sat down at the large table, scarred from years of work done at it. Truth be told, he felt more comfortable here than he did in Tess's ornate parlor. Besides, there was something pleasantly intimate about being here with her, almost as if they were husband and wife.

He tried to keep any hint of what he was thinking from showing on his face, knowing that such feelings would not be welcome and would only embarrass his sister-in-law. He was not the man for her, and he would never fool himself into thinking that he was. Tess had loved Shelby, and there had never been two brothers more unalike than he and Shelby.

Shelby had been the golden child of the family, handsome and lithe, a will-o'-the-wisp, charming and quick. He had loved horses and dancing and had worked only because he had to. He had been equally adept at managing Tess's family's plantation and orchestrating the extravagant social life of a wealthy, influential planter. Everyone who met Shelby had immediately fallen under his spell. He had been a perfect match for Tess.

Unlike himself, Gideon knew. Quiet, slow-spoken, and stolid, he had none of Shelby's smoothness and charm. Around Tess Gideon felt like a clumsy giant, and he was certain he would never appeal to her, certainly not as a possible husband.

Besides, Tess was still in love with Shelby. To this

day she mourned him, and she had no interest in marrying again. Gideon had heard her tell his mother that.

"Would you like something to eat?" Tess asked. "Or coffee?"

"Coffee'd be nice. But I have to save room for Ginny's cookies." He winked at his niece, who was fairly bouncing about the room in her eagerness to peek into the oven.

Tess poured two mugs of coffee and brought them to the table, sitting down across from Gideon. Ginny plunked herself down beside him and grinned up at her uncle.

He looped his arm around her shoulders and gave her a squeeze. "You going to help me nail that old fence together?"

The eight-year-old beamed. "Sure!" She glanced over at her mother. "May I, Mama?"

Tess pursed her lips in thought, looking from her daughter's eager face to Gideon's. She sighed. "I suppose. But run upstairs and put on one of your old dresses."

"All my dresses are old," Ginny reminded her.

"I mean one that's too worn out to wear anywhere but to work in the garden."

"All right." Ginny bounced out of her chair and started toward her bedroom. She paused at the kitchen door and turned back. "Don't go outside without me," she instructed her uncle firmly.

Gideon's lips twitched, but he said solemnly, "I won't. I promise."

Ginny flashed him a smile and scooted out the door. Seconds later, he could hear her feet pounding up the back stairs to the upper floor.

They were silent for a moment, then Tess said, "You know, in the past I wouldn't have let Ginny play carpenter's helper. It's not exactly ladylike behavior. I hate to think what *my* mother would have said if I'd asked to help nail a fence." She laughed mirthlessly. "Well, *I* wouldn't even have dared to ask. But now I guess it doesn't matter so much whether a woman ruins her hands with scratches and calluses." She glanced down at her own slender fingers. "I hardly recognize mine anymore. I remember when I used to spread lotion on them constantly to keep them soft and pretty. I never went outside without gloves, and if I was foolish enough to forget, I'd put on cucumber paste to get rid of the freckles."

She shook her head and said softly, "Things are so different now."

Gideon gazed at her sadly. "I know. I'm sorry you've had to suffer."

"Don't be. It's not your fault. And I don't mind so much. In some ways it's been . . . I don't know, almost freeing, I suppose. Not worrying about whether you're going to freckle saves loads of time. And I don't get bored any longer," Tess pointed out, making light of her troubles.

Gideon wanted to tell her that he would take care of her, that he would make sure nothing bad ever happened to her again. He wanted to pull her into his arms and cradle her there, sheltering her from the world. He wanted to kiss her.

It always came back to that, he thought: his carnal hunger for Tess. There was no escaping it, no amount of honor or duty or family loyalty that could purify his love into something selfless and noble. The lust was there, would always be there, mingling inextricably with his love.

Sometimes he thought he should stop coming around, should cut himself off from Tess entirely. Surely over time, then, his pain would stop, his desire would ease, his love for her would lessen and die. But that was the one thing Gideon was certain he could never do. No matter how frustrating it was to be around her, knowing he could never have her, it didn't compare to the misery of being without her.

"I'm ready!" Ginny burst into the room.

Gideon had to smile at her appearance. She looked like an urchin in the worn dress several inches too short for her, seam marks showing where it had been let out, but it didn't dampen her enthusiasm for life a whit. "So I see," he commented lightly. "Well, come on, then. We'd better get to it." He stood up and held out his hand.

"You two run and play," Tess teased.

Gideon kept smiling, but inside his heart ached. He thought he would have given anything in the world if only this were really his family: this girl, his daughter, and this woman, his wife.

But that could never be. Even with Shelby lying in his grave, Tess and Ginny would always be his brother's family. And he could be nothing but their caretaker.

5

Maggie and her mother strolled along the aisle of the mercantile, eagerly assessing the wares. Willy and Ty had long since grown bored and left to roam up and down the main street. But for the two women, shopping was a treat, even though neither had any extra money to spend. During the War, there had been so few things in the stores even to look at! Besides, the jaunt provided an opportunity to chat with townspeople they rarely saw otherwise.

As they idled by a display of calico, the front door opened with a jingle of its bell, and in stepped Benton Conway, a balding, middle-aged man whose expensively tailored clothes could not disguise his distinct paunch. He had a fleshy face dominated by pale, almost colorless eyes, and he walked with deliberate arrogance, hardly glancing around him, as if expecting all obstacles to clear deferentially out of his path.

Beside him was his daughter, Rosemary, a small, slender girl with mousy brown hair, her eyes effectively hidden by a pair of wire-framed spectacles as she shyly gazed down at the floor.

Rosemary faded into insignificance beside the third member of the party, a stunningly beautiful redhead. The woman's eyes were a vivid blue, her complexion soft rose and white, and her form and face almost perfectly modeled. Her blue silk gown was cut in the latest fashion, not an old dress resewn as Maggie and many of the other women wore, and it was ornamented beautifully. Her hat, reticule, and gloves likewise proclaimed elegance and wealth, and her slippers were of fine, supple leather. She was Benton Conway's second wife, Linette. The woman who had once been engaged to Maggie's brother Hunter.

Jo Tyrrell's mouth tightened as she looked at the Conways, but she said nothing. She wasn't one to air family troubles in public. But Maggie knew there were few people her mother despised more.

Jo had once been very fond of Linette; the girl had seemed a perfect match for Hunter, sure to be what he needed to make him settle down. But when Hunter had mistakenly been reported killed in battle, Linette had married Benton Conway with callous, indecorous haste, casting both her love—and her character—into dubious shadow. When he finally returned, Hunter had been devastated to learn that the woman he loved had so blithely wed another, and he had never been the same since. He had left town and headed west, and Jo would never forgive Benton and Linette the hurt they had caused him and his family.

The Tyrrells, however, were not the only people in Pine Creek who disliked the Conways. Benton Conway was one of a group Southerners sneeringly called Scalawags; after the War, they had befriended the conquering Yankees and the carpetbaggers who had swooped down upon the South to profit from its defeat. Conway had accumulated a great deal of money in that fashion, but as his wealth grew, the esteem in which he was held by the other citizens had dropped. If there was one thing the people of Arkansas admired, it was loyalty— to family, to homeplace, to state.

Indeed, secession sentiment had barely edged out the anti-secession vote in Arkansas—it was not a large slave-holding state, with few of the grand plantations that provided the insatiable demand for labor in which slavery had taken root—yet the loyalty of the rest of the citizens had sent them into war. One stood by one's own, no matter what the price. Therefore, someone like Benton Conway, who would turn his back on his own people and associate with the enemy just to make money, was thoroughly despised.

By now he had spotted Mrs. Tyrrell and Maggie, and he stopped and smiled. "Good afternoon, Mrs. Tyrrell. Mrs. Whitcomb. How nice to see you."

Maggie stared coldly at him while Jo gave him a short nod and said stiffly, "Mr. Conway. Mrs. Conway." Her eyes slid over Linette coolly, but she smiled at Benton's daughter. "Good afternoon, Rosemary."

"Good day, Mrs. Tyrrell." Rosemary, a shy, bookish creature, looked rather like a scared rabbit.

Linette was as cool and reserved as ever. Maggie had never understood exactly what had happened to the vivacious, laughing girl Hunter had loved. Linette Sanders had once been Tess's best friend, as well, but after her marriage she had dropped Tess, too, turning into this remote, icy beauty who rarely took part in the social life of Pine Creek. Maggie wondered if any of them had ever known the real Linette, or if the girl had been playing a part all along, interested only in snagging a man. It was hard to imagine that she had been so cold and skillful an actress, yet it was equally hard to imagine that she had changed so abruptly into a completely different person.

The Conways strolled through the room, pausing near a couple at the sales counter. The man grudgingly shook Benton's hand and spoke to him. His wife flushed and looked away.

"No doubt that man owes Mr. Conway money," Jo commented acidly. "I suspect Benton lends people money for the sheer pleasure of owning them afterward."

At that moment, another customer came in the front door. When his eyes fell on Conway, he stopped, staring blearily. Then he straightened his shoulders and began stalking across the floor. Everyone in the store turned to watch, wide-eyed, as the man lurched toward the Conways.

His name was Robert Bowlin, and he had owned the cartage company and a warehouse in Pine Creek before the War. But, with business faltering badly, he had sold out to Benton Conway two years ago. Since then he had tried working at other trades, but he had been unable to make a go of anything, and his wife had started taking in sewing to make ends meet. Maggie had heard that Robert had stopped even trying to work and had taken to drinking and roaming the streets, muttering about his misfortunes to anyone he could buttonhole. Judging by his unsteady gait, Maggie suspected he was in such an inebriated state right now.

His wife, Samantha, who had been looking at buttons when he came to retrieve her, gasped when she realized her husband's condition—and his intent. Quickly she fluttered toward him. "Robert, please . . . !"

"God damn you," Bowlin growled, grabbing Conway by the arm and whirling him around to face him.

Jo and Maggie exchanged shocked looks. Such behavior in public was scandalous, so much so that for a moment everyone froze, unsure what to do.

Conway sneered at Bowlin. "You're drunk, Robert."

"At least I'm not a lying, swindling son-of-a-bitch like you!" Bowlin shouted, his hands balling into fists at his sides.

Samantha Bowlin moaned, clamping a hand to her mouth. Bowlin swayed a little, but there was no uncertainty in his taut face and blazing eyes.

"Daddy . . ." Rosemary tugged at her father's arm, her eyes wide and her face as white as paper. "Let's go." Linette simply stood by stiffly, her face pale, her eyes unreadable.

"Nonsense." Conway faced his accuser squarely, his face red with anger. "I won't be run off by some bourbon-swilling failure who—"

"You bastard!" Bowlin roared.

At that the curtain over the doorway into the back twitched open, and the owner of the store peered out. His eyes bulged when he saw what was happening, and he hastened out onto the selling floor.

"Robert!" he snapped, motioning toward his clerk for help. "That's enough!"

But Robert Bowlin was too filled with rage to hear him, and he continued to rant at Conway. "You stole my business! You've stolen half the money you've got! You lie down like a whore with the enemy—why, you're lower than a goddamn Yankee! Lower than a snake that crawls on its belly!"

Mr. Macklin reached the two men and clamped a hand firmly around Bowlin's arm. "Robert," he said through clenched teeth, "you forget, there are ladies present. Come on, let's you and I go outside."

"Let go of me!" Robert tried to shake off Macklin, but the clerk had reached them now, and he grabbed Bowlin's other arm.

The two men dragged him toward the front door, but Bowlin dug in his heels and struggled, shouting back at the other customers, "He's cheated everyone he's ever had dealings with! He lent me money—'Here, take it, Robert,' he said. 'I know you'll pay me back, and I won't dun you for it.' Then he pulled my business right out from under me! Called my note due and took it all. Took everything I'd ever worked for! And old

Geoff Carter—he stole his farm from him, had his Yankee friends raise his taxes till he couldn't pay them and they took his land away. Look who bought it for a pittance! He's a liar and a thief, and the truth isn't in him! I'm not the only one he's ruined! He likes to do it. Look at him!"

Everyone in the store watched in appalled fascination as Bowlin was dragged out of the store and the door closed, cutting off his tirade. As Samantha Bowlin followed, weeping, Maggie couldn't help but steal a glance at Conway. His smug expression suggested the accuracy of Bowlin's statements. Catching her gaze, Conway smiled at Maggie and bowed, his eyes so cold that Maggie shivered.

Jo turned to the man's daughter, conspicuously ignoring Benton himself, who didn't spare a glance for the embarrassed, frightened girl. "Rosemary, are you all right?" Mrs. Tyrrell asked solicitously.

"Yes." Rosemary's eyes filled with tears, negating her words. "I'm fine. I'm sorry."

"Nonsense," Jo said stoutly. "*You* did nothing wrong."

"Papa, please, let's leave," Rosemary whispered.

"Don't be absurd," Benton responded scornfully. "Robert Bowlin is just a noisy, whining drunk. Pay him no mind and do your shopping, girl."

Since it was obvious that Rosemary found it painful to be the object of so many curious stares, Maggie and her mother gave a reassuring smile and turned away, walking to the other side of the store and pretending to be interested in a display of threads.

"Poor girl," Jo whispered indignantly. "Her life must be very difficult, having to live with that man and *her*."

Maggie nodded. "Do you suppose he really did those things Mr. Bowlin said?"

Jo snorted. "I imagine Robert barely scratched the surface." She sighed. "That unpleasant scene has taken away all my pleasure in looking at things. Let's go to Tess's while Gideon finishes up."

"All right." As they made to leave, Maggie glanced back at the Conways. Mr. Macklin had returned and was profusely apologizing to Benton, who was visibly preening under the man's effusiveness. Rosemary looked as if she would like to sink through the floor. Her stepmother had moved aside and was idly fingering a bolt of delicate lace.

Linette glanced up, as if she had felt Maggie's gaze on her, and for an instant her blue eyes were huge pools of sorrow. The sadness was so deep, so intense, it took Maggie's breath away. Then suddenly the woman's eyes were shuttered again, the pain gone, and Maggie wondered if she had only imagined it.

Linette turned back to the fabric. Maggie hesitated, then followed her mother out of the store.

Will hummed tunelessly as he sloshed the paddle of the butter churn up and down. Maggie glanced at him and smiled. Churning was one of Will's favorite chores. Its rhythmic quality seemed to soothe him, and it was something that, given his superior strength, he could do better and more quickly than either Ty or Maggie, allowing him the rare pleasure of excelling at something.

Will looked up from his task and grinned. "Sing," he entreated. When she raised her eyebrows at him, he quickly added, "Please."

Maggie smiled. "All right." Will loved to hear her sing, and the song didn't matter much. Children's ditties, hymns, ballads—anything delighted him.

Maggie started with a light and lively Stephen Foster tune. Will joined in on the chorus; he didn't have a particularly good voice, but he belted out the words with enthusiasm, keeping time with his foot and the butter paddle. Maggie liked to sing when she worked.

Ty had loved it, too, when he was younger. But now she supposed he had decided that the practice was childish.

She looked at Will and smiled at the picture he made, his face glowing with good spirits, his hips bouncing a little on the stool as he churned enthusiastically. Unlike Ty, Will would always be a child, staying by her side, reveling in a simple song, not bored by a repetitive task, loving her with uncritical devotion. The thought touched her with a melancholy sweetness. She walked over to him and bent to kiss him on the forehead, smoothing back his hair. He looked up at her, smiling.

Maggie found herself searching his face for some sign of the old Will, some spark of intelligence or memory or even mischief. But there was nothing akin to adulthood or experience in his eyes. She remembered how she used to feel, gazing into those eyes—the excited racing her heart would start, the breathless, tingling anticipation. She remembered how he would glance at her sometimes across the supper table, a certain glow in his eyes and a softness to his mouth that told her he was thinking about making love to her when they went to bed that night. And she remembered, too, how her own blood had heated at that look.

She straightened and stepped away. It was better not to remember such things. They made her too sad, made her wish for things she couldn't have. Usually she was better at keeping them at bay. Over the past few years Maggie had become good at quite a few things she had never imagined she would need to do.

"Where's Ty?" Will asked.

Maggie bit back a sigh. It was no use getting irritated with Will, either; he couldn't help being the way he was. "You know where he is, Willy," she said calmly. "I told you a while ago. He's under the willow tree, reading and preparing for his lesson with Mr. Prescott, remember?"

"Oh." Will nodded, satisfied. Ty spent nearly every morning studying. Will often forgot that, though, and would look around or ask where he was. However, he always accepted the answer equably, never pestering Maggie to allow him to go out and be with Ty instead of finishing his tasks.

All in all, Maggie knew, Will was very easy and biddable, and she should thank her lucky stars for that. Not everyone whose minds went were as docile as he. She remembered Celia Porter's elderly father, who had gotten extremely cantankerous as he lost his faculties. Celia was apt to find him wandering around outside in the middle of the night, with no idea of why he was there or what he was doing but likely to explode into a rage when she tried to make him come in. Once he had even thrown a washbasin at her head. She had ducked, fortunately, and the basin had broken harmlessly against the wall, but Celia told Maggie that she had sat right down on the floor and cried, she was so tired and upset.

If Will had turned mean or feisty, Maggie didn't know what she would have done, for he was too large and strong for her and Ty to handle.

Still, despite his gentle disposition, there were times when she almost couldn't stand the feeling of pain and regret that would squeeze her heart. In the past few days, since Reid Prescott had been at their place, she seemed to have had more difficulty with that kind of feeling.

"Oh, Ma, come look!" Will sucked in a breath, his attention suddenly riveted to the open doorway.

"What is it?" Maggie wiped her floury hands off on her apron as she walked toward the door, knowing it was as apt to be a bright red cardinal Will had spotted as anything more dramatic.

She looked out. "Oh, my Lord," she breathed, and her hands went up to her mouth, whether to stifle a giggle or a gasp of alarm, she wasn't sure.

Outside in the yard, Reid Prescott was tacking a roll of chicken wire onto one of the four slender posts he had sunk into the ground around the peach tree. Maggie had asked him to erect a fence around the young tree this morning because the goat was continually nibbling at the tender bark and new leaves. But now the mean-spirited billy goat was standing not twenty feet behind Prescott, eyeing his posterior as he stooped to secure the wire.

The goat, ornery as he admittedly was, would never have attacked something as tall as a man. However, bent over, Reid made a perfect target, and Maggie knew the goat would never pass up such a golden opportunity.

"Mr. Prescott!" she called in warning. But just as she did so, the goat lowered its head and charged.

Reid twisted and looked over his shoulder toward the house, still reaching down to hold the springy wire in place. His eyebrows arched questioningly, but he couldn't speak for the two nails he held between his teeth.

"Look out!" Maggie shrieked, pointing. "Behind—"

At that moment the goat hit him squarely in the seat of the pants, and Reid sprawled forward, the nails flying from his mouth and the hammer from his hand. His shoulder hit the post, pushing it askew, and he went down in a tangle of chicken wire and fence poles.

Will burst into laughter, and Maggie had to press her hand hard against her mouth to keep back her own giggles. This undignified view of lean, laconic Reid Prescott was just too comical to resist a chuckle.

The goat, its foe thus vanquished, didn't spare a glance for the man. It planted its front legs on the slender tree trunk and stretched its neck up to tear off a sprig of leaves. Then it dropped back to all fours and stood beside Reid, chewing away.

Maggie reined in her giggles and hurried out into the yard, flapping her apron at the goat. "Git! Get away! Go on, you stupid old goat. Git!"

For a moment the billy goat regarded her with its

bright black eyes, leaves dangling foolishly out of its mouth. Maggie clapped her hands. "Go on, you, git!"

Haughtily the goat finally turned and pranced away. Maggie looked toward Reid, who had kicked and rolled, trying to get free of the chicken wire, until he was even more tangled up in it. Maggie couldn't contain a giggle, and he glared up at her.

"I'm sorry," she said, choking back her laughter and bending down to pull the wiring away from him. "I should have told you to tie up the goat before you attacked his favorite nibbling place."

Reid grimaced and pushed away her helping hand. "I'm afraid I'm not very familiar with billy goats."

"I'm sorry," Maggie repeated. "I don't mean to laugh."

Reid pulled the wire from his legs, unhooking it from where it had caught on a button on his trousers. But the bouncy wire caught on the back of his shirt, and in frustration, he jerked at the mesh, hearing a loud rip as at last it pulled free. "Blast!"

"Oh, no, you tore your shirt!"

Reid twisted to look over his shoulder at the V-shaped rent. His brows drew together, and he cursed under his breath. Then he cast a glance at Maggie. Seeing the twinkle in her eyes and the way her mouth twitched, he scowled and struggled to his feet, shoving the quivering wire aside. As he stood, however, the wire sprang back and caught his foot. Disgusted, he shook it off, and as he did so, his gaze went to Maggie again, who had now clapped both hands to her mouth and looked as if she were about to explode. He glared at her, then back at the curling wire.

Maggie was sure he was going to storm off. But, to her surprise, his shoulders began to shake, and she realized that he was laughing, too. Freed from her self-restraint, she burst into giggles, and soon she was guffawing, holding her sides against the almost painful waves of laughter. Reid, too, became helpless with laughter, setting her off yet again.

Will joined them, looking in happy puzzlement from one to the other, and Ty, who had been reading under the willow, came around the side of the house at the commotion. The three of them tried to relate to him what had happened, all the while fighting their laughter and gasping for air.

When Ty finally made sense of their words, he stared at Reid in astonishment. "You mean you didn't tie Euphemia up?"

"Euphemia!" Reid repeated in equal amazement. "You named that son-of-Satan Euphemia?"

Ty nodded, and Reid went off into another storm of laughter.

Will smiled, too, pleased that for once he understood the joke. "It's silly, isn't it? 'Cause Euphemia's a billy goat, not a nanny."

"Well," Ty protested, "I couldn't help that. I didn't know he was a boy, and he looked like Aunt Euphemia."

"You mean you named him after someone?"

"Yes," Maggie replied, grinning a little shame-facedly. "Will's aunt. And"—she giggled—"Ty was right. She looks exactly like that goat—except for the beard, of course."

At that they all began to laugh again, and it was some time before they calmed down. Finally Maggie said, "I really am sorry about your shirt, Mr. Prescott. Let me sew it up for you."

He hesitated. "You don't need to do that, ma'am."

"It's no trouble. After all, that blasted Euphemia is my goat."

"Then I reckon you have trouble enough already," he commented dryly.

Maggie smiled. "No, really, please let me do it. I'll feel better." She thought how much younger and more handsome Reid looked with his face lit with amusement. This was a man who *should* smile, she realized.

Her eyes went to his mouth. His lips were full, parting over even white teeth. At the sight she felt suddenly breathless, and her brain went blank. Her gaze flew to his, and for an instant heat seemed to flicker in his eyes, but it vanished so quickly that Maggie wasn't sure she had really seen it. Flustered, she stepped back, hoping she wasn't blushing.

"All right," Reid said finally. "Just let me change into another shirt." And he headed for the barn.

While he was gone, Maggie tied the goat to a fence post at some distance from the tree, and the boys replaced the fallen poles. Reid returned a few minutes later and held out his torn shirt. Remembering the strange feelings that had afflicted her earlier when she had looked at Reid, Maggie was almost reluctant to touch it. It suddenly seemed too personal, too intimate, as if touching the cloth that had lain against his skin would be like touching his skin itself. Maggie forced her fingers to curl around the fabric, wondering if she felt or only imagined that it retained a trace of the heat from his body. Tongue-tied, she said nothing, yet she could not seem to move away.

Beside her, Will shifted impatiently. "Look, Reid," he said, too eager to wait. "Ty and I set up the posts."

His words broke whatever spell had held both Maggie and Reid motionless. Reid turned to Will, who was standing proudly beside the posts. "Yes, I see. Thank you both. That was good work."

Maggie finally started toward the house again. She didn't like the jangly feeling in her stomach. Whatever was the matter with her?

"I'll finish up here," she heard Reid say, "and then you and I can get started on our lessons, Ty."

"Can I do it, too?" Will asked, his voice laced with disappointment and longing.

Maggie stopped and looked back at the three of

them. Will had that hopeless, hangdog look on his face that he got whenever he felt abandoned in some way. Maggie's heart ached. She hoped Reid would let him down easy; Will's feelings were so easily hurt.

Much to her surprise, Reid replied lightly, "Sure, Will. After Ty and I get through this afternoon. How would that be?"

Will's face lit up. "Really?" He turned to Ty, beaming, and nudged him with his elbow. "I'm going to school, too!"

Ty smiled. "That's terrific, Will." But his eyes flickered worriedly toward his mother.

Maggie bit her lip. Obviously Reid didn't understand about Will. "Boys? Hadn't you better get back to work? You know, Willy, that butter'll never set if you don't go back and churn it."

"All right." Will sighed and trudged past her to the kitchen. Evidently even the butter churn didn't hold as much appeal as the prospect of lessons with Reid.

Ty picked up his book and walked back toward the willow tree, and Maggie knew that he understood she needed to talk to Reid.

"Mr. Prescott . . ." she began uncomfortably, returning to his side.

He looked at her questioningly. "Yes?"

She stopped beside him. "I—well, I'm not sure you realize what condition Will is in. He wants to be like Ty, to read and study, but he can't."

Reid shrugged. "We never know what the human brain is capable of. I've heard of cases that were considered hopeless, but—"

Maggie interrupted him. "It doesn't matter what you've heard of. This is Will we're talking about, and I won't have you raising his hopes that he might be able to read or learn the things that Ty does. It's cruel."

Reid cocked an eyebrow. "You seem awfully anxious not to let him try. Why? Is it easier to let him stay the way he is?"

Hot, choking anger rushed through Maggie. "Easier! You think I've done what was *easy* with Will? You think I didn't try to bring him back to himself, didn't try to teach him to read and write again? That I didn't sit with him for hour after hour with Ty's slate and chalk, trying to teach him the alphabet? Not even a word, not even his name, just simple letters! He couldn't do it! He would try to copy them, but he'd get the letters backwards, or he'd be missing something, and he couldn't really understand what was wrong with them. He couldn't retain anything. He'd grasp a word one day, be able to read it, but the next day it would be as if he'd never seen the word before."

Tears sprang into her eyes at the memory, and Maggie clenched her fists, burying them in her skirts. Her voice caught, but she plunged ahead, too wrought up to stop. "I wanted my husband back. I was sure that if I worked with him long enough, tried hard enough, he'd get back to the way he had been. I kept trying to make his mind well, telling myself that I could do it, just like I'd made his body well again. But I couldn't! Will wasn't there anymore!" She pressed her hand against her forehead and struggled not to give way to tears.

"I'm sorry." Reid stepped forward quickly, taking her arm. "I didn't know."

"Nobody knows!" Maggie replied fiercely. "Everybody says, 'How good you are with him, Maggie, how kind.' And, 'Well, at least he's not much trouble.' They don't know what it's like to look at a man every day and know that this is my husband and yet to know that, inside, he's gone. He's as far away from me as if he had died. I wanted so badly to get him back. I tried so hard!"

"I'm sure you did." Reid led her over to the scarred tree stump used for chopping wood and gently pulled her down to sit. "I apologize for what I said. I wasn't thinking. So many people *will* take the easier way. They won't change even if it means helping someone. They'll cling to the old ways. I should have known you weren't like that. I'm sorry. I didn't mean to upset you."

Maggie looked up at him. He bent over her, his eyes for once plainly kind and worried. She almost felt as if she were seeing a different man from the cool, reticent stranger who had lived with them for the last couple of weeks. She wanted suddenly to pour out all her troubles to him, to give her burdens into his hands.

But that was foolish, she reminded herself. Reid Prescott was a drifter, a wanderer, the kind of man who took on no responsibility, even for himself.

Maggie sighed. "I'm sorry. I don't know why I got so worked up about it." She gave him a faint smile. "I reckon sometimes I have a mighty short temper. Gideon used to say I was like tinder to loose gunpowder."

"You had every reason to be angry. I made an unfair assumption about you." He paused, then squatted down beside her. "What happened to Will? Was he wounded in the War?"

Maggie nodded. "Yes. The Battle of Pea Ridge. He took multiple hits. They were able to remove the bullets from his arm and shoulder but not the shrapnel in his skull. They didn't dare go digging around inside. Gideon told me the doctors who operated on him more or less assumed he wouldn't live."

"But he did."

"Yes." Maggie let out a mirthless chuckle. "They obviously didn't know Will. He always was as stubborn as the day is long."

"Your brother Gideon was with him?"

"Yes. They were the best of friends—had been since they were children. Ma used to call Will her other son. Will loved coming to our house. He said he liked it because we were always laughing. Will loved to laugh."

"You talk about him as if he weren't here anymore."

"He isn't," Maggie replied simply, turning her clear gaze on him. "That's not the man I married. It's as if a different person came back from the front. Will was never scared of anything, but Willy is. He gets hysterical over a thunderstorm. A lot of my husband's mannerisms, the habits that he had—they're gone. It's odd, and I can't explain it well, but he doesn't make the same expressions. He has no interest in hunting now, and he used to enjoy it. Used to be he didn't really care much about music, and now he loves it. He can sit for hours and listen to me sing. But he can't dance a lick any longer. He didn't remember us—any of us—when he came back. He loves us now, but it's a love that's grown in the past few years—because we cared for him, not because he felt affection for us when he saw us."

"It must have been very hard for you," Reid said quietly.

Maggie nodded, remembering. "Yes. I reckon I didn't think much about it at the time—I was so busy just trying to keep Will alive. Gideon had written to me to tell me what had happened, that he was afraid Will would die of his wounds. The care in the hospitals was —well, they had so many and all, and I guess they couldn't pay him much mind."

Reid nodded, the lines around his mouth deepening. "I know what the field hospitals were like."

"So I went up there to get him."

Reid's eyebrows rose in amazement. "All the way to northwest Arkansas? By yourself?"

Maggie nodded. "What else could I do? There was nobody else to do it. Will's father was dead, and mine was, too. All my brothers were fighting. We didn't have any servants. So I left Ty with my mother, and I got in the wagon and drove up there."

Reid stared at her, flabbergasted. She spoke as casually as if she'd taken a trip to the next town, instead of undertaking an arduous journey through mountainous, half-wild territory with two opposing armies ranging over it.

Maggie frowned at him. "What else could I do?" she demanded again.

He shook his head. "I'm sure *you* couldn't do anything else." He suddenly smiled, looking young again. "I'd like to have seen the doctors' faces when you drove up in your wagon, telling them you'd come to fetch your husband."

Maggie flashed a fleeting grin. "They did seem surprised. One of the doctors told me I couldn't take him —said I'd kill Will hauling him home. I told him that I couldn't kill him any more surely than they were doing right there in the hospital."

The fire from the remembered confrontation faded from Maggie's face. "But all the way home I was scared to death they were right. He was so sick, crazy with fever. He babbled all the time, but he didn't make any sense; it didn't even sound like words, only noises. He was burning up, and I kept stopping to wash him down with cool water. He was just skin and bones; I could hardly get him to eat anything. One of his wounds had formed pus and was draining, and I had to keep rebandaging it. I was afraid he'd get lockjaw, die." She shook her head. "It was a nightmare," she said softly.

"But you got him home, and you got him well."

"Yes." Her eyes were vague, focused inward. "Even after I got home, it was hard. More than once I thought I was going to lose him. Ma helped me nurse him, and so did Aunt Euphemia. Finally he began to recover. But . . . it was clear that he didn't recognize any of us. He didn't know the house or the town or anything. At first he could hardly talk. He couldn't remember the right words for things. As he got better and stronger, it became obvious that his mind was . . . was wounded worse than any of the rest of him. He was a child again." Her mouth twisted in remembered pain. "He didn't know my name. When he called me anything, he called me Ma, like Ty did."

"I—I'm sorry," Reid said a little huskily.

"You never know what life has in store for you,"

Maggie mused. "When I was sixteen, and Will was courting me, I never would have imagined . . ."

"But you never gave in to despair." Reid's voice seemed laced with reluctant admiration. "Most of us would give up. But not you. You simply keep on fighting."

Maggie shrugged. "That's the way I was raised, I guess. My mother didn't believe in quitting. Especially when family's involved."

She glanced at Reid and saw that he was gazing at her with an odd expression in his eyes. She wondered what his thoughts were. Then it occurred to her that he was probably thinking how tough she was, how unfeminine. A blush spread up her face. She couldn't recall the last time she had worried about whether or not she appeared feminine. The fact that she was doing so now made her blush even harder. It really didn't matter what this stranger thought about her, she told herself. He was nothing to her, only a hired hand.

But she couldn't help remembering how things had been when she was young and flirting with Will—how protectively he had draped her shawl across her shoulders when they were leaving the house, how carefully he had helped her up into his buggy. He had thought her so sweet and utterly womanly. She remembered how she had smiled up at him, deferred to him. But that was back before she had learned that she had no one to depend on except herself. Now she hardly knew any other way to be; she made decisions and ran her life—ran Ty's and Will's, too, if the truth be known. She didn't give a second thought to whether people thought her bossy or hard or even masculine. Until now . . .

Maggie looked away quickly. Her heart began to pound in her chest. What did she care what Reid Prescott thought of her? But there was no denying that she did. She didn't want to think about what that implied.

She stood up abruptly. "Anyway, what I meant to say to you to begin with was, when I tried to teach Will to read and write, he'd get frustrated and angry. Once he even screamed and threw the slate across the room. It was too hard on him. He knows that he's not normal, and he wants so much to be. It hurts him to fail. I don't want him to feel like that again."

"I don't, either." Reid had risen when she did. "Look, I promise I won't push Will past his abilities. I wasn't sure how much he might be able to learn, but now that I know, well, we'll only do things that are within his reach. I'll tell him stories, say, about events or people in history. I could read aloud to him sometimes. Don't you think that would make him feel better, more competent, as if he were learning new things, like Ty? Make him feel, oh, I don't know, not so left out?"

"Yes! Oh, yes, I think it would. He'd love it." Maggie gazed at Reid with shining eyes, amazed by his perceptiveness. "That's very kind of you. Most people don't even think about how Will might feel. Usually they just ignore him, or worse."

Reid shrugged. "I like Will. I'd like to do this for him. I won't push him to learn, and if he gets upset about it, we'll stop immediately."

Maggie spontaneously reached out to lay a hand on his arm. "Thank you. You're a good man."

Reid looked uncomfortable, and almost immediately he stepped back, so that her hand fell away. "Don't make me out to be any more than I am."

"I'm sure I'm not." Maggie smiled at him, then turned and went back into the house.

Reid watched her walk away, seeing the womanly sway of her hips and the flash of ankle as she lifted her skirts and petticoats to climb the three steps to the back door. Heat stirred in his abdomen. She was a desirable woman, Maggie Whitcomb. But she was more than that. She was strong. She met life head on, without dodges or complaints. He wondered if she'd always been like that, or if the War had changed her.

He went back to the peach tree, shoved down on the

slender posts, and tamped the earth securely around them. The work couldn't take his mind off Maggie, however, nor her story about Will. He thought about her driving a wagon halfway across the state by herself. He thought, too, about what she hadn't said: how it must have felt to walk into the roughhewn field hospital and see Will lying there, one of row upon row of disastrously damaged men.

Reid closed his eyes. He could see those rows of men. He could see them torn and shattered and bloody, on litters, on the ground, lying there waiting for their turn on the table—and by the time it came, half of them would no longer have need of it. He could almost feel the sweltering heat under the tent, the perspiration rolling down his face, his back, his clothing sticking to him, the moans and cries of the wounded rising hopelessly around him. Some of them cursed, some prayed. There was that one after Sharpsburg who'd called out "Oh, Lord, forgive me" over and over again, all through the day, all through the night, until Reid had thought he would scream. And always there was the persistent drone of flies as they buzzed around the tables, around the litters.

Reid gritted his teeth until his jaw hurt, and slowly he sank down to the ground. He held tightly on to a slender post and leaned his head against it. Beads of sweat formed on his brow. He didn't want to think about it. But the memories were rushing over him in a wave, forcing him down into an ocean of pain, filling his eyes and ears and nostrils with the sights, the sounds, and the thick, distinctive stench of blood, the odor of the slaughterhouse. It was everywhere—on the tables, on the men, on his own clothes, soaked into the ground. It was a scent you could never forget, one that he'd spent months trying to scrub off him. It mingled with the odor of urine and feces released as death gripped its victim, with the smell of festering wounds and amputated limbs stacked in inhuman piles behind him. It was the smell of death, stifling, sickening, and the memory was so real it almost gagged him. Forcibly wrenching himself free of the hideous vision, Reid rose shakily to his feet, leaning against the diminutive peach tree. Finally he looked at the yard around him, and gradually it returned to the same pleasant place it had been, grass and dirt dappled with sunlight.

How had he ever managed to stand it? Just the thought of it made him ill now. How had he stood there after each battle, cutting and sawing and prying out gore-covered bullets?

Because he had had to. Because if he hadn't, they would have died. That's what he had told himself then. But looking back on it, he thought truly he had been in a fog, shocked into numbness, the raw horror too much for his mind to absorb.

Reid looked toward the barn. He thought about going to his room there, digging out his few possessions, wrapping them up, and heading out. He looked down at the posts and chicken wire and took a step away from them.

Then he heard Ty's voice as the boy came around the corner of the house. "Hey, Reid, I'm done! This book was wonderful!" he bubbled.

Reid turned slowly and looked at him.

Ty was grinning as he trotted toward him. "Here, let me help you, and then we can get to studying quicker. I want to talk to you about this book!"

Ty reached for one end of the fencing and flattened it against a pole for Reid to hammer. His gray eyes were sparkling with excitement over the upcoming lessons.

Something from the dimmest recesses of his past stirred inside Reid.

And he picked up the hammer.

6

That afternoon, when his lessons were through, Ty brought out his old slate and a piece of chalk, and Reid sat down with Will, helping him to copy letters. Will was pleased at first but quickly lost interest in the alphabet and began to fidget. Reid then told him it was time to move on to their history lesson, beginning with Greek mythology. Enthralled, his mouth open in fascination, Will listened raptly as Reid wove stories of the jealous, warring gods of Mount Olympus.

When Reid had finished, Will let out the breath he'd been holding in his excitement. "I liked that," he said earnestly, and his eyes, usually vague, glowed.

"Good. That's the end of the lesson for today."

"Was that really school?" Will asked in disbelief.

"I learned it in school, yes," Reid said.

Will grinned. "I like your school."

"I'm glad." Reid stood up, stretched, and started toward the barn.

Will trailed along beside him. "Ma tried to teach me

to read," he confided. "But I couldn't. I reckon I'm just a big dummy." His mouth crumpled a little, and pity washed through Reid.

"Your—Maggie doesn't think that, and neither do I."

"It's true, though. I heard Jack Scott say so."

"Well, I don't know Jack Scott, but he sounds like an ignorant fellow to me. I don't see any reason you should listen to him."

"That's what Ma said. I mean, Maggie." He gave Reid a sheepish grin. "She likes for me to call her Maggie, but I forget sometimes."

"I'm sure she understands. Mrs. Whitcomb loves you."

Will frowned uncertainly. "Mrs. Whi—" His face cleared. "Oh, you mean Maggie."

"Yes. Maggie." Reid liked saying her name. It was like her—warm and homey and strong, yet pretty, too. "You know, Will, nobody understands everything. There are always things that people don't know. There's nothing wrong with your not knowing how to read. You can still learn by listening. And there are plenty of things you know that I don't know. I can't milk a cow, for instance."

"Really?" Will looked at him, wide-eyed.

"That's right. But I bet you can."

Will nodded. "I'm not as good as Ty—sometimes I spill the milk—but I know how to do it."

"I tell you what. I'm teaching you some school things. Why don't you teach me how to milk a cow?"

Will's face lit up at the idea. "You mean it?"

"Of course."

"I'd be real careful. I'd teach you real good."

"I know you would." Reid paused, glancing at Will, then went on. "You know, it's not your fault, your not being able to remember things, not being able to read. It's because of what happened to you in the War."

Will nodded slowly. "I know. I used to be smarter. I can't remember anything before I was sick, though."

"That's what the shrapnel did to you. When it went into your head, it hurt part of your brain, and that took away your memory. It's the same as a man who's lost his leg, or the other wounds you got. It's a sacrifice you made for your country. It's not something to be ashamed of. You should be proud."

Will looked at him, frowning in concentration. "Really?"

"Yes, really."

"Oh." Will smiled. "That's good, then." With innocent interest, he pulled open his shirt. "You wanna see my scars?"

Reid hid his amusement; he could imagine Will using this parlor trick on some local matron come to call. He merely nodded and examined the jagged white scars. "I'd say the bullets and shrapnel cut into you pretty deeply. You're lucky to be alive. If it weren't for your . . ." He paused; it stuck in his throat to call Maggie this boy-man's wife. "If it weren't for Maggie, you probably wouldn't have made it."

Again Will nodded enthusiastically. "Maggie took care of me. She always takes care of me. And Ty takes care of me, too."

"He's a good boy."

"I take care of him, too," Will pointed out proudly.

"Do you?"

"Uh-huh. I can reach things he can't. And I can lift things. Once he fell down." He gestured toward the ground, moving his hands in a circular way, apparently unable to express the circumstances. He frowned and abandoned the attempt. "I pulled him out."

"I'm sure he was glad you were there to help him."

"That's what he said," Will agreed. He smiled sweetly at Reid. "I like you. I'm glad you're living with us."

Reid started to remind him that he would not be staying long, but then he stopped. It was pointless, he thought; Will wouldn't remember it. Besides, he couldn't bring himself to dim that happy expression on the man's face. Instead he said only, "I am, too, Will."

One morning Ty returned from his egg route with an envelope in his hands. "Letter from Uncle Hunter," he said excitedly as he entered the kitchen.

Will was right behind him. "Read it to us. Please!"

"Later," Maggie told him firmly as she snatched the letter, smoothed it out, and studied the well-traveled envelope as if she could somehow divine her brother's presence in it. "After I've had a chance to read it."

She glanced up to see Reid Prescott watching her from the breakfast table, and she blushed, thinking that she must look foolish mooning over a letter that way. "Hunter's my brother," she told him by way of explanation. "He's been away a long time."

"I remember—the one in Texas, right?"

Maggie smiled. "Yes, that's Hunter."

"You're very close to your family," Reid guessed, still studying her face, which was warm with love and excitement.

"Oh, yes. There are those who say we Tyrrells are downright clannish. But I don't think that's a bad thing, do you?"

He shrugged as if in indifference.

Maggie had trouble imagining how someone could not be strongly attached to one's family. It had always been the very bedrock of her existence. Even Will stared at him in astonishment. There were Whitcombs and Tyrrells all over the Pine Creek area, and they were always involved in one another's doings.

Reid shifted uncomfortably under their gazes. "I have no close living relatives."

Maggie could see that he was uneasy with the conversation, so she turned back to the stove and began to dish up their breakfast, tucking Hunter's letter away in her pocket. She would take it out later when she had the time to savor it.

A letter from Hunter was a big event, one that didn't happen more than three or four times a year, and she usually pored over each missive several times, reading parts of it aloud to the boys. Will and Ty loved to hear Hunter's descriptions of herding cattle and driving them north, or of the wild terrain and the threat of Indian raids as one moved west into New Mexico—all the things that made Maggie's hair stand on end. She worried so about his safety.

Though it was true that Maggie was close to everyone in her family and loved all her brothers, Hunter had always been her special favorite. Because he was closest to her in age, they had played together often when they were little. Gideon and Shelby, several years older than they, usually ignored them and left them behind when they went on their big-boy outings. Like any brother, Hunter had teased Maggie, but he had been fun and daring, always ready with a quick grin and a mischievous idea. It had saddened Maggie terribly to see war—and Linette Conway—wipe away that fun-loving smile.

Ty and Will washed their hands and joined Reid at the table as Maggie finished setting out the serving platters. They were silent as they passed around the food and dished it out into their plates, too hungry to waste time talking.

After the meal, Maggie shooed Ty and Willy out the door with Reid, then hurried through washing the dishes. Afterward, she went out to the front porch, where she could sit in the shade with the cool spring breeze blowing across her, and read Hunter's letter in peace.

Dear Mags,

Forgive this henscratching. I am writing with the nub of the only pencil I could find in the bunkhouse and a stub of candle for light. Tomorrow we begin the spring roundup, so it will be some weeks before I draw a free breath again.

I hope this letter finds you and all the family well. If I do not have a chance to write Ma, please tell her that I love her and think of her often. I think of you, too, and miss you. How is Ty? And Will?

I've been remembering the farm in the spring lately. It must be April by the time you're reading this. I was thinking about Ma's jonquils in front of the house—that's always when you know spring has truly arrived. Sometimes I think I can even smell the earth freshly turned from plowing, moist and thick and black like the darkest of chocolate cakes.

But I'm no farmer like Gideon, and I know I wouldn't be able to settle down there if I came back.

Tears filled Maggie's eyes, interrupting her reading. She held the letter to her chest and gazed out across the yard. Actually, it was May, rather than April, and her own bright yellow jonquils along the fence were nearly dead. The dogwoods and redbuds were in bloom now, and the air was thick with the scent of honeysuckle.

The sights and smells Hunter wrote of were infinitely dear to her. She loved this spot on earth—her town, her home. They were as much a part of her as her unruly curls or the scar on her arm from the time a nail caught her when, at age nine, she crawled through the slats in a fence on some urgent childhood escapade.

As she'd read of Hunter's nostalgia, her heart had leapt in hope that he might be coming home. But his next line had dashed that hope. Maggie sighed and blinked away her tears, then continued reading. He told her that he had started work on a ranch near San Antonio and would probably be there for the next few months, so she would be able to write to him there. He described the ranch and its owner, Rayfield Minter, added some details about the coming roundup, then closed with his love.

Maggie read the letter once more, then folded it and put it back into the capacious pocket of her skirt. She sat reflecting for a moment, pushing with her toe against the floor to make the swing move a little. At least Hunter was thinking about coming home. He missed the farm and his family. He might not be ready to return right now, but at least there was hope that he might someday.

It was a pleasant morning, not yet hot as it would be in a few weeks, and Maggie was content to do nothing for the moment except breathe in the scents of spring and think about the possibility of her family being together again.

Except for Shelby, of course. The realization saddened her.

Maggie sighed and stood up. There was work to be done, and it wouldn't get done if she sat around thinking about the way life ought to be. Life was as it was, and you had to do what you could with it; Maggie had learned long ago that no one was going to come along and make it right. She straightened her skirt, patting the pocket containing her precious letter, and went back into the house.

That night when Maggie finished the supper dishes, she wandered out onto the small back porch. All the while she was washing, she had heard the boys laughing and playing in the yard, and now she was drawn to join them.

When she stepped outside, she found Reid Prescott sitting on the top step, watching Ty and Will in the mellow dusk. Maggie hesitated. She wasn't sure Reid would want her company; he often seemed to prefer to be alone.

He turned and looked up at her. His features weren't clear in the dim light, so she couldn't tell what he was thinking.

"The boys are chasing fireflies," he told her, and there was something relaxed and almost friendly in his voice.

Maggie sat down beside him on the step. After all, she told herself, it was her porch. The man could always leave if he didn't like being with her. She hoped he wouldn't, though; somehow tonight she felt like company—adult company. She supposed Hunter's letter had left her feeling lonely.

"It's getting close to summer," she remarked, looking out across the yard. Ty and Will were running around, cupping their hands to catch the brief glimmer of light when a firefly flashed.

"We used to do that when we were kids, out on the farm." Maggie smiled, remembering. "You'd have thought we'd be tired, the way we worked all day, but somehow we always had enough energy for that. Papa and Mama would sit on the porch, rocking, and Papa would smoke his pipe—I can still remember how it smelled." She drew in a deep breath and sighed. "Evenings like this seem to me about as close to heaven as you can get on earth. I can't imagine living anywhere else," she mused. She glanced at Reid. "I could never live as you do, traveling from place to place, no home to call your own."

"I don't mind it."

"Maybe it's different when you don't have family," Maggie suggested.

"Maybe." His voice was noncommittal. "Tell me more about your family."

Maggie glanced at him, surprised at the uncharacteristic inquiry. She wondered if he really wanted to know or if he just wanted to change the subject from himself. However, it never took much to get her talking about the ones she loved.

"That's a dangerous thing to ask," she warned him. "Mama always said I'd talk the ears off a cornstalk."

"I'll risk it."

"All right. What do you want to know?"

"Are all your relatives fighters like you?"

"Fighters!" Maggie chuckled. "Is that what you think of me?"

"What else would I think of a woman who greets me with a shotgun? Or who drove to the front to retrieve her wounded husband?"

"Well, if that's what you mean by fighting, I reckon we are. Mama and Papa had to be. The land was still rough when they moved here with their families. They were children really, back in the thirties. They got married and started their own farm when Mama was just sixteen and Papa nineteen. They lived in a little house, hardly more than a shack, for the first few years, even after Gideon was born.

"Papa died right before the war. He was a wonderful man, very sweet and kind. He didn't talk much—I take after Mama that way. But he'd put me on his lap sometimes in the evening and hold me, and it was worth more than a thousand words. I can remember leaning against his chest while he rocked, and I can smell the pipe smoke again like it was yesterday." Tears glittered in her eyes, and she blinked them away.

"You must have loved him very much."

"I did. I love Mama, too, of course, but she couldn't be more different. She's always bustling and doing things; she never rests. She's rock-hard in her convictions. She was the one who would get after us about our mischief. Papa was too soft-hearted to punish us— at least most of the time. I remember only one time he whipped Hunter—when he caught him gambling with Stoney Carter out behind the mercantile. Afterward Papa shut himself up in his room all evening; I think he cried over it. He took it harder than Hunter, I imagine."

"So there were three of you children—you, Hunter, and Gideon?"

"I had another brother. Gideon's the oldest. Then there was Shelby. He died in the War." Her voice grew a little husky, but then she smiled, remembering. "Shelby was the best at everything: running, jumping, climbing trees, fishing, riding. You name it, he could do it perfectly. He was a wonderful dancer, and, oh, my, he was handsome. Lots of girls used to cozy up to me, thinking they'd get to be around Shelby." She chuckled. "Not that it did them any good. Shel liked women, but he liked to be footloose and fancy free, too. Until he met Tess Caldwell, that is. That's the woman he married. They had a little girl, Ginny. She's nine now. Shelby never even saw her."

She swallowed and blinked away tears. "He was killed in the Wilderness campaign. He joined up as soon as they fired on Fort Sumter. He had to be in on the adventure, and he was afraid it wouldn't last." Bitterness mingled with the sorrow in her voice. "At least Will and Gideon waited awhile; they were concerned about Ma and me and the farms. But Shel was never one to think about practical things. He rode with J.E.B. Stuart, and he seemed to have a charmed life. He was wounded a couple of times, but he went right back. That was Shelby for you. None of us really thought anything bad would ever happen to him. The fighting had gone on for so long, and we thought for sure that—"

She stopped, biting her lower lip. After a moment, she continued. "It was a shock when we got word."

"I'm sorry." Reid's voice was soft and understanding. He reached over and took Maggie's hand, startling her to the core. It was a sympathetic gesture, she was sure, one that didn't mean anything, but his touch made her skin tingle, and suddenly her heart was pounding and her throat was dry.

She couldn't think of anything to say. She thought her heart might jump straight up out of her throat if she so much as opened her mouth. She gave a sidelong glance, but she couldn't make out Reid's expression in the darkness, only that he was watching her. His palm burned hot against her skin, and Maggie was afraid her fingers might begin to tremble. She thought that she ought to pull her hand away, but she couldn't bring herself to.

"Thank you," she said shakily, striving to act as if there was nothing abnormal about her hand being in Reid Prescott's. "I—I'm sure you must have lost people in the War, too. We aren't the only ones."

Reid dropped her hand and shoved his into his pockets. He turned to look straight ahead. "There's no point talking about it."

"You mean, you don't like to let anybody see inside you that much."

Prescott glanced sharply at her. For a moment she thought he was going to say something biting or perhaps just get up and leave. But finally he shrugged. "Maybe."

"You're a mysterious man, Mr. Prescott."

"And you are an inquisitive woman." His tone was more teasing than sharp, though.

Maggie felt old, coquettish instincts rising up in her, inclinations she had thought long dead. It made her excited and a little breathless; years seemed to drop away from her. She wanted to flirt, and the thought scared her. Worse than that, it enticed her, too.

She remembered the way Reid's hand had felt on hers; her skin began to tingle again where he had touched it. This wasn't right; she shouldn't feel this way. She knew that she should get up and leave, walk away from this situation. Yet she lingered, unable to pull away, unwilling to draw closer. A confusion of emotions tumbled within her, heady and frightening.

"Ma!" Ty's voice broke into the quiet that bound them. "Look! I caught a firefly!" He raced over to them, his hands cupped tightly around his prize.

Maggie's heart thudded back into place, and her breath came more naturally. She was, she reminded herself, just an old married woman, and Reid's teasing hadn't meant a thing.

7

Tess awoke early and went to her window, leaning out to breathe in the cool, moist dawn. The eastern sky was turning pink and pale yellow with the approaching sunrise, and the air smelled clean and invigorating. It was a perfect time to work in the garden.

Quickly she whisked off her nightrail and put on her oldest dress. She pinned her hair up haphazardly and covered it with a calico square. Then she crept down the back staircase, careful not to awaken her mother or Ginny. Much as she loved both of them, she would just as soon not have Ginny's "help" this morning or one of her mother's lectures on how she was ruining her soft hands and white complexion.

From a small shed behind the kitchen, Tess grabbed her work gloves, a hoe, and a trowel, then walked around to the front yard to begin her work. Ornamental shrubs graced the foundation of the house, lending particular beauty in the springtime, when the azaleas and rhododendrons produced brilliant splashes of color against the gleaming white clapboard. In the summer red and pink roses took over.

Tess had struggled to keep up the landscaping over the years, but with all her other chores, she could do little more than weed and water. Tess's mother bemoaned the overgrown bushes, missing their pre-War manicured appearance, but Tess rather thought she liked them better this way, spreading out wildly however they happened to grow.

The flower beds, however, she couldn't ignore. Of all the work Tess did nowadays, the one chore she truly loved was gardening—especially in the flower beds, which brought forth such splendor. She liked planning them and planting, liked watching the new green life emerge. And then, most beautiful of all, came the budding of the flowers, glorious in their color and variety. It was soothing, somehow, to work with the soil, to dig and turn it to bury a bulb or seeds, and she got a certain satisfaction from jerking up the weeds that threatened to crowd out her blooms. And through all the work, there was the pride of knowing that she was accomplishing something wonderful with her own two hands, the thrill of helping something grow, of being part of the process of creation and life.

Tess toiled happily as the sun rose, scarcely noticing the passage of time. She paid scant attention to the sounds that began to come from the street—a wagon passing, someone walking, the hoofbeats of a horse. However, the creaking of her front gate did penetrate her thoughts, and she looked over her shoulder, curious to see who had come calling. She dropped her trowel and stared at the man striding across her yard. What on earth was Benton Conway doing here?

Hastily, Tess rose to her feet, brushing the dirt from her dress. A blush rose to her cheeks to be caught in this state of dishabille, let alone by someone like Benton Conway. Nonetheless, she lifted her chin with all the hauteur she could muster. "Mr. Conway?"

"Hello, Tess."

Tess raised her eyebrows. Though she had once been good friends with Linette Sanders, now Conway's second wife, she certainly was not on a first-name basis with the man. And since she had just greeted him as Mr. Conway, his use of her Christian name was rude, overly familiar, insulting. However, she said nothing; she didn't want to talk to the Scalawag any more than she had to.

Conway tipped his hat. "Linette sends her regards."

"I see little of Linette anymore," Tess replied evenly. "I'm sure you're aware of how our circumstances have changed."

"Indeed, I am." A thin smile touched his lips, and his odd, colorless eyes swept down her body. "You must find a widow's lot hard and lonely."

Tess was suddenly aware that this old dress she wore to garden in dated from her late teens, before she and Shelby were married, and it was now too tight across the bosom, as well as worn thin. The way Conway looked at her made her cross her arms over her breasts.

"Why are you here, Mr. Conway?" she asked bluntly.

"Why, to make you an offer, ma'am."

"A what?" Tess couldn't imagine what he was talking about.

"An offer." He gestured toward the grand structure behind them. "I want to buy your house."

Tess was too stunned to speak.

"There, I can see I've taken you by surprise. But surely you must have realized that sooner or later someone would be happy to take this place off your hands. It's beautiful, but awfully big for only two women and a little girl. Hard to maintain, too, I'd imagine. Why, this place really needs a whole staff of servants." His eyes traveled significantly down her old dress to the heavy work gloves on her hands.

Finally Tess's tongue began to function again, and

she said crisply, "Let me assure you that I have absolutely no intention of selling the house I was raised in, the house my father built for my mother. It will be my daughter's when I die. I wouldn't think of selling it. I'm afraid you've wasted your time."

If she had disappointed him, it didn't show on Conway's face. He said mildly, "Now, don't be too hasty, ma'am. This is something you ought to think over. I know you're a reasonable sort of woman, not like some of the stiff-necked people in this town. After all, you sold Farquarhar Jones your plantation."

"Mother and I did disencumber ourselves of the property, but that was an entirely different situation. We could not use it; it was simply a burden to us, what with the taxes and all. But this is our home. I would never sell it."

"Never say never," Benton cautioned, his tone amiable but with a glint in his eyes that sent a shiver down Tess's spine. "Sometimes you have to eat words like that."

Tess looked at him, frowning in puzzlement. "Why would you want this house so much? There are plenty of other lovely homes around, including your own, for that matter."

"Ah, but yours is the most beautiful. The one I want."

"You have more than enough money to build one far grander than this."

"But I don't want to build another house. I want this one." He came a couple of steps closer, until he was uncomfortably near. Tess wanted to step back, but she was afraid Conway would interpret that as weakness, so she held her ground.

His voice was low and somehow intimate as he went on. "You know, you might not necessarily have to leave this house. Any of you. I could buy it, but you could continue to live here."

Tess stared at him, baffled by his words as well as by his conspiratorial manner. "I don't understand."

"Come, come, Tess, you're a bright woman. I think you can understand how a man might be happy to let a pretty woman like you be a tenant. Provided he came by often to collect the rent."

His voice had dropped almost to a whisper, and there was a hot gleam in his eyes. It was quite clear to Tess now what he was getting at, and she was instantly aflame with fury and indignation.

"Get out of my yard!" she hissed, her eyes blazing. "How dare you come here and make an indecent proposal to me? Surely you can't really believe that I would actually agree to—to be your *mistress!*" The repulsion in her voice was clear.

Conway's mouth narrowed to a razor-thin line, the skin around it going white with suppressed anger. "There are quite a few Pine Creek ladies who wouldn't mind having such a proposal from me. Many of them would be thrilled to be offered money *and* a lovely house."

"Then make the offer to them," Tess retorted flatly. "I can assure you that I'm not interested. Nor would any other *lady* be. Your disgusting offer is an insult not only to me, but to your wife!"

His pale eyes glinted again in a lascivious way. "An insult? Why, my dear, quite the opposite." He ran his eyes lewdly down her body. "You are the only woman I know whose, shall we say, physical assets can compare with my wife's. Possessing the two most beautiful women in town—one as my wife, the other my mistress —would be rather like having an elegant matched pair draw one's carriage. A source of pride to all concerned. And it makes it even more . . . touching knowing that my dear little Linette is fond of you. Rather like bedding sisters, you know." He smiled in a way that nearly made Tess ill.

Instinctively she lashed out, slapping him hard across

the face. "Shut your filthy mouth! Don't you ever speak that way to me again!"

"Or what?" he sneered. "You think you're so special, that different from any two-bit whore? I can tell you, you're not. That ain't gold you got under your skirts just 'cause your name's Caldwell—oh, excuse me, Tyrrell. The Tyrrells are no better than anybody else, just a lot more sanctimonious. Why, I could tell you stories about your dear husband that'd—"

"Stop it! Get out!" Tess's voice was trembling with anger, her fists clenched at her sides. "I don't ever want to see your face again. If you show up here with your filthy suggestions ever, *ever* again, I will tell Mr. Tyrrell. At least the Tyrrell men know how to fight. They didn't sit out the War safe at home." Her words were a calculated jab, since Conway had not gone to fight for either side.

"The Tyrrell men," Conway repeated scornfully, though Tess was certain she had seen a flicker of fear in his eyes. "I would say that their fighting spirit has done little to protect their women the last few years. I certainly had no trouble wedding Linette, Hunter Tyrrell notwithstanding. Go ahead and sic that oaf Gideon Tyrrell on me; I have no objection to seeing him in jail."

"I don't know how Linette could have married you. It makes me sick to think that she did. Even if she was as mercenary as you, she deserves something better than a husband who offers to set up a mistress practically in her face!"

A humorless smile twisted Conway's face. "Believe me, she'd probably regard it as a blessing. Linette cares for no one. She's as cold as ice."

"Any woman would be cold to you!" Tess spat out. "You're not a man; you're a devil." To her dismay, tears of rage filled her eyes. The last thing she wanted was for this evil man to think he had the power to make her cry.

"I wouldn't be so high and mighty if I were you."

Conway's voice was as cold and flat as his eyes. "You're no longer sitting on the top of the heap. I am, and so are my friends. You might need a favor from me someday."

"I'd never ask a favor of you. Not even if I were starving to death. You're lower than a snake. You're worse than any Yankee or carpetbagger who's come here to loot this state. You've betrayed your own people; you've cheated and stolen from your neighbors and the people who used to be your friends, like that poor Robert Bowlin. I can't think of any scum worse than you."

A nasty smile spread across Conway's face. "You know, Mrs. Tyrrell, I've been thinking. A fine property like this must have a pretty large tax on it. Isn't that so?"

Tess stared at him, flabbergasted by his sudden change of subject. What was he talking about?

"It's a shame how high property taxes have gotten these days," he went on, the smile still on his face and his eyes boring meaningfully into hers. "Why, I've heard of cases where they've doubled, even tripled, this year. I know, because I have some very good friends in the tax assessor's office. It'd be hard for you to pay if they were to raise your taxes like that, I reckon."

A chill ran through Tess. "You're threatening to raise my taxes because I won't sell my home to you? Because I won't be your mistress?"

"Now, ma'am, I'm threatening no such thing. We both know that raising your taxes is not in my poor power to do. I'm just saying it's a likely thing to happen, knowing the tax situation as I do."

Tess refused to show the fear that ran through her at his words. She stared back at him without a hint of yielding, and her voice was clear and vivid with anger as she said, "Whatever happens, I'm not selling. I hope I make myself clear. I would never sell this house to you.

Now, I want you to get out of my yard, and don't ever come back here again. Do you understand? Get out!"

With exaggerated courtesy that displayed more insult than respect, Conway tipped his hat and left the yard.

Tess watched him go. Only after he was out of sight did she let herself sink to the ground, suddenly weak and trembling in the aftermath of the ugly scene. Fear and dismay flooded her, washing away her defiant stance. Benton Conway had become a very powerful man in the last few years, and he had good friends in both the local and state government. What if he could get them to raise her taxes? To even double or triple them? She could never pay that much money! Why, she was struggling just to get by now.

Would he do it if he had the clout? It seemed absurd to think he would go to that much trouble just to get this house. On the other hand, Conway seemed to enjoy wielding his newfound power. He seemed to enjoy hurting people, taking away their money and businesses and land.

Firmly she fought down her panic. There was no reason to worry yet. Conway hadn't actually done anything, only made insinuations. Likely as not he didn't actually have the power to get her taxes raised.

"Tess?" Her mother's call from the front porch interrupted Tess's fretting. "Oh, there you are, dear."

"Hello, Mama." Tess turned to greet her mother, forcing a smile onto her face, automatically hiding her anxiety. George Caldwell had always protected his wife from life's unpleasantries, and when he died, Tess had inherited the role. Amanda Caldwell, a small, fluttery woman with the same porcelain-doll coloring that Tess had, seemed somehow too frail to face up to the same burdens others carried.

"Why are you up and about so early?" Mrs. Caldwell asked, coming down the porch steps toward Tess.

"My gracious, child, whatever are you doing out here without a hat on? You'll freckle dreadfully."

"I haven't been in the sun, Mama. It's barely up. That's one reason I started so early." Tess fought down her irritation. Sometimes her mother's preoccupation with frivolous concerns drove Tess nearly to distraction. Right now it was especially difficult to pay polite attention to them with Benton Conway's threats still ringing in her ears. However, Tess knew it was unfair of her to do otherwise. Her mother was older and had a great deal of difficulty accepting what the world had become.

"Mama!" The front door opened, and Ginny came running out. "I looked all over the house for you!" She took the two steps leading down from the porch in a single jump and skipped across the grass toward them. Her blond hair was done in straggly braids, and she still wore her nightdress. There were no shoes on her feet.

"Ginny!" Mrs. Caldwell scolded. "You're not decent! You shouldn't come out here like that. Why, anyone could see you."

"Oh, Mama, she's only a child." Tess's smile deepened as she looked at her daughter. She held out her arms to Ginny and engulfed her in a hug. "Hello, sweetheart. Did you have a nice night's sleep?"

"Yes, and I'm starving!" Ginny squeezed Tess's neck, then bounced back out of her arms, not one to be held still for long. "Binnie's cooking flapjacks. I could smell them all the way upstairs."

"Well, let's get in there and eat them, then." Tess laughed. "Come on, Mama. I think we could use a little sustenance, too."

She and her mother followed Ginny toward the house.

"Tess, what was that awful Benton Conway doing here?" Mrs. Caldwell asked. "I could hardly believe my eyes when I looked out the window and saw you two talking. I thought to myself, why, if only George were alive, he'd throw that man right off the place. George never could abide him, you know, even back before the War, when they had some business dealings. Your father always had such knowledge about people; I've never known him to be wrong."

Tess had known her father to be wrong on more than one occasion, about people *and* about business. Investing all his cash in Confederate bonds had been one such glaring error. But when she had pointed that out to her mother, Mrs. Caldwell had burst into tears, calling Tess an unnatural and ungrateful daughter for turning against her father. To Amanda Caldwell's way of thinking, her husband had been the epitome of all fine masculine attributes, and his downfall had been precisely because he was so loyal, honorable, and true to his beliefs. Tess, though she'd loved her father, saw him in a slightly more critical light, but she was careful now not to express such thoughts to her mother.

When Tess said nothing, Mrs. Caldwell prodded, "Darling, what's the matter? Is something wrong?"

"Of course not, Mama. Don't be silly. Mr. Conway was, uh, just asking if I knew where Papa bought that—the chandelier in the entry," Tess improvised. She couldn't tell her mother any of the things Conway had said. The older woman would worry herself sick. She had already lost so many of the things that had been dear to her, and Tess knew she was often sad, thinking about her husband and the parties they had given here and the lovely dresses she and Tess had worn, now all vanished. To lose her home, this grand house her beloved husband had built for her, would be the ultimate blow. Tess couldn't bear to worry her needlessly.

"The chandelier? Why, how strange. Why would Benton Conway want to know about our chandelier?"

"I don't know," Tess replied. "Perhaps he wants to buy one like it."

"Well, I suppose it is the finest in town—why, maybe in the state. I'm not at all sure that there's anything like it even in Little Rock." Her eyes glowed, and a reminiscent smile touched her lips. "I remember when your father and I went to New Orleans to buy it. That was the grandest trip. Did I ever tell you about it?"

The truth was, Mrs. Caldwell had recited the story many times, especially since the War, and the trip grew grander and grander with each repetition. But it was a harmless enough pleasure for her mother, and it led away from the subject of Benton Conway, so Tess smiled encouragingly and said, "Tell me again, Mama."

"All right." Mrs. Caldwell preened. "I recall I purchased the most beautiful satin gown there, too, and lovely little matching slippers with rosettes on the toes. It was quite a trip, let me tell you. . . ."

Maggie stepped to the window and looked out at the drive once more. Ty and Will were very late. Breakfast was nearly ready, and Reid had already come in from his chores and cleaned up. Frowning, Maggie went back into the kitchen.

A few minutes later Ty's wagon rattled over the drive, and soon Ty was walking in the door. But his nose was bloodied, and one eye was swollen. Will, behind him, was in tears.

Maggie gasped in horror. "Ty, what happened?" She went over to him and took his chin in her hand to examine his face. Ty twisted away and set his mouth stubbornly, refusing to say anything. Reid calmly rose to wet a cloth.

"Here," he ordered. "Sit down and tilt your head back." He pressed the rag to Ty's nose. "What happened, Will?" Reid asked, surprising Maggie; usually she didn't even try to get any information out of Will when he was upset.

But Will, looking anguished, said in a low voice, "Billy Sattler told Ty his daddy was a dummy."

"So Ty hit him?"

Will nodded.

"Oh, Ty . . ." Maggie moaned. A similar name-calling incident had happened once before, when Will had first recovered enough to start going into town with Ty. Ty had come home furious and hurt, but at least he hadn't gotten into a fight.

"That's understandable," Reid commented. "I imagine I'd blow up if someone insulted my family. 'Course, I'd probably use words instead of my fists. I suspect this Sattler boy is someone you could outsmart, Ty."

Ty tried to sneer, then winced at the pain the movement caused. "Of course I could. *He's* the one who's a dummy."

"If I were you, I'd think up what to say next time something like that happens. Then you can end it quickly—without getting blood down the front of your shirt."

Ty looked at Reid's calm face, and a faint smile touched his lips. "Maybe I will."

Quietly, Maggie went to a still distraught Will and put her arm around him, pulling him out onto the porch to calm him down, leaving Reid and Ty to their quiet conversation on honor and power.

That evening when Reid was sitting on the back porch, watching velvet darkness settle over the farm, Maggie went out and stood behind him for a moment. The breeze lifted tendrils of her hair, cooling her after her evening chores. She could hear Will calling to Ty in front of the house.

"You were awfully good with Ty this morning," she said, putting her hand on Reid's shoulder and sitting down beside him.

Reid turned his head and looked at her. His hand came up and covered hers for a moment, squeezing it gently. "I'm glad you thought so. I was afraid you might have been angry with me for interfering in your business. I didn't mean to usurp your authority."

Maggie hadn't really thought about touching Reid; it had been a simple gesture to draw his attention. But when she felt the warmth of his hand on hers, she realized what she had done, and a tingle ran through her. A little shakily she withdrew her hand, letting out a breathless laugh.

"Oh, no, I didn't mind. I wasn't worried about my 'authority.' Frankly, I was relieved. It's . . . hard sometimes for a woman to raise a son alone. There are some things a father can deal with better than a mother. But, of course, Will . . ."

Maggie thought she saw regret touch Reid's features when she withdrew her hand. The thought made her nervous . . . and excited. To dismiss the feeling, she turned away slightly, looping her arms around her knees and clasping her hands together. She gazed out across the yard at the red-tinted horizon. The sun was completely out of sight now.

"I was grateful," she went on. "You did a much better job of talking to Ty than I would have. I would have lectured him about the evils of fighting, and all the while I would have been so furious inside that I would have wanted to go out and whip Billy Sattler myself for making him and Will unhappy."

Reid studied her profile in the dim light, thinking how pretty she was and knowing that he shouldn't be thinking that. Still, it was hard not to, just as it was hard not to imagine how soft she would feel in his arms, how sweet.

He pulled his mind back to the subject at hand. "It's harder, I imagine, when you're the parent. An . . . outsider can look at the situation a mite more objectively."

"That's true, I reckon. I always get caught up in worrying what people will think of me if my boy gets into fights. I guess it shouldn't matter, but it does." Maggie smiled sheepishly. "Even so, it seemed remarkable to me that you knew so well what to say to him."

"Oh, I understand him, I reckon. Ty's not that different from me when I was a boy. He's sharp; he wants to do what's right and be a man. Sometimes it's hard to find your way." He gave her a wry grin. "Even when you're thirty-five. Unfortunately, when we're older I guess we don't think so much about what's right or wrong when we make decisions."

"What do you consider then?"

He shrugged. "Expediency, maybe. What's easiest."

"Surely that's not all." Maggie turned to look at him. "When you stayed here, I doubt that was the easiest thing for you. You've been doing hard work, work that doesn't come easy to you."

"That obvious, huh?" He smiled faintly.

"Stop trying to make a joke. What I'm saying is true."

"It's easier to sleep on a bed than to tramp around the countryside, never knowing where your next meal is coming from."

"That wasn't why you stayed. You stayed because you wouldn't leave a sick woman with a household to look after. That's morality, not expediency."

Reid shifted. "I think you find more morality in me than is there. It's yourself you're seeing, reflected in other people."

"Why do you say that? Why do you write yourself off, pretend you aren't the good man you are?"

"I'm just saying I'm no model of anything. Don't build me up to be, or you'll wind up disappointed."

"It's no wonder you understand Ty. Ty carries his hurts inside him, too. And he turns them against himself. Like you do, I suspect."

Reid shot a quick glance at Maggie but deflected her last comment. "Ty was troubled," he agreed, deftly shifting the conversation away from himself. "What the Sattler boy said angered him. He didn't want Will to be hurt. But that wasn't all." He paused and gave her a considering glance. "I hope you'll understand how he feels. Much as Ty loves his father, he, well, feels a little ashamed of him, as well, particularly when Will says or does something odd."

Maggie nodded sadly. "I understand it. I've felt the same way myself. No matter how hard I've fought it, no matter how much I love Will, there are times when his behavior is glaringly inappropriate for a man his age, and I feel humiliated. I remember once I even snapped at him in public because he had dropped a piece of stick candy on the ground and he'd begun to wail about it. I was so embarrassed. Then, you know, I was ashamed of myself for feeling that way. Because he can't help it."

"No, he can't. But neither can you or Ty help feeling embarrassed. Ty felt that shame about his father, and he felt that same guilt, too, which made his anger worse. He wanted to smash the boy's face in to make up for his own guilt and shame, as well as for the insult. I just tried to help him see that he wasn't a bad person for feeling that way, that it was natural."

Maggie sighed. "I should have talked to Ty about it before this. I didn't think—I guess I was so busy trying to hide that I felt that way sometimes that I didn't even think about how Ty felt."

"You can't take care of everything."

"I know. That's why I'm so glad for your help."

Impulsively Maggie wanted to ask him to stay on the farm for good. Life was better with him here, easier. She was coming to depend on him. But she sensed that the idea of someone coming to depend on him would only send Reid Prescott running. He would think that she was trying to tie him down, and obviously he was a man who couldn't bear that. So she said nothing else. But inside she made a wish, as she had when she was a little girl, finding the evening star hanging low in the sky and thinking, *"Please, oh, please, let him stay."*

8

"You know, boys," Maggie said at supper one evening, "the Lyceum's coming up next Saturday."

Ty brightened. "Really?"

Will perked up. "What's that? I want to go."

Maggie and Reid chuckled.

"I'm with Will," Reid put in. "What is the Lyceum?"

"It's fun," Ty told them. "Don't you remember it last year, Will? They sang and played the piano."

"Really?" Will looked even more interested. "Can we go, Ma—Maggie?"

"Of course." She turned to Reid to explain. "The Ladies Guild formed a year ago to try to encourage what they call cultural endeavors. One of their projects is to build a public lending library in Pine Creek. They put on the Lyceum to help raise money for it. It's an evening of performances. Some women play the piano, some give dramatic readings. That sort of thing."

"Ah, an evening of arts and culture."

Maggie grinned. "Yes, right here in Pine Creek, Arkansas."

Will turned toward Reid. "Are you going to come with us?"

"Well, I don't know." Reid smiled at Will's eager face. "I hadn't given it any thought." He glanced at Maggie.

"You might like it," she told him. "And we'd be glad of the company."

"Perhaps I will, then." There was a certain sparkle in his eyes as he looked at her, and Maggie found herself smiling at him. It did funny things to her insides when he wore that youthful, lively expression.

"But you have to dress up," Ty stuck in, his nose wrinkling in disgust.

"Horrible," Reid sympathized.

Ty glowered at his mother. "Ma makes me wear a jacket and have my shirt buttoned up to here." He pointed at his throat and demonstrated by pretending to choke.

"Ty!" Maggie protested, chuckling. "It's not that bad."

He rolled his eyes as if to say, *What do mothers know about such things?*

"It seems only fair that I should suffer, too," Reid assured him with mock solemnity. "Unfortunately, I haven't got a Sunday-go-to-meeting suit."

"You could wear one of my pa's," Ty responded. Then he looked quickly toward his mother. "Couldn't he?"

"Well . . . I . . . yes, there's a suit of Will's from before the War that's in good condition." Will was heavier now than he had been in his youth, and he could no longer wear the handsome coat he had worn on their wedding day twelve years ago. But because it held such memories for Maggie, she had never had the heart to cut it down for Ty. It would probably fit Reid Prescott well enough if she hemmed the sleeves and pant legs a little. "I could take it up easily enough."

Reid hesitated. "If you're sure you wouldn't mind my wearing something of Will's."

"Of course not." It gave Maggie a funny feeling to think of Reid wearing the suit Will had donned to marry her, but that didn't seem sufficient reason not to let him. She was too practical to hold something as a keepsake when it could be used. "I'll bring it down from the attic tomorrow."

"All right. Thank you."

"Good. Then it's settled."

The next morning Maggie climbed the narrow ladder into the attic. It was dim and dusty but not yet as hot as it would be later in the day. Stooping a little to avoid the sloping roof, she crossed to the humpbacked trunk and opened it, releasing a faint scent of the cedar chips she had put in to preserve the clothes. On top lay the pressed flowers from her wedding bouquet, and beneath that Will's coat. She gently set the flowers aside and lifted out the suit. It was still in good shape. Will hadn't worn it many times before the War. As she reached down to put the flowers back in, she stopped when she saw the dress that had lain beneath the suit. It was her wedding gown, folded neatly, and to one side lay her veil. She ran her hand over the satin and lace, and for a moment there in the dusty attic she was lost in the past, remembering the day she had married Will—the nerves that danced in her stomach, the way the church had looked as she walked down the aisle, all her friends and family swiveling to watch her.

Her throat closed, and tears misted her eyes. She lifted the dress out and looked at it, then glanced at the one beneath it. That one was a pink silk, decorated with a collar of delicate lace now aged from white to yellow. She had worn the dress several times during the year she and Will were courting. It had been Will's favorite, and Maggie had to admit it had looked especially good on her. She held it up, smiling as she remembered the parties and dances, the church socials, all the magical moments of that year of carefree happiness.

It had been four years before the War started, and she had been only sixteen. Back then she had never dreamed that anything bad could happen to her, that her world could fall apart.

As she fingered the dress she had put away when her figure had filled out, she pondered the momentous changes that had occurred—the election of the Republican president, the secession of Arkansas along with the other Southern states. Like flotsam, she had been carried along on the tide of events, her life shattered on the rocks of politics.

She gazed down at the dress. Maybe with today's style—a narrower skirt caught up in the back and flattened in front—she could alter the dress so that it fit her fuller figure. There was a small swatch of pink-and-white striped material downstairs that she could use to make a new collar, maybe even insets for the sleeves to suit the new fashion.

Maggie smiled, the raw sorrow she had felt a few moments before settling into its usual place in the back of her mind. It would make a lovely dress, almost brand new. If she worked quickly, she could wear it to the Lyceum. The pink would still be pretty on her, giving color to her cheeks, which needed it more now than they had in the flush of youth. She set her wedding dress and the pressed flowers back inside the trunk and closed its lid. Then, carrying her booty, she climbed back down the ladder.

When supper was over that evening, Maggie said to Reid, "I brought down Will's suit from the attic. If you'd like to try it on, I could hem it this evening."

"All right."

Will and Ty put their plates on the counter by the

washbasin and immediately banged out the back door, unwilling to hang around for something as boring as clothes measurements.

Maggie brought Reid the suit, saying, "You can change in the parlor." Then she went upstairs to her bedroom to get her sewing basket.

When she returned, she hesitated outside the parlor door. Had Reid had enough time to change?

She thought about him taking off his work clothes inside that room, and she blushed. What an improper thing to be thinking about! She busied herself by hunting in the basket for her tape measure. After she found it, she glanced once more at the closed door.

At that moment it opened right in front of her, and she let out a squeak of surprise. Reid looked startled, too. Then he chuckled at her reaction, and Maggie released a nervous laugh.

Reid backtracked into the middle of the room. "I'm all yours," he said, lifting his arms up and out to the sides. Then, oddly enough, he blushed.

Maggie was dumbstruck to see it. She never would have figured Reid Prescott for a man who embarrassed easily. Why, she didn't think he had blushed even on that first night when she'd taken the blanket out to him and caught him in the altogether.

At the thought, the image of him naked flashed into her mind. She remembered his chest, ridged with muscle and lightly furred with dark, curling hair. He was strong, fit, wiry, with no excess flesh on him anywhere. His long, lean torso tapered down to narrow hips, where the skin was stretched tautly across the points of his pelvic bones.

Maggie blushed now, too, at the direction her thoughts were taking. The worst thing about that night, she knew, was that she hadn't covered her eyes at the first glimpse of the stranger's nudity. No, she had stood there gaping at him, unable to move. It had been most unseemly behavior for a lady. Maggie would have thought she'd be so appalled that her instinctive reaction would be to whirl and run away. Yet she had not. The reason she hadn't didn't bear thinking of.

Knowing why *she* had blushed suddenly made Maggie wonder why *he* had blushed just now. Then she recalled what he had said. *"I'm all yours."* It had been an innocuous enough statement . . . until, evidently, his thoughts, like hers now, had made it otherwise. . . .

What was going on here? Maggie wondered in confusion. It was crazy for two adults to be acting this way over something as simple and innocent as measuring a man's sleeve. Why, she had measured her brothers and father, Ty, and Will for shirts and suits, and she couldn't remember once feeling embarrassment. But now, as she reached out and took one of Reid's arms, pulling down the sleeve so that it was straight, her fingers trembled.

Reid's wrist was warm where her fingers grazed his skin, and Maggie was suddenly acutely aware of how close to him she was standing. His breath ruffled her hair as he looked down at what she was doing. She found she couldn't look up into his face. With fumbling fingers she turned the end of the sleeve under and pinned it. It and the other sleeve seemed to take forever as her hands brushed his over and over again, awakening her to the texture of his skin, which was far rougher than her own.

It was a relief when she was done and could step back. When she had said that she would alter the suit for Reid, it hadn't occurred to her the intimacy it would entail.

Then she realized the worst was yet to come.

"I—I need to measure the trousers now," she said, surprised at the huskiness of her voice.

Pincushion in hand, she knelt in front of him, unable to ignore the suggestiveness in the posture. Nor could she avoid having to smooth the fabric down over each muscular leg before turning the hem and pinning it. Flushing madly, she wondered if Reid could feel the tremor in her fingers.

When she finished the second hem, she experienced a wicked urge to run her hand back up his leg. She was shocked at herself. No lady would even think of such a thing! She couldn't imagine why she had, and it made her more awkward and embarrassed than ever.

It was fortunate, she thought desperately, that Reid Prescott could not read minds. No doubt he would be stunned at the bizarre images running around inside hers. She certainly was.

Maggie quickly rose to her feet, careful to avoid Reid's eyes. "There. That should do it."

"Thank you, Mrs. Whitcomb. This is most kind of you."

"You're welcome." Maggie glanced at him, then away. There was something in his eyes she didn't want to think about, didn't want to see. She turned aside to pick up her basket, and Reid stepped back. She walked past him and up the stairs to her bedroom.

Her heart was pounding, and her breath was suddenly shallow and fast. She put down her sewing basket, then stood gripping one of the bedposts until she heard the parlor door close. A few minutes later it opened again, and she listened to Reid's footsteps in the hallway below. The back door swung shut, and Maggie released a long breath she hadn't even realized she was holding. Her knees felt weak, and she sat down heavily on the bed, staring at her hands clenched in her lap, her mind a determined blank. She would not think about it. Nothing had happened.

Yet it was nearly a half hour before she was able to get up and go back down to the kitchen to work. And she had been able to think of nothing except Reid Prescott.

*   *   *

The night of the Lyceum, the whole family was dressed and ready long before they needed to leave, and they sat in the kitchen, waiting for Reid to join them.

Before long Reid came up the back steps. Oddly, he looked handsome and at ease in Will's formal suit, as though this was the kind of clothing he was accustomed to wearing. Will and Ty, on the other hand, were so twitchy and obviously uncomfortable that it was apparent they had been forced to dress up.

"My, we're certainly elegant tonight," he commented of the two.

"Why, of course," Maggie retorted. "This is the social event of the season."

She stood up to go, then instantly felt self-conscious. She thought she had done a good job on the dress. The skirt was pulled back and draped over a small bustle, and the pink-striped accents gave it a fresh look. It had seemed pretty upstairs in her small dresser mirror, but now she wondered how it appeared to Reid.

He turned to her, his face softening. "Mrs. Whitcomb, you look beautiful."

Her doubts thus banished, Maggie couldn't keep from grinning. "Why, thank you, kind sir. You're very grand yourself."

"That is entirely due to your skills, I'm afraid."

It wasn't, of course. The most one could say was that her needlework was good enough that the alterations didn't detract from the debonair figure he cut. She thanked him anyway.

"Let's go," Will stuck in eagerly. "Let's go!"

Reid held out his arm to Maggie courteously, then hesitated, glancing toward Will as if he had just remembered that it was her husband who had the right to escort Maggie, not he.

However, Will was already heading out the door behind Ty, without a second glance toward Maggie. A little shyly Maggie took Reid's arm, and they followed the others.

They headed for the schoolhouse on the edge of town. Ty and Will walked in front, sometimes darting ahead, sometimes lagging to collect pebbles or explore other objects of interest. The evening was mild and smelled of spring, and Maggie's step had a decided lilt.

It seemed almost no time before they reached the schoolhouse, a plain, sturdy structure with a squat bell tower and two front doors, one for boys and one for girls. The desks had been moved out, leaving rows of benches, which were already nearly filled.

Maggie suggested they sit near the back on an aisle. She wasn't sure the performances would hold Will's interest throughout the evening, and she wanted him to be able to slip outside without calling too much attention to himself. Right now, however, he was happily engaged in looking around at all the townspeople crowding the room.

Reid, too, was surveying the audience with interest; he hadn't yet met any of the residents of Pine Creek proper. Sitting on the other side of Ty, he had to lean across the boy to ask Maggie questions. After several such consultations, Ty changed seats with him.

Maggie felt a bit odd sitting beside Reid Prescott in this public gathering. It was almost as if he were her escort. She couldn't deny, though, that it was also a little exciting. She could smell the scent of soap and the lotion he had used after his shave, faint but intriguing. She could feel the heat of his body, and she knew that if either of them moved a fraction, they would be touching.

Maggie glanced around, looking for something to distract her thoughts. Her mother and Gideon hadn't driven in from the farm, but she saw many people she knew, and she smiled and waved to them. Tess and her mother sat near the front, Ginny squirming beside them with impatience. Maggie slipped up to talk to them for a few moments.

Shortly after she returned to her seat, a murmur ran

through the audience. Maggie and Reid swiveled slightly to see what had caused it.

Benton Conway, his daughter, and his wife had just entered the schoolroom and were making their way toward seats close to the front.

"Who are they?" Reid whispered to Maggie. Stiffly, she told him their names. Reid quirked an eyebrow. It was obvious from Maggie's manner and the tension in the room that there was a great deal more that she was not telling him.

Conway stopped in the aisle beside them and made it a point to address Maggie. "Well, Mrs. Whitcomb," he said with false joviality, a malicious gleam in his eye, "how are you and your family?"

Cool as a mountain stream, Maggie looked him straight in the eye. "We are all quite well, thank you." Her gaze flickered briefly to the women beside Conway. "Linette. Rosemary."

Linette nodded politely, her face expressionless.

"Mrs. Whitcomb." Rosemary bobbed her head shyly, looking pale and rather frightened. "It—it's nice to see you."

Maggie's voice thawed a trifle. "It's good to see you, too. I understand you're reading tonight?"

The girl looked more scared than ever and nodded.

"Girl's a genius," Conway commented with a loud chuckle. "Can't imagine how I wound up with a blue-stocking for a daughter. Be more help, don't you think, if she found a husband instead of reading all those books!"

"Papa!" Rosemary cried in a low voice, blushing up to her hairline.

Maggie felt like kicking the boorish man. "I don't see why Rosemary can't be intelligent *and* have a husband. Otherwise only stupid women would marry." She gazed at him with a deceptively bland expression. "Or do you think that's the case, Mr. Conway?"

Conway's mouth tightened. Reid thought he saw a

flicker of amusement in Linette Conway's cool blue eyes. The man didn't answer Maggie's question, only nodded stiffly and said, "Good to see you again, Mrs. Whitcomb. Please tell your family that I said hello. Especially your lovely sister-in-law."

"I will." Maggie bit out, glaring at Conway as the trio continued down the aisle.

When they were out of earshot, Reid whispered, "What was that all about?"

"Benton Conway is an evil, wicked man," Maggie replied in a heated whisper. "A scalawag. I don't know why he singled out Tess that way, but I'm sure it can't mean anything good for her. It worries me." Maggie frowned.

"But obviously the girl isn't Mrs. Conway's daughter."

"Heavens, no. Her mother, Benton's first wife, died, oh, ten or twelve years ago, when Rosemary was still a little girl. I imagine that's one reason she's so painfully shy."

"If Rosemary is so shy, why is she giving a reading tonight?"

"She loves literature, and you have to perform somehow if you're in the Ladies Guild. The Lyceum is the biggest thing they do. Besides, the library was largely her idea. And I suspect Benton wants her to participate. She's his link to Pine Creek society."

"And that's important to him?"

Maggie nodded. "Yes. I think he misses having stature in the community. Before he started sympathizing with the carpetbaggers, he was, well, maybe not really *well*-liked, but he was accepted. After he turned traitor, he was virtually ostracized by everyone, except, of course, the other turncoats and carpetbaggers. He likes the money, of course, too much to give up what he does. But most of the people he associates with are"— she wrinkled her nose—"carrion."

Reid glanced at Maggie, and an amused smile tipped

up the corners of his mouth. "I don't reckon anyone ever accused you of being reluctant to express your opinion."

Maggie laughed. "No. You're right." She sighed reminiscently. "Will and I used to have some terrible fights. He'd tell me I ought to agree with my husband, and I'd tell him I didn't see any reason I should when he was wrong."

"Who won?"

"Neither one of us, most of the time." Her eyes darkened in a secretive, sensual way. "Will'd start ki—" She stopped abruptly and blushed, realizing that what she'd been about to blurt out was hardly fit talk around a man. "That is, well, we'd make up and forget about it," she finished weakly. And she turned to stare straight ahead at the makeshift stage, too embarrassed even to glance at Reid.

Reid, however, continued to watch her profile. He could guess how she and Will had made up, and the thought of it sent a hot quiver of passion through him.

He gazed at the smooth curve of her brow, the straight line of her nose, the softly rounded silhouette of her lips. A man would enjoy arguing with Maggie, he thought, if she brought equal passion to the lovemaking afterward. And he was suddenly sure that she would. She might be calm and strong, but no one could accuse her of not feeling deeply.

She would be wild and unfettered in bed, he decided. It wasn't the first time he had considered the matter; his mind had gone to that image many times in the last few weeks. Maggie Whitcomb wasn't exactly pretty; her features were too compelling for so tame an adjective. But her looks were deeply sensual—from the delicious curves of her hips and breasts to her slightly untamed eyebrows. Her lower lip had a soft fullness, which gave an almost little-girl pout to features that might otherwise have been too strong. Reid doubted that any man could look at such a woman and not feel some stirrings of sexuality, and he was no better than any other male in that regard. Indeed, perhaps he was worse. For he was hungering for another man's wife. And that man was a likable, sympathetic wreck left by the War.

Reid knew that Maggie would never betray Will. She was not the sort of woman to treat her wedding vows lightly, no matter what the circumstances. She had taken Will for better or worse. Well, this was the worse, and Reid was sure she was determined to bear it.

Every time Reid looked at the big blond farmer's open, vague face, he felt a twinge of guilt that it was this kindly family man, rather than himself, to whom this had happened in the War. However, he couldn't help thinking that Will Whitcomb would neither know nor care whether Maggie remained true to their wedding vows. There would be no pain for him if Reid and Maggie made love.

And Reid's temptation was growing daily. Maggie was always *there*. Every day he could see her and listen to her, laugh at the clever things she said, witness her admirable strength and courage. Being around Maggie was like standing in the sun. For the first time in years he felt warm, connected to someone, interested in where he was and what he was doing. For the first time he woke up in the morning looking forward to the day.

With a stir at the front of the room, the program started. Mariana Hill, the Ladies Guild president, announced their first performer, who would offer a medley of songs. The local woman performed with gusto if with little ability. Next the shy Rosemary Conway read an essay by Lamb in a voice so soft it could hardly be heard, all the while looking as if she might faint. It was something of a relief when she ended and sat down. But then an older, gray-haired woman took the stage, playing a violin concerto so lovely that it seemed to twine around one's soul. A large matron with a prominent jaw and a jutting bosom read a stirring poem, and a dimpled girl played a rollicking, if somewhat inexpert, tune on the piano. All in all, the array of acts was varied and energetic enough to hold the children's attention and make the evening a success. For Reid, he thought it was enough simply to sit beside Maggie for an entire evening, inhaling her faint lilac scent and feeling her warmth beside him.

After a bit of hearty socializing with friends and neighbors, they walked home in the same manner in which they had come, with Ty and Will some distance in front of Maggie and Reid. Their steps were necessarily slower because of the dark, and they looked at the stars as they ambled along, talking in soft voices. The night wrapped around them like velvet, soft and secretive and sensual, and Reid felt his blood stir in response. It was so easy, so natural to be with Maggie that he took her hand, holding it as they walked, for all the world like a couple courting.

Then Ty and Will turned back toward them, asking a question about the constellations, and Maggie, abruptly coming to her senses, dropped Reid's hand like a hot potato and moved away from him. Suddenly her heart was pounding in her throat, and she felt flushed and hot. It seemed bizarre to her that she could have been so casually holding hands with Reid Prescott. The rest of the walk home, she stayed a good foot and a half from his side. They said little, the silence between them now awkward.

As usual, they took the path that cut through the side yard to the back of the house, ignoring the rarely used front door. It was too dark to see well, and the yard was dotted with mud puddles, especially where it was shaded by large trees. Maggie lifted her skirts a fraction, slowing her steps and moving carefully, unlike Ty and Will, who bounded ahead to the house.

Despite Maggie's care, she stepped squarely into a puddle. She let out an exasperated sigh.

"What's the matter?" Reid was beside her in an instant, his hand on her elbow to steady her.

"I—I stepped in the mud." Maggie felt his touch throughout her body, and it was all she could do not to shiver in reaction. To cover it, she complained, "These are my best slippers, too."

"Come on. I'll clean them off." He turned toward the barn, his hand still on her elbow, and Maggie went with him.

The barn was black inside, but Reid quickly reached for the lantern, lit it, and hung it on a hook by one of the stalls, then opened the heavy wooden toolbox and removed a metal scraper. He closed the lid and took off his suit jacket, laying it across the top of the trunk. "Here. Sit down."

Maggie lowered herself to the trunk lid, intending to unlace her high-topped shoe and hand it to him, but, to her surprise, Reid knelt and took her foot in one hand and with the other began to scrape the mud from her sole. She looked down at him. His head was bent, so she saw only his thick, shaggy hair, his powerful shoulders, and the firm, lean muscles of his arms beneath his shirtsleeves as he worked on her slipper.

It gave her a funny feeling in the pit of her stomach to watch his strong, slender fingers curve around her ankle, even with the leather of her shoe between them and her flesh. His hands had always fascinated her, so graceful and quick in their movements, yet so masculine, with thick tendons rippling and a light sprinkling of black hair across the backs. To see his hands actually touching her somewhere almost took her breath away, making her imagine them on her more intimately, sliding down her bare arms or caressing her shoulders.

Maggie knew she shouldn't think these thoughts. She had been trying to stop for weeks now. Reid was as far away from her as the moon. She was a married woman, bound by law and religion to Will. It would be a sin to touch another man, to kiss him, to let him make love to her.

Besides, it was silly to think Reid even wanted to do

those things. She was no longer a sweet young thing. She was almost thirty now, and she had borne a child. A man as handsome as Reid Prescott could have any woman he wanted; there was no reason to think he'd even look twice at her.

Just because she felt all knotted up inside whenever she looked at him didn't mean that he felt the same way about her. Just because her eyes sought him out every chance they got didn't mean that he was always looking for her. It didn't mean he thought about her or dreamed about her in the hot, sultry nights, nor that he lay awake thrashing in his bed, longing to feel her skin beneath his hands.

Maggie swallowed hard, heat rising up in her at her thoughts. She hoped Reid wouldn't look up, wouldn't see the color in her cheeks or the sudden sparkle in her eyes.

Reid wiped the scraper with a handful of straw, then returned to peel off the last bit of mud on the instep of her shoe. His movements were slow, his hand tight upon her ankle, and it seemed to Maggie as if an eternity had passed while he worked on her foot. She wondered if she had gone mad or if Reid was actually lingering over the job. She told herself she must be imagining it; he couldn't be feeling the same tingling sensations in his fingers that she did when he touched her.

He laid down the scraper and picked up another handful of straw. This time he wiped her shoe with it in long, slow strokes. But now it was actually his hand moving across her foot, with mere straw and leather between them. Maggie thought that she could feel the heat of his hands, and again she wondered if she were imagining things. Her breath caught in her throat; her heart raced.

She didn't know if she made a noise, but at that moment Reid glanced up at her. His face looked flushed beneath its tan, and there was a soft curve to his wide mouth. For an instant something glittered in his eyes, hot and primitive, and a thrill ran through Maggie. He was as stirred as she. *He wanted her!* It was as clear as if he had spoken.

He dropped the straw, but his hand returned to her foot, sliding up over the leather almost possessively. Maggie sensed that he was about to straighten up from his crouch, reach for her, and pull her into his arms, his lips seeking hers.

For an instant, they were motionless, frozen on the edge of action, caught in a tangle of desire and duty. Then Reid lowered her foot and slowly started to rise, his eyes blazing into hers. As if his movement had released her from her trance, Maggie jumped up.

"Thank you," she told him breathlessly, her voice sounding like a squeak to her ears. And she turned and hurried from the barn. By the time she reached the yard, she picked up her skirts and fairly flew toward the house, running as if the hounds of hell were after her.

Behind her Reid stood up, frustration and hunger mingling within him. Letting out a wordless cry, he turned and hurled the metal scraper at the barn wall.

9

The next morning Maggie peered at herself in her mirror. Did she look old? Was she still attractive? She hadn't thought about such things in years, but she did now. She studied her face, leaning forward to search for telltale lines and wrinkles. But she had always been careful to protect herself from the blazing sun of the Arkansas summer, sparing her skin the leatheriness some women's acquired as they grew older. Hers was still white and creamy. Reassured, she stepped back to look at herself full length. Thank Heaven her body, too, was still firm and slender.

She wasn't pretty, she knew, in the way Tess or Linette Conway were. They had the sort of looks that swept men off their feet. But her parents had always assured her that she was appealing in a different way, and, sure enough, her wide eyes, full lips, and thick, straight eyebrows gave her an exotic aura that had often drawn masculine attention. When she was a marriageable girl, she had had her fair share of admirers. And, fortunately, hers were the kind of looks that didn't fade with the passing of youth. If anything, the slight fleshing out of maturity had subtly enhanced her appearance.

Maggie looked down at her faded old dress and sighed. All her clothes, even her church dresses, were tired and worn. She considered her image thoughtfully once more, then began rummaging through her drawers until she found a crocheted collar. She pinned on the neckpiece with a brooch and looked at herself again. A prettier hairstyle would help, too. She brushed it out, then pinned it up in a fuller, looser style that softened the angularity of her features.

She didn't examine why she did these things; she didn't want to know. It was simply fun to think about her looks again, to feel that little lift when she looked at herself in the mirror in the morning and saw that she was still attractive. She had lived too long in plainness.

Maggie ran lightly down the stairs. She felt faintly excited this morning. A little embarrassment mingled with her excitement, for she wasn't sure what Reid would think about what had happened in the barn last night. But then she reasoned that, after all, nothing *had* happened. She had left, and nothing had been said, nothing had been done, that either of them should regret.

So when Reid came in for breakfast with Will and Ty, she smiled easily at all three of them and did her best to act as if nothing untoward had occurred. She could not, however, keep from shooting glances at Reid all through breakfast. Nor could she help noticing that he kept looking at her, as well.

After breakfast, she and the boys drove into town for church. As was their custom, Tess and Ginny joined them after the service, and they drove out to the Tyrrell farm for Sunday dinner. Sometimes Tess's mother joined them, but this time Amanda went to her sister's house for the noon meal. Ginny, Will, and Ty sat laughing and playing in the back of Maggie's small wagon, their feet dangling off the end, while Maggie and Tess chatted on the front seat.

Tess looked over at her sister-in-law. She hadn't told Maggie about Benton Conway's disturbing visit a few weeks ago. It had seemed too awful and embarrassing a thing to talk about, even to Maggie. Besides, she had hoped that his threats were merely empty blustering.

But then, two days ago, she had gotten a notice from the tax assessor. The taxes on their house had been hiked astronomically, just as Benton had threatened. When she realized that it would be impossible for her to raise the money she needed, she had sat down on the stairs and wept.

She could see no way out of the horrible fix. She wanted to tell Maggie about it—Maggie was the sort of person in whom it was easy to confide—yet she could not let herself. She knew the Tyrrells. They would attempt to shoulder responsibility for her without her even asking. They would think that they should help her raise the funds to pay the taxes, or, worse, Gideon might decide to solve the problem with his fists, and then Benton's friends in the government would throw Gideon into jail.

This was simply something she had to solve herself. She had to be strong for Ginny and her mother's sake. She had to figure out a solution. So instead of saying what weighed on her mind, she smiled at Maggie and asked brightly, "How is the hired hand working out?"

Maggie, who had been concentrating on turning the wagon out of the churchyard, glanced over at her. "Reid?" She colored, thinking of the night before, and hoped Tess wouldn't notice. "Mr. Prescott, I mean? Well, he's—I—" she faltered. "Actually, I'm not really sure," she conceded.

"What do you mean?"

"Well, he can chop wood and mend fences and things like that, but I don't think he'd know a tomato plant from a weed, he can't milk a cow, and he didn't have any idea how to slop the hogs until Ty and Will showed him. He was going to break ground for a vegetable garden for me, but he didn't know how to harness the mule to the plow."

"That doesn't sound like much of a hired hand," Tess said doubtfully.

"Well, he never claimed to be a farmer. He's from the city. Savannah. But I think it's more than that. I don't think he's used to doing any kind of manual labor. I suspect that maybe he had money and lost it in the War."

"Oh, I see. You mean he's useless, like I was." Tess's teasing smile and dancing eyes took the sting of self-pity from her words.

"Now, Tess, I never said that."

"I know. You were much too kind to. But I saw that stunned look on your face the time you had to show me how to turn the feather mattresses."

Maggie couldn't help but giggle. "Oh, my, I'd forgotten that. Well, yes, I guess that is the way Mr. Prescott is about his chores. But at least he learns quickly. You never have to explain anything to him twice."

"Well, it's good that he's smart."

"Yes, but you know, that's an even stranger thing about him. He's obviously very well educated. He helps Ty with his studies, and you can see how much he knows. So why wouldn't he use that education? I mean, why wouldn't he get a job teaching or something? He could easily clerk or read for the law, I'm sure. Why would he just wander like that, never really accomplishing anything?"

"Maybe he was too devastated by losing his fortune. Or maybe he was too proud."

"So proud that he'd rather be a vagrant and sleep in people's barns and never know where his next meal is coming from?"

"Well, I admit it doesn't make much sense. Haven't

you asked him why he doesn't teach school or something? Why he became a drifter?"

"No. Even I don't have that much courage. It's obvious he doesn't like to talk about his past. He'll answer if you pose a direct question, but he never volunteers anything more than what you ask. About all I know about him is that he's from Savannah and that his parents are dead."

"Aren't you afraid that means he's hiding something awful?" Tess's eyes widened dramatically. "What if he's dangerous? What if he's a criminal?"

"Now you sound like Gideon. Prescott's not a criminal—I'm sure of it. When you meet him, you'll see. He's just, well, reluctant to talk about himself. And I don't think he likes people much."

"He doesn't sound very agreeable."

"Oh, no, it's not that," Maggie hastened to assure her. "Now I've given you the wrong impression. He's not really gruff or disagreeable, just . . . aloof. Though I'll admit he doesn't smile very much, he can be quite pleasant. And he's kind to the boys, and he has good manners. It's obvious that he's a gentleman. He's quite handsome, too."

"Handsome? Really?"

"Yes." Maggie thought of Reid's smooth features and his clear hazel eyes shaded by thick, dark lashes.

"Why, Maggie, you didn't tell me that," Tess teased lightly. "Now, I would think that'd be one of the first things you'd mention."

Maggie grimaced. "Tess, I'm a married woman!"

Tess chuckled. "Well, that doesn't mean you're dead."

"Tess!" Maggie snapped.

Did her sister-in-law suspect something? Maggie wondered anxiously. But how could she? There was nothing, absolutely nothing, to be suspicious of, she reminded herself. Still, an odd, stifling sensation rose in Maggie's chest. She had felt it several times lately. She wasn't sure what it was, only that it clutched at her throat, made her feel as if she were choking.

"Now, Maggie, I didn't mean to upset you." Tess leaned over, putting her hand on Maggie's arm. "Don't go all stiff and prickly on me. I certainly didn't mean to imply anything wrong. I was just being silly. I'm sorry."

Maggie forced a smile. "I'm sorry, too. Sometimes I'm an old grouch. I shouldn't have snapped at you."

They were nearing the farmhouse now, and Maggie pulled on the reins to steer the mule into the long drive. Within moments, the house loomed up ahead, sturdy and familiar.

Maggie usually felt a welcoming lift of her spirits whenever she saw it. But, somehow, today it seemed as if the knot in her chest only grew tighter at the thought of seeing her mother and Gideon. Jo would ask her what she'd learned of Reid Prescott's background, and Gideon would probably be all big-brotherly and lecture her on the dangers of hiring a stranger. It startled Maggie to realize that for once she really wasn't looking forward to her Sunday visit at home. Whatever was wrong with her?

Grimly, she set her jaw and slapped the reins across the mule's back.

Gideon walked down the hall for the fourth time in thirty minutes and looked out the open front door. There was still no sign of Maggie's wagon. He turned and frowned at the clock in the hall. Surely that wasn't the correct time. It seemed to him as if he and his mother had been home from church for hours.

But he knew it hadn't been that long, that the clock was right. He was simply eager for Tess to get here. Well, Maggie, too, of course; he loved his sister. But it was Tess's arrival that made his chest tighten and his heart speed up.

He wandered back down the hall and into the

kitchen, where his mother was cutting potatoes into a pot of boiling water. She glanced up at her son, and her face softened.

"There, now, don't worry about them," she told him. "You're just like a mother hen with her chicks."

"Ma . . ." Gideon looked pained.

"It's true. You always looked out for the other three."

As the oldest child of hardworking parents, Gideon had often been left in charge of his younger siblings, responsible for keeping their toes out of the fire and their hands out of the cookie jar. It was he who warned off bullies at school, he who fixed Maggie's porcelain doll when Hunter, teasing her by holding it out of her reach, had accidentally dropped it. It was he who covered for Shelby when he sneaked in late the night before, smelling of whiskey, and couldn't get up to do his chores the next morning. He had been part father as well as brother and friend to them.

"Not well enough." His voice was laced with bitterness.

Jo frowned. "Gideon . . . it's not your fault. You couldn't help what happened. You couldn't keep the War from coming or Shelby from dying. You couldn't make Will better or Maggie happier."

"I know." They had touched upon the subject before, yet the fact was that, no matter how irrational it might be, Gideon couldn't help feeling he had failed his brothers and sister. He had been unable to protect them, unable to keep them safe. And now he had made that failure worse by falling in love with Shelby's widow.

"Then don't worry so. You've done the best you could, and that's all anyone can do."

"You're right." Gideon stared down at a chair back, unconsciously picking at a patch of peeling paint. "But, Ma . . ."

"What?"

He shrugged. "Oh, nothing. It's just, well, I'm not one to cry over spilt milk, but sometimes I wish so badly that things could be the way they were before. Just the other day I was thinking about the way Shel used to laugh. You remember?"

"Oh, yes, I remember." Jo turned misty-eyed. "You couldn't help but laugh, too, when you heard him."

Gideon nodded. "I wish I could hear him laugh again. I wish—I wish I hadn't told him he was an irresponsible fool to run off to war like that when he had a wife depending on him and a child on the way. He made me so mad at the time. I only wanted him to stop and think about what he was doing. To not be so impulsive."

"You aren't the only one who felt that way," Jo assured him. "You aren't the only one who tried to get him to change his mind. But I've never known a Tyrrell who wasn't bound and determined to do exactly what he wanted. Nothing could have stopped Shel. And nothing you said made him die."

"I know. Still . . ." He couldn't tell her the real reason he felt so guilty about Shelby.

"Listen." Jo cocked her head.

Gideon went still. Then he smiled. "You're right. I hear a wagon."

He strode down the hall to the front door again. This time he saw Maggie's wagon bouncing up the drive. "They're here!" he called back to his mother, and Jo came hurrying out to join him on the front porch.

They waved as the wagon drew up in front of the house, and for the next few minutes everyone was busy climbing down from the wagon, greeting each other, hugging, and laughing.

"My, don't you look handsome today," Maggie told Gideon, linking her arm through his as they walked inside.

Gideon frowned down at his sister and said gruffly, "Just church clothes."

Maggie chuckled, shaking her head. "You never could take a compliment. Tess, what are we going to do with this man?"

"I don't know." Tess, walking ahead beside Jo, flashed a dimpled smile back at them. "He certainly isn't like Shelby. Now, that man loved a compliment."

"That's the truth. In fact, he'd even ask for them!" Maggie agreed.

The two women smiled in fond remembrance, and neither saw the pain that flashed across Gideon's face at the reminder of how little chance he had with Tess, being so unlike the man she loved.

As was usual at a Tyrrell family gathering, dinner was accompanied by plenty of laughter and animated talk as the heavy bowls and platters of food were lightened of their load. Perhaps the fare was plainer and less plentiful than before the War, and some of the faces were missing, but there was still the old closeness and ease, the same humorous and loving ways.

They talked of many things, from the weather, always of prime importance to farmers, to the latest gossip from town. Maggie told them about the letter she had gotten from Hunter and her hope that he might return to Pine Creek someday.

Jo stopped, her fork in midair, and stared at her daughter. "What did he say, exactly, Maggie?"

"Well, he wrote that he missed the farm and all, reminiscing about what it was like in the springtime. Of course, he said he wasn't a farmer like Gideon, so coming back wouldn't make much sense, but I reckon he wouldn't have brought it up if he hadn't been thinking about it."

"Oh." Jo looked disappointed. "Well, at least he misses us."

"It'd be nice to have Hunter home again," Tess contributed.

Gideon looked over at her. That was one of the few things Tess had said during the whole meal. She hadn't been her usual bubbly self at all, and he was beginning to wonder if there was something wrong with her. Was she sick? Unhappy? And why had the only thing she'd said been about Hunter?

Sharp teeth of jealousy began to nip at his insides. Gideon knew it was ridiculous to make anything out of her simple remark; Hunter was family, and it was only natural that all of them wanted him to come home. Hunter was Shelby's brother, too, just as he was, and Tess was still mourning Shelby. She wouldn't have any interest in Hunter as a man.

Still, he couldn't help but start thinking of all the ways that Hunter was more like Shelby than he was— the charm and hotheadedness, the dashing good looks, the way he had with women. The thought that Tess might feel something, even a little something, for Hunter was like a knife slicing right through his chest, and for a moment he selfishly hoped that Hunter never came home.

But as soon as he thought that, Gideon was disgusted with himself for it. It was bad enough to be jealous of a long-dead brother, but to wish for his other brother to stay away just because Tess had expressed a small degree of interest in him was, Gideon admitted, the height of selfishness.

To make up for the momentary disloyalty, he said, "If Hunter came home, things would be easier. Maybe then Maggie wouldn't have to hire some stranger to help out around her place."

Maggie rolled her eyes. "Honestly, Gideon, you're like a dog with a bone."

"You mean Reid?" Ty asked, his brows drawing together in a frown. "But I like Reid. I want him to stay."

"Then it's a good thing Uncle Gideon doesn't have anything to say about it, isn't it," Maggie responded firmly, fixing her brother with a stern glance.

Gideon ignored both her look and Ty's comment. "How's he working out? Has he stayed in line?"

"Yes, Gideon," Maggie answered with heavy sarcasm. "He's been a perfect gentleman."

Gideon flushed a little. "I know you think I'm being priggish about the whole thing," he said stiffly. "But I can't help but be concerned about my sister. If anything happened to you, I'd hold myself responsible."

Maggie reached across the table to pat his hand. "Gideon, you take on far too much responsibility for everyone else's problems. But we all have to learn to make it on our own. Isn't that right, Tess?"

"What?" Tess glanced up at Maggie, then at Gideon. "Oh. Oh, yes, that's right. We have to take care of ourselves. We can't expect you to pull us out of the ditch every time we fall in."

Damn. Independence was the last thing Gideon wanted from Tess. Her reliance on him was the most important link he had to her, and her words only made him feel worse. "Now, ladies," he said, making a joke of his worry, "you're going to have me feeling absolutely useless if you keep this up. What am I going to do with myself when you two are completely self-reliant?"

Maggie made a face at him, but Tess smiled sweetly.

"I'm afraid you won't have to worry about that," Tess told him. "I sometimes wonder if I could ever reach that state."

"Nobody reaches that state," Jo put in firmly from the head of the table. "Believe me. You can't be rich enough or strong enough or old enough to never need anyone else." She cast a look at Maggie. "And you, young lady, ought to be grateful for your brother's help, not griping about it."

"Yes, Mama," Maggie said contritely. "I'm sorry, Gideon." She smiled at him, then added the little-sister face she had made at him often over the years: eyes crossed and tongue stuck out.

Gideon laughed. "I accept that apology in the spirit in which it was given."

After the meal was over, Gideon herded the children outside while the women cleaned up. Later in the afternoon, hot and sweaty from their rambunctious games of hide-and-seek and tag that roamed all over the farmyard, he retreated to supervise their activities from the sidelines. As he drew close to the porch, he saw Tess perched on the rail, leaning back against one of the square posts. Seemingly lost in thought, she was gazing off into the distance, a faint frown between her eyes, and Gideon was reminded of how preoccupied and quiet she had been during the meal. Now that he thought about it, Tess hadn't really seemed herself for the last few Sundays.

"Penny for your thoughts," he said quietly.

Tess started. Worrying over her problem with the taxes, she hadn't even heard Gideon approach. "Oh." She tried to smile. "You startled me."

"Sorry. Didn't mean to." He came up the steps, wiping the sweat from his brow, uncomfortably aware of how he must look, dusty and dirty from chasing about, his hair probably sticking out every which way. Tess never saw him at his best, he realized sadly. Never saw him all slicked-up and clean, dressed in a suit and carrying flowers, the way she had seen Shel and her other beaux before she married.

Gideon wished he could come to call on her, carrying a bouquet of sweet-smelling roses or a bunch of long-stalked irises, their blooms complemented by the heady scent of honeysuckle. He would call her Miss Tess and tell her how lovely she was. And he *wouldn't* talk about how much ground she wanted broken for her vegetable garden or whether a board on the porch steps needed replacing.

A silence stretched between them. Gideon watched Ty and Ginny and Will playing in the distance, then cast a sidelong look at Tess. "I noticed you didn't talk much during dinner today. Is something wrong?"

Tess glanced at him, startled. "I—well, no, of course not. What would be wrong?"

"I don't know. I thought maybe you were unhappy about something, or worried, or sick. You just didn't seem quite yourself."

"I'm fine," Tess assured him quickly, but there was a false note in her voice that made him uneasy. "You worry too much about all of us."

"I can't help but worry," he objected. He paused, then pressed on. "Tess, I know that something is bothering you."

Tess hesitated, tempted to pour out her tale of woe into his sympathetic ear. Then she shook her head. "No, really, Gideon, it's something I need to handle myself."

"What is?"

"No, honestly, Gideon, you already do too much for me."

"No, I don't. I want to help you. Don't you realize that?"

He looked at her with worried eyes, and Tess longed to lay her troubles at his feet. He was always so strong, so resourceful. Perhaps somehow he could think of a way to help her.

But Tess knew that was the way of the weak. Gideon shouldn't have to shoulder her burdens. "I know, but . . ."

"Please. Let me help you." His voice was low and persuasive.

Tess looked at him, torn. "I—it's pointless. There's nothing you can do. Nothing anyone can do."

Gideon looked alarmed. "Why not? What do you mean?"

"I—oh, Gideon." Her breath caught, and suddenly she felt as if tears were filling her up, pushing against her eyes, aching to get out. Again she shook her head.

She simply couldn't let herself break down in front of him.

"Tess!" Visibly upset, Gideon moved closer.

She drew a deep breath, then said quickly, "I'm afraid I'm going to lose the house."

"What?" Gideon stared at her. "What did you say?"

"My house—they've raised my taxes, and I can't pay them. They'll take it away from us."

"But why?"

"Benton Conway wants it."

"Conway!" Disgust twisted Gideon's features.

"He wanted me to sell it to him. It's only half mine; Daddy left it to both Mama and me, but Mama would agree to sell if I asked her to. I told him I wouldn't, of course. Then he insinuated his Yankee friends might raise the taxes so high that I couldn't pay them, and they'd take the house away from me. Then he could buy it cheaply."

"Why didn't you tell me this earlier? God, Tess, how long have you been carrying this burden around, keeping it a secret?"

"I don't know, two or three weeks, I guess. I was hoping he didn't really mean it, that he wouldn't go through with it. But I got the tax notice Friday, and it's so high I couldn't possibly pay it."

"Well, it can't happen. We won't let it happen." Seeing the fear in Tess's eyes, Gideon felt like tearing somebody apart. He wished he had that slime Benton Conway in front of him right now.

"But how can we stop it? I don't have that much money. We didn't get much for the plantation, and then there were a lot of debts to pay. We've used up almost everything. I thought about taking in sewing—I'm fairly decent at it—but that wouldn't raise enough money. Besides, Mrs. Bowlin is already doing that, and she's a better seamstress than I am. Bettina Cryer opened a boarding house. Maybe we could do that, too—though I can't imagine what Mama would say—but we still couldn't make money quickly enough to pay off the taxes."

She thought it best not to mention Benton's other suggestion of a way in which she could keep the house. She was desperate enough that she had thought about it a few times over the past couple of days since receiving the tax notice. For it was true that the only thing she had ever been trained to be was a wife, her only assets her beauty and social graces. But the only way she could use those assets to save her house would be to become Benton's mistress.

Yet she hated to think of that loathsome man even touching her. Everything about him repulsed her. She couldn't imagine how Linette could stand to sleep with him. Would she be able to endure it if it meant saving her home for her mother and daughter?

It would mean the ruin of her, of course. Word would get out, even if Conway was discreet, which she doubted he would be. In a town the size of Pine Creek, little could be kept hidden, and his visits would be noticed. Soon everyone would know, and they would all shun her. Worse, they would shun Ginny and her mother as well. Tess's stomach knotted at the thought of people slighting Amanda Caldwell, or of Ginny hearing someone say that her mother was Benton Conway's whore. She could imagine, too, how Gideon would look at her, with disgust in his eyes. No. Nothing was worth that, not even their home.

Not looking at Gideon, Tess went on. "I've thought that we could sell the last of our jewelry and our better furniture. That would raise some money. But I don't think it would be enough."

"No! Oh, God, you shouldn't have to sell everything you own! Tess, it doesn't bear thinking of."

"But what other choice do I have? How can we leave that house?" Tears clogged her voice. "It's where I grew up; it holds all our happy memories."

"I know. It must mean the world to you."

"I don't think I can bear to lose it!" She began to cry, and her hands flew to her face.

Without thinking, Gideon leaned to put an arm around her shoulders, and Tess clung to him, crying into his chest. Gideon gently wrapped her in his arms, bending his head down over hers.

Even in the midst of his sympathy for her, he couldn't help but notice how perfectly Tess fit into him, how soft and sweet-smelling her hair was beneath his cheek. He thought that he could hold her this way forever. Of course his body would soon begin to stir in a decidedly un-sweet, very masculine way, if he did not let her go, but for the moment this was enough, all he could ever want—to hold her in his protective embrace and let her cry out her pain into him. To be, at least for now, the man she turned to.

"It'll be all right," he told her soothingly when at last her tears subsided. "You'll see. We'll find a way. I promise. I'll help you pay the taxes."

"No." Tess stepped back from him, shaking her head decisively. "That's exactly why I didn't want to tell you. I don't want you to try to pay the taxes for me."

"Tess, this is no time for pride."

"You might think about that statement yourself," Tess retorted. "We both know that you haven't any extra money. You're struggling, just as we all are. You have enough worries keeping the farm going by yourself without trying to scrape together enough money to pay someone else's taxes."

"I can't stand by and watch while your home is taken away from you, can I?" Gideon looked insulted. "What kind of a man would I be?"

"A sensible one. Where would you get the money? How could you do it? It would be impossible."

"I'd get it," he grated out. "I could sell a piece of the farm."

"Gideon! Don't even mention such a thing!" Tess looked truly shocked. "The farm is your birthright. All the Tyrrells' birthright, Ginny included. And rightfully it belongs to your mother."

"She'd be as happy to sell some of it to help you as I would be."

"Perhaps, but I won't take it. My home is precious to me, but not as precious as this land is to you. I'd sell the house ten times over before I'd see you sell a bit of the farm."

Gideon stared at her. "You are the stubbornest female. . . ." He stopped, then grimaced. "Well, except for my sister and mother, of course. What is it about Tyrrell women, I'd like to know?" he grumbled. "Even the ones who only marry Tyrrells."

Tess chuckled. "That's easy to answer: it's living with Tyrrell men. It makes you as stubborn as they are."

Gideon had to grin. "I reckon you're right about that." Then his laughter stilled, and he sighed. "Oh, Tess . . ."

He was filled with frustration, wanting to protect Tess from pain, yet feeling powerless to do so. This state, this town, was his home, yet he and his family and friends—because they wouldn't take the oath required—were disenfranchised, strangers to the new government, enemies, even.

"Don't worry, Gideon. I'll get by somehow. If I do lose the house, it won't be the worst thing that could happen. I'll still have Ginny and Mama, and we still have our health. That's more than some folks have."

Though she had found no solution to her dilemma, Tess felt better than she had earlier. Just talking to Gideon seemed to have taken some of the weight off her shoulders. Besides, by having to cool his temper, she had managed to calm herself down, as well. Losing her home would be terrible; she dreaded the thought. But it really *wouldn't* be the worst thing that could happen to her. That would be to take Conway up on his proposal, to give up her good name, her honor, her character, her very self, in order to stay in her house.

"Have you thought about talking to Linette?" Gideon asked after a moment. "She should be able to influence Conway. Surely she doesn't want to take your house away from you."

Tess shrugged. "I don't know what Linette wants anymore. I haven't talked to her in ages. We haven't really been friends since she married."

"But, even so, don't you think she'd retain some fond feelings for you after all the years you were friends?"

"I don't know." Tess gazed at him evenly. "Could a woman who married someone else only weeks after her fiancé died have any feelings for anyone? I've wondered sometimes."

"I guess you're right," Gideon admitted, thinking that Linette Conway was indeed a cold, hard woman. It was probably foolish to think she might help Tess for the sake of an old friendship. For all they knew, Linette could be egging Conway on, wanting to live in a house she had always admired. He sighed. "But I hate it that I can't do anything, that there's no way to fight this thing!"

Tess smiled, warmed a little by his vehemence. "You do more than enough, believe me."

Gideon looked at her, thinking how beautiful she was, how kind and understanding. Shel had been a lucky man to be married to her, he thought.

Almost immediately guilt stabbed him. How could he even think that Shelby was lucky when he was buried in some lonely grave off in Virginia? It was he who was the lucky one, to be sitting here alive, able to talk to Tess and admire her beauty, while Shelby was cold and silent and alone. The thought made him shiver, and he looked away.

"We've got time yet," he said. "Let's think on it. Maybe we'll come up with something." Then, dissatisfied with half measures, he took her hand, looked her in the eye, and said earnestly, "I'll find a way to help you. I promise."

He had to, he knew. Or he'd never be able to live with himself.

10

Maggie was in the kitchen washing dishes and pondering what she would make for the noon dinner when she heard Will scream.

She set a dish down with a clatter and ran to the open back door. Will was standing under the large black oak tree near the barn, wringing his hands over a prone figure on the ground. Ty!

Fear clutched at Maggie's stomach. She picked up her skirts and ran full tilt out of the house and across the yard toward the tree. "Ty!"

Will glanced toward her but continued to hover over Ty's motionless form, his face twisted with alarm. He was whimpering and saying Ty's name when Maggie reached them.

"What happened?" she asked sharply, forgetting in her fright that her tone would upset Will even more.

"I told him!" Will cried, his voice shrill with fear. "I told him he was too high. I told him to come down."

He began to cry, then broke into a run. Maggie didn't spare him a glance as he galloped toward the house. She knew he would run up to his room and hide, hands over his head, as he always did when a crisis occurred. But she didn't have the time to worry about that now.

She dropped down onto her knees beside her son. He was lying there so pale and still that for an awful instant she thought he was dead. Then his eyes opened and rolled in terror, and she breathed a sigh of relief. At least he was alive. His fall from the tree had just driven the air from his lungs.

"It's all right, sweetheart," she soothed, placing a hand on his forehead. "Just relax. You got the wind knocked out of you, that's all. You'll be able to breathe soon. Just calm down."

She ran her eyes down his body, and a chill touched her. His left arm was twisted at a peculiar angle. Oh, God, he had broken it!

Panic engulfed her. Over the years she had become accustomed to handling whatever problem arose, from a sick animal to Ty's measles to a leaking roof. But one thing she had never had to deal with was a broken bone. It would have to be straightened and immobilized to knit properly, and Maggie knew that could be an agonizing experience; she had seen the doctor set her father's leg after a mule had kicked him. Though her father had downed an enormous amount of sour mash, she well remembered his white, sweat-beaded face as Dr. Daley pulled the tibia back into place. The thought of her son suffering that kind of pain made Maggie ill.

But the situation was even worse than that, for Dr. Daley had died a few years back, and there was no longer a physician in town—or, indeed, any closer than Sharps, a good fifteen miles away. It would take the rest of the day to ride there and locate his house, and what if he wasn't in? What if he wouldn't ride back through the night but insisted on waiting for daylight? It could be a whole day that Ty was in pain, and she would have to worsen it by moving him. She might even damage the arm further. But what other choice did she have? She couldn't leave him lying out here all night. And she knew she couldn't set the bone herself. Even if she could steel herself to hurt Ty so, she was afraid that she wouldn't put it back together right, and Ty would grow up with a twisted, maybe even useless, arm. Why, even with a physician setting her father's leg, he had walked with a slight limp thereafter.

Maggie looked down at Ty, doing her best to hide the fear that raged inside her, knowing she had to appear calm to keep him from panicking. She brushed back a lock of his hair and tried to smile. Ty struggled to breathe, and as he finally managed to suck some air into his lungs, he whispered, "It hurts. Mama, I hurt."

"I know, honey. You've had a bad fall. Just stay calm and breathe. I'll . . ." But she didn't know what she was going to do, and she let the sentence trail off vaguely.

"Maggie!"

Maggie's head snapped up at the sound of her name. Reid was running toward them from the field. Relief flooded her. Reid was here; he would help her. She didn't question why she was so sure of this, especially given his aloofness, but somehow she knew that she wasn't alone anymore.

He reached them, explaining breathlessly, "I heard a scream, and—" He broke off as he got a good look at Ty, and he dropped down on his knees beside the boy. "What happened?"

"I'm not sure," Maggie answered. "He was climbing the tree. When I looked out, he was on the ground. Will said he climbed too high."

Reid smiled down at Ty. "Well, now, it looks like your spirit of adventure got you into a little trouble here." With care he moved his hands over the boy's body, avoiding the obviously broken arm.

Maggie was amazed at Reid's calm demeanor. Even though he had run here, obviously alarmed by a scream, he was now as cool as a cucumber, chatting lightly to Ty while he examined him. When he touched the boy's side, Ty winced and let out a groan.

"That hurts?" Reid asked, cautiously returning to the spot.

Ty nodded, holding his breath until Reid's hand moved on to another location. Finally Reid finished and sat back on his heels.

"Well, son, I think you've managed to break your arm and probably crack a rib or two, though I don't think they're broken. But you're pretty lucky; that's it, except for a few bumps and bruises."

Lucky? Maggie stared at Reid. Had the man gone mad? With no doctor within miles, he considered a broken arm lucky?

Reid smiled reassuringly at Maggie. "He's going to be all right. Don't worry. I'll set the fracture. First I'll need a couple of thin slats, and I think I saw a crate behind the barn that I can cut down to size. Meanwhile, you can tear some strips of cloth to secure the splints and to wrap around his ribs. That should provide some relief."

Dazed by Reid's easy assumption of command and his seeming knowledge of what to do, Maggie nodded and went to the house to do what he had asked. She grabbed an old sheet from the linen closet and tore it into wide strips. When she was through, she paused by Will's door. He was lying on his bed, huddled into a ball.

"Willy? Honey, Ty's all right. He's going to be okay. He broke his arm, but that's all."

Will gazed at her, wide-eyed with fear, and she knew that he needed more reassurance, but right now she didn't have the time. She had to help Ty. "I'll be back when Ty's fixed up. All right?"

He nodded but remained balled up on his bed. Maggie knew it would be some time before he worked up the courage to come back downstairs.

Reid was with Ty when Maggie returned, and he had two wooden slats sawn to the length of Ty's upper arm.

He looked up at her as she approached. "I'll need your help," he told her. "Can you manage it?"

Maggie's knees felt weak, but she set her jaw and nodded. She would have to manage it; there was no one else around to help. Will, though far stronger than she, would be worse than useless at the task.

She knelt. "Just tell me what to do."

Reid smiled at her. "I knew I could count on you. When I get his arm positioned, hand me the splints. Then you'll need to hold his arm while I secure them."

Maggie's stomach lurched at the thought, but she nodded grimly.

"I promise you, I'll be as gentle as I can."

Maggie trusted him. Given his ineptness at farming chores, she wasn't sure why exactly. But something in his calm manner inspired confidence that he knew what he was doing and could handle it without a hitch.

Carefully, gently, Reid slipped his hands around Ty's narrow arm, lifting it and pulling the broken bone back into place. Ty let out a short cry; then his eyes rolled back in his head.

"He's fainted!" Maggie bit her lower lip until it bled.

Reid continued concentrating solely on the boy's arm. "Good. That way he won't feel the pain. Now, hand me the first splint."

Maggie did as he requested, watching as he carefully positioned the slat. Then she put her hands on Ty's arm where Reid instructed, holding tightly while he arranged the other splint. Holding the two sides together with one hand, he swiftly and expertly wound the strips of cloth around and around the splints until the arm was immobilized so the bone would knit cleanly.

"There." Reid tied a knot at the lower end of the bandage and looked over at Maggie.

Maggie sank back on her heels, suddenly drained of

all energy in the aftermath of her fear and sympathetic pain for her son.

"Are you all right?" Reid reached out to touch her arm.

Maggie nodded. "I feel like a limp washrag, that's all."

He smiled with understanding. "It's a common reaction. In moments of stress, people sometimes perform extraordinary feats they wouldn't normally be able to do, but afterward . . ." He shrugged. "Rest for a minute, and you'll feel better. I'll bandage his ribs and carry him in. We might as well get that done before he comes to."

He unbuttoned Ty's shirt and propped him up against his knee, then wound more of the bandages around the boy's thin chest. When he was through he picked Ty up in his arms and carried him into the house and up the stairs to his bed, with Maggie hurrying in front of him to lead the way.

Ty woke up during the process and groaned. Reid looked down at him and smiled. "Hey. It's all right. It's all over, and your arm's set."

Ty looked pale but relieved. "I still hurt."

"Unfortunately, there's not much I can do about that."

When they entered the boys' bedroom, Will looked up, terror in his face at the sight of Reid carrying a helpless Ty.

"He's all right," Reid hastened to reassure Will as he laid Ty down on his bed. "He's just broke an arm, and he's worn out from having the fracture set."

Will crept over to Ty's bed, and the boy smiled up at him weakly. "Hi," he whispered, reaching out a hand to Will. "I'm fine. See?"

Will took his hand but turned to look anxiously at Reid. "He's all right?"

"Yes, only a little worse for the wear. I'm afraid

these things happen to adventurous boys like our Ty here."

Will nodded emphatically. "I told him. I did." He gazed at Reid with an earnest expression, as if trying to convince him that he had done all he could. "I told him to come back. He was going too high."

"I'm sure you did." Reid laid a hand on Will's arm. "It wasn't your fault. Anyway, there's no permanent harm done, though I'm afraid Ty may not feel too chipper for a while. His ribs are cracked, and that hurts." He looked at Ty and told him, "They'll probably cause you more pain than your arm."

He turned to Maggie. "Let him rest, but I'd advise not letting him sleep for the next few hours. I don't think he has a concussion, but it would be safer not to chance it."

"All right."

Reid left, and for the next hour Maggie fussed over Ty, scolding him for climbing so high in the tree and then kissing his forehead and telling him how happy she was that he was all right. She also had to comfort and reassure Will. Before long her own nerves were calmer, and she left Ty to rest, with Will watching over him.

She went back downstairs, hoping to thank Reid for all his help, but he was nowhere in sight. How like him, she thought, to vanish without even giving her a chance to express her appreciation or to ask the hundred and one questions crowding her mind. She had often wondered about Reid's background, certain that he was no ordinary vagrant, but after his performance this afternoon, her questions were even more pressing.

The morning was almost gone, however, so Maggie quickly started the noon meal cooking. When it was ready, she carried Ty's and Willy's upstairs and returned to the kitchen to lay the table for Reid.

Before long he entered and began to wash up. "How's Ty feeling?" he asked.

"Pretty well, considering, but he says his chest hurts."

Reid nodded. "The ribs. They'll probably bother him for a couple of weeks. But he didn't do any serious damage." He dried off his hands and turned toward the table, looking it over appreciatively. "Mmm, smells delicious."

"Don't think you can flatter me out of asking you about what you did," Maggie told him sternly.

"What do you mean?" He gazed at her with an innocence so bland that it had to be fake.

Maggie scowled. "You know good and well what I'm talking about. You're a doctor, aren't you?"

Reid looked at her for a moment. "I used to be."

"Used to be? I don't think that's something you can just stop being, is it?"

"Let me put it this way—I no longer practice medicine. But I do remember a few things, and I've had plenty of practice with fractures."

Maggie continued to look at him, frowning. "I don't understand why . . ."

"Why what?"

"Why did you leave medicine? Why are you roaming around the countryside like a . . . a common vagrant?"

"I *am* a common vagrant," he told her with irritating calm. "I *used* to be a doctor."

"Hogwash," Maggie retorted succinctly. "It doesn't make any sense. I mean, I knew that you were educated and that you'd likely come from money, but I figured that you'd probably lost your holdings in the War and didn't have any skills." She stopped, realizing her remarks had sounded rude. "I mean, practical kind of skills—that is, things, you know, that you could use to work. . . ."

She trailed off, realizing she was digging herself in deeper the longer she talked. "I'm sorry," she said lamely. "I didn't mean . . ."

Unexpectedly, Reid grinned. "You didn't mean that I'm unable to do most things necessary to run a farm, so you assumed I was a well-educated, useless sort who must once have had a lot of money and never had to take care of himself?"

Maggie blushed. "No! I mean, yes, I suppose so, but I wouldn't have put it like that!"

"No, I'm sure you'd have been more polite. But since it's basically the truth, why bother? One thing I like about you is that you seem incapable of lying. No need to start now." He sat down, dismissing the subject. "Now, how about some of that wonderful-smelling food?"

"Reid Prescott, if you think you're going to get away that easily, you'd better think again." Maggie followed him to the table and plopped down at the place across from him. "You can't just tell me you *used* to be a doctor and then nothing else."

"Why not?" Reid scowled, all trace of amusement gone from his face. "It's the truth."

"But there has to be more to it than that!" she exclaimed in exasperation. "Why are you so secretive?"

"I'm not secretive," he snapped. "I just don't see any reason to sit around dwelling on the past. It's over, and I'd rather put it behind me, forget about it."

"You can't forget your past! Nobody can. It's there; it happened. If you cut it out, it's like cutting out part of *you.*"

"Maybe that's better," he said stonily.

"No! How could it be?"

He slammed a hand down on the table and leaned toward her, his eyes bright with anger. "It is if you don't like the person you were. If you want to get away from it, from him. From everything he did and didn't do."

Maggie sat back, folding her arms over her chest and gazing at him calmly. "It still eats at you. Why else are you so reluctant to talk about it? If you're running from something, you can't have forgotten it. It's there inside you every minute of every day. You're letting the past control you completely."

"Damnation! You are the stubbornest woman I ever met! You just won't let a subject die, will you?"

"Not if what you're doing is hurting you and others." Maggie leaned forward earnestly, flattening her palms on the table. "You could do so much for people. I mean, think of all the things you know, all the ways you could help. Why would you stop?"

Making an exasperated noise, Reid stood up, shoving his chair back. "Blast it, you just don't understand! Not everyone is strong like you. There are some of us who simply give up."

"Not you. I don't believe it."

"No?" Reid raised one eyebrow quizzically, his mouth a cynical line. "That's because you ascribe your own qualities to other people. You're the kind of woman who picks up and goes on, no matter what, who takes whatever is given to her, good or bad, and makes the best of it."

"What else can you do?" Maggie asked blankly.

"That's exactly what I mean: you wouldn't know how to be weak. You wouldn't give up or run away just because your life was in ruins. You'd roll up your sleeves and get to work rebuilding it. But not all of us have that . . ." He paused, searching for the right word. "That strength. That determination and grit. Some of us surrender." He looked away, and his voice was barely above a whisper when he went on. "We surrender and run away."

Maggie gazed at him in consternation. It was clear that some tragedy ate away at him. She wished she could help him, and she wondered what had happened to make him feel so defeated. But she knew she shouldn't pursue the subject; it obviously caused him pain. And it was, after all, none of her business, she reminded herself. Reid Prescott had a right to his privacy, and if he wanted to leave his past behind him, then she had no right to bring it up and make him feel the hurt all over again. She looked down at her hands, abashed.

Then, to her surprise, Reid sat back down and quietly began to speak. "I joined the Army when the War started. I thought I could save lives with my skills, that I could help the South. My people. The places and things I loved. I . . ." His voice trailed off, and his shoulders slumped.

"You don't have to tell me this," Maggie put in. "I shouldn't have pressed you."

"No, you have a right to know. I've put myself into your lives, so it matters what sort of person I am. Perhaps I'm simply reluctant for you to find that out."

"I know what kind of person you are," Maggie said gently. "You're kind and good. Whatever you tell me won't change that." She gazed at him, her eyes clear and trusting.

Reid looked into those eyes. He realized, amazed, that he wanted very much to tell this woman the tortured burden of his past, the sins and sorrows that had weighed him down, crushing him into the still numbness of his recent existence.

"I worked in the field hospitals for four years," he began. "It was . . . closer to hell than anything I've ever seen. I amputated arms, hands, feet, legs. I tried to patch men up, sew the wounded back together. But mostly I watched them die. Man after man, and then, more often, boy after boy. Yankees and Rebs—there was no difference between their pain, their screaming, their delirium." He paused, seeming to look deeply inward.

"I wasn't a doctor; I was a butcher. Sometimes the men I managed to save would have been better off if I'd let them die with some dignity."

Maggie's heart melted with sympathy, and she

reached across the table for Reid's hand. "It must have been horrible."

He gripped her fingers hard. "I was a doctor!" The words tumbled out of him; he was incapable of stopping them now even if he tried. "I was committed to saving lives. Yet there I was in those charnel houses, serving in an army committed to killing. With no medicine to ease pain, rarely even any chloroform for surgery."

"But you did save lives," Maggie protested, wanting to comfort him. "Surely there were men who would have died without your care. Surely there are wives and mothers and sisters all over the South grateful to you because you returned their men to them. It wasn't you who killed. You were a savior."

Maggie saw the wet gleam of tears in his hazel eyes.

"I tried to tell myself that. At first I even believed it. But as the months wore on, then years, I realized I was simply part of that awful grinding machine of war, patching soldiers up only to throw them back into its maws. I realized I no longer gave a damn about the Confederacy or that ephemeral idea of states' rights or Georgia or much of anything, really. I wanted only an end to it all, to go home to my wife and child, to let them cosset me and soothe away the horrors."

Maggie felt her stomach clutch. *Reid was married?*

"Then, when I finally did get back to Savannah, I had a house but no home. A house . . . but no family. No wife, no child."

"Oh, no . . ." Maggie squeezed his hand. "I'm so sorry."

"They had died toward the end of the war, after communications were disrupted—you know, because of Sherman's March." His voice was thick with emotion, and he looked down at the table, tracing the whorls in the wood with a finger that trembled slightly.

Maggie said nothing. She had read horrifying accounts in letters from her cousins of the swath of destruction General Sherman had cut through Georgia.

"Savannah was occupied. Diphtheria was rampant. First it took Sally, our little girl, and then my wife." He pulled his hand away from hers and dug his palms into his eyes, as if he could force back the darkness and despair welling up inside him. "They had no doctor. If I had been there . . ." He swallowed hard, and for a moment he could not speak. Then he went on in a tortured voice. "I had to go off and play war hero—and they died!" His shoulders began to shake. Tears leaked out from beneath his eyelids and slid slowly down his cheeks.

"Oh, no, it wasn't your fault!" Maggie cried.

Impulsively she jumped up from her chair and went around the table to him. She smoothed her hand over his hair, tried to urge his head up. Instead, he threw his arms around her waist and buried his face against her breasts. He shook convulsively, giving way to deep, masculine sobs that seemed as if they would tear him apart. Years of suppressed torment came pouring out of him, thawed by her warmth and concern. Aching for him, Maggie stroked his hair, his shoulders, his back, soothing him and letting him release his sorrow.

At last the storm in Reid subsided, but he did not relinquish his hold on her. Gradually Maggie became aware of the intimacy of their posture, and heat began to rise in her body. She eased herself away from him.

Reid dashed the tears from his cheeks and cast her a shamefaced look. "I—I'm sorry for that outburst."

"There's no need to be. It's no sin to be sorrowful. It's trying to hide it that eats away at a soul. I—I'm glad I was here."

Reid pushed back his chair and stood. "Damn. I've never told that to anyone. I closed up my house and walked away and never went back. Don't you see? I don't want to remember it! I've spent years trying to forget it!"

"But you can't keep on running all your life. And you can't keep on blaming yourself. It wasn't your fault that your wife and daughter got ill."

"No?" he responded sarcastically. "If I had been there, they might have lived."

"Then again, they might not have," Maggie retorted. "You aren't God, you know. There's no guarantee that your medical skills could have saved them. You aren't all-powerful, no matter how good a physician you are. People die even as doctors fight to save them. You don't make the decision whether a person lives or dies. Only God does that. Don't you see? If it was that person's time to die, there's nothing you or anybody else can do to change it."

"I wasn't there when they needed me," he insisted.

"A doctor has duties to other people, too, though. And you were following that duty, saving lives. I'm sure your wife understood that. I didn't like it when Will and my brothers went off to fight—I was scared they'd get killed—but I understood why they had to. I imagine your wife did, too."

Reid's mouth twisted—in a smile or a grimace, Maggie wasn't sure. "Olivia wasn't like you."

Maggie felt a stab of pain in her chest. Of course she wasn't like his wife. How could she be? She came from a farm, not a city, a hardworking country family, not high society. Olivia. Even her name was exotic, so unlike plain old Maggie. Doubtless she had been sophisticated and delicate, ladylike. Maggie wondered whether she had been beautiful.

"Olivia wasn't strong," Reid went on. "She depended on me. She was very upset when I left. She cried and clutched at my arm the morning I rode off." His face darkened. "I was irritated with her. That's the memory of my wife that I carried into war: my irritation with her."

"Don't destroy yourself over it," Maggie told him gently. "You did what you thought was best. No one can do more. Besides, guilt won't help anyone—not your family, not you. Turning your life into a desert won't, either. The past is over and done. All you can do is get on with your life and make the best of it."

"Some of us have a difficult time doing that," Reid snapped. He turned away and walked toward the door.

"Where are you going?" Maggie waved a hand toward the table. "What about dinner?"

"I'm not hungry." And he walked out the door, striding quickly toward the barn.

Maggie watched him go, feeling terribly uneasy. Had she ruined everything by making him talk?

His head lowered, his hands jammed into his pockets, Reid stalked into the barn. Emotions were roiling within him: renewed pain at all he had lost, bitter anger at himself, irritation with Maggie for bringing it up, shame at breaking down in front of her. She must think him weak; she faced everything so bravely. How could she understand someone who had run from his demons instead of battling them?

He sat down on the edge of his bed, resting his elbows on his knees, and sank his hands into his hair. His fingers pressed into his scalp. He wished he could squeeze hard enough to push all his thoughts out of his skull.

Things had been easier before he came here. He wished he had never stopped, that a storm hadn't driven him into Maggie Whitcomb's barn.

Maggie was stubborn, pushy. She didn't know when to stop. If he stayed here, she would continue to poke and pry into his life, probing all the dark corners. That was insane; it was too painful. He didn't want to remember Olivia and the baby. He didn't want to see all those nameless soldiers again, looking to him for help.

He dropped back onto the bed, covering his eyes with his arm. Still, tears leaked out from beneath his eyelids. Now, having opened up the past, he couldn't seem to close the door on it. Fresh waves of pain washed over him.

"Damn the woman!" He jumped to his feet, dashing the tears away with his hand. He went to the chest and jerked open the bottom drawer, pulling out his bedroll. He laid it out on the bed and began to pile his possessions in it.

He would leave this place, forget about Maggie and Will and their child. He would escape the desire she aroused in him—and the fear that she would expect more from him than he had inside him. He would leave her and her strength and Will's trusting eyes and Ty's admiration.

He picked up his bedroll and left the room. He paused at the barn door, looking across the yard toward the house. He thought about walking away and never seeing this place again. He thought about not being here when the cherries ripened and the vegetables came up in Maggie's garden. He thought about not unwrapping Ty's splint when the time came. Not sitting beside Maggie on the porch steps in the evening.

He stood still for a moment in an agony of indecision. Then, cursing himself for his probable folly, he turned and walked back to his room, tossed down the bedroll, and went back to work.

11

Ty *was up* and about the day after his accident. At first he was quite proud of his splint, eager to show it off at church. An added benefit was that he couldn't milk the cow or muck out the stalls. However, neither could he climb trees or run fast or even hold a book easily. Worst of all, it interfered with fishing. By the time a week was up, he was fretting about how long it would be before Reid took the nuisance off.

The wild plums ripened in the thickets along the road and down by the creek, and Ty and Will spent many hours picking the small, tangy fruit, one task Ty could do with a broken arm, although at a slower pace than he was accustomed to. Home they would come with brimming baskets, and Maggie made jar after jar of preserves, her fingers continually stained red from plum juice as she peeled, pitted, and sliced, a pot left stewing on the stove nearly every hour of the day. Maggie knew that next winter she would appreciate the preserves, but at the moment she was heartily sick of plums.

During those weeks Maggie was careful not to mention Reid's past again. Recalling it had obviously been very upsetting to him, and it seemed to Maggie that there had been a coolness in his attitude since the day she had pried the information of his medical expertise out of him. He seemed more remote, the way he had been when he first came to the farm, speaking to her less and often stilted and stiff.

Their renewed awkwardness around each other only added to another underlying tension. For between them still lay the memory of the night of the Lyceum, when he had held her hand and later taken her to the dim barn to clean her shoe. When heat had risen between them at the touch of his hand on her foot. When they had almost kissed.

Maggie was aware of Reid all the time now. Again and again during the day she found herself going to the window and looking out, searching for Reid. She realized what she was doing, and she tried to stop it, but somehow she could not. Yet, strangely, whenever he was near, when the family was sitting at the table eating or he was discussing some task he was undertaking, she was reluctant to look at him, afraid to meet his eyes, as if she would find something there that she did not want to see—or, worse, he would see something in hers that she didn't want to reveal.

Even so, she kept watching him in brief, secret glances whenever she could, noticing every detail about him. And whenever he was close to her, she felt his strength and heat almost as if he'd touched her. It was an unsettling sensation, and she tried her best to ignore it. But it could not be ignored forever.

The days grew hotter, creeping toward the almost unbearable heat of midsummer. They left all the windows open now, even at night, and as Maggie lay in bed, waiting for sleep to come, the drone of insects seemed to complement the thrumming in her nerves, adding to her restlessness. Each night she found it more and more difficult to fall asleep.

On washdays, Maggie set up her washtub and scrub board in the shade cast by the cherry tree, just beyond its drooping limbs. The boughs were now heavy with pink blossoms, and it was pleasant to work beside such beauty. One day as she was laundering, she heard the thwack of an ax. Glancing up, she saw that across the yard Reid was splitting wood. She watched as he raised the heavy ax above his head and brought it down in a smooth sweep, slicing into the wood. His sleeves were rolled up, and she could see the muscles of his forearms bunching under his skin. When the log split through, he bent and set up the halves to chop them into quarters. Maggie's eyes followed the strong, graceful movements of his body as he worked. Then she realized she was staring, and hastily she returned to her scrubbing.

Mechanically she wrung out the sheets, unable to keep her mind off Reid's presence nearby. She wished she could stop thinking about him, stop seeing his lean torso as he twisted, arms arcing up and then swinging down to chop the wood. But it seemed that the harder she tried to ignore him, the more she found herself glancing back at him.

Even though he, too, was working in the shade, the heat of summer and the hard labor had made him sweat. His shirt clung damply to his skin, and perspiration shone on his face. Maggie imagined wiping the sweat from his face with her hands, first his brow, then down along his jaw and across his upper lip. . . .

She swallowed and looked back down at the washtub. Her hands were plunged into the water, but they were motionless, locked in a death-grip on a sheet. She shivered and began scrubbing frantically, rubbing harder and faster than was necessary. Then she quickly wrung out the sheet and dropped it into the rinse water.

The rinse water was getting soapy, she noticed. She would have to change it. Wringing out the sheet, she dropped it into the basket of clothes to be hung on the line. Then she grasped the rinse tub and heaved it up.

It was heavy, and Maggie staggered back under its weight before she steadied herself. The water lapped up over the top and splashed onto her shirtwaist. She started toward the bare patch of ground where she emptied the soapy water, and with each step more water sloshed over onto her blouse.

"Here, let me do that," Reid called from behind her.

Startled, Maggie almost dropped the tub. She looked back over her shoulder and saw that he had trotted across the yard and was only a foot or two away from her. He had unbuttoned his shirt partway in the heat, and her eyes were drawn to his damply gleaming chest.

"What?" It took her a moment to register what he had said. "Oh. Why, thank you."

As he took the tub from her, his gaze dropped from her face to the front of her shirtwaist and lingered for a moment. A flush rose in his cheeks, and he quickly turned away and went to empty the tub.

Maggie glanced down and realized why he had stared. The water sloshing over the tub had completely soaked her front, and the light blue shirtwaist might as well have been transparent. It clung to her breasts, outlining them and even revealing the darker circles of her nipples. Reid could hardly have seen her breasts more clearly if she had been naked.

Heat flooded Maggie's face, and she retreated quickly to the cherry tree. She dumped several shirts into the washtub and began to scrub furiously.

A few minutes later Reid returned, carrying the rinse tub now filled with clean water from the cistern. As he set it down on the worktable, he was within inches of Maggie, and she was terribly aware of his presence. She didn't dare look at him, yet as he continued to stand there beside her, she couldn't resist the impulse, either. Finally she raised her eyes to his. And blood rushed to her face at the hot, slumberous look in his. Her hand flew to her throat, and she found it difficult to breathe.

His gaze slid down from her face to her breasts. Maggie wanted to cover them, yet at the same time she wanted to stand there brazenly before him, letting him look his fill. His chest was rising and falling in rapid, shallow breaths, and Maggie trembled, fighting the urge to take the short step that would bring her up against him.

"Maggie . . ." It seemed to be all he could utter.

Maggie looked at his mouth—mobile, soft, sensual. And she knew that she wanted to touch it, wanted to feel it upon her own lips.

She drew in a ragged breath, and that was all it took to break Reid's trance. He stepped closer to her, grasped her shoulders, and began to move her backward, under the drooping limbs of the cherry tree. He swept aside a limb, scattering pale pink blossoms, and it fell back into place behind them. A drapery of blossoms hung all around them, creating a fragrant, shady cave, secret and beautiful.

Maggie's senses were suddenly sharpened, intensifying everything around her. The smell of the cherry blossoms was heady, mingling with the scent of Reid's skin; the sunlight beyond the curtain of branches was blindingly bright; the summer hum of insects buzzed in her ears, combining with the loud thump of her own heartbeat. Maggie felt as if she might faint, as if she might begin to shiver or cry and never be able to stop.

"You're the most beautiful woman I've ever known." Reid's voice was low and hoarse, barely more than a whisper.

Maggie backed up a step, a little frightened by the glitter in his eyes—and by her own wild, rushing emotions. "No . . . please."

"I can't help it." His eyes looked tortured now, and he reached up to grip the low-hanging branch above him. His knuckles shone white with the strain, as if only by holding on to something could he keep his hands from doing what they wanted to.

"Damn it!" he exclaimed and shoved hard against the branch, sending blossoms cascading down around them. "I can't think about anything but you. Kissing you. Holding you."

Fragile pink blossoms fell onto Maggie's hair and shoulders, and Reid reached out and plucked one. His fingers trembled, but he did not draw his hand back, instead letting it drift down her dark hair and onto her cheek, caressing the velvet smoothness of her skin.

"We mustn't," Maggie protested weakly. She felt as if her knees were about to give way, and she sagged back against the tree trunk.

But, as if he had not heard her words, Reid leaned closer. He gazed down into her face, his eyes holding hers hypnotically. "I want to kiss you. I want to touch you. I want to see your breasts . . . feel them in my hands . . ."

Maggie could hardly breathe. Her heart was racing in her chest. Reid reached for the top button of her shirtwaist, and he began to undo it. She knew she should protest, should move away, but she could not. She didn't want to. She felt, suddenly, as if she would die if she left this spot, lost this moment. She *wanted* to feel his hands upon the fastenings of her clothing, wanted to feel them on *her*.

A faint breeze stirred the branches, lifting a tendril of Maggie's hair and kissing her hot skin. She shivered and looked down, following the movement of Reid's tanned, roughened fingers on the buttons of her blouse, loosing first one, then another from their carefully stitched buttonholes. She could see the pale flesh of her upper chest appear, and then, as another button fell to him, the wet white fabric of her chemise, now as transparent as gauze.

Reid drew a shuddering breath as his fingers moved to the last button above the waistband of her skirt. He, too, watched his hands as they grasped the sides of her blouse and gently pushed them aside, revealing her breasts beneath the thin covering of the wet chemise.

Maggie looked at Reid's face and saw the stark hunger there, the desire-slackened features. His expression sent heat piercing through her, driving down through her chest to explode in her abdomen. She must have made a noise, for he looked up into her face. She gazed into the hazel depths of his eyes, and she knew that she was lost. Reid turned her insides to molten wax, made her a stranger to herself, evoked a wild and wanton creature she had not even known existed within her.

"Please . . ." she said again, but this time her meaning was completely different.

Reid's lips drew back in something that was too fierce and hungry to be a smile. He hooked his fingers in the top of her chemise and pulled it down, his knuckles rubbing slowly over her heavy breasts until at last they burst free from the fabric.

He groaned as his eyes roamed the silky smooth globes. Her breasts were as white as milk, with a faint tracing of blue veins beneath the skin. Her nipples were large pink circles, and they tightened now under his gaze, pointing into small nubs. Entranced, he raised a finger and brushed it across one nipple, watching it prickle into an even tighter pebbled bud.

Maggie closed her eyes, feeling as if she might explode. She wanted more than anything else on earth for Reid to touch her, to kiss her. When he cupped her breasts in his hands, lifting them, she trembled, feeling a hot, damp yearning blossom between her legs.

"You are so beautiful," he murmured again as his thumbs circled her nipples. "And I want you."

He moved forward, pressing his body against hers, and his hands rose to dig into her hair. With a groan, he wrapped his arms around her and kissed her, his lips opening her mouth to his tongue, his tongue exploring the hot cave as his body rubbed against hers. He kissed her as if he would never stop, as if he could claim and know and keep her all in this one fiery kiss.

Maggie clung to him, lost in sensual delight. She felt possessed by him, consumed, yet she ached for more. She yearned to wrap her naked legs around him, to take him inside her. All the heat and passion that had lain dormant in her for years came to life, setting her ablaze. She kissed him back hungrily, her hands sinking into his thick, glossy hair.

He shuddered and moved his hands down over her body to her hips, lifting her even more tightly against him. She thought she could feel every muscle and bone of him, the insistent hardness of his desire for her.

Reid lifted his head and gazed down into her face. His eyes glittered, and Maggie knew that he wanted to pull her down on the ground right there and take her. It was what she wanted, too.

Then, in the distance, came a trill of boyish laughter, followed by the deeper cadence of Will's voice. The sounds were like cold water tossed in their faces. Reid went rigid for an instant, then his eyes closed and he groaned, his arms going lax around Maggie. For a moment Maggie stood rooted to the spot, horror dawning as she realized what they, in their madness, had been about to do—and with Will and Ty playing in the field just beyond them! The boys might have come upon them at any moment.

She felt sick, choked with guilt. Whirling around, she buttoned up her dress with shaking fingers, then hurried out from under the tree to her worktable. She stood gripping the sides of the washtub, trying to blot out of her mind what had just happened. Behind her she heard the rustle of branches as Reid emerged from their retreat and walked away from her.

Gideon paced back and forth across the kitchen floor. His mother watched him patiently. "Gideon," she said at last, "you're going to wear a trough in that floor if you don't stop soon."

"What? Oh, I'm sorry, Ma. I didn't realize what I was doing."

"You've been this way for over two weeks now," Jo went on. "When are you going to tell me what's the matter?"

Gideon looked at her in an agony of indecision. "It's —it's not really mine to tell. It's . . . about Tess."

"Tess! What's wrong with Tess? Is she ill?" Jo sat up straighter, frowning in concern.

"No, she's fine. At least, her health is. Look, she wouldn't want this to get out."

Jo looked offended. "Gideon! You know I wouldn't tell anyone anything you said to me in confidence."

"I know. But Tess wouldn't want even you to know. She tried to hide it from me, too." Sighing, he sat down across from her at the table. "But I have to tell you, because one of the few things I can think of that would help her, you would have to agree to."

"What's that? Gideon, tell me what you're talking about right this minute. You aren't making any sense, and you're scaring me silly."

"Tess is in trouble. She's going to lose her house."

"What! But how—why, I thought they had enough to live on after selling the plantation."

Gideon shook his head grimly. "Apparently there were a lot of debts. I knew they were being frugal, but I didn't realize how close to the bone Tess was having to cut it. They were managing to survive, but now . . ." Succinctly he related Benton Conway's offer and threat and the subsequent raising of Tess's property taxes.

Jo stared at her son in amazement. "I never would have believed it, even of Benton. To turn two widows and a child out just because he's taken a hankering to their house. That man is a devil!"

"He is that." Gideon nodded. "Anyway, ever since

Tess told me, I've been trying to figure out what I can do. We have to help her out of this, Ma."

"I agree. Well, if worse comes to worst, she can always come live with us. All three of them can."

Gideon thought about having Tess living in the same house with him, seeing her every day. Eagerness welled up in him, but firmly he shoved it aside. "I know, but she won't want to live on anyone's charity. She wants to keep her home and family intact."

"But, Gideon, how can we fight Benton Conway? He's far wealthier than we ever thought of being, and he has friends among the new government, whereas you can't even vote because of that Oath."

"I've thought about going over there and hauling him out and making him see reason." Gideon's fists knotted, and his eyes glinted.

Jo looked at him in exasperation. Gideon was the most reasonable and peaceable of any of her sons—the Tyrrells had always tended toward hotheadedness—but his fighting instincts had been roused, and she could see that he would like nothing more than to beat Benton Conway to a bloody pulp.

"Gideon, I know how you feel about Tess," Jo said, reaching out and covering one of his hands with hers. Gideon looked up at her, surprise stamping his face. Jo nodded. "You care for her—perhaps a little more than in a brotherly way, I think."

"Ma . . ."

"I understand. You don't want anyone to know."

"She's Shelby's widow, Ma."

"So? That doesn't mean she isn't a woman. A very attractive woman. And it certainly doesn't mean you couldn't fall in love with her."

"I want to help her because she's Shelby's widow," Gideon insisted stubbornly.

"All right, dear," Jo said with a sigh. "You want to help her because she's Shelby's widow. But beating Benton Conway half to death won't help her any. It'll just land you in jail. Surely you realize that."

"I know," Gideon said regretfully. "I wouldn't be able to raise money in jail. And that's what I need to do —help Tess raise the money."

"But how?"

"I have a couple of things I could sell. Pa's pocket watch, for instance. My rifle. It's a good hunting gun."

"Oh, Gideon, your father's watch? He left you that —he wanted you to have it. And your rifle—how would you go hunting?"

"I could use Pa's old gun," he said impatiently. "The thing is, I don't think they'd bring in enough money, and I can't think of anything else to sell except land."

"The farm?" Jo gazed at her son searchingly. "You'd be willing to sell the farm?"

"We wouldn't have to sell all of it, just some."

"But, Gideon, you've always loved this land so. It's practically a part of you."

Gideon glanced away from her. "I know," he said in a low voice. "But I have to help Tess. I'll just have to work harder so I can buy it back someday."

"I can't imagine it's possible for you to work any harder than you already do!" Jo exclaimed.

"Ma, this is Shelby's widow—we have to help her! Are you going to stand by and let some scalawag throw her out on the street?"

"Of course not!" Jo's eyes snapped. "How could you even say such a thing? Tess is a Tyrrell now. Why, her daughter is my grandchild. If—if there's no other way, then we'll try to sell part of the farm. But I'll tell you the truth, Gideon, it tears my heart out to think of it. This farm is your heritage—all of you children. It's part of what makes you a Tyrrell. Isn't there anything else we can do? Maybe I should write Hunter; he might have some money saved from working out West. Heaven knows what he could spend it on out there."

"I'm sure he could find something," Gideon commented dryly. "Besides, by the time you wrote him and heard back, it might be too late."

"I'd borrow the money, except I don't know anyone who has any money anymore. Except Benton Conway." Jo sighed. "In fact, who's going to have enough money to buy the land if we do offer it for sale?"

"I'm not sure."

"And what about next year? How will we come up with enough money to pay the taxes then? And what if they raise them again?"

Gideon hesitated, then said, "There is one thing I thought of."

"What?" Jo frowned at his expression.

"Nothing illegal," he assured her hastily. "Not threatening Conway or anything. But I happened to think of Linette . . ."

He glanced at his mother, trying to gauge her response. Her opinion of Linette was not at all good; Jo never forgot a hurt to one of her children. Unable to determine her reaction, he forged ahead. "Tess didn't want to ask for her help. She said she didn't know Linette anymore and wasn't sure how she'd behave. But I think it's more because Tess is too proud. She can't bear to beg a favor, especially from someone who used to be her friend. The thing is, I don't know but what Linette might want to help her if she knew the situation."

"*She* may be the one who wants the house." Jo sniffed.

"That's possible," Gideon agreed judiciously. "But it might also be that she doesn't know anything about it. She might have retained some degree of feeling for Tess; surely their friendship wasn't just pretense on her part all those years. And Linette's bound to have her husband wrapped around her little finger."

"I'm sure that's true." Jo's tone made it clear that she wasn't paying the woman a compliment. "So what are you suggesting?"

"*I* could call on Linette. I could tell her what happened and ask for her help."

"And you, of course, are not too proud," Jo murmured.

Gideon colored. "Ah, hell, Ma, you know good and well that it sticks in my craw to ask that woman for anything. But I can't let my pride stand in the way of helping Tess. At least it isn't as bad for me; it's easier to ask a favor for someone other than yourself."

Jo nodded. "You're right. Go see Linette. Maybe we'll find out she has a spark of warmth left in her after all. And if not . . . well, we'll start selling things. There's that old silver salt cellar of my granny's; we don't need something like that."

Gideon smiled. "Ma, you're the best." He jumped up and came around the table to kiss her on the forehead. "I'll go see Linette tomorrow."

The next day Gideon dressed in his Sunday best, slicked down his hair, and drove into town to the Conway mansion. It was a red brick structure, large and well kept, obviously the home of a wealthy man. It was not as grand nor as elegant, however, as the Caldwell mansion. Gideon stopped at the house and sat there for a moment, looking at the front door. He didn't want to go in.

Finally he told himself that he was acting like a coward, and he drew a deep breath, climbed down from the wagon, and tied the mules to the black wrought-iron hitching post. Then he walked up the wide brick pathway to the door and knocked.

A maid answered, and Gideon squared his jaw and forced himself to say, "I'd like to see Mrs. Conway, please."

The black woman gave him a puzzled look. He suspected she had some idea of who he was—and that he didn't belong here—but she said simply, "And who shall I say is calling?"

"Gideon Tyrrell."

"Mr. Tyrrell!" Rosemary Conway was coming down the stairs that curved into the entry hall, and she stopped, staring at him. "What are you . . . I mean, uh . . ." She fumbled to a halt.

"Mr. Tyrrell is here to see Mrs. Conway, ma'am."

"Oh." If possible, Rosemary looked even more confused than before. "I see. Well, certainly, Essie, go tell her he's here. I'll show Mr. Tyrrell into the front parlor."

Rosemary came over to Gideon, giving him a nervous little bob of her head in greeting. "This way, please." She led him across the hall into a large, gloomy parlor, the drapes drawn against the sun. Rosemary quickly opened them, but even the light coming in could not dispel the oppressive atmosphere of the room with its massive, expensive, black walnut furniture.

"I—I'm sorry. I'm forgetting my manners." A faint flush touched the girl's pale cheeks. "Could I get you something to drink? Some coffee or tea or—or July might have made up some lemonade. It's awfully good."

"No, thank you." Gideon clenched the brim of his hat. He was, he thought, almost as uncomfortable as Rosemary.

"Gideon?" Linette's voice, steeped in amazement, came from the doorway.

Gideon whirled around. "Linette. It's—uh—good to see you." That was a lie, but for the moment he couldn't think of anything else to say.

The woman was as breathtaking as ever. Her vivid, auburn-haired beauty had always intimidated Gideon, though he wouldn't have admitted it to anyone. Still, he hadn't envied Hunter. Linette had been too stunning, too bright, the kind of woman with whom he had trouble making conversation—or even completing a sentence, the truth be known. In recent years that vividness had turned into a more icy, remote loveliness, but Gideon found that her present style left him no less clumsy and tongue-tied.

"Thank you." Puzzlement chased across her features, giving her face a trifle more warmth and humanity. "I'd say the same, except that, frankly, I feel more confused than anything. I wouldn't have expected to see you here."

"Well, it's not my choice," Gideon admitted bluntly. "I had to talk to you." He glanced uncomfortably at Rosemary.

The young woman blinked. "Oh. I—uh, why don't I go see about getting us some refreshments?"

"Thank you, Rosemary." Linette smiled at the girl, then turned back to Gideon, gesturing toward a chair. "Won't you sit down?"

He nodded and took the chair. He looked down at the brim of his hat, which he rolled back and forth between his fingers. Linette sat down across from him and gazed at him with her cool blue eyes, her face as immovable and ungiving as a statue's.

"The reason I came . . ." Gideon drew a deep breath, then released it. "It's about Tess."

"Tess Caldwell?" Linette's eyebrows vaulted upward in astonishment. "I'm sorry, I mean Tyrrell." Gideon nodded. "But what in the world—she—she's not ill, is she?"

"No. If it were that, I wouldn't need to come to you. I don't know if you have any regard for her still, but I remember that she was once your friend."

"Of course. That's not the reason we aren't—well, you must know that I am not the most popular woman in this town these days. I wouldn't put Tess in that kind of position."

Gideon studied her for a moment. He couldn't tell whether she spoke the truth; she was too smooth and cool. That lovely voice and expressionless face could have hidden almost anything. "Then why are you taking her house away from her?" He dropped the question in quietly, watching her.

Linette's mouth dropped open, and she stared at him. In that instant she looked almost like the girl she had once been. "What? What are you talking about?"

"You don't know about your husband's plans?"

The astonishment left Linette's face, and her eyes went carefully blank. "I'm not sure what you mean."

"I mean that Benton has been trying to buy the Caldwell mansion. It's the only property they have left; you know how the War left them."

Linette nodded. "Yes, I . . ." She hesitated, seeming to choose her words. "I wanted to help her, but I . . . I didn't imagine anyone with the name Tyrrell would accept anything from me."

"Oh, Tess wouldn't want your charity," Gideon agreed with feeling. "And, believe me, I wouldn't have come here if I could have thought of a better way to help her. But your husband's had her taxes raised sky high because she wouldn't sell out to him. Obviously, he plans to buy the house from the government when they take it back for uncollected taxes."

"Oh." Linette's face was as fixed as marble. She looked down at the floor. "I see."

Gideon got up and began to pace. He couldn't continue to sit still, thinking about Tess's dilemma. "It's the house Tess grew up in. It will kill her to leave it. Her mother, too. I thought you might still feel enough friendship for her to stop your husband from doing this to her. He can buy another house; he could make this one grander if he wanted. But that house is all Tess has."

Linette sat silently for a moment. At last she looked up and cast him a wry smile. "I'm afraid you have overestimated my influence with my husband. He hadn't even told me that he was trying to buy the Caldwell house."

Gideon grimaced skeptically. "Come, now, Linette, there's no need to play coy. Any woman who looks like you is bound to be able to influence her husband."

"No doubt many people think so." Linette's mouth hardened. "However, I'm afraid that isn't the case. Benton is not buying the house for me, believe me; he is buying it for himself. If he's adamant about it, I'm sure nothing I could say would change his mind."

"Then you aren't going to help?" Gideon demanded, his mouth twisted in disgust.

"I didn't say that. I was simply pointing out that there's probably little hope that I can change his mind. However, I will talk to him about it."

Gideon couldn't imagine that Linette didn't have Benton Conway eating out of her hand. She was far younger than he and quite beautiful; Gideon would have guessed that Conway was utterly besotted with her. He wondered if she was devious enough to pretend that she would try to help Tess, when all the while she coveted the Caldwell house and intended to have it.

"I promise," Linette said, as though she had guessed his thoughts.

"Please," he said in a low voice. "Please do. I can't bear to see Tess thrown out of her home."

Linette turned her face aside. "I will do what I can. That's all I can promise."

"Thank you." Gideon knew he would have to be content with that; he sensed he would get nothing more out of Linette. But his chest felt heavy; he didn't think her promise held out much hope for Tess.

He turned and walked toward the door. Linette's next words stopped him in his tracks. "Do you hear from Hunter?"

He glanced back at her. She was gazing at an ornament on the table beside her, as though only mildly interested in his answer.

"Sometimes we do," he replied.

When he said nothing further, Linette went on, still not looking at him, "How is he?"

"He's well." He didn't add that he couldn't imagine why she would care, given what she'd done to him. "He likes Texas."

Linette gave a little nod. "That's good. I'm glad."

Gideon guessed that the news somehow salved her guilt, made her feel that it hadn't been so wicked to marry Conway before Hunter's memory was even cold. He didn't like giving her even that bit of surcease, but, on the other hand, he wasn't about to admit to her that Hunter had never been the same after hearing the news. His brother was too proud to want her to know that. He'd rather she think he was fine, unaffected by her betrayal.

He looked at Linette, wondering what lay behind her icy demeanor. But he could read nothing in her posture or in the lovely profile of her face. He turned and left the room.

Outside the house, he drew a deep breath. He had done everything he could think of for Tess. But it didn't help the heavy feeling in his chest to realize that it probably would not be enough.

12

Maggie could no longer pretend to herself that she did not feel desire for Reid. There under the cherry tree she had been eager for him to take her. She had wanted to feel his hands on her—on her breasts, on her legs, everywhere. She had wanted to hear his voice thick with passion.

For years she had successfully pushed any thoughts of the act of love to the back of her mind, knowing it was impossible for her. She had remained faithful to Will, even thinking a little smugly that she was above passion. Then, in an instant, she had been knocked off her moral pedestal, and she realized grimly that she had simply never been tested before.

No. It hadn't really happened in an instant. She knew that. Though she had tried to wish it away, to pretend that it didn't exist, desire had been building inside her for weeks. The day under the cherry tree the flame had simply been touched to tinder long piled up and waiting.

Maggie considered telling Reid that he would have

to leave the farm. It was frightening how much that idea pained her. She didn't want him to leave. She relied on him. She wanted his company. And, besides, she reminded herself, Ty and Will both adored him; they would be crushed if he left. Surely there must be some other way. Surely there would be no harm in his staying on as long as she was strong and didn't give in to temptation. She reasoned that she had erred this time only because she had been unprepared, because she didn't have her defenses up. Now she knew better. She would be wary. She would avoid being around Reid, and on those occasions when she could not avoid it, she would force herself to be strong. She was not a weak person, after all; she could win this struggle over her baser nature.

However, she soon discovered that the temptation was always with her, even though Reid did not touch her or kiss her again. She was aware of him all the time, and she was aware of her body as she never had been before. Her breasts felt faintly swollen and tender, achy, and there was a sensual heaviness in her abdomen. Whenever she saw Reid, a tingle raced across her skin as if he had brushed his fingers over it. Whenever he looked at her, warmth flooded through her. At night she lay awake, unable to sleep for the sensations playing through her body. She was restless and yearning, unsatisfied, and as she lay in her bed, thinking about Reid, the warmth deep inside her turned into a slow, throbbing ache.

At those times, she would grit her teeth and dig her fingers into the bedclothes, wishing, praying, that there was some release from this feeling, a way that she could magically be rid of it. But she knew there was not. She knew what it would take to satisfy it, and that was something that could never happen.

The fact that she had known the marriage bed made it worse, she thought. She knew what it was like to make love. She knew exactly how a man could touch

JOIN THE
TIMELESS ROMANCE READER SERVICE
AND GET FOUR OF TODAY'S
MOST EXCITING HISTORICAL
ROMANCES FREE,
WITHOUT OBLIGATION!

Imagine getting today's very best historical romances sent directly to your home – at a total savings of at least $2.00 a month. Now you can be among the first to be swept away by the latest from Candace Camp, Constance O'Banyon, Patricia Hagan, Parris Afton Bonds or Susan Wiggs. You get all that – and that's just the beginning.

PREVIEW AT HOME WITHOUT
OBLIGATION AND SAVE.

Each month, you'll receive four new romances to preview without obligation for 10 days. You'll pay the low subscriber price of just $4.00 per title – a total savings of at least $2.00 a month!

Postage and handling is absolutely free and there is no minimum number of books you must buy. You may cancel your subscription at any time with no obligation.

GET YOUR FOUR FREE BOOKS TODAY ($20.49 VALUE)

FILL IN THE ORDER FORM BELOW NOW!

YES! *I want to join the Timeless Romance Reader Service. Please send me my 4 FREE HarperMonogram historical romances. Then each month send me 4 new historical romances to preview without obligation for 10 days. I'll pay the low subscription price of $4.00 for every book I choose to keep — a total savings of at least $2.00 each month — and home delivery is free! I understand that I may return any title within 10 days without obligation and I may cancel this subscription at any time without obligation. There is no minimum number of books to purchase.*

NAME_____

ADDRESS _____

CITY_____STATE_____ZIP_____

TELEPHONE_____

SIGNATURE _____

(If under 18 parent or guardian must sign. Program, price, terms, and conditions subject to cancellation and change. Orders subject to acceptance by HarperMonogram.)

GET
4
FREE
BOOKS
(A $20.49
VALUE)

AFFIX
STAMP
HERE

her and kiss her, where his hands would drift, and what it would feel like to have his maleness fill her, satisfying the empty ache in her loins. There was none of the fear of the unknown or of pain that helped to cool the heat in a young girl's blood. Maggie knew what would happen, and she knew that there would be no pain involved now, only pleasure.

But at the same time she had no familiarity with Reid's body, and the thought of discovering his planes and angles, of learning the special spots that brought him pleasure, of coming to know the feel of his hands and mouth on her, were tremendously exciting.

Try as she might, Maggie could not banish such thoughts and feelings. She kept thinking about Reid, kept looking out the window, hoping for a glimpse of him working in the yard. Each night before she crawled into bed, she went to the window again, looking out toward the barn. Sometimes she saw him standing in the doorway there, seeking the coolness of an evening breeze. And she would wonder whether he was thinking about her, too.

She would get into bed and try to sleep, but visions of Reid would flood in on her. She would think about how his hands would feel on her body, imagining him stroking her leg, cupping her breast, toying with the bud of her nipple until it was hard and swollen. Closing her eyes on the wave of pulsing pleasure, she would think of his kiss, of his wide lips covering hers, pressing into her. She would imagine his naked body, the hard planes and curves, the ridges of muscle and bone, the swelling evidence of his desire for her. . . . And by then she would be so suffused with heat that there was no possibility of sleep for several long hours.

It was impossible to avoid the man altogether. He ate all his meals with them, and he was constantly around, working in the yard or repairing something in the house or helping Ty with his studies. There was simply no getting away from him.

More than that, there was no getting away from his desire for her.

Not that he said anything outright or made any untoward advances. He was unfailingly correct and polite, and his conversations with her usually centered on the farm or Ty. But Maggie sensed that his hunger equaled her own. It emanated from him like heat; it was almost a tangible thing. She could see it in the tension in his body and in his eyes when he looked at her, especially when she turned and caught him watching her unawares. The force of his desire was like a bellows to her own, feeding the flame.

It wasn't fair! She had always been a good and moral person; she had never even thought of being unfaithful to her husband before. Why had Reid Prescott had to come into her life and complicate it so? Why had he had to appear at her doorstep, so handsome and kind and appealing? Why did he have to have eyes that crinkled up so attractively when he smiled, or long, thin fingers that could move so easily and quickly over any task, drawing her eyes to them, drawing her mind to thoughts of them on her skin?

If he did have to be so handsome, why couldn't he then at least have a disagreeable personality? A man that good-looking should be vain or at least too bold in his speech, accustomed to women falling at his feet. He shouldn't be quiet or solemn or gentle or kind.

But he was those things. And her pulse picked up whenever he was near. She couldn't keep from grinning foolishly whenever he smiled or winked at her. She couldn't harden her heart when it melted at the sight of him listening patiently to one of Will's rambling, stumbling communications. She was, foolishly, crazily, falling in love with him! And that was something she simply could not allow herself to do. That way lay only heartache. She could never marry him; she already had a husband. The only way she could have Reid would be for Will to die, and Maggie could never wish for that!

She was in a horrible tangle, and she knew no way out. All she could do was go from day to day, trying her best to avoid Reid, to suppress her emotions, hoping against hope that somehow it would all work out.

The hot summer days crawled by. The cherries ripened and began to fall. Will and Ty picked them, Ty clumsily retrieving them from the ground as Will shook the limbs of the tree. Maggie baked pies and tarts and laid up cherries and cherry preserves for the winter months. The early vegetables were ready now, too, and their meals were feasts of fresh peas and beans and carrots, little round new potatoes dripping with butter, and tart red tomatoes still warm from the sun. She canned all day long every day so her family could have vegetables long after the growing season was done. The excess produce Ty and Will took into town and sold to the store.

Despite her long, hard days, Maggie found it more and more difficult to sleep. She felt as if she were waiting for something to happen, for something to change, hanging on but unable to take any action to move her life one way or another. The summer heat filled her with lassitude, sapped her strength, yet at the same time she felt a curious kind of energy building inside her, a restlessness that had no outlet but simply burgeoned and grew—and ached for fulfillment.

One late day in June was particularly hot. It had rained the night before, and the air was thick and heavy; it seemed to soak up the heat, holding it close around them. No one did much work; Reid even called off Ty's lessons, and the boys spent most of the afternoon halfheartedly fishing in the shade of the willow by the pond, dangling their feet in the water to cool off.

Maggie thought with longing of going down to the pond herself. She would have liked to jump into the water in only her chemise as she had when she was little. She could imagine the coolness enveloping her, soothing her heated skin.

Then she imagined Reid in the pool with her, streams of water sluicing down his bare chest, and suddenly all thought of coolness was gone. She went hot all over, and her nipples hardened, pressing against the thin cotton of her dress.

Maggie blushed, thinking with scorn how wanton she must be to have such notions in the broad light of day and without any provocation. Nowadays her body seemed to have a will of its own, reacting to the merest thought. And her mind was wandering to such errant thoughts at the most inappropriate times.

The heat grew no easier throughout the day, and neither did Maggie's mood. She was irritable, angry at herself inside and snappish with the others. She fixed a cold supper that evening, too hot and out of sorts to work over a stove. Then she felt bad for putting an inadequate meal on the table and apologized to Ty, Will, and Reid for not cooking. She felt absurdly close to tears.

Ty stared at her, and Will frowned, looking confused.

"Ma?" Ty asked, his voice vaulting upward. "Are you all right?"

"Of course I'm all right," she answered impatiently, and immediately she regretted her tone. "Oh, Ty, honey, I'm sorry." Tears welled up in her eyes, and she had to blink them back, disgusted with herself. "I don't know why I'm being like this."

"It's the heat," Reid assured her. "Don't worry. We all feel the same way. I don't even want a hot meal tonight, and I'm sure Will and Ty feel the same way."

"Sure," Ty chimed in.

Will nodded. "That's right. Don't be mad."

"I'm not mad!" Maggie felt stricken as she looked at Will's uncertain expression. He was so innocent, like a child, despite his size. She felt guilty for snapping at him, and she thought she must be the most evil woman on earth for thinking about betraying him with another man. It didn't matter that he would never know or care. She would know. "I'm just . . . I don't know. You're right. I'm sure it's the heat."

Reid reached across the table and laid his hand over hers, giving it a little squeeze. She looked at him and saw that he was gazing at her with warmth and concern; there was no hint of sexuality in his gesture. Yet the moment their eyes met, desire crackled like lightning, hot and relentless, and suddenly the air was alive with it.

They pulled their hands apart instantly and looked away, but now Maggie was unable to think of anything but him and the look of hunger in his eyes. She tried to recall what she had felt only a moment before—the guilt and disgust at the thought of betraying Will—but now, stronger than that, was the yearning. The sheer force of her desire shook her. And she wondered how she could *not* sleep with Reid.

She jumped up from her seat. "I—I'm afraid I don't feel very hungry right now. I—uh—you all go on and eat. I'm going to lie down for a bit."

Behind her she heard Ty asking anxiously, "What's the matter with her? Is she all right?"

"I'm sure she's fine," Reid assured him. "It's just the weather. It gets on people's nerves. Grown-ups especially."

Maggie fled up the stairs, leaving the sound of their voices behind. She went to her room and closed the door and flung herself down across her bed. She felt like a fool, like a silly young girl unable to control her emotions. Back when she was turning into a woman she had been full of volatile, intense feelings, happy as could be one minute and a few minutes later sad and lonely or furious at a teasing brother. But why was she acting the same way now, when she was a grown woman with an eleven-year-old son? Why couldn't she control herself?

But she knew the answer to those questions: *Reid Prescott.*

She couldn't lie still for long. She was too nervous, too chock-full of turbulent emotions. She got up and began to pace back and forth, until finally that motion itself began to get on her nerves, and, sighing gustily, she flopped down into her rocker and stared out the window. Her thoughts wandered back downstairs, and she wondered if the men were through eating yet. She wondered if Reid was still there or if he had gone to the barn, leaving it safe for her to return to the kitchen. Somehow just thinking that he was there in the house with her made her more keyed up.

Maggie wondered if she were going mad.

Or perhaps she was going through the Change. But it was far too early for that. She refused to think about what else it might be. She would not allow herself to.

As the sun began to slip toward the horizon, again she got up and paced. Finally she went downstairs and cleared off the table, substituting the old, familiar tasks for thinking.

As she washed the dishes, it seemed to grow dark very quickly, and when she looked out the west window, she saw why. Clouds, stacked high like a looming cliff, had built up on the horizon, blotting out the setting sun. Lightning crackled through the clouds, making them glow from within, then forked across the sky. There was no rain or thunder, just the wild display.

Maggie watched in fascination. It seemed as if the very air around her were charged. Ty and Will came running into the kitchen to exclaim excitedly over the silent phenomenon. Will was a little afraid of the lightning, but without the thunder his fear was countered by awe.

Slowly the storm moved on, and Maggie was able to get the boys to go to bed. Finished with her tasks, she followed them upstairs, but even though she undressed and washed and put on her nightgown, she could not bring herself to retire yet. Off in the distance she could still see the heat lightning, and somehow it added to her jittery feeling.

She took down her hair and attempted to brush it out, but the charge in the air made the strands crackle and cling to the brush, and finally she stopped and simply tied it back with a ribbon. She paced to and fro. She turned down the covers and stretched out on her bed, but it was too hot to sleep, too hot even to lie still. Once more she got up and went to the window, hoping for a breeze to cool her.

The storm had finally disappeared, and her eyes turned toward the barn. Pale yellow light spilled out the open barn door. Reid was standing in the lantern's glow, a dark silhouette of angles and lines. But Maggie could imagine his features. She could imagine the tan skin of his arms and chest dotted with sweat in the heat of the evening. She could imagine his eyes turning upward toward the house, seeking her.

Maggie almost stepped back at that thought. But a perverse something in her wanted him to see her, ached for him to. Desire was raw within her; she could feel it pulsing in her throat, in her wrists . . . between her legs, hot and damp and primitive. She drew in a shaky breath and turned uncertainly toward the door. She felt hot and desperate, as if she might explode if she stayed penned up within this room another minute. With a last glance toward the window, she turned and hurried out of the bedroom. She went lightly down the stairs, her feet barely whispering upon the wood, and out into the night.

Maggie stopped at the edge of the porch and looked across the yard. Reid was still standing outside, and he turned at the sound of the back door closing. When he saw her, he straightened and took a step forward, his eyes fixed on her statue-still form. Almost without volition, Maggie started across the yard toward him. His stride lengthened, and her steps quickened in response.

Something deep inside her quivered with alarm, but she refused to listen; she didn't want to think. She was all emotion now, and she could do nothing but hurry toward the man she loved.

They did not speak. When he reached her, Reid grasped her and pulled her the last step to him. She went eagerly, her arms going up to twine around his neck, her mouth lifting to his like a leaf turning toward the sun. He kissed her. And if ever there had been a moment when they could have turned back, it was gone now.

Their mouths clung, and passion surged through them, overwhelming all reason. Reid squeezed her to him tightly, pressing her soft flesh into his. Her breasts flattened against his chest; his masculinity pushed against her abdomen, insistently demanding satisfaction. The pressure of it neither surprised nor alarmed Maggie; she reveled in the feel of it and rubbed her pelvis against him provocatively. Reid groaned, and Maggie smiled against his mouth, his passionate reaction increasing her own desire.

Reid lifted his head, breaking their kiss, and gazed down at her, his eyes dark and desperate, his chest rising and falling in harsh, fast gasps. Then he bent, sweeping her up into his arms, and walked rapidly toward the barn. Maggie lay quiescently in his embrace, her face buried in his shoulder, her arms looped around his neck. She breathed in his scent, felt the heat of his skin through his shirt. Her senses were wildly alive, her body throbbing with a deep, primitive passion.

He carried her through the barn and into his sleeping quarters at the back. He kicked the door closed behind him and set her down. Then he reached back and dropped the heavy bar into place across the door, sealing out the world. Maggie felt the thud deep within her abdomen, intensifying the heavy throb of desire there.

Reid began to unbutton his shirt. Maggie's heart

knocked furiously against her ribcage as she watched him, and heat flooded her face.

Reid saw the slight widening of her mouth, the heaviness of her eyelids, the way her gray eyes darkened and her cheeks flamed, and it heightened his own desire almost unbearably. He tugged his shirt off and let it fall to the crude plank floor, and they came together again in a long, deep kiss, their bodies straining as if seeking to melt into one. His hands roamed over her back and down to her hips, pressing her tightly against him, his fingers sinking into the flesh of her buttocks.

Maggie let out a little whimper of yearning, stretching up on tiptoe to press her lips even deeper into his. His tongue was hot and hungry against hers, the sensation wiping out all awareness of time and place. His hands swept back up to the fastenings of her shift, fingers fumbling on the little buttons. At last he shoved it down onto her arms, exposing her soft white shoulders and upper chest, and his mouth left hers to trail feverishly down her neck. His tongue crept out to circle the vulnerable hollow at the base of her throat, and Maggie could not hold back a groan.

Reid cupped one breast in his hand, searing her skin even through the fabric of her shift. The nipple tightened and pressed against the cloth, begging to be touched. He dragged his thumb across it slowly, and the breath caught in Maggie's throat. She trembled with pleasure, and his mouth, hot and velvety, moved down her chest, inching ever closer to the tight, aching bud. His thumb stroked back and forth across it, sending tremors through her. Heat pooled in her abdomen, and she could feel the moisture of desire form between her thighs. She squeezed her legs together, seeking some release from the almost painful pleasure, but the movement only heightened her hunger.

Sensing her need, Reid brought his hand down her back and over her buttocks, delving between her legs and pressing her nightgown tightly against her. Her damp heat made him groan, and he moved his fingers ever so slightly against her in a way that made Maggie writhe and whimper. With the other hand he thrust her shift down farther, exposing her full, luscious breasts, and hungrily he took one engorged nipple into his mouth. He licked the little button delicately and circled it with his tongue.

Flooded with a pleasure so intense she could barely stand it, Maggie gasped, her head lolling back. "Please," she panted, too dazed even to express what she wanted. "Reid, oh, please . . ." But he knew instinctively what she wanted, and he pulled her breast more deeply into the hot, wet cave of his mouth, sucking gently.

A chord of fire shot straight to her loins, and she cried out, her fingers digging into his bare shoulders. Passion, suppressed for so many years, rushed through her, and as his mouth nuzzled her breast and his fingers caressed the very center of her desire, a tidal wave of pleasure crashed within her. Sobbing, she jerked convulsively, then went limp against him, stunned by the passion that had just overtaken her.

Reid took her weight against him, cradling her in his arms, and, holding back the desire surging within him, he raised his head and brushed his lips against her temple, murmuring meaningless, soothing sounds of love. Then, guiding her to sit down on the bed, he gently removed her gown completely and laid her back against the pillow, his eyes feasting on her nakedness as he finished undressing and lowered himself onto the mattress beside her.

Maggie looked at him—at his lean, tan, muscled flesh, at the hard evidence of his desire, obviously still unsatisfied—and she felt longing stir inside her once more. It surprised her that as completely and stunningly as her hunger had been fulfilled just moments before, she could still feel the prickle of need. She wanted to give Reid the same pleasure she had received, but she ached for the satisfaction of feeling his maleness inside her, too. She wanted to experience that wild explosion of pleasure again.

Expertly his hands roamed over her body, fanning the embers of her passion into flame once more. His mouth and hands explored her, finding the sensitive spots that made her melt and moan and move restlessly against the sheets. Then Maggie's hands made to do likewise for him, and she was rewarded by the quick intake of his breath. She trailed her fingers over his shoulders and chest, delighting in the smoothness of his skin, the rougher texture of his body hair, the satiny sleekness of his belly. He jerked and groaned when she touched him there, but when she started to move away, he whispered, "No, please, go on," his face taut with wanting. "Touch me."

Gently her fingers circled the root of his desire, then curled up around the shaft, which was hot and throbbing, engorged with passion. His hands dug into the sheets beneath them, and with a groan he rolled to position himself between her legs.

Gazing deeply into her eyes, he thrust into her, and Maggie let out a cry of satisfaction as he filled her. Nothing had ever felt this good, this right. Joy welled in her, so strong and beautiful that she almost wept.

But there was more. He began to move inside her, thrusting deep, then almost withdrawing, caressing her with long, slow strokes. Maggie wrapped her arms and legs around him and moved with him, her own pleasure and passion at one with his. He groaned again, and she dug her fingers into his back. Her reaction seemed to enflame him even further, and he began to thrust more quickly, rushing toward the pinnacle of their lovemaking.

Maggie cried out as her pleasure peaked, and Reid shuddered as he found his own release. He let out a low, hoarse moan and collapsed against her. Maggie buried her face in his shoulder, a long sigh escaping her.

Then, to her own surprise, she felt tears streaming down her cheeks.

"Maggie." Reid's voice was low and concerned. "Maggie darling, don't cry. What's the matter? Did I hurt you?"

"No." Maggie shook her head, unable to stop crying. "No, it was beautiful."

He rolled to one side, cradling her in his arms. She laid her head on his shoulder and gave vent to her tears. She couldn't explain why she was crying; she was a jumble of intense emotions—happy, filled with pleasure, stunned by the beauty of their lovemaking, and yet now, with her mind working again, awash in guilt and sorrow, too. Tears seemed the only release.

Reid did not question her further. He thought he knew why she was crying: she had remembered Will and was thinking how they had betrayed him. And there was no way he could save her from that guilt. He felt it, too. So he stroked her hair and back, giving her the only solace he could.

He bent to kiss the top of her head. "I'm sorry, Maggie, I'm sorry. I never meant to cause you any pain. That's the last thing I wanted to do. Please don't hate me."

"Hate you?" Maggie gave a watery chuckle. She wiped at her tears and sniffed, her bout of crying subsiding at last. "I could never hate you. I love you."

"Oh, Maggie!" His arms encircled her tightly, and he kissed her hair again, burying his face in the sweet-smelling curls. "You don't know how much I've wanted to hear you say that. For weeks, maybe months—maybe from the first moment I saw you standing there with that gun in your hands, so pretty and brave and so damned full of life."

Maggie smiled; he could feel it against his bare shoulder.

"I thought I detected something other than affection in your voice at the time," she pointed out.

He chuckled. "I didn't say you didn't scare the hell out of me, too." He picked up a tendril of her hair and idly played with it, twining it around his fingers. He sighed. "You don't know how much I've thought about this, longed for it. I could hardly keep my hands off you some days. I don't think there's any way I've seen you that I haven't thought you beautiful."

Maggie's arm, thrown across his chest, tightened convulsively. "Oh, God, Reid, what are we going to do?"

"I don't know." His voice roughened. "Please, just don't ask me to leave. Don't ask me to give you up. I don't think I could do that."

"No!" Fear squeezed her chest. "I—I don't want you to leave. I couldn't bear it. It's just . . . oh, Reid, how can I do this to Will? I feel so awful. So wicked."

"Hush! You're not wicked. You couldn't be wicked if you tried. You're a courageous, good woman, and surely it's no sin for you to want some happiness for yourself."

Maggie sat up, pulling her knees to her chest and wrapping her arms around them, bending her head so that her hair fell like a waterfall around her, all but concealing her nakedness. "But it's wrong to break your marriage vows. A sin. I pledged to be faithful and true to Will before God and my family and everyone. It's my duty, and it doesn't matter that Will has changed, that he's . . . incapable of being a husband. He's still my husband; I pledged myself to him for better or worse."

"And you've been steady as a rock through the worst," Reid assured her. "No one could have been more true or faithful than you have. Good Lord, woman, you saved his life. You brought him home and cared for him, and you've been patient and understanding and loving with him for all these years."

Maggie turned her head and fixed him with her clear

gray eyes. "And do you honestly believe, then, that it's all right for me to break my marriage vows? To . . . to cuckold him?"

He lowered his eyes in the face of her unwavering gaze and sighed. "Ah, Maggie, I know it's a violation of what you believe in, and that's a painful thing for a woman like you. You're too responsible, too full of duty and honor, to seek another man's bed. But giving in to love, to desire, after all that you've gone through for so many years doesn't make you wicked. Lord, Maggie, you're not meant to be a saint."

"I know. But if it went on . . . if I continued to sleep with you, it wouldn't be just a mistake anymore. It wouldn't be something forgivable. It would be conscious, planned. I'd be intentionally unfaithful. An—an adulteress. I can't be your whore, no matter how much I want you!"

"Don't say that!" Reid said fiercely, sitting up and grabbing her arm. He turned her to look at him. "You could never be anyone's whore! You are the best woman I've ever known."

"Oh, Reid!" Tears streamed down Maggie's cheeks, and her voice broke. "I love you so. I never felt this way about Will, never felt this way in bed with him. That's part of why I feel so bad! I've not only betrayed him, I've betrayed the love we used to have."

"No! Please don't say that. Please don't feel bad about loving me—or about loving differently from the way you loved Will." His hand trailed up her arm. He leaned his head against hers, whispering in her ear, "It makes me feel like I could conquer the world when I hear you say you love me."

Maggie swallowed. "Reid, I . . . I have to go now."

"No, not yet," he murmured. "Stay with me." He kissed her naked shoulder, and his hand trailed down her back.

"I can't. I—this isn't right. I have to go, and we can't let it happen again."

"Maggie, no!" He began to rain kisses over her neck and shoulders, delighting her senses and weakening her resolve.

Maggie was shaken by the power he had over her, how easily he could arouse her into mindless passion. How would she ever be able to withstand the temptation Reid was to her?

"No. No!" Her voice was panicky, and she pulled away from him, scrambling out of the bed. "I have to go. Please don't try to persuade me to stay." Her voice was anguished. "Reid, if you have any feeling for me, let me go. Please don't try to make love to me again— tonight or any other night. I can't live like that!" She began to pull on her shift, tears streaming down her face.

"Maggie . . ."

"Please! I mean it!" She gazed at him earnestly, unaware of how her half-naked body aroused him even while her tears pierced his heart. "Promise me that you won't tempt me, won't try to persuade me to sleep with you again. I can't do it. I wouldn't be able to live with myself. Please, promise me!"

Reid's face contorted with pain. "Maggie, you're killing me."

"Reid, please!"

"All right! Yes, yes, I promise I won't pursue you."

A sob of relief escaped her. "Thank you. Oh, God, thank you."

Maggie wiped the tears from her face and hastily finished dressing. She hurried to the door, then turned and looked back at Reid. The hunger in his face was so stark that she almost cried out. She knew that she should leave immediately, but she couldn't resist the urge to taste his lips one last time. She returned and bent to kiss him. Her hair swung down around them, enveloping them in a silky veil. Their mouths clung in a brief, hard, desperate kiss. Then Maggie pulled back, her hand flying to her lips, as if she could somehow hold in the kisses that yearned to tumble out into Reid's mouth. And she turned and ran.

13

Maggie hoped that at least the night of passion she and Reid had shared would ease the strain that had been between them over the past few weeks. After all, now that they had satisfied their desire, surely it would lessen.

It didn't take her long to realize that she had been naive to think so. As soon as Reid walked into the kitchen the next morning, the air almost crackled with tension. Maggie felt his presence without even turning around. She *couldn't* turn around, afraid of what her face would reveal when she looked at him.

It was some time before she allowed herself to glance in his direction. Reid was washing his hands, and her eyes immediately went to them. They had always fascinated her—long and slender and skillful yet intensely masculine as well—but now she knew their talents even more intimately. She blushed at the thought and pulled her gaze away.

As the family sat down to eat, Maggie continued to avoid Reid's eyes. But she could feel him watching her, and his gaze seemed to draw her. She felt impelled to look at him yet at the same time was reluctant to do so. Finally, toward the end of the meal, Maggie decided she was acting the coward, and she made herself meet Reid's eyes. Instantly heat flooded her face. He was looking at her, his eyes heavy-lidded with desire, and she knew as clearly as if he had spoken that he was thinking of their lovemaking.

Trembling, she jumped up from the table and carried her plate to the counter, setting it down with a clatter. "Hadn't you all better get to your chores?" she asked abruptly.

"Sure, Mama," Ty said, glancing at her curiously. Will looked as puzzled as Ty. Reid's face was drawn into hard lines, but he said nothing. He merely got up and left the kitchen.

The situation got no better as the days passed; if anything, it grew even worse. Maggie found herself by turn distracted, irritable, excited, furious, and scared. Sometimes it seemed as if she felt all those things at once. She could not imagine how she was going to survive without either going insane or giving in to the demon of desire that gnawed inside her.

One evening after supper, Reid remained at the table talking to Ty. While Ty wrestled with his thoughts concerning *Macbeth,* Reid idly began to trace whorls and lines in the wooden tabletop with his forefinger as he listened. Maggie's eyes were drawn to his hand, mesmerized by the slow, sensual motion, and her breath caught in her throat, almost as if it were her flesh he was stroking. She grew flushed and damp and jittery, and when she glanced up, Reid's eyes locked with hers, and she knew that he felt the same thing she did.

She sprang from the table, overturning her chair. Hastily, she bent to right it, blushing furiously. Reid rose abruptly and strode out the door.

"What's the matter?" Ty asked, staring at his mother.

Maggie feigned ignorance. "What do you mean?" She turned away, unable to look at Ty.

"You're acting funny, all jumpy or something. Reid's the same way. Usually he stays and talks longer."

Maggie shrugged. "Probably the weather. It's too hot, and you know that gets on people's nerves."

"Do you like Reid?" Will asked suddenly.

Maggie went rigid. "What do you mean, Will?" she asked tightly.

"I thought maybe you were mad at him. I thought he'd done something wrong."

"No. Of course not. I . . . like Reid. I'm just a little edgy lately, that's all."

"Oh. Good. 'Cause I like him."

"Yeah, me, too," Ty agreed. "He's smarter than anybody I ever met."

"And he's nice," Will added.

"Yes, he is." Maggie kept her voice carefully neutral. "We all like him."

She was glad when the boys dropped the subject and went outside to play. She left the dishes sitting where they were and went out onto the front porch, where she sank into the rocking chair and leaned her head back, closing her eyes.

It would be easy, she thought, so terribly easy, to go to Reid's bed, to let their love take its natural course. After all, who would know? Who would be hurt? It would be almost like being married, for they already shared so much of their lives. Ty and Will would have no idea what was going on; she could slip out to Reid's room at night. No one in town would have any idea that she and Reid were secretly lovers.

Unless, of course, she got pregnant.

The thought chilled her. Part of the reason she had been so edgy since the night they'd made love had been fear of the consequences of that moment of passion. If she got pregnant, everyone in Pine Creek would know it was not Will's child. The natural suspect, of course, would be the new hired hand, living right there on the farm with them. Everyone would turn from her in contempt, thinking her no better than a whore. Oh, they might have sympathy for her plight now, having a husband like Will, but that sympathy would end as soon as she stepped over the line. It had been a distinct relief this morning when she found she had started her monthly flow.

However, the fact that she had escaped that fate this once didn't mean she would continue to do so. If she returned to Reid's bed, the threat of repercussions would be forever hanging over her head. And even if she should manage not to get pregnant, even if no one ever found out about her and Reid, Maggie knew that she could not, must not, allow herself to have an affair with him. After all, *she* would know. *She* would care. She could not live with herself if she sneaked around like that, betraying her marriage vows and her duty to Will. She would hate herself, despise what she had become.

Her resolve strengthened, her nerves calmed, Maggie sat up and went back to the kitchen to continue her work. She would find a way to get through this, she told herself. And surely as time passed it would grow easier.

She soon learned, however, that that hope, too, was naive. With every passing day her desire grew, not diminished. In some ways it was worse now, for she knew exactly how wonderful it felt to be in Reid's arms, how much his kisses and caresses stirred her. She ached to feel his hard masculine force inside her again, to have his weight pressing her into the bed, his mouth feasting on her breasts. Thoughts of their lovemaking popped into her head at the most inappropriate times, making her blush as she felt the familiar heat in her loins again.

The minister of their church had often said that once one committed a sin it was far easier to do it again. Temptation, he would tell the congregation, grew stronger, not weaker, after one had yielded to it. Too late Maggie was realizing that his words were all too true. As the hot days of summer dragged by, her desire for Reid grew more and more intense, until sometimes she thought she would burst from the sheer urgency of it.

She thought about him, dreamed about him, remembered each vivid detail of their lovemaking. She could see in his face, too, that he wanted her more than ever. The strain began to tell on her. It was difficult to sleep. Her appetite dropped off. When she looked at herself in the mirror, she saw hollow cheeks and a haunted, desperate look in her eyes. And Reid looked much the same.

Once he walked into the kitchen while she was pulling the bread from the oven, and when he saw her straighten tiredly, her hand reaching to massage her spine, he went to her without thinking and began to knead her shoulders. With a sigh, Maggie leaned back against him. Almost before they knew what was happening, his lips were trailing down the side of her neck and she was melting into him. Suddenly it struck them exactly what they were doing, and they sprang apart guiltily. Maggie stared at Reid, wide-eyed, her cheeks flushed.

"I'm sorry," he said hoarsely and left the kitchen, not returning that evening. But Maggie had to wage a battle with herself all through a meal she hardly tasted and far into the night to keep from following Reid out to his room.

Another time, when Maggie went into the springhouse to get a jug of milk cooling there, Reid came in after her and pulled the door shut, enveloping them in darkness. He took her in his arms and kissed her thoroughly, his tongue searching her mouth, his hands moving over her body. Finally he broke away, panting.

"I'm sorry." His voice was harsh and uneven. "God, I seem to be saying that all the time now. But sometimes

I look at you and want you so much, I feel as if I'll burst if I don't touch you or kiss you." He made an aggravated noise and whirled away, banging his fist against the wall. "Damn it! I can't live like this!"

"Reid!" Fear made her voice sharp. "What are you saying?"

"I don't know!" he exploded. "I only wish I did. All I know is that I love you, and I can't bear to be away from you. But I can't bear to be around you and not touch you, either! I think I'm going mad. Where is it going to end, Maggie? What are we going to do?"

"I don't know!" Tears sprang into her eyes. She wanted to scream in frustration, and at the same time it was all she could do not to throw herself back into Reid's arms. "I don't know!"

He left the springhouse then, and Maggie sat down, her knees suddenly too weak to carry her. Despairingly she put her head in her hands and wondered what was to become of them. Deep in her heart, she was afraid she knew the answer, but she would not allow herself to look at it. For she also knew it would leave her life in ruins.

Tess had decided to sell her last remaining jewelry and what furniture she could. It might not bring enough to pay her taxes, but she had to try.

Gideon hated for her to part with her prized possessions, but there was little he could do to dissuade her. However, when Tess asked him if he would drive her into Sharps so she could catch the train to Little Rock, he put his foot down.

"You're not going to Little Rock by yourself," he said with finality.

"But, Gideon, how else am I going to sell Mama's and my jewels? Little Rock's the only place big enough for—"

"I didn't mean that. I agree about Little Rock, but a lady can't just go running off by herself like that."

"I'll take Mama and Ginny with me."

"You'd need protection," he growled. "What good do you think your mother and daughter will do? I'll take the things for you. I'll ride up there and—"

"No." Tess's voice was firm, and she looked him straight in the eye. "You're a dear man, Gideon, and I appreciate your trying to spare me the embarrassment. But this is something I have to do myself."

He glowered at her. "Then I'll come with you. We'll take the big wagon for the furniture."

Tess contemplated the offer. "All right, Gideon. Thank you." Then she stopped, frowning. "But we can't make the trip in a day. We'd have to camp out. We couldn't go, just the two of us alone. It wouldn't look right." Tess suddenly felt herself blushing. "I mean, of course, I know that you would be a perfect gentleman. I don't mean to imply, well, you know . . . but people might talk."

She stumbled to a halt, her face fiery red. She knew it was ridiculous to even consider such a thing in regard to Gideon. Gideon would never try to take advantage of any woman, much less his brother's widow. And, of course, he had absolutely no interest in her, anyway; he had never shown by the slightest word or gesture that he thought of her as an attractive woman. Indeed, he might wonder if her mind was in the gutter that such an objection would even occur to her.

Gideon's face looked as if it had been touched by the same fire as Tess's. "No, of course not. I would never try to . . ." He trailed off nervously. It scared him to think that Tess might distrust him. Had she somehow guessed how he felt about her? Did she suspect that he burned with desire for her? That at night he woke, sweating, from hot, lascivious dreams of her? Had he somehow let it slip? He cleared his throat. "But we have to consider your reputation. We'd, uh, need a chaperone."

Tess reflected for a moment. "Such a hasty trip would be hard on Mama." Then her face brightened. "We'll take Ginny with us! And Ty and Will could come along, too. They'd love the ride. And with three relatives along, no one would ever dare to think that, well, that anything wrong was going on."

"Of course." Gideon smiled, relieved.

When Gideon told Maggie the plan, he was surprised that she seemed less than enthusiastic about having Ty and Will go along. He'd thought she'd relish a couple of days of peace. But despite whatever reservations she had, she ultimately agreed, and one Monday in July Gideon picked up Ty and Will at the farm and drove into town, where they loaded a large mahogany buffet and a few other elegant pieces of furniture into the wagon. Then, with Ginny and Tess in tow, they set off for Little Rock.

The children and Will, who all sat in back, were in tearing high spirits. To them the journey was an adventure. Even Tess had color in her cheeks and a sparkle in her eyes. No matter how sorry the occasion, a trip to Little Rock couldn't fail to be exciting; she had been there only a few times in her life. Besides, at least she was doing something to try to defeat Benton Conway, and, Heaven knows, that was better than sitting around bemoaning her losses.

Tess glanced at Gideon, sitting next to her on the high seat of the wagon, and, sensing her gaze, he turned his head toward her. Tess smiled at him. He smiled back, looking suddenly rather vulnerable and shy.

The thought surprised Tess. Gideon, vulnerable? Surely she had been mistaken. Though reserved, Gideon was the strongest, steadiest man she knew, the one to whom others turned in their hour of crisis.

She glanced at him again. His eyes were on the road now, and there was no reading his expression from this angle. Tess looked at the strong set of his shoulders, the stubborn thrust of his jaw. No, there was nothing soft or vulnerable about Gideon. And yet . . .

She thought of his kind blue eyes, of the way he melted whenever he saw Ginny, of the surprising sweetness of his smile. Physical strength, or even a calm, steady nature, didn't make one invulnerable. She knew he had felt great pain at Shelby's death. She knew how much he loved his family, how deep his roots were in this land. Of course, a man like that could be hurt—and deeply.

Tess wondered why she had never thought of Gideon this way before, and she concluded that she must have been terribly selfish. She was always seeking Gideon's help, never offering him her own. It made her feel small to realize that, made her wish she had paid better attention to him. Had there been moments when he had needed something from her, even just an attentive ear, and she hadn't given it? Tess wished she could make it up to him. But she didn't even know where to begin.

They camped that night near a stream, on a slight rise that afforded them a view of the road. Gideon, Tess noticed, always kept a watchful eye out, protecting them from any danger.

She watched him lay the fire, his motions quick and competent. He had big, square, workman's hands, callused and hard, with wide palms and large fingers very different from Shelby's long, slender digits. Tess closed her eyes, remembering the way Shelby's hands had felt on her body, his soft caress. Then somehow she was thinking not about Shelby's hands any longer, but Gideon's. She imagined the rough feel of his callused palms, the gentle way he would stroke her, his big fingers spreading out over her skin.

Tess's eyes popped open, and she drew in a sharp breath. Whatever was she thinking of? She had actually been imagining her brother-in-law caressing her! Her skin felt suddenly hot, her breathing irregular, and she only hoped that if Gideon had happened to glance over at her, he had seen no clue on her face as to what she had been thinking. He would be appalled, she was sure.

Gideon treated her like a sister. He thought of her as nothing but his dear brother's widow. As Ginny's mother. She was not a woman to him, someone he might desire. It was wrong and quite wanton for her to have such wayward thoughts of him.

Tess stole another glance at him. He had the fire going now, and he was showing the others how to cook over it. He smiled as he talked, his lips parting over strong, white teeth. Tess gazed at him, wondering why she had never noticed before how attractive his features were, how sensual his mouth, how healthily muscled his arms and shoulders.

Tess couldn't believe that she was thinking such things. It was wicked of her. Downright lustful, in fact. If Gideon had any idea what she was picturing, she would be utterly humiliated. Resolutely pushing the errant notions from her mind, she turned and looked toward the road.

But she found that once the idea had entered her mind, it was next to impossible to get rid of it. Having thought about Gideon's physical attributes, she discovered that she couldn't *stop* thinking about them. The best she could do was pretend, keep a false mask of indifferent friendliness on her face—when all the while her eyes were straying to the long, bulging muscles of Gideon's thighs beneath his workpants or the hard, sun-browned forearms showing below the rolled-up sleeves of his shirt.

After supper, Gideon unrolled a thin down mattress and spread it out beneath the high wagon. "Here's where you and Ginny can sleep," he said. "It doesn't look like rain, but you never know. Will and Ty and I'll bed down over there, so we won't be far away if you need anything."

He glanced up at Tess, looking faintly uncomfortable, and she wondered if he, too, found it awkward being with her like this. And if so, had he, too, had any surprising thoughts about her and their sleeping arrangements sometime during their day together?

Tess's cheeks flamed, and she chided herself for the absurd notion. "All right. Thank you." She turned to Ginny. "Come on, honey, why don't you and I go down to the creek and wash up? It'll be time for bed soon."

Tess felt almost as if she were fleeing from Gideon. It was all very unsettling and strange. She didn't feel like herself at all, and suddenly Gideon seemed like someone she didn't even know.

When she and her daughter returned from the stream, she found that Gideon had hung a canvas tarp over the wagon wheels, providing a curtain for her and Ginny. He had laid the men's bedrolls on the ground beyond, close enough for her to call him for help, yet far enough away for her to have some privacy. He was such a thoughtful man, she realized anew.

Gideon, Will, and Ty were clustered around the campfire, and Gideon was telling them stories. Ginny, of course, had to join them. Tess perched on a low, flat rock behind the girl to brush her hair and plait it for bedtime. Without thinking, Tess then continued her nighttime ritual, pulling the pins from her own hair and letting it tumble down. She massaged her temples with her fingertips, luxuriating, as she always did, in the release of the weight of her tresses. Then she began to brush them a hundred strokes, half-listening to Gideon's silly story about a man who lived up a tree in the Ozarks.

Gideon's voice slowed, then stopped, and Tess opened her eyes, wondering what had happened. Gideon was staring at her, and there was a strange heat in his eyes. A shiver ran through her. Shelby had often looked at her that way, silently signaling his hunger for her. She sucked in her lower lip, her brush stopping in mid-stroke.

Then she realized suddenly what an intimate thing she was doing in public. No man ever saw a woman brush out her hair except in the privacy of their bedroom. A combination of embarrassment and excitement rippled through Tess. She didn't know what was the matter with her. She felt like a hussy.

"Come, Ginny," she said breathlessly. "It's time for bed."

"But, Mama, Uncle Gideon hasn't finished yet!"

"Ginny!" Her voice came out short and sharp.

"Do as your mother says," Gideon told her softly.

Tess hurried to the wagon and crawled under it. In the darkness and with the canvas over the sides, they were protected from anyone's sight, yet she felt clumsy and shy as she unbuttoned her blouse and skirt and slipped them off, as if Gideon could see her. She folded her clothes carefully, then Ginny's, and laid them at the foot of their makeshift bed. Then she arranged the blanket for sleep.

With only half an ear, she listened to her daughter's childish prayers. The canvas fell two or three inches short of the ground, and lying down like this, Tess could see out. She watched as Gideon banked the fire and moved to the bedrolls. He turned and glanced toward the wagon, and for one foolish moment Tess thought he was looking at her. But that, of course, was impossible, she realized.

Gideon pulled off his boots and slid into his bedroll, wondering how he was going to make it through the night. He wouldn't be getting any sleep, that was for sure. Not with Tess lying only a few yards away from him.

He could make out the dim outline of her form beneath the wagon. He wondered what she was wearing under the blanket, if she was still dressed or if she had pulled off her outer garments. Or perhaps she was wearing nothing at all. He bit down on his lip to stifle a groan and rolled over, facing away from the wagon and Tess.

It didn't do any good. He could still see her in his mind's eye. He could imagine her naked, with only his blanket atop her, just as he could picture peeling the blanket back and revealing her feminine curves. He thought of his hands, big and tanned, on her milk-white flesh.

The thought made him hard, and he told himself he was a lust-driven fool. Tess trusted him, had given herself and her daughter into his care. It was dishonorable to betray that trust, even in his mind. It was disgusting, perverted, even, to think such things with children around. Yet it seemed as if the more he tried to banish the thoughts, the more they stayed in his mind, until finally he gave up trying and let the images overtake him, sweeping him with red-hot desire.

It was hours before he finally slept.

Tess felt uncomfortable around Gideon the rest of the journey. Sitting beside him on the wagon seat, she could think of almost nothing to say. Instead of the usual thoughtful conversation that flowed between them, they were reduced to talking about the heat and the beauty of the countryside around them. It was a relief when they finally reached Little Rock.

They stayed with Tess's cousin in the city, and the next morning they left Will and the children at the house and went downtown to sell Tess's jewelry and furniture. There Tess was grateful for Gideon's presence. He bolstered her courage; without him she was afraid she wouldn't have had the nerve to go through with her plan. He bargained for her, and she was certain the shopkeepers gave him a better price than they would have given a woman.

Still, what they got was not nearly enough to pay her taxes. Tess had feared as much, but she decided to put her worries aside for the moment so that Ginny and Ty and Will could have a pleasant outing as she and Gideon took them on a tour of the city that afternoon.

On the way home the following day, Tess and Gideon were quiet, and even the children and Will, in the now-empty back of the wagon, were uncharacteristically subdued, worn out from their big adventure.

Since they had gotten a very early start, they forged on all the way to Pine Creek without camping out a second time. When they arrived at the Caldwell house, Gideon walked Tess inside, carrying her carpetbag. Ginny went tearing up the stairs to find her grandmother and report on all the wonderful things she had seen in the big city of Little Rock. Tess turned to Gideon and held out her hand.

"Thank you. I don't think I could have managed without you."

"It was too little," Gideon replied grimly, squeezing her hand quickly and releasing it.

"I know." Tess shrugged. "But it's a start. Maybe if I have enough time, I can come up with the rest of it."

"Maybe." Gideon hesitated, then pulled a small pouch from his back pocket. "This should help a little."

Tess stared at the pouch he laid in her hand. He nodded. "Go ahead. Open it."

She pulled the drawstring and poured out the contents: several silver coins. Her jaw dropped. "But—but, Gideon, what's this?"

"Ma and I sold a few things we didn't need."

"Oh, Gideon, no! You shouldn't have done that. What did you sell?"

"A silver salt cellar. A pocket watch."

"Not your father's pocket watch!"

Gideon shrugged and nodded. "Yeah. I never wear it except on Sundays, so it's not much use to me."

"But, Gideon, you loved that watch. I know. Shelby told me how much it meant to you." Tears filled Tess's eyes. "I can't let you do that."

"I've already done it." He hesitated, not sure if he should tell her the rest. But he hated the idea of her continuing to worry about her home. Finally he said, "I —I think I can get the rest of the money, too."

Tess's eyes widened. "Where? How?"

"I'm going to talk to Farquarhar Jones."

Tess stared. "The Yankee? But why?"

"Once he wanted to buy a piece of land from me. I'm going to see if he's still interested. I'd lay odds he is."

"The farm? Gideon, no! You can't do that! I won't let you!"

"Just a small piece of it."

"Gideon, you can't sell him even part of the farm! You love that place. It's part of you."

"I can't stand by and let you get hurt, either. I'm not farming that meadow he wants, anyway."

"But you could someday. Or you could raise cattle there or something. Besides, that farm is your heritage! Ginny's and Ty's and your children's heritage!"

"I don't have any children. And there'll be plenty left for Ginny and Ty."

"But you *will* have children. You're bound to get married someday and have children, and then you'll regret giving up even a part of their inheritance." Tess wasn't sure exactly why pain stabbed her chest as she said those words, but she suddenly felt overwhelmed by sadness.

Gideon shook his head. "I don't think that's too likely. You know what a confirmed old bachelor I am."

"I'm sure there's someone who's right for you, and when you meet her and fall in love—"

"Tess, forget it! You can't argue me out of this. I've

talked to Ma about it, and she agrees. We can't see any other way to save you from being put out of your home, and I won't let that happen. Whatever it takes, I'm going to do."

Tess looked at him. His jaw was set in that stubborn Tyrrell way, and she knew that there would be no moving him. "But I can't let you make that kind of sacrifice," she cried helplessly.

"You don't have any choice. If Jones will buy that piece of land, I'll sell it to him."

"I won't take the proceeds," Tess decided, lifting her chin. "I can be just as stubborn as you."

Gideon scowled. "Then I'll give the money to the tax collector directly. You aren't losing this house."

Tess glared at him, planting her hands on her hips. "You can be really aggravating at times, did you know that?"

"So I've been told." Gideon crossed his arms and gazed back at her implacably.

They stared at each other intransigently. Finally Tess whirled around and walked away from him. "Oh, all right! If you're blamed determined to squander your land, then go ahead and do it. But what are you going to do next year, when I have to pay the taxes again? And the year after that? Do you plan to keep on selling off pieces of your property until you don't have anything left?"

"This will buy us enough time to do something about Conway's scheme. We'll be back in power someday, and his kind will be out. Or I'll figure out another way to stop him."

Tess sighed and looked at him worriedly. "You're too kind and generous for your own good sometimes. I know how much you loved Shelby, but you really shouldn't do this."

Gideon couldn't tell her that it wasn't Shelby for whom he was sacrificing his beloved land. He was ashamed to admit that he had scarcely thought about

Shelby the whole time he'd been working to save Tess's house. It was Tess who concerned him. But he couldn't let her know that. His love would just embarrass and concern her, and no doubt she would feel even worse about what he was doing.

So he said only, "I have to."

"Oh, Gideon!" She flung her arms around his neck and hugged him.

Startled, Gideon froze. Then his arms went around her, gently cradling her to him. She was soft and warm, and her head seemed to fit naturally against his chest. Gideon closed his eyes, luxuriating in the pleasure of holding her. At this moment, he could almost believe that he had the right to hold her, that she was his woman, not his brother's. It would be delightful to slide his hands down her back, to press her more closely against him.

Tess raised her head and gave him a peck on the cheek. Her lips were wonderfully soft on his skin. Suddenly Gideon's whole body was hot. He twisted his head, meaning to pull back, but at the same moment Tess moved, too, and their lips touched.

It was only for an instant, but their mouths remained just a breath apart. Then Gideon, without any conscious thought at all, leaned that fraction of an inch forward and kissed her. Tess went up on tiptoe, her mouth pressing into his. Gideon groaned deep in his throat and pulled her hard against his body.

He pressed her to him tightly as his mouth moved over hers. Her lips opened to him, and all the frustrated hunger he had felt for her during the trip rushed up in him, sweeping over him like a river at flood. His mouth devoured hers, his tongue roaming the honeyed cave. His blood roared in his ears; his fingers dug into her hips.

"Darling, I'm so glad— Tess!" A woman's voice shocked them both out of their haze of desire.

Gideon's head jerked up, and he stared at Tess's

mother standing in the doorway of the kitchen. The realization of where he was and what he had been doing rushed over him. His arms fell away from Tess, and he stepped back.

"Oh, God," he murmured. He looked from Mrs. Caldwell back down to Tess. Her face was soft, her lips faintly swollen from his kisses. She looked devastatingly desirable, and his body stirred in response. But Mrs. Caldwell's presence had effectively returned his sanity to him. "Oh, Tess. I'm sorry. I—" He broke off, shoving a hand through his hair. "I'm so sorry" was all he could say. Then he turned and rushed out the door, leaving Tess staring after him.

"Tess, what in the world do you think you were doing?" Amanda Caldwell asked in a horrified voice. "Standing right here in the middle of the house, kissing a man! Just like white trash! Why, Ginny's right upstairs. There's no telling what she might have seen. And Shelby's own brother, too!"

"Oh, hush, Mother!" Tess snapped, whirling around and glaring at Amanda. "Will you just be quiet!"

Then she turned and ran up the stairs.

14

After Will and Ty left for Little Rock with Gideon and Tess, Maggie's emotions were in turmoil. She couldn't keep from thinking about the fact that she and Reid were alone on the farm. While in theory it should make no difference, given her resolutions, in actuality there was something exceedingly tempting about the idea. There was an illusion of freedom, an aura of intimacy, a hint of secrecy, all of which served to heighten Maggie's unwanted desire. But it was also frightening to think of what might happen. Of how easy it would be to give in to temptation.

Halfheartedly Maggie worked in the kitchen all morning. After she had kneaded the bread and left it to rise, she stood uncertainly in the middle of the room, unable to decide what to do next. There were many things she *could* do; there always were on a farm. But there was nothing that absolutely had to be done at that moment.

Her eyes strayed to the window. Reid was nowhere in sight. She wondered if he was working in the barn.

Was he trying to keep his distance, occupy himself as best he could so he wouldn't be tempted to come to her?

Finally, disgusted with herself for idly mooning about Reid, Maggie straightened her shoulders and went upstairs to dust and sweep the bedrooms. Once she started, she decided to wax the floor, as well. Hard physical labor was the best way to keep her mind off her worries. So she rolled up her sleeves and threw herself into it.

However, she found that no matter how hard she swept or scrubbed or polished, she could not keep her thoughts from straying to Reid. Suddenly she heard his voice calling to her from downstairs, and, with a guilty start, she jumped to her feet.

Only then did she notice that the sun was high overhead, blazing down with all its strength. It was time for dinner, and she hadn't even noticed! Her stomach growled as if to drive home the point. Hurriedly, she dropped her scrub brush into the pail and flew out of the room toward the stairs, rolling down her sleeves as she went.

At the foot of the stairs, she almost bumped into Reid, who had wandered into the hall looking for her.

"Oh!" She stopped abruptly, grabbing the rail to steady herself.

Instinctively Reid reached out to her, and his hand went around her arm. But he dropped it immediately, as if it had burned his fingers, and he took a step backward. "I'm sorry. I was getting worried. . . ."

"I know. I'm terribly late. I was busy, and I lost all track of time." She could still feel a circle of heat around her arm where his hand had been. Just that touch had made her heart thump crazily. "I'm sorry. It won't take but a few minutes to throw something together."

"That's all right. I didn't mean to rush you. It was just that when you didn't call me in to eat, and then I

saw that the kitchen was empty, I got a little nervous."
He grinned ruefully. "I don't know exactly what I
thought—that you'd been spirited away by elves or
what."

"Thank you for being worried," Maggie said,
warmed by his concern for her.

She headed for the kitchen, and Reid stepped back to
let her pass. She didn't dare look up into his face for
fear everything she felt at his nearness would show in
her eyes. She busied herself with the food, keeping her
back to Reid, but as she heard him sit down at the table
behind her, she realized she could not stifle her awareness of him.

He was watching her, she knew, and she wondered
what he was thinking, what she would discover in his
eyes if she whirled around quickly. She had seen the
look of passion on his face before, and the thought of it
made her weak in the knees. Better not to think of it,
she chided herself. But how?

Maggie had rarely felt so clumsy as she did while she
prepared the noon meal that day. Yet at the same time,
she was aware of an ever-growing heat deep inside her,
a warmth caused not by embarrassment but by desire.
She despised her own weakness, her seeming inability
to keep her mind off carnal thoughts. But she could not
stop them. All she could do was ignore her impulses—
and she prayed she was up to doing that.

She finally had the repast ready, and they sat down
together to eat. Maggie looked at Reid, overwhelmingly
cognizant of the intimacy of their situation. He gazed
back at her, and a light flickered in his eyes. Quickly
Maggie dropped her gaze to her plate.

Despite her hard work this morning, she suddenly
didn't feel hungry at all. She picked at her food, glancing up surreptitiously at Reid now and then. He cut up
his food mechanically, but the dogged way he avoided
looking at her now was as pronounced as if he had
stared at her all the way through the dinner.

Neither of them could think of anything to say, and it was a relief when the meal ended. Yet, perversely, Maggie ached when Reid left, missing him already. Irritated with herself, she returned to her work upstairs and spent the rest of the afternoon in a frenzy of cleaning.

By the time she cooked the evening supper, she was exhausted and sweaty. Before she called Reid in to eat, she went back upstairs to her bedroom with a pot of hot water and stripped to wash away the dirt and sweat of her exertions. As she rubbed the damp washcloth over her breasts, her nipples stood up in response. Maggie looked down at the thrusting points, remembering how Reid's loving ministrations, with his hands and lips and tongue, had turned them into hot, hard buds. At the thought her nipples hardened even further, and a pulsing warmth began deep in her abdomen. Maggie bit her lower lip, her face flushing with a strange combination of embarrassment and passion. Was she such a wanton that she could think of nothing else? she wondered.

At supper she could not bring herself to meet Reid's eyes. When they finished eating, she carried their dishes to the counter, clenching her teeth to keep from asking him to stay with her. She forced herself not to look over her shoulder when she heard the scrape of his chair on the floor. He took a few steps, then hesitated. Maggie stood rigidly, hardly breathing, waiting. He had been walking toward her, she was sure. And she wanted him to come to her. Yet she prayed he would leave.

With a low curse, Reid strode out the door. Maggie let loose a long sigh and wilted against the counter.

He was gone, and that was best. Still, she wanted to cry.

Wearily she cleaned the kitchen, then sat down to mend some clothes. The heat was stifling, the stillness oppressive. All the doors and windows were open, and she could hear the buzz of insects and the croaks of tree frogs. The hypnotic, repetitive sounds should have made her drowsy, but she didn't feel the least bit sleepy. Rather, the night noises seemed to thrum along her nerves. She couldn't keep her mind on anything but Reid—and her empty bed upstairs. Finally she gave up any attempt to work and retreated to her room. She changed into her night rail and got into bed, but she couldn't sleep.

The night stretched on endlessly. Maggie tossed and turned. She arose several times and went to the window, sure it must be close to dawn. But still it was dark outside, moonless, the barn and trees slightly denser shapes in the blackness. She turned and padded back to her bed, fighting the urge to slip down the stairs and out to the barn as she had that one night. No one would know, she reminded herself. No one would care.

Except Maggie herself.

She could not live with herself if she gave in to her desire. Such yielding went against all her beliefs.

But neither could she live in any comfort *without* giving in to that same desire. Maggie buried her face in her pillow, muffling her groan. Why did it have to be so difficult?

The next day was much the same, the air full of tension between Maggie and Reid. No matter how hard Maggie worked, she was still unable to sleep when she went to bed that night. Then, in the middle of the night, she heard a noise. She lay still, listening. There was another sound downstairs, and she sat straight up in bed, her heart pounding.

She waited, clutching her bedcovers, every nerve alert. The stairs creaked, and she heard footsteps on the treads. It occurred to her that she should be frightened, that perhaps a burglar had broken into her house. But she didn't believe that. She knew it was Reid, pulled to her, unable to resist, just as she had been pulled to him that other night, desperate with passion.

A dark form filled the doorway, and whatever modicum of fear she had that it might be someone come to do her harm melted away. She knew the lines of Reid's body, the stance, the faint tilt of his head; in such a short time she had come to know him as well as herself.

He paused for a moment, then moved forward into the room. Maggie watched him, her mouth too dry to speak, her pulse thundering. He stopped at the end of the bed, resting his hands on the footboard, and looked at her. Maggie gazed back. Her hands let go of the covers, and they slid down her body to pool in her lap.

This time, she knew, it could not be written off as a mistake. This time they would have to face the consequences. They would have to face themselves. There was no more innocence, no more naivete.

Reid drew in a sharp breath, and in an instant he was around the bed and at her side. Maggie went up on her knees to meet him, her arms sliding around his neck. His body was hard and warm against hers; her body fitted against his naturally. Maggie felt as if she had come home. She let out a little sigh as his mouth claimed hers.

He kissed her again and again, murmuring her name. Maggie clung to him, returning his kisses with equal fervor. Their passion, suppressed for so many weeks now, soared, and they tumbled back upon the bed. Lost in desire, they rolled across the mattress, their hands roaming each other's bodies, their tongues and lips telling everything their hearts wished to. There was no time, no world, except this moment, this place, no reality except the hammering of their hearts and the sweet ache of their desire.

They made love with a wild, unrestrained eagerness, surging together to an explosion that rocked their very souls. For one blinding moment they were as one, locked together so tightly in mind, body, and heart that there was no telling where one left off and the other began.

Shaken by the glory of their lovemaking, they clung

to each other, arms and legs still entwined. They dozed and woke to make love again, this time with all the leisure and gentleness in the world. They explored and teased and pleasured. Reid caressed her breasts, kissing the nipples to hardness. Maggie smoothed her hands over him, tracing the curves of his musculature, and her lips trailed over his skin, tasting the faint saltiness of it. Slowly, lingeringly, they fed their desire until at last it burgeoned out of control, catching them up and flinging them into a wild maelstrom of rapture.

Afterward, they lay still, her head resting on his chest, his arm around her. There was no need to hurry this time, no place to go or anyone else to worry about; they had the night to themselves and could luxuriate in their sensual exhaustion.

"I love you," Reid murmured for the first time, kissing the top of her head as his fingers trailed lightly up and down her arm. "I've never known anyone who could do to me what you do. I want to be with you every minute, every day, for the rest of my life."

Maggie's breath caught in her throat. It was what she wanted, too. There were a million reasons it was impossible, but she refused to think beyond this moment. There would be ample time later for rationality and regret, for sorrow and despair. Now she simply turned her head and pressed her lips against his arm. "I love you, too. With all my heart."

Maggie awakened the next morning to see Reid propped up on one elbow, gazing down at her with a faint smile on his lips and abiding love in his eyes.

She smiled back. "What are you doing?"

"Watching you sleep."

She quirked an eyebrow. "Doesn't sound very exciting."

His smile turned sensual. "Exciting enough for me." He reached out and trailed a finger down her cheek.

Maggie's heart picked up a beat, sweet anticipation filling her. A time of reckoning would come, she knew. For once more she had fallen off the moral path, and she had only herself to blame. She had knowingly betrayed her husband. She might even be pregnant.

But stubbornly she turned her mind away from such thoughts. For a little while, at least, she wanted to enjoy her love; she wanted to grab whatever bit of happiness she could. So she tossed her hair back over her shoulder and grinned at him saucily.

"Is that right? You must lead a boring sort of life."

"If this is boring, that's the way I like it." He cupped her chin and skimmed his thumb across her lips. Teasingly Maggie caught it between her teeth. Reid sucked in his breath, his eyes darkening. "You, I can tell, prefer to live dangerously."

He bent and kissed her, and once again they were lost in the swirling mists of desire.

When at last they emerged from the bedroom, they made an attempt at a normal day. Reid milked the cow, which was lowing impatiently at the delay, and Maggie gathered the eggs and cooked breakfast. Then she pulled Ty's wagon into town to make his deliveries while Reid started his other chores. But when Maggie returned, she found it difficult to keep her mind on her tasks. She kept going to the window to look for Reid.

Before long, he returned to the house on the pretext of asking a question Maggie suspected he already knew the answer to. However, she was too happy to see him to point that out. Instead, she offered him a cup of coffee, and they sat for a while, chatting and looking at each other, their fingers interlaced on the tabletop.

Finally Reid said, "I don't want to leave you."

"I don't want you to."

He grinned. "Why don't we play hooky today?"

"From work?"

"From the world."

Maggie's smile was as broad as his. "It sounds wonderful."

"Good. Let's do it."

Maggie packed a picnic lunch, and they carried it down to the pond, where they sat beneath the shade of the willow and watched the sunlight sparkling on the water. They talked and fished and napped in the soporific heat of the afternoon. Later Maggie peeled off her shoes and stockings, hiked up her skirts, and waded into the water, laughing at the feeling of the cool mud squishing between her toes. She hadn't felt this young and carefree since she couldn't remember when, and it was wonderful.

Reid shucked off his shoes, rolled up his trouser legs, and followed her, and they splashed and played like children until the water soaked their clothes into clinging to bodies that showed how little they were still children. Then Reid scooped Maggie up in his arms and carried her back to the blanket beneath the willow, where they made love with sweet abandon.

For this one day it was easy enough to live for the moment, to pretend that no one and nothing existed except the two of them. When they ate supper at the table and afterward sat together on the back porch talking of planting a cash crop next spring, they seemed for all the world a married couple planning for their future.

In the velvet night, it was sweet and precious to make love and whisper promises, to dream of what might be.

Late in the night, as morning crept closer, Reid awakened and held Maggie close. She came to sleepily at the tightening of Reid's arms around her, and he kissed her hungrily, making love to her in a kind of silent desperation.

Afterward, his arms still tight around her, Reid said hoarsely, "We could go west, you know. To Texas, or even farther. Where nobody would know us. We could take Ty and Will and be a family. Live as husband and wife. I could sell my house in Savannah, so we'd have something to start with."

Maggie went perfectly still. For a moment a vision of the life Reid proposed shimmered in her mind. She would be Reid's wife; no one would know any different. Ty and Will would be happy. They could say that Will was her brother, and they could be a family.

She wanted it so badly she could have cried. She wanted to believe that it could happen, that it could be the way he described. She clung to him, kissing his chest. "We can't, Reid. You know we can't," she whispered, her voice clogged with tears. "Oh, God, what am I going to do? I love you so much."

Maggie knew that whatever they might dream now in the darkness, the light of day would chase it away. They could not take Ty and Will and flee. They could not escape their lives. And Maggie could not leave Pine Creek. This was her home, the place where her roots grew deep and strong. Here were her family, her friends. Away from here, she feared she would wither and die. And no matter how far away they ran, they could not escape themselves. They would know how wrong they were. No, these few nights of bliss could not become forever. Her conscience would never allow it.

"Then say you'll come." Reid's voice was tortured. "Please, Maggie. We could be happy. We could have a home together. Will wouldn't know; he'd be pleased."

"But *we* would know," Maggie answered. "We would know. I—I can't do it."

It wasn't the same after that. They dressed the next morning with heavy hearts, and whenever they looked at each other, there was pain in their eyes. They could not bear not to touch each other, not to link hands as they walked down the stairs or not to kiss as they parted to start their day's work. Neither talked about it. But both knew that their magical time together was over. Gideon would bring Ty and Will home tonight. And they would have to face their lives.

It was dark when the wagon came rumbling into the yard and Will and Ty tumbled out, full of excited chatter about their adventures in the big city. Gideon, clearly exhausted and rather grim-faced, didn't say much and left quickly. Maggie listened to Ty and Will, forcing herself to smile, but she didn't really hear a word they said, only a jumble of cheery noise surrounding the cold emptiness inside her. Finally Ty and Will wound down.

"Whew, I'm tired," Will admitted, giving a jaw-cracking yawn.

"Yes, it's time for you two to get into bed," Maggie agreed. She could not keep her eyes from sliding over to Reid.

He was as still as death, his eyes fixed on her face. Finally, he said prosaically. "You're right. Good night, Ty, Will." He glanced back to Maggie. "Good night, Maggie."

She nodded, too choked with tears to speak, and watched him turn and walk out the door. She hated herself, but in that moment, Maggie almost wished that she had never driven the wagon to the field hospital to bring Will home.

After they had washed up, Maggie tucked the boys into bed and gave them each a good-night peck. For the first time she could remember, she hesitated briefly before she bent and kissed Will's cheek. He didn't know, but her own heart was too laden with guilt for her to feel completely at ease with him. With tears staining her cheeks, she fled into her bedroom.

But everything in the room reminded her of the night before. She closed her eyes, and heat rose in her again, just remembering. She wanted to cry, to rage and scream like a two-year-old. But she simply sat down and stared out the window for a long, long time.

She was weary and leaden and aching with remorse.

It would rip her heart out to lose Reid. But she knew that she could not live this way any longer, so torn by her love, her desire, and her duty. She knew that there was only one thing for her to do, or she would be lost forever.

She had to tell Reid to leave the farm.

Reid ate his breakfast in terse silence the next morning, unable to look at Maggie. Immediately afterward he went back to the barn. Ty and Will followed him. Reid glanced over at them, wishing he could think of a tactful way to be rid of them this morning. Given the turmoil of his thoughts and feelings, he was in no mood for company. But he couldn't get mad at the two, he thought, looking at Ty's lively face and Will's open, innocent one. They weren't to blame for this mess, after all. He was.

"You should have gone with us to Little Rock," Ty was saying enthusiastically, the third time he had voiced that opinion. "You'd have liked it."

"Lots of people," Will put in. "And buildings!"

"You've never seen such big buildings!" Ty agreed. Then he paused judiciously and admitted, "Well, maybe you have, but I never did."

"I'm glad you had a good time." Reid smiled at them, his irritation subsiding.

"I liked it," Will announced. "But I like home better."

Ty didn't look quite as certain that he felt the same way, but he nodded. "Yeah. It's nice to be back. But I sure do hope we go again sometime soon."

Reid looked around the yard. "Tell you what, I don't have that many chores today. Soon as I finish, why don't we go down to the pond? We can do our lessons there, and afterward we can fish."

"That'd be terrific!" Ty piped. After his exciting trip,

a change of pace added zing to the otherwise mundane return to routine. "We can go swimming, too."

Will's face lit up. He enjoyed both swimming and fishing, and it pleased him to take part in the lessons.

They pitched in and helped Reid finish his chores, then took their books, fishing poles, and a basket lunch and headed for the pond.

Reid couldn't help thinking of the day before, when he and Maggie had gone to the pond. He glanced at Will, swept anew by guilt. He had come to like Will very much, even love him in a way. Yet there were times he almost hated the man for being the obstacle that lay between him and Maggie. And he hated himself just as much for feeling that way, after the deception and treachery he had engaged in.

When they reached the pond, Will settled down to fish, and Ty proudly produced a book of mathematics. Reid picked it up, surprised. "I haven't seen this before."

Ty nodded, grinning. "I know. Uncle Gideon bought it for me in Little Rock. He found it in a box of things at this place where he went to sell Aunt Tess's furniture. It's not new, but it's in good condition. See? Uncle Gideon thought it'd help."

"Oh, yes. It goes far beyond your old arithmetic book."

They settled down to study it, and they were soon engrossed.

Will sat patiently waiting for the fish to bite, but this morning they seemed more patient than he, and before long he grew bored. Glancing back at Ty and Reid, he sighed. It was obvious from their intent expressions that they would not be through anytime soon. He stood up and wandered around the edge of the pond, trying to skip stones across the water. Finally he decided to go for a swim, and he shucked off his clothes down to his underwear and waded into the pond.

He swam for several minutes before he spotted the

snowy white bird standing on a thick exposed root of a huge old oak that grew right at the water's edge, the soil long since eroded from beneath the aged tree.

He swam closer, moving as quietly as he could so as not to disturb the bird. The bird, perhaps sensing his presence anyway, hopped farther back on the tangle of roots. Will crept forward. Here, near the shore, he could stand upright and walk. Just as he edged around the outthrust roots of the tree for a better look, the ground suddenly disappeared from beneath his feet and, with a yelp, he dropped down into the murky water.

He flailed his arms in momentary panic and splashed back up to the surface. Submerged roots jabbed him and twisted around him, doubly frightening him, and just as he drew in a gulp of air and started to swim, something caught at his underclothes. He reached down to tug himself free, but it seemed as if the more he struggled, the more the roots tangled and snatched at him.

He panicked and screamed, kicking his legs frantically, and as he went under again, his ankle was wedged in the tangle of thick roots.

15

Ty and Reid looked up at Will's scream. Shielding his eyes against the sun, Reid saw the man struggling in the water. He jumped to his feet and raced toward the water, tore off his shoes, and dove in.

Ty stood frozen on the bank for a moment, then jerked off his shoes as Reid had done and jumped into the water after him.

Reid swam toward Will in strong, smooth strokes and reached him quickly. He grabbed the man around the chest and pulled him toward the surface. But Will, in his panic, flailed around, knocking Reid's arms loose and hitting him in the face. Reid persisted, but just as Will's head broke the surface and he grabbed a gulp of air, he came to a sudden halt, and Reid lost his grip on him. Reid grabbed him again and tugged, but Will's large body wouldn't budge, and his wild movements carried him back under.

By now Ty had reached them and had grabbed one of his father's arms to pull at him, too. Will clawed desperately at them, and his hand slapped against Ty's head, knocking him aside.

"Careful—he'll pull you under, too!" Reid shouted to Ty. "He's caught on something!" He pointed to indicate what he was doing and dove down into the murky water, made even dimmer by Will's churning.

Narrowly evading Will's kicking leg, Reid groped for the trapped leg. He found it and followed it to the clutch of roots where Will's foot was wedged. He tried to move the foot, but it wouldn't budge. Will's thrashings had grown weaker, and Reid knew that he was probably blacking out. If he didn't get him out of here soon, it would be too late. Desperately he put his heel against the roots and shoved with all his strength.

Will's foot slid free.

Lungs bursting, Reid shot to the surface, encircling Will's chest as he went. He drew in a gasp of air and turned to look at Will. The farmer was unconscious. Reid locked one arm under Will's chin to keep his head above water and began to tow him back to the bank. Ty swam ahead and scrambled onto the bank to help pull his father out of the pond.

With much tugging and pushing, the two of them managed to get Will's limp form onto firm ground. Reid sank down on his knees beside him and rolled Will over onto his stomach. He pressed down on the man's back until water dribbled out of Will's mouth. Will coughed, and more water came up. He struggled to breathe, coughing violently. Finally his eyes opened, and he looked around in confusion.

Ty sank back onto his heels, his pale face beginning to regain some of its color. "Thank God. He's all right."

Reid nodded and sat down, suddenly exhausted. Will coughed some more and slowly sat up. "Ty? Reid? I . . . I couldn't get loose."

"Your foot was caught in some submerged roots," Reid explained.

"Reid saved you," Ty informed him. "He got you free and pulled you to shore. He even started you breathing again."

Will turned to Reid and threw his arms around him. "Thank you! I was so scared!"

"I know." Reid hugged him and patted his back. "But it's all right now. You'll be fine." He smiled faintly. "Except, of course, for explaining to Maggie how we all got into this condition." He glanced ruefully down at his soaked, muddy clothes, then at Ty's.

Ty chuckled, and Will grinned proudly. "Not me. I took mine off first."

Reid ruffled his hair affectionately. "That's true." He smiled into Will's clear gray eyes. He wondered how something so sweet and gentle as Will's childlike gaze could make his heart feel as if it were breaking inside him.

"Come on, you two," he said. "We'd better get back."

Maggie was startled the next morning to step out onto the back porch and find Reid sitting on the bottom stair, his hands clasped around his knees, watching the sun come up in pink and pale gold behind the oak trees. The last time she had seen him had been early yesterday afternoon when he had brought Ty and Will home, all of them soaking wet, and explained how Will had almost drowned in the pond. Then he had left while she was fussing over Will and getting Ty into dry clothes. She had assumed that he had gone out to his room to change into dry things, too, and that he would return later, but he had not. He hadn't even come in for supper; she had sent Ty to the barn with a tray of food and told him to make sure Reid was feeling all right. Ty had come back and assured her that Reid was fine, that he was just tired from the events of the afternoon.

Maggie knew better. He was avoiding her. It was a

relief, actually, because otherwise she would have had to talk to him about leaving, and that was something she dreaded doing. Her whole heart and soul cried out against his leaving, no matter how necessary her mind knew it was.

"Reid?" she said now. "What are you doing here?"

He turned and looked up at her, then stood. He had his hat, and his bedroll lay on the ground beside him. "I was waiting for you."

Fear clutched at Maggie's heart. She knew what he was going to say, and she wanted somehow to stop it, even though she knew it was inevitable and right.

"I'm leaving," he told her bluntly.

Maggie said nothing, though her world rocked around her. She was expecting this, had even planned to initiate the conversation, but still the reality of it shook her to the core. She looked at him, her eyes big in her pale face.

Reid twisted his hat brim in his hands, looking down at it as his fingers worried it. "I . . . I spent most of yesterday afternoon and night thinking." He cleared his throat. "Yesterday, when Will was drowning and I jumped in after him, I did it instinctively—I didn't even think. But as I swam toward him, I realized: if I don't rescue him, he'll die, and then Maggie'll be free. I knew I could have you. All I had to do was let a man die."

He looked at her with agony in his eyes. "I was tempted, Maggie. I wanted to swim slowly, to not try too hard to save him. I wanted Will to die. I wanted to betray everything I ever believed in—because I want you so much."

Tears filled Maggie's eyes, and she clasped her hands together, aching inside for his pain. "Oh, Reid. Reid . . ."

"I was a doctor. I made a sacred vow to save lives. Nearly all my life that was what I wanted to do. Yet here I was, wishing a man would die, wanting to *let* him die."

"But you didn't," Maggie said quietly. "You saved Will. You brought him back."

He nodded. "I couldn't do it. I'd given up medicine, quit everything—my whole life—because I had lost all faith in myself. I had failed everyone who trusted me, those I was supposed to protect—my wife, my child, the soldiers. Why had they—a sweet, innocent little child! —died while I had been spared? The world and everything in it no longer made sense. I couldn't believe in anything—not me, not medicine, not God. That's why I began roaming—running, actually. But I couldn't ever get anywhere, because what I was running away from was myself." He paused, looking pained, then collected himself to forge ahead.

"Then I came here. I fell in love with you. And you, you gave me back myself. You taught me to love again, to believe in myself, to trust and want and *feel* again. Your love saved me." For a moment he almost smiled. But then he went on with grim determination. "But I couldn't be the man you loved, the man who loved you, and let another man die. I had to save Will, or I would have been the same dead, sorry wreck I've been for the past four years. Worse, even. So I pulled him out." Again he paused. "And when I realized that, I knew I had to leave."

"I—I know." Maggie's voice was low and choked. Tears streamed unheeded down her face, and she took his hands in her smaller ones, hugging them tightly to her chest. She didn't think she had ever loved Reid more than she did right now. Now, when she was losing him. What bitter irony that the courage and honor that made her heart swell with pride and love for him were exactly the qualities that would make him leave her!

"I can't stay," Reid went on, easing his hands free, his voice raw with emotion. "For a while I fooled myself into thinking I could. Thinking I could control my desire." He smiled bitterly. "Or that if I couldn't, I could deaden myself just enough to live with the deception." He frowned. "It wasn't possible. It was a contradiction in terms." He gazed into her eyes. "I wanted so badly to be around you. It tears my heart out to leave you, to think that I'll never see you again or hear you laugh or even listen to you calling Ty . . . and Will . . . home in the evenings." He paused, dragging a hand across his face. "Oh, God, Maggie . . ."

Then don't go! Maggie wanted to cry out. But she knew that she would not. Could not. Reid had to leave, no matter how much it hurt. And she had to be strong enough to let him go.

"I've tried living around you without touching you, and I can't," he went on. "We both know that. We've said before that we'd stay away from each other, but in the end, we can't. I can't look at you every day without wanting you. I can't live this close to you and not love you more and more, not want to be with you in every way. No matter how much I promised, no matter how hard I tried, I know that one day, sooner or later, I wouldn't be able to control myself anymore. I'd come to you again. I'd betray Will; I'd drag you into sin with me. I'd—I'd do anything, just to make love to you again. That's why I have to go. You know it as well as I do."

Maggie nodded reluctantly. She couldn't speak for the teariness tightening her throat. She felt as if she were being torn apart. If Reid stayed, there was nothing that would manage to keep them apart for long; they had already found that out. The desire, the love between them, was too strong.

She knew he was right. He had to leave. Yet it seemed horribly unfair, some sort of diabolical jest.

If he stayed, it would destroy him, so if she loved him, she had to let him go.

If he stayed, she would betray everything she believed in, everyone she had held dear all her life. She needed Reid's love so desperately, she knew that without him she would never feel whole again. Yet if she kept that love, she would lose her very soul.

"Good-bye," she whispered, all her love for him shining in her eyes. She longed to throw herself into his arms one last time, but she wasn't sure she would ever be able to let him go.

"Good-bye."

Maggie wished she could feel his lips against hers once more.

"I love you, Maggie. I always will."

"I love you, too." She took a step back, swiping the tears from her face and trying desperately to hold on to her fragile self-control. "You—you'll stay to say good-bye to Ty and Will, won't you? They'll miss you so much. I—"

"I'll talk to them." Tears shimmered in his eyes. "I wouldn't leave without saying good-bye to them. I—I love them, too."

Maggie drew a ragged breath, forcing herself to ask, for her son's sake, "Do you know where you're going? Ty would want to write—" She broke off, unable to continue.

"I'll write to him. I think I may head back to Savannah. At least for a while."

Maggie nodded. Summoning all her strength, she turned and started into the house.

"Maggie, wait!"

She whirled around, her eyes searching Reid's face as though trying to memorize every line of it.

"I can't go without holding you one last time," he said. "Please."

With a wordless cry, Maggie launched herself into his arms. Tears choked off any words she might have uttered. She could only cling to him and bury her face in his chest, breathing in the scent of him, wishing this moment could last for the rest of her life.

Reid's arms were tight around her, crushing her to him. He rubbed his cheek against her hair. A soft groan rose up from his throat. Almost roughly he put a hand beneath her chin and tilted her face up to him, bending to take her lips in one final kiss. Maggie felt the wetness of his tears upon her skin. A tiny sob escaped her; she trembled in his arms.

Reid raised his head, sucking in a breath. "Oh, God."

Maggie tore herself away from him and ran into the house. She ran up the stairs to her room, flinging the door closed behind her, and threw herself across the bed, sobbing.

Dimly, in the midst of her storm of tears, she heard Reid climb the stairs, no doubt to talk to Ty and Will. She heard him leave their room, too, and for an instant her heart leapt with the hope that he would come to her one last time. But he walked on down the stairs, and her tears burst forth anew.

She felt drained, empty of tears, empty of everything. She stood and walked to the mirror above her washstand. She had to take care of Will and Ty. They would be hurting, too, Ty most of all. Will would miss Reid, but Maggie thought that the sorrow would not last with him as it would with Ty. Maybe Will was lucky in that he could easily forget. When their dog, Blackie, had been killed, Will had cried off and on for a day or two, heartbroken, but within a week he no longer seemed to think about the animal. Ty, on the other hand, had silently carried the hurt with him for months and months, never weeping openly but secretly carrying flowers to the loyal mutt's little grave.

Ty had suffered so many losses. It would break his heart that Reid had left. At least for a while, Reid had become for Ty the father Will could never be. Maggie was riddled with guilt that it was because of her that Reid had gone and her son would be so unhappy. If only she had been a better person, none of this would have happened, and Ty would not have to face this misery.

Maggie drew a deep breath. Well, there was nothing she could do about that now. She had learned long ago that regrets were useless; one had to deal with what was at hand. The thing for her to do now was to help Ty and Will through their unhappiness over Reid's departure.

She grimaced at herself in the mirror. She looked a horror, she thought dispassionately. Her face was blotchy from crying, and her eyes were swollen. Bits of hair had come loose and were straggling down around her face. At the moment, she didn't really care how she looked, but she knew it would disturb Ty and Will to see her this way. For their sake, she had to put on as good a front as she possibly could. She had to be the rock she had always been. She had to put aside her own feelings and carry on.

Maggie wet a cloth with cool water and daubed her face and burning eyes. Then she smoothed back her hair and repinned the stray strands into place. She examined her image in the mirror again. There. She didn't look wonderful, but at least she looked more herself.

She headed downstairs and automatically began her chores, going out to pick the eggs, then starting breakfast. She felt no hunger at all, but she knew that even sorrow wouldn't rob Ty of his appetite. Though her fingers went about their usual tasks, she felt heavy and sore inside, as though bruised from within, but as long as she kept busy, she managed not to think too much.

Before long, Will appeared in the doorway. He stood watching her until Maggie felt his gaze and turned. "Hello, Will."

She summoned up a smile, but he didn't smile back. He looked utterly woebegone. "I wish Reid were here."

Tear sprang into Maggie's eyes at his forlorn words, and it was all she could do not to burst out sobbing again.

"I know, honey," she said tightly, shoving down her own surge of despair and loss. She held out her arms, and he came into them, burying his face in her shoulder and crying.

"Why'd he leave?" he wailed.

Maggie didn't know how to answer him. She couldn't tell him the truth. "Didn't Reid explain it to you?" she hedged.

Will shrugged, stepping back and wiping his eyes with his fists. "Yes, but I don't understand. He said he had to go. He said he never stayed anyplace long."

"Some people are like that," Maggie told him gently. "Restless. They can't settle down. They need to travel a lot."

"I wouldn't like that."

"No, I'm sure you wouldn't. I wouldn't, either. I reckon we're both homebodies."

"But I thought Reid liked it here," Will went on doggedly. "Didn't he? Didn't he like us?"

"Yes, sweetheart. He did like it here, and he loves you and Ty."

"And you."

Maggie hesitated, not sure what to say.

"He'd have to love you, too," Will insisted.

"Yes, he . . . loved me, too. He didn't leave because he didn't like you or Ty or me. It was just . . . something he needed to do."

"Will he come back? Maybe he'll miss us and come back."

"I don't think so. He will miss us, I'm sure, but I don't think he'll be back."

Will's spate of queries subsided, and he turned away and sat down heavily at the table. Maggie turned her attention back to the stove, hoping he wouldn't raise the issue again.

Ty still had not shown up. Maggie went out onto the porch and, cupping her hands around her mouth, called him several times. Still he didn't appear.

Finally, she and Will ate without him. Fear nibbled at Maggie. She was sure that Ty was upset by Reid's departure. What if he had run off into the woods to be alone with his sorrow and had gotten lost? No, he knew the woods well, and he was old enough and clever enough that he could find his way back even if he did get a little off track. But what if he had taken it into his head to follow Reid? Between her worry over Ty and her grief over Reid, she could hardly choke down her food.

She was relieved when Ty finally came in a few hours later, looking tired and hungry, his eyes red from an obvious bout of tears. His mouth was turned down sullenly, and though he shot her a wary look, as though afraid she would take him to task for not showing up for breakfast, he gave no apology or explanation for his absence. Maggie didn't need one. She knew full well what had sent him off, and she could hardly get angry with him for being miserable.

Instead, she smiled sympathetically at him and heated a plate of food. He ate with a young boy's appetite, but he remained steadfastly silent. Maggie didn't try to talk or jolly him out of his mood. She knew his sorrow went too deep for that. He wasn't like Will, who could be petted and cajoled out of his disappointments.

But when he got up to carry his empty plate to the counter, she reached out and laid a hand on his shoulder. He turned and looked up at her, misery and confusion mingling on his face.

"Oh, sweetie . . ." She ached for her son. It wasn't fair that he should have to suffer because *she* had been unable to control herself. However unhappy she was, she at least knew that it was punishment for her own sin. But Ty was being punished, too. Guilt and shame burned inside her.

"Why did he have to go!" The words exploded from Ty, his voice sliding upward in a squeak of anger and frustration. "Why couldn't he stay?"

"I'm sorry, honey." Maggie slid her arm around his

shoulders and bent her head to rest her chin against his hair. "I'm so sorry. I wish there had been some other way."

"But why wasn't there?" Ty insisted. "Why couldn't Reid stay here?" He clung to her as he had when he was little. "I thought he liked it here! He acted like it. Didn't he seem happy?"

"Yes, he did. And I know he liked you very much. You and Will mustn't think that his leaving had anything to do with you. He just needed to leave, that's all. Didn't he explain that to you?"

"Yes." His voice turned sullen, and he pulled back, straightening his thin shoulders defensively. He faced his mother with an air of defiance. "But I don't believe him."

Maggie looked at her son in consternation. She should have known that Ty was too perceptive to believe Reid's story about his restlessness and need to wander. While that might have been true earlier on, it was obvious that Reid had found a home here. He *had* been happy. He *had* come to like the farm and to love Ty and Will . . . and her. Her throat tightened, and she couldn't speak.

Ty's eyes narrowed as he gazed at her. "You know why he left, don't you? Why won't you tell me?"

"Ty, I really . . ." Maggie floundered. She had never been good at lying, especially to someone she loved. Yet she couldn't tell him why Reid had really left. He was too young to know of such things. He would be shocked and horrified if he heard that his mother and the man he admired so much had committed adultery. She couldn't expect him to understand; he would be even more upset.

"It was because of you, wasn't it?" he asked shrewdly.

Maggie gasped, and her hand unconsciously flew to her throat. How could Ty possibly know?

"It *was* you!" Ty gaped at her, astounded. "But why . . . how . . . what did you do to make him leave?"

Maggie realized then that he didn't really know what had happened; he had only guessed that it had something to do with her. He didn't know about her infidelity, her sin. But her reaction to his words had clearly confirmed his suspicion that she had had something to do with it.

"Ty, you don't understand."

"No, I don't!" he shot back. "How could you make him leave? Why?"

"I didn't make him leave. He told me, just like he told you, that he was going. I didn't have anything to do—" But the words stuck in her throat. She *did* have something—everything—to do with Reid's departure.

"How could you?" Ty's gray eyes, so like her own, blazed, and it seemed almost as if it were Will himself gazing at her with rage, accusing her. "I liked him! He liked me! He was . . . he was . . . he understood. He talked to me."

"I do those things, don't I?" Maggie asked, pained.

"It's not the same!"

She knew it wasn't. Reid had become a father figure to Ty. Ty needed a man to talk to, to help him with the business of growing up. A mother could provide love and guidance but not that missing masculine quality.

"Oh, Ty . . ." she whispered, tears sparkling in her eyes. "I'm sorry."

"What did you do? What did you say to him? And why?"

"Ty, it was time for him to go. You don't understand it now. Maybe if you were older—"

"Why? Tell me why he left!"

Maggie looked at him in anguish. She couldn't lie to Ty; she had always made it her policy to tell him the truth, at least in a form he could understand. But this was one thing about which she could not tell him the truth. He was too young to hear about such things.

More than that, he was her son. She couldn't speak freely about a man and woman's desire to her own son. He would only despise her if he knew the truth, and Maggie could not bear that. "Sweetheart, this time you'll just have to trust me. It was for the best."

"Better for who?" Ty asked scornfully.

"For all of us. For Will and you . . ."

"Will and me! You didn't consider Will and me at all, or you never would have sent him away. We loved him! Reid was nice to Will, nicer than anybody, even Uncle Gideon! And he taught me things! He—he told me I was so smart, I ought to study at a college when I grew up. He told me about William and Mary and how he went there and—"

Ty broke off, his voice cracking, and he dashed away his tears with the back of his hand. He swallowed. "You didn't think about Will and me at all," he repeated in a low voice. For the first time Maggie could remember, her son looked at her with eyes as hard as stones. "I'll never forgive you for sending him away. Never!"

He turned and stalked out of the house.

"Ty!" Maggie cried, but he did not stop or turn around.

Maggie stood still for a moment, gazing at the empty doorway, her heart leaden within her. Then she sat down heavily at the table and put her head down on her arms, and, for the second time that day, she cried her heart out.

16

Tess *was in* a turmoil after they returned from Little Rock. When Gideon had stormed out, she had run up to her room and thrown herself across her bed, flinging an arm across her eyes to shut out the world, her heart racing, her insides trembling from his kiss. She had never experienced anything like it, not even with Shelby. She felt as if she had been turned inside out. She was hot and waxen inside, and she pressed her legs together tightly to stop the ache there.

She would have given anything if Gideon had stayed. She longed to run after him and beg him to come back and make love to her. But that was the thing—was it love? Or was what she felt only lust?

It seemed insane. How could she be in love with Gideon—after all these years? He was her brother-in-law; it seemed almost wicked. And yet . . . Tess thought about Gideon, seeing his face in her mind: the absurdly thick lashes, the straight nose, the serious blue eyes. Her lips curled up into a smile, her heart warmed within her chest, and she felt as if she might swell up with so much joy that surely she would explode. Of course she loved Gideon! The only thing odd about it was how long it had taken her to recognize it.

She thought of how much she looked forward to Gideon's visits, how much she enjoyed talking to him or just spending time with him, how much she relied on his help and opinions. Tess felt as if she were looking at the world like a blind person suddenly given the gift of sight. Why had she never realized before how very dear to her Gideon was?

Lying on her bed and thinking about Gideon, Tess could hardly stop grinning. She thought of each little endearing thing he did, remembered every aspect of his looks, the way he talked, the things he said. She didn't know when or how it had happened, but somehow she was head-over-heels in love with him.

The only problem was . . . did he love her?

In the days and weeks that followed, that problem rolled over and over in her mind. Sometimes it seemed obvious that he must love her. Why else would he have kissed her with such fervor? She remembered the thudding of his heart through his jacket, the heat of his skin, the hungry way his mouth had claimed hers. It had been the way Shelby had kissed her, except that there was more desperation to Gideon's kiss, a wilder sort of hunger.

But that could be simply desire, and Tess was worldly enough to know that, particularly for a man, love and desire were not invariably one and the same. Gideon liked her, she knew; he had always been kind and helpful to her. But that wasn't necessarily love, either. There had been none of the flowery sentiments or sentimental flowers Shelby had wooed her with. Gideon had never held her hand and kissed it lingeringly or murmured that he could barely live from day to day when he didn't see her, that he thirsted for the sight of her the way a man in the desert thirsted for water.

And yet . . . that kiss! That had held more yearning for her than a thousand well-said words. Gideon wasn't like Shelby. He was a quiet man, one who did things rather than saying them. And his feelings ran deep and strong and true. There was no flightiness or changeability in him. How could a man like Gideon hold her like that, kiss her that way, and not love her?

But if Gideon loved her, why didn't he express it? He had never said anything to her to even hint at such feelings. He might be quiet, but he wasn't mute. He was seldom unwilling to state his opinions or beliefs. Why would he be reluctant to tell a woman that he loved her?

Tess wondered if possibly he, like she, had been unaware of his feelings until their trip together. But if so, wouldn't he be back at her house the first chance he got, telling her how much he loved her? Tess felt as if she could scream it from the rooftops.

But Gideon did not come visit her. In fact, he avoided her. The first Sunday after the trip, Tess rode out to the Tyrrell farm with Maggie, hardly able to sit still in anticipation of seeing Gideon again. But when they arrived, Jo told them that Gideon had gone home with the Johnsons from the small country church she and Gideon attended to help them build a lean-to behind the house. Tess's heart had fallen down to her feet, and it had been all she could do to keep the tears out of her eyes.

She was certain then that Gideon did not love her. If he did, he would have been eagerly awaiting her visit. Instead he had run from her, using an excuse that anybody could see was flimsy. No doubt he regretted their impulsive kiss and did not want to have to face her expectations of his love.

It took all her self-control to get through the afternoon, trying to smile and make small talk until Maggie was ready to leave. When she finally reached her house, she ran to the privacy of her room and cried.

After that, she told herself to forget about Gideon,

that there would never be anything between them. But it was hard not to hope. Time and again she would think that maybe he hadn't meant to avoid her on Sunday. Maybe he had just been overwhelmed with shyness or something. Maybe he was nervous. Or maybe the Johnson man had been very insistent, and Gideon had owed him a favor. She wavered back and forth, telling herself that she was being foolish to hope, yet unable to completely repress that hope.

The following Sunday, she was relieved to see that Gideon had remained at home. Her heart seemed to leap in her chest at the sight of him, and she had trouble keeping her lips from breaking into a silly grin. However, her rising spirits were quickly dashed when Gideon studiously avoided her as much as he could the remainder of the afternoon. He almost never looked in her direction, and when he did, he didn't meet her eyes. He spoke to her only when he had to. After the meal was over, he escaped to the barn.

Tess could do nothing but grimly survive the afternoon. Only a short time before they were about to leave, Gideon came up to the porch where she was sitting. Tess looked up hopefully, unable to keep her heart from starting to pound in anticipation. He didn't look at her, but rather at the floor. He cleared his throat.

Finally he said, "I—I wanted to make it clear about —about what happened the other day. At your house."

Tess waited. She could think of nothing to say. She just wished the moment was over.

"I'm sorry. I wanted you to know that. It was wrong, I know, and it won't happen again. That's a promise."

Tess felt as if her heart were cracking right down the middle. There was no hope for her at all. Gideon thought that their kiss had been wrong, and he regretted it. That meant that he did not feel any love for her. Why else would he call it wrong, unless he knew that he desired her but did not love her? He had felt only lust for her. She couldn't pretend otherwise.

"It's . . . it's all right," she responded in a low voice, fighting back tears.

"No, it's not. What happened was—well, it shouldn't have happened. It was entirely my fault, and I apologize."

That was so like Gideon, to shoulder the responsibility. He was far too kind to place the blame at her doorstep, even though she had kissed him with equal fervor. But ladies were supposed to be higher-minded than men, to be able to restrain their passion better, and Gideon was graciously allowing her that pretense.

Tess shook her head, not looking at him, unable to speak without bursting into tears. Gideon stood there for a moment longer, then moved quickly off the porch and back toward the barn.

After she got home that afternoon, Tess sat for a long time in the upstairs parlor, staring out the window. She had never felt so low. At last she had fallen in love again, and with a wonderful man. But he didn't love her back. She was on the verge of losing her home. And she didn't even know where she could go after that. Where would she and her mother and Ginny live? Her aunt would take in Amanda, but there wasn't room enough in the woman's small house for all three of them. Jo, of course, would tell them to come live with her and Gideon on the farm. Once she would have been able to, although it would have been hard to accept even their charity. But she could hardly live in the same house with Gideon now, given the way she felt about him.

She had nowhere to go. Yet she could not let Gideon sell part of his farm to help her keep her house. He loved that farm like a part of himself. She simply could not let him make that sacrifice. But how was she to find the money?

Tess rested her head in her hands wearily. She had

thought and cried and prayed about this until she was at her wits' end. She didn't know what to do.

"Mama?"

Tess glanced up at her daughter's loud whisper. Ginny was standing in the doorway with an odd look on her face. "Mama, there's a lady here to see you. A fancy lady."

"A fancy lady?" Tess was puzzled. She couldn't imagine who it could be. She stood up and followed her daughter downstairs. When she reached the bottom of the curving staircase, she came to a dead halt. Linette Conway was standing in the entry hall.

"Linette!"

Linette, who had been looking back out through one of the glass insets by the door, turned. "Hello, Tess."

She looked elegantly lovely, as usual, making Tess very conscious of her own faded green dress. Once she wouldn't have dreamed of wearing a dress this old; now it was her Sunday best.

"I—I— Won't you come in?" She showed Linette into the sitting room, her mind racing frantically to think of what she could serve as refreshments. "Would you like something to drink? Or eat?"

"No, thank you. I can't stay long."

The two women sat down, facing each other. There was a long silence. Finally, Linette said, "I'm sure you must be wondering why I'm here."

"Well, I . . ." Tess didn't know what to say.

Linette squared her shoulders, as if about to perform a difficult but necessary duty. "I know how you must feel about me, because of my marrying Benton."

"I never understood it," Tess admitted.

Linette's smile was thin and bitter. "Perhaps there's nothing to understand. Sometimes people . . . do foolish things. But that's far beside the point now. I came because, well, I just couldn't bear to have you think any worse of me than you already do. I didn't want you to think that I didn't try. I asked Benton not to take your house away from you. I begged and pleaded, but—" She sighed and looked away. "It didn't do any good. Benton was adamant. He wants this house." Linette's eyes glittered, and for an instant Tess wondered if there were actually tears there.

"You asked Benton to . . ."

"Of course. Did you really think that I wouldn't?"

For the first time, Tess noticed that there were faint lines around her old friend's lush mouth, giving her an almost weary look.

"Your opinion of me is even lower than I thought," Linette continued. "I asked him that evening after Gideon told me what he was doing."

Tess stared at her. "What did you say? Gideon told you?"

Linette looked a little puzzled. "Yes. He came to my house and told me what Benton was up to. He asked me to help you."

"He—he asked you to help me?" Tess realized that she sounded foolishly like a parrot, but she was too stunned to say anything else. She had never dreamed that Gideon would go to Linette for help on her behalf. The Tyrrells were all enormously proud, and their dislike of Linette Sanders Conway was well known. Tess could hardly believe that he had swallowed his pride like that for her sake. Suddenly she felt like crying, and her heart swelled with warmth and tenderness. Why would Gideon have done that for her if he didn't love her?

"Yes. Didn't you know?"

Tess shook her head.

Linette grimaced. "That shouldn't surprise me, I suppose, knowing Gideon."

Tess looked at Linette. She was still flooded with tenderness by Gideon's gesture, and she was touched by Linette's concern. It was almost as if they were close friends again. "Linette, I don't know what to do," she said in a low, urgent voice. "Gideon plans to sell off part of the farm in order to pay my taxes. I can't let him do that! He's already done so much for me, and I just can't let him make that sacrifice. It won't be just this year, either. I'll have to pay the taxes again next year, and what will I do then?"

"I don't know." Linette lowered her head, seemingly unable to meet her old friend's eyes. "I'm sorry."

It was hard to believe that a woman as lovely as Linette wouldn't be able to influence her husband. However, since Benton wanted to take Tess herself as a mistress, perhaps he was no longer interested in his wife. In fact, he had seemed to take perverse delight in choosing a mistress who would be most hurtful to Linette.

"I have a little money saved," Linette said suddenly. "I don't know if it would be enough to help, but you're welcome to it. And Rosemary has a little, too—I'm sure she would lend me some if I asked her."

"Rosemary would help somebody thwart her own father?" Tess looked doubtful.

"She's a sweet girl. She wouldn't want to go against her father, but if I asked her for help, she'd do it. She's quite kind."

Tess sighed and looked down at the carpet. "I could give up the house if I had to. It would hurt; I love it. But I could do it, I think. But somehow I just can't bear for *him* to have it."

She glanced up guiltily, realizing what she had just said. Linette was, after all, Benton's wife. "Oh, Lord, I'm sorry. I didn't think."

"There's no need to apologize. I have few illusions about my husband."

"I can't let Gideon sacrifice his land, and, no matter how grateful I am for your offer, I can't take money from you and Rosemary. Yet I have to take care of Mama and Ginny." Tess groaned. "I don't know what to do."

Linette gazed at Tess thoughtfully. "Tess . . . I just

thought of something my uncle once did. It might just work. It would mean having to give up ownership of your house, but it would keep Benton from getting it, and you and your family could still live in it."

Tess blinked. "Are you serious?"

Linette nodded, her usually cool face tinged with excitement. "Well? Would you be willing to give up ownership of it if it meant you and your family could stay here, Gideon could keep his farm, and Benton would have his hands tied?"

Linette's enthusiasm was contagious. Tess nodded her head resolutely. "Yes," she said firmly. "I'd do it."

Linette grinned. "All right. Now, listen . . ."

Tess walked slowly down the stairs. She had dressed carefully for the Ladies Guild meeting this morning, wearing the very best gown she had, one she usually didn't wear even to church, and putting on the pearl earrings Shelby had given her when they married. Gideon had insisted she keep them back from the sale.

She paused in the parlor doorway. Her mother was sitting in the once-elegant green velvet chair, her feet on the small matching footstool. She looked up at her daughter's approach, and Tess saw tears glitter in her eyes.

"Oh, Mama . . ." Tess went to her and knelt beside her chair, reaching out to hug her. "I'm sorry."

Amanda sighed. "Your father was so proud when he brought me here. He carried me over the doorstep just as if I were a bride again."

Tess nodded. "I remember." She had been only seven, but the occasion had been such a joyous, exciting one that it was imprinted forever on her memory. "He loved you very much."

It had taken some doing to get her mother to agree to Linette's plan, and there had been moments when Tess had been hard put to hold on to her patience and explain again how they would lose their home entirely if they did not do this. Tess thought that the thing that had finally convinced her mother was the fact that it was Benton Conway who would otherwise take their house from them. Amanda had sighed and said at last that she would do anything to keep her beloved house from "falling into *that* man's hands." However, even after her mother had agreed, Tess hadn't felt easy about it until they had actually signed the deed.

"Would you like to go with me to the Ladies Guild meeting?" Tess asked.

"Oh, no." Amanda shook her head decisively. "It would be too humiliating." She rose from her chair, her handkerchief raised to her eyes, and hurried out of the room.

Tess sighed and stood up. She wasn't sure whether her mother would ever really accept what she was about to do. She glanced around the parlor. It was hard enough for Tess to accept it herself. It seemed as though everywhere she looked the past few weeks, she had seen some precious memory. It would be so sad to see this room changed. Still, they would be able to keep their home, and that was what mattered.

Slowly Tess trailed through the downstairs rooms, looking them over one last time. She opened the sliding pocket doors between the front and back parlors, remembering how they would pull them wide for a party, clearing out most of the furniture, leaving only a few chairs against the wall for the older ladies to sit and watch the dancing. They would roll up the heavy oriental rugs, now long since sold, and stash them away in the sitting room, and then they would dance for hours on the gleaming wood floors.

She could remember the first time she'd seen Shelby here. Or, rather, the first time she'd seen him with her skirts let down and her hair put up, old enough at last for him to notice her. She had idolized him for years, a giggling little girl far too young for him to heed. But then there had been that dance when she was sixteen, and she had swept down the stairs and across the hallway, pausing for a moment in the doorway as her mother had taught her, so as to attract the eyes of everyone inside. The ploy had worked. Shelby, who had been lounging against the mantel talking to Tommy Self, had turned, and his eyes had widened with astonishment.

Tess giggled to herself even now, remembering the faintly dazed expression on Shelby's face. She closed her eyes, seeing him walk across the floor toward her and bow elegantly in front of her. "Miss Caldwell?" he had said in that lazy, husky way he had of talking. "I had to come over and meet my future wife."

Tears welled up inside Tess. Oh, how could she give away this house and all its precious memories! It was too difficult to bear. She hated Benton Conway for forcing her to this. Her hands curled up into fists at her sides.

"Tess?"

Gideon's deep voice startled her out of her reverie. Her eyes flew open, and she whirled around. He was standing in the open front door, looking at her sympathetically.

"Gideon!" Suddenly everything seemed a little easier, just because he was here. "What are you doing here?"

"I figured you could use a friend when you went to the meeting today."

"Thank you." Tears filled Tess's eyes, but her smile was dazzling. Gideon was the dearest man in the world. He was a good, true friend to her, coming to help her through this ordeal even though things had been so awkward between them lately. She felt petty for wishing that he loved her. His friendship was far more than what many people had; she should be grateful for it and not wish for more.

"You're still willing to go through with it?"

Tess nodded. "Yes. I was just remembering things, that's all."

Gideon glanced into the parlor. "Like that party the night Shelby fell in love with you?"

Tess looked at him, astonished. "You mean my six-teenth birthday party? Were you there?"

Gideon smiled wryly. "Yes, along with about a hundred other people. It's just that Shelby's the only one you saw that night."

Tess chuckled. "I guess that's true."

He gestured toward the music room on the other side of the hall. "And that's where Mary Sue McHenry spilled punch all over her skirt at your engagement party."

"Oh, my Heavens, you're right! I'd forgotten about that." Tess laughed. "I was so mad at her, making such a commotion right when Papa was making the announcement!"

She glanced around again, sobering. "It will never be the same again."

"Nothing ever is."

Tess nodded. "I guess you're right about that." She sighed, then straightened and put on a smile. "All right. We might as well go. I don't imagine it'll get any easier."

Gideon thrust out his elbow in a courtly manner and with his other hand made a sweeping gesture toward the front door. "Mrs. Tyrrell? May I escort you to your carriage?"

Tess looked out the door to the street, where Gideon's heavy farm wagon was waiting. "Why, thank you, kind sir," she returned, dimpling. "I would be most honored."

The Ladies Guild meeting was being held at Rosemary Conway's house. To Tess it seemed like a sign that fate was on her side. It was a fitting place for her announcement, a way of throwing her answer defiantly in Conway's face.

Gideon escorted Tess up the steps of the mansion and in through the front door, but he stopped at the parlor filled with women. All the ladies turned to look, their faces curious.

"Why, Tess!" Mariana Hill, seated at the front of the room facing the others, stood up, smiling. "How nice to see you. Do come in." Her eyes flickered to Gideon looming in the doorway, but with well-bred restraint, she made no remark. "Have you come to sit in on a meeting of the Guild, Tess?"

"No, but I'd like to say something to the club if I may." Tess's voice trembled slightly, but she kept her chin up firmly.

Gideon, watching her, thought that she had never looked so much the lady as she did right now, pale and brave, and his heart swelled with pride in her. He wondered what Shelby would think if he could see her now. The girl his brother had fallen in love with had grown into a full, strong woman.

Light footsteps sounded in the hallway, and Gideon glanced over to see Linette Conway approaching. She came to a stop beside him and looked into the parlor. A faint smile played on her lips as she watched Tess walk to the front of the room.

Tess reached Mrs. Hill and spoke to her in a low voice. The other woman listened, her eyes growing big with amazement. Then a smile burst across her face, and she nodded eagerly at Tess.

"Ladies, ladies. I am giving Mrs. Tyrrell the floor. I know it's rather unorthodox, but when you hear what she has to say, I'm sure you'll agree with me that it's well worth breaking a few little rules."

She stepped back, beaming, and Tess turned to face the women. "I'm sure most of you know my family's home. You also probably know that it's rather large for just the three of us women to rattle around in. Mama and I decided that we wanted to do something for our community, and therefore we decided to help in a project I know you ladies are interested in."

"Tyrrell!"

A man's voice sounded behind him, and Gideon turned and saw Benton Conway standing on the stairs, glowering at him.

The man came down the last few steps and strode toward Gideon. "What the devil are you doing in my house? Linette, what's the meaning of this?"

Linette shrugged, stepping back a little to give her husband room to stand in the doorway beside them. Gideon brought a finger to his lips in a silencing gesture, nodding toward the parlor, where the roomful of women sat listening attentively to Tess. Conway followed his gaze and abruptly stopped blustering.

"What's going on, Tyrrell?" he asked in a stage whisper, frowning suspiciously. "Why are you here at the Ladies Guild meeting?"

"I brought Mrs. Tyrrell." Gideon watched him, arms folded, as Conway glared toward the front of the room, where Tess was addressing the assembled women.

"What's she doing?"

Gideon smiled faintly. "Why don't you just listen? I'm sure you'll find it interesting."

Gideon turned his attention back to Tess, and beside him Conway fell silent. He cast a puzzled, angry glance toward his wife, then turned back to look at the slender figure at the front of the room.

"Mrs. Hill." Tess handed a document to the meeting chairwoman, who smiled broadly. Tess glanced toward the back of the room, knowing that Gideon's support would give her strength. She saw Benton Conway standing right beside him, and she nearly faltered for a moment. But then she met Gideon's warm, steady gaze. Her spine straightened, and she spoke in a loud, clear voice. "Mrs. Hill. Miss Conway. Ladies of the Guild. I know that a town library is a very special project to all of you. Rosemary Conway in particular has made heroic efforts toward that goal."

Rosemary blushed, looking puzzled but fascinated.

"This is the deed to the Caldwell house on Main Street," Tess went on. "My mother and I are donating it to the Ladies Guild, to be used as the future home of this town's first library."

A gasp went up around the room, and the women burst into delighted chatter.

Rosemary let out a cry and jumped to her feet. "Truly? Oh, Mrs. Tyrrell, how can we ever thank you?"

Gideon cut a glance toward Benton. The man stood motionless, his pale eyes fixed on Tess, and the cold fire flaring in them was frightening.

He turned to Gideon, not bothering to mask his hatred. "Damn you! You're the one who put her up to this, aren't you?"

Gideon grinned, enjoying Conway's frustrated, helpless wrath. "Actually, I'm afraid not. Personally, I was more in favor of using physical persuasion to change your mind."

Conway's mouth twisted. "No doubt Mrs. Tyrrell thinks she's quite clever, thwarting me. But I promise you, she'll live to regret what she did today."

He turned and stalked away.

Smiling with wry contempt, Gideon watched him go. Then he turned back toward Tess. She looked across the room at him and smiled triumphantly.

17

Grief engulfed Maggie. She had never imagined what a hole Reid's departure would leave in her life. He had been with them only a few months, but in that time he had become precious to her. The depth of her love and consequent sorrow surprised, even horrified, her. How could she possibly live the rest of her life with this pain inside her? What if it never went away? In the past, if anyone had asked her, she would have said that she could bear anything, but now she was not so sure. She didn't think she could bear a lifetime of missing Reid.

She struggled to get through the days, holding on to the hope that someday, somehow, it would get better, that she would be happy once more, that she would eventually cease to think of Reid, cease to miss him. But thwarting that hope was the knowledge that each day she seemed to miss him more, not less.

To make matters worse, Ty had not forgiven her for what he thought of as her dismissal of the man for whom he cared so much. Maggie could not think of any satisfactory way to explain to him why Reid had had to leave. All she could do was pray that with time he would let down his guard. As it was, there was a strain between them that had never been there before, and it pricked at her constantly.

She worried, too, that she might have gotten pregnant, and with each day that passed, her worry increased, for she did not start her next monthly period. At the prospect Maggie swung between abject fear and odd exhilaration. Having an illegitimate child would mean certain ostracism by the town, and she dreaded the shame that would fall on her family. Yet the thought of having Reid's child to love, since she would never again have him, was wildly sweet. Then, unexpectedly, almost a month late, her flow started. She hid in her room and sobbed, uncertain whether she wept tears of sorrow or relief.

Autumn came. The mornings were nippy, the afternoons mellow and sweet. The leaves began to turn, flooding the countryside with yellow and orange, the rich amber of sweetgum, the blazing scarlet of sourwood and blackgum trees. Maggie had always thought this wonderful cool weather a magical time before winter got its grip on the world; as a child she had thought that if she awoke early enough she would see fairies dancing among the crystals of frost on the grass.

This was the time for juicy apples, crisp and sweet, for filling up the root cellar with potatoes and onions and pumpkins. It was the time to go gathering nuts, shaking the pecan trees to release their bounty, the anticipation of the holidays already hovering in the air.

This year, however, Maggie didn't feel the joy, didn't see the beauty. She merely tried to put on a good show for the boys' sake.

In October, Ty received a letter. When Maggie picked up the envelope at the post office and saw the dark scrawl across the front, her eyes flew to the return address on the back. When she saw the name *Reid Pres-*

cott, her unruly heart felt as if it were breaking all over again.

Still, she was pleased for her son. She handed the missive over to Ty and watched his face light up.

Although she knew that any contact between her and Reid would only prolong their love and agony, Maggie had half hoped that Ty would read the letter out loud. He did not. He went out to the wagon and sat down in the back with Will, reading intently. As she drove home, she could hear Ty and Will talking, but over the jangle of the harness and the rumble of the wheels she could not make out the words.

When they stopped in the drive, she swallowed her pride and asked Ty what Reid had said.

Ty looked at her scornfully. "What do you care? You're the one who sent him away."

Maggie's eyes flashed. "Ty, I will not have you taking that tone of voice with me."

Ty set his mouth mulishly and crossed his arms, looking at the ground. Will looked anxiously back and forth between them. He hated it when Ty and Maggie quarreled, and the last few weeks, he had been frequently upset by the palpable tension between them.

"You don't have to tell me what Reid said. I won't pry into your private letters. But you *will* show me the proper respect. Do you understand?" Maggie continued.

"Yes, ma'am." Ty replied sullenly and went into the house.

Maggie sighed. Will came over to help her unharness the mule. "Ty told me Reid's gone to Sa—uh—" His brow wrinkled in concentration.

"Savannah?" Maggie suggested.

"Yes." Will's face cleared. "That's right. He said he's . . . cleaning his house."

"Is he? That's good." Tears sparkled in Maggie's eyes as she reached out and patted Will's arm. "Thank you, sweetheart."

"That's all I can remember," Will said, looking woebegone.

"Don't worry. That's all I wanted to know. It was nice of Reid to write, don't you think?"

Will nodded. "I wish he'd come back."

Maggie blinked back her tears. "So do I, honey," she said in a broken voice. "So do I."

That evening Maggie saw Ty bent over the kitchen table, scratching away on a piece of paper, and she was sure he was answering Reid's letter. He wrote frequently over the next few weeks, and Reid responded every week. Maggie often heard Ty telling Will something Reid had said, and she blessed Reid for remembering them both. She wished with all her heart that she would get a few lines from him, but she knew it was better this way. Any contact would only encourage her wayward heart in loving him. Still, she couldn't help but begin to wonder bleakly if Reid had already ceased to love her.

The year ground on toward Christmas. Maggie could work up no enthusiasm for the holiday, but she had to try for the boys' sake. She cracked the nuts the two brought home and set them aside for fruit cakes and other holiday dishes she would make. In her spare time, she worked on presents for her family. At least, she thought, all the work left her little time to think about Reid.

As always, Maggie and Tess and the children drove out to the Tyrrell farm each Sunday for dinner. Maggie found the weekly meal more and more trying. Her mother looked at her each time with worry knitting her brow and asked seemingly endless questions about her health and state of mind. Maggie knew she had lost weight and often looked tired and sad, and she had tried her best to put on a more cheerful face, to pretend that nothing was wrong. But Jo Tyrrell was no fool, and she didn't believe Maggie's assurances.

Maggie hated lying to her mother, but she could not possibly tell her the truth about Reid's departure and her subsequent grief. Josephine Tyrrell was a woman of strong moral principles. She would be shocked and disapproving—worse than that, disappointed—in Maggie if she knew of her sin. All of them would be—Gideon and Tess, too. Maggie didn't think that she could bear that, not the way she felt right now.

"Maggie, are you feeling all right?" Tess asked one Sunday a couple of weeks before Christmas as the wagon rumbled down the rough road, rutted by fall rains, to the Tyrrell farm.

Maggie managed to summon up a smile. "Why, of course I am."

"You've just seemed—oh, I don't know, awfully tired and sort of low for weeks. Longer than that, even. For months."

"Getting ready for Christmas is tiring. You know that. I'm just about worn out from making fruitcakes and gifts and all that. Aren't you?"

Tess shrugged. "Somewhat. But it's different with you. Something's the matter—I know it is."

"Now, what could be the matter with me?" Maggie tried a light laugh.

"I don't know. That's why I'm asking," Tess said seriously. She cast a cautious glance back toward Will and the children. Satisfied that they were happily talking and laughing out of earshot at the other end of the wagon, she went on. "You haven't seemed yourself for a long time. Ever since your hired hand left."

Maggie glanced sharply at her sister-in-law. Tess looked only concerned. She would have loved to pour out her troubles into Tess's sympathetic ear, to tell her all about Reid and her love for him and her loneliness and sorrow since he'd left. Tess was a good friend, and a widow, too; if anyone would know the ache of losing a lover, she would.

But something always held her back. She felt too ashamed of herself, too scared of what Tess would think of her. She would hate to see disgust or horror in her friend's eyes. After all, Tess had been a widow for years; unlike Maggie, she was free to love another man, yet she had remained alone, her loyalty to Shelby too strong for her to fall in love again. Wouldn't she scorn Maggie's unfaithfulness, consider her weak and immoral, unworthy of her friendship? Tess had never seemed particularly judgmental of other's mistakes, but then, Maggie had never seen her react to as monumental a sin as hers before.

"I—really, there's nothing the matter with me," Maggie said in her brightest voice. "Let's talk about something more interesting. How's the library coming?"

"Fine. They want to have some kind of party to celebrate its opening next month." Tess's eyes were still shadowed with concern, but she followed Maggie's change of topic without protest. "They're moving the furniture out of the front parlor and the music room and putting in bookshelves. Rosemary plans to turn the study into the library office. You know, I've seen a lot of her recently; she's a very nice girl. I like her."

"Yes. It's hard to believe she's Benton's daughter."

Tess nodded. "Isn't that the truth? She's pleasant and intelligent and hardworking. Unfortunately, she's so shy, it's hard for people to get to know her."

Maggie turned the wagon into the drive leading to the farmhouse. Both women fell silent for a moment. Then Tess drew a breath and said quickly, "I have to try again before we get to the house. Please, Maggie, I want to help you if there's anything wrong. Wouldn't you feel better if you talked about it? I remember how I kept it quiet about Conway and his threats, and it made me feel all the worse."

Maggie looked at her. She wanted to talk to Tess about Reid; she ached to. Yet the words stuck in her throat. Finally she just shook her head silently.

Tess sighed. "All right. I don't mean to stick my nose in where it doesn't belong." She paused. "But if you ever want to talk . . ."

"I know." Maggie managed a smile and a nod.

They pulled up in front of the house and got out. Gideon and Jo came hurrying out to greet them, and they all hustled inside, the warm, cozy house making them freshly aware of how cold it was outside.

It should have been a normal Sunday. They were all together again, the topics were familiar, the food, the usual favorites. But something was missing. Neither Ty nor Maggie talked as much as they used to, and they spoke even less to each other. Where once they had been so close that they could communicate without words, now there was an awkwardness between them. Sadness hung around Maggie even when she made her best effort to laugh or chat. Her face was drawn, her eyes appearing over-large. Jo frowned in worry and glanced down the table at her son. Gideon looked across at Tess, and she shrugged in pantomimed ignorance.

Later, when the women were clearing the table, Gideon turned to Ty, suggesting quietly, "Why don't we take a walk?"

Will started to pop up, eager to go, but Tess jumped in to distract him. "Will, would you come put up this canister for me? The shelf's too high to reach."

Will hurried to oblige her, pleased to be needed.

Gideon and Ty strolled out of the house and across the farmyard toward the trees. The air was chilly, but it still felt good to be outside. Ty liked being with his uncle. It wasn't the same as with Reid, of course, but there was a masculine strength, a familiarity about Gideon, that was comforting.

"You and your ma having problems?" Gideon asked casually.

Ty cast him a sharp glance. "Is that why you wanted me to come out with you?"

"What do *you* think?"

Ty shrugged. "I don't know. I reckon now you're going to tell me how I ought to be nicer to Mama, what all she does for me and everything."

"No. I suspect you know those things already."

"That's what Gran told me."

"Well, Gran is your mama's mother, and mothers tend to be awful protective of their children. You know, the way Maggie'd be if somebody said something unkind to you."

"So what are you going to tell me?"

"I don't know. I didn't have anything planned. I thought we'd just walk. I thought you might want to talk to somebody. Another man. Sometimes it's tough to say what you think to a woman, even blood kin."

"She treats me like a baby," Ty blurted out.

"She does?" Gideon raised his eyebrows. "You know, that surprises me. I'd have said Maggie gave you too much responsibility for someone so young."

"Nah." Ty looked at his uncle askance. "I can do anything she asks me to. It's not that."

"How does she treat you like a baby?"

"She won't tell me why Reid left!" The words exploded out of the boy. His face was fixed and intense, his hands shoved hard into his pockets.

"Maybe she doesn't know."

"Oh, she knows," Ty responded bitterly. "She as much as admitted it. It's because of her, somehow."

"Reid left because of Maggie? How do you know?"

"I guessed it. I could tell by the look on her face that I'd gotten it right. Only then she wouldn't explain it. She said I didn't need to know, that I ought to trust her."

"Maybe you would be better off not knowing."

"I don't believe that," Ty told him scornfully. "Do you? Would you rather not know why somebody up and left?"

"No, I imagine I'd want to know," Gideon admitted. "You know, Ty," he went on, "sometimes it's hard for a mother to realize that you're not a child anymore, to tell you things adult to adult."

"Do you know why he left?" Ty looked up at his uncle, his eyes narrowing.

Gideon shook his head. "No. I didn't know Reid that well, and Maggie hasn't taken me into her confidence. I don't think she's told Ma or Tess, either, if that's any consolation to you. It's something she evidently doesn't want to talk about to anyone."

"It's her fault."

"How do you know?"

"It's gotta be something she said or did that made him leave."

"Why?"

"'Cause Reid liked us! He told me that. He told Will. I could see that he liked being with us. He and I used to talk about all kinds of things, and he told me that he liked my curiosity. He did!"

"I believe you." Gideon glanced down at his nephew. They had reached the edge of the yard, and the woods stretched away from them on one side, the fields on another. Gideon squatted down, picking up a stick and beginning to idly break it into pieces. Ty squatted down beside him. They sat for a moment in comfortable masculine silence.

Finally Gideon said, "I don't understand one thing, Ty. Why does it have to be that either Maggie or you and Will drove this man off? Why couldn't he have left on his own?"

"He wouldn't have," Ty insisted stubbornly. "He wouldn't have left us like that. He wouldn't have been like he was and then just left."

"Did you ever think that maybe there was no particular reason he left—that maybe it was just his time to move on?"

"There's gotta be some reason!" Ty cried, looking at him with anguish in his eyes. "He wouldn't leave without a reason."

"Well, all I'm saying is the reason might not be what you think it is." He paused. "Now, I don't know what the true answer is, but there are some things I can guess at. I don't know whether your mama sent him away or he left of his own accord, but I can tell you one thing: Maggie liked the man. I don't think she *wanted* him to leave. But sometimes what you want may not be what's good for you. Maybe leaving was the best thing for him to do."

"How? Why?"

Gideon sighed and stood up. He looked off into the distance, considering his words. "You know, Ty, your mama's a pretty woman. Maybe we don't pay much attention to it, because we're related to her and we see her all the time. But she's very attractive, and she's good-hearted, too. She's the kind of woman a man could fall in love with real easily. I don't *know* that that's what happened, but it wouldn't surprise me if your friend Reid started falling in love with your ma. Being around her all the time like that, it'd be easy."

Ty gazed at Gideon with wide eyes. "With Ma? You think he fell in love with Mama?"

Gideon shrugged. "I told you, I don't know. But it's possible. It might even be that Maggie started to care for him, too."

Ty frowned. "I don't know . . ."

"This isn't exactly the kind of thing you think about your mother, I know. But it could be how Reid felt. And since your ma's married to Will, well, Reid would know it was useless to love her. He couldn't ever marry her. Sometimes the one woman a man wants is the very one he cannot have."

The ache in Gideon's voice was so strong that Ty

stared at him. Gideon felt his gaze and glanced down at him. Then he grinned and clapped the boy on the shoulder. "Hell, Ty, I'm no expert on love. But I do know one thing: couldn't anybody love you any better than your ma does. Whatever her reason, whether she's right or wrong, she didn't do anything to hurt you. If she did anything, she did what she thought would be best for you. You and Will. You all are who she cares for, who she always thinks of first. I can swear to that."

"Yeah. I guess you're right." Ty looked away, scuffing at the dirt with his toe. "It's just that nothing feels good anymore."

"I know that feeling," Gideon agreed grimly. "Hey, I'll tell you what. Why don't you stay here with Ma and me for a few days? You and Will both. Would you like that? You could help us get ready for Christmas. We'll get Ma to telling stories about when Shelby and Hunter and your ma and I were kids. She loves to complain about all the trouble we got into. And after three or four days, you could hike back to your farm. It's not far when you cut through the woods. Will and I used to go back and forth that way all the time."

Ty brightened. "I'd like that."

"Good. Then it's settled. Now, come on, let's get back to the house."

When Gideon relayed the news to Maggie, she looked a little reluctant, but when she saw the eager expression on Ty's face, she gave in. It had been a long time since she'd seen him excited about something. So she drove back to town with Tess and Ginny and spent the next three days by herself.

It was lonely, but there was a curious peace to being by herself. She didn't have to keep up any pretenses of happiness or well-being. She could sit staring out the window if she chose or cry in her bed at night without worrying whether Will and Ty might hear her. And for the first time, she felt a faint hope of healing.

* * *

Ripe for the adventurous hike Gideon had suggested, Ty and Will set out for home early Thursday morning. They would take the shortcut through the Tyrrell fields and the stretch of woods that poked like a broad finger into Whitcomb and Tyrrell land.

It was just past dawn, damp and cold. Fog hung above them and lay lightly atop the creek. Dew clung to the needles of the pines and dotted the grass and vines, catching the sunlight as it began to filter through the trees. The birds were trilling and chirping, their wings darting flashes of color, and a brown squirrel sat on a branch, staring down at them with bright, impudent eyes.

They walked quietly. Even though they had been in these woods many times, it was still a little frightening in the deepest part. It heightened their excitement and faint sense of danger to know that this finger of trees ran back into much denser growth, and that if they took a wrong turn, they could wind up hopelessly lost in the forest, where all kinds of wild animals besides squirrels and birds lurked.

But after a while they could see that they were drawing nearer the edge of the woods that ended behind their house, and they began to relax.

Will, trudging along with a serious look on his face, said, "Ty . . ."

"What?"

"How come Reid left?"

Ty glanced at him. It was a question Will had asked many times before, but he answered patiently, "I'm not sure."

"Do you—" Will's face contorted as he struggled to organize and express his thoughts. "Was it . . . because of me?"

Ty stopped and stared at his father. This was the first

time Will had expressed *that* thought. Will stopped, too, and faced him unhappily.

"Because of you?" Ty said. "What in the world—why would you think that?"

Will shrugged helplessly and moved his head from side to side. "I don't know, exactly. But sometimes—I don't know—he looked at me funny."

"Looked at you funny?"

Will frowned, refusing to meet Ty's eyes, and squatted down on the path. He picked up a stick and began to draw aimlessly in the dirt. "I don't know. Like—like he was sad. Like I *made* him sad. Not like Uncle Gideon, not stiff. But kinda . . . mad-sad." Will looked up, and Ty saw that there were teardrops welling in his eyes.

"Oh, Will, no . . ." Ty knelt beside him. "Don't think that. I'm sure he didn't leave because you made him sad or anything. Mr. Prescott liked you. Everybody knew that."

"Really?" Will's face brightened a little. "You think so?"

"I know so. Look, you know I don't lie to you, isn't that right?"

Will nodded earnestly.

"Well, I'm not lying to you now, either. Mr. Prescott liked you. A lot."

"Honest?" A smile spread across Will's face. But then he frowned. "Then why'd he leave?"

Ty squirmed. "I don't know." Suddenly he understood what his uncle had meant the other day. He didn't want to explain his thoughts on the subject to Will, didn't even know how to. It made him feel awkward, and there wasn't any point, anyway, because Will wouldn't understand. Maybe that was what Uncle Gideon had meant about Ma not being able to talk to him about it because he was her son. Were there things you simply couldn't say, no matter how much you loved someone? he wondered now.

But Will demanded no further explanation. "I'm glad it wasn't me," he said simply. He snapped the twig he had been holding in two, then broke each piece. "But I wish he hadn't gone."

"Me, too." Ty swallowed the lump in his throat. He stood up, holding his hand out to his father. "But I reckon there's nothing you or I can do about it. Come on, or it'll be noon before we get home."

Will nodded and took his hand, rising to his feet, and they started off down the path again. Will scuffed at dead leaves, liking the crunching sound they made. Ty smiled, remembering how much he had liked to do that when he was younger. He still did, in fact, he discovered. He kicked a great swoop of leaves, sending them flying, and Will chuckled.

Then he saw a flat, smooth rock, with a pinkish swirl of color lying just off the path, and he stopped. "Hey, Will, look at that."

Will went over to it eagerly. Ever since Ty could remember, Will had liked minerals. The two of them squatted down, and Will picked up the stone, turning it over carefully in his hands.

Then Ty heard the snort.

He glanced up and immediately went still. In the shadow of the trees, only yards away from them, stood a razorback boar. It looked at them with feral little eyes. Two long tusks curved out of its vicious snout. Ty knew just how dangerous these big, tough-hided animals were. Tusks aside, their mouths were full of long sharp teeth. The best thing to do was to avoid the creatures, and Ty was always careful to look for them when he ventured into the woods. He had never seen one this close to the house before, though. But winter had come hard and early this year, and he had heard that many animals had been moving out of the deepest woods and closer to civilization in search of food.

Home, which had seemed so close only moments before, now seemed very far away. Ty tried not to move, hoping the wild hog would lose interest in them, decide that they were not a potential meal crouching there on the ground.

Will, sensing something odd in Ty's manner, looked up. When he saw the razorback, he jumped to his feet, yelling, "Run, Ty! Run!"

The boar let out a loud snort and began to charge. Ty screamed as loudly as he could, hoping they were close enough to the house that Maggie would hear. But he knew, too, that it wouldn't matter if his mother heard the scream and came running with a gun to kill the razorback. He couldn't outrun the animal.

His only hope was to climb a tree. But the trees closest to them were pine, difficult to climb, with long, smooth trunks bare of branches until far above his reach. He ran for an oak tree, but he knew he'd never make it. Will, with his longer legs and greater muscle power, might; he was already several feet ahead. But Ty realized that the boar was too close and the tree too far away for him. He would have to try a pine. He jumped as high as he could at the nearest tree and wrapped his arms around it. Desperately he began to shinny up the trunk, gripping with his knees and arms and moving like an inchworm.

The razorback slammed into the trunk just below him, so near that Ty could feel its hot breath on his ankles. The tree shuddered under the force of the hit, and Ty almost lost his grip. He slid, frantically grappling to stay on. The bark ripped his shirt and scraped his skin, but he didn't feel the pain. He was too filled with terror. If the boar hadn't backed up to make another charge at the tree, his legs would have been within reach of its dangerous tusks.

"Ty!" Will shrieked, his voice matching the terror inside Ty.

In desperation, Ty tried to scramble up the tree, but it seemed as if his legs slipped back as much as they moved upward. The razorback was charging again; Ty could hear the thunder of its hooves. He knew he shouldn't, but he couldn't help but look.

The boar was rushing at the tree. But suddenly there was Will, running into the animal's path, wielding a branch he'd swooped up off the ground. "No!" Will bellowed, and he swung the branch with all his might.

"Will, don't!" Ty screamed. "No!"

The branch connected with a mighty *thwack,* landing hard across the boar's head.

"Hurry!" Will screamed. "Climb! Climb!"

The wild hog staggered under the blow and backed up a little, shaking its head. Will went after him, swinging the thick branch again. This time it landed harmlessly across the animal's bony ridged back, and the makeshift weapon cracked and fell apart.

Will turned and ran, but the razorback had recovered from its momentary stunned state, and it thundered after him. Will didn't have time to make the tree, and both he and Ty knew it. Ty watched with helpless horror as the razorback charged full tilt into Will, sending him to the ground.

"No!" Ty screamed and let go of the tree, jumping to the ground. "Pa! No!"

Will rolled and struggled to get up, although blood was spurting from the backs of his legs. But the wild boar rushed at him again, slamming his head into Will's side. Ty shrieked, tears streaming down his face, as he ran toward his father, stooping to pick up whatever he could find on the ground and fling it at the creature.

But the pine cones and rocks he hurled at the razorback's thick hide didn't distract it. The animal was intent upon his kill, and he charged into Will's prone body again, trampling and jabbing.

"Stop it! Damn you, stop it!" Ty screamed, tears streaming down his face, and he hurled a rock with all his might.

This time Ty's missile landed on the animal's more sensitive snout, and it let out a squeal of pain. The razorback swung around and saw Ty. Its head went down, and he charged the boy.

18

Maggie was putting loaves of bread into the oven to bake when she heard the shouts. Frowning, she went to the back door and opened it, listening. She heard the call again, at some distance, but she couldn't make it out. Then a scream pierced the air, echoing out of the woods. She whirled and ran into the hall to grab the rifle. She didn't know what was wrong, but she recognized her son's scream, and she knew that, whatever it was, it was serious. It might be an animal, or it might be that one of the boys had fallen or otherwise hurt himself, but she had learned long ago that the safest course was to take a gun when she didn't know what she might be facing.

Maggie hit the back porch at a run and took the path into the woods, loading the gun as she went. She heard Will's shouts mingling with Ty's, and then Ty let out a scream so chilling that the hair on the nape of her neck stood on end. Maggie fairly flew down the path.

Ahead of her in the trees she saw Ty. He was running as fast as he could, and not twenty feet behind him was a ferocious razorback, tusks bloodied, pounding after him. Maggie didn't stop to think. Instinctively she brought the rifle to her shoulder, drew in a breath, aimed, and fired. She had a clear shot at the beast, and she hit it. The wild hog let out a squeal and stumbled. His front legs folded under him, and he came down hard. But he rose to his feet again, lowered his head, and, blood pumping out of him, ran after Ty.

Maggie had immediately loaded again, and now she fired once more. This time the bullet hit the animal in the head. It jerked, squealing in pain, and fell to the ground. Maggie went limp with relief.

"Mommy!" Ty ran to her like the little child he had once been and threw his arms around her, burying his face in her chest. "Pa! It got Pa!"

"Will?" In the terror of the moment, seeing her only child being chased by a vicious predator, it hadn't even registered on Maggie that Will was missing. But now a new stab of fear went through her. "What? Where?"

Ty broke from her and ran, pointing, and Maggie followed. She could see Will now, a still form lying in the leaves. As she drew closer, she saw the red staining the ground and Will's clothing, and she remembered the blood on the razorback's snout and tusks.

"Will!" Maggie froze, staring at him, her voice barely a whisper. For an instant she couldn't move, paralyzed by the fear of what she would see if she went closer. For a moment everything—land, trees, sky—seemed to swirl around her, and she closed her eyes, drawing in deep breaths to steady her. Then she walked forward.

Will was still breathing, but his breath made an odd wheezing sound as it went in and out. His trousers and jacket were soaked in blood, and he clutched his stomach, his face knotted in agony.

Maggie dropped down on her knees beside him, moaning, "No, no . . ." Her voice was racked with pain. Will was only inches from death.

He opened his eyes and looked up at her. "Mags." His eyes, normally vague, were brightened by pain, and, strangely, he looked almost himself again. "Ty?"

"He's all right," Maggie assured him, reaching out to cover one of his hands with hers. He gripped it tightly. Tears welled in her eyes.

"I saved him." A faint smile touched Will's lips, and there was pride in his eyes. For an instant he looked like the man he had once been. Then the light faded from his eyes, and they fluttered closed. He groaned softly, and an odd bubbling sound came into his breathing. He went still.

"Will? Will!" Panic rose in Maggie. It couldn't be true. This couldn't be the way it would end. "No!" She began to sob. "No, please, don't. Don't . . ."

She clung to his hand, crying. For some reason, all she could think about was the way he had looked when he had first asked her to dance with him. She had thought that all her grieving for him was past, that she had lost and mourned him years ago when she brought him home from the front with the mind of a child. But now she knew she had not. Whatever had ended between them then, she had loved and cared for him in the years since. And now she had lost him all over again.

Ty put a hand on her shoulder, and Maggie turned and looked up at him. His face was pale and old beyond his years. "He—he's dead, isn't he?"

Maggie nodded, unable to speak past her tears. Ty sank down beside her and threw his arms around her, and they held each other tightly, silent tears streaming down their faces.

Will's funeral was held two days later. Gideon built a coffin, and they buried him in the cemetery in town beside his parents. The weather was chilling, damp and windy, and Maggie couldn't keep from shivering as she stood watching the casket lowered into the ground. After they returned to the house, Maggie climbed the stairs to her room to take off her cloak and gloves and tidy her hair before the visitors arrived. She sat down for a moment in her rocker and stared out the window at the gray afternoon. She wondered how she was going to carry on now. She wasn't sure she could this time. She had, she thought, reached the end of her rope.

There was a small tap at her door, and it slowly opened. Maggie looked up to see Ty standing in the doorway. She smiled faintly and motioned for him to draw closer. He closed the door behind him and came over to her chair.

"Mama?"

"What, sweetheart?" Her heart ached for him, and she took his hands, easing him down into her lap. He was much too big to sit there, of course—his feet hung almost to the ground, and his head was higher than her own—but it was good to hold him once again. Ty laid his head against hers; she could feel the wetness of his tears in her hair.

"Mama, I'm sorry," he whispered in a small voice.

"For what?"

"For being mean to you. About Reid. I'm sorry."

"Oh, honey." Tears choked off her voice. She squeezed Ty more tightly to her. "I love you."

"I love you, too." They cried, holding each other.

For the rest of the day the small house was crammed with people coming to pay their respects. Jo moved in for a week to take care of the house and her daughter, and after that Tess took over for a week.

Soon Christmas was upon them. Maggie prepared special treats for the subdued family gathering, but inside she was miserable. She tried to put a happier face on things for Ty's sake, and Christmas night, when they had returned home from her mother's, she gave him the shirt she had made and the brand-new puzzle she had saved her pennies to buy.

When Maggie opened Ty's gift to her, a wooden cow he had carved himself with Gideon's help and instruction, her lips trembled. She pulled him to her and held him tightly, struggling not to give way to tears.

"Mama," he whispered, his voice strained, "why does everyone leave us? Will I always lose people? Doesn't anyone stay?"

"Oh, Ty, no, you haven't lost everyone!" Maggie exclaimed, alarmed and saddened by the direction his thoughts had taken.

"But Pa died, and before that Reid left. Before that Uncle Hunter left, too."

"But I'm here, Ty. And your Grandma. Aunt Tess. Uncle Gideon. Your father couldn't help dying, and Reid couldn't help leaving, either. Neither one of them wanted to leave you."

"I know Pa didn't want to die." It was easier for Ty to call him Pa now that he was gone and his childlike nature wasn't evident every day.

"Of course not."

"But it's hard, and—oh, I don't know. It's kind of scary to think about how people disappear. They're here one day and then they're gone. There's nothing you can do about it. You can't hold on to them no matter how much you want them to stay."

"Sometimes that happens," Maggie agreed, and she squeezed him tightly to her again. "I'm sorry it came twice so close together for you. But it doesn't happen every time you love someone. It doesn't even happen most of the time. I promise you."

He nodded, but Maggie knew he wasn't convinced. Reid's departure and Will's death had come too hard and fast for him. She prayed that Ty wouldn't lock his heart away, afraid to love anyone lest they leave him.

Later, after Ty went up to bed, she opened the present Will had given her. It was a wooden figure, too, a clumsy attempt to imitate what Ty had carved. Maggie held the crude figure to her breast and cried.

*   *   *

The opening of the new library was to be the biggest social event Pine Creek had seen in years. Several of the women of the Guild had spent a good deal of their time after Christmas decorating the bottom floor of Tess's house for the January occasion. On the day of the party, the Conways' servants brought in box after box of food, taking over the kitchen to prepare the evening repast.

Tess knew how much Benton hated seeing the library get the house he had wanted, but because he wanted to stay in the good graces of Pine Creek society, he put on a pretense of being delighted for the Ladies Guild. Because of his daughter's involvement, he had made a show of throwing himself behind the social event, paying for the food and decorations. It irritated Tess that he was passing himself off as a benefactor, but her annoyance was offset by the knowledge that privately Benton was gnashing his teeth over his loss.

Tess dressed for the occasion carefully. The last thing she wanted was to look threadbare at the gala. She hated to think of people pitying her or Amanda or guessing that they had had to give up partial use of their home in order not to lose it altogether. Therefore, she had spent part of the money she had received from what they'd sold in Little Rock on some elegant royal blue silk for herself and some dark wine velvet for her mother. She and her mother had spent their spare time sewing the dresses, and Tess had carefully clipped rows of lace from an old ballgown to decorate the hems and necklines.

When Tess was dressed and her hair done up in a cluster of long finger curls, the pearls Shelby had given her on her earlobes, she was quite pleased with what she saw. With the fingerless black lace mitts on her hands, she doubted anyone would guess that she had spent yesterday washing and waxing floors.

Tess and Amanda stood in the receiving line with Rosemary and the president of the Ladies Guild. Tess could see that, despite her earlier dismay, her mother was having more fun than she had had in years. Wearing a new evening gown and graciously greeting her lifelong friends and acquaintances, she might have been back at one of her own parties ten or fifteen years ago.

Tess enjoyed it somewhat less; she had lost most of her taste for such social events. Once the excitement of wearing a new dress and looking her best began to wear off, nodding and smiling at each new guest grew more tiresome than anything else. Her back ached from scrubbing the floors yesterday, and she was hungry and thirsty. She was thinking with longing of breaking away from the receiving line and trying to sneak a plate and cup from the buffet when the front door opened again, and the Tyrrells came in.

As always when she saw Gideon these days, her heart tightened within her chest. She could not be around him without thinking about her love for him—and the fact that he did not return it. Gideon always seemed to feel as awkward as she did. "Gideon. Mama Jo."

Tess kissed Jo on the cheek, taking her hands and squeezing them. She nodded formally toward Gideon. Jo cast a speculative glance from Gideon to Tess but said nothing.

"I'm sorry Maggie couldn't be here," Tess said. "But I understand."

"Yes." Jo sighed, looking worried. "Will's death has hit her hard. I tried to get her to come with us, but she said she just couldn't face it. You know, I think people expect her to be relieved that Will's dead, but she loved that man. It hurts her."

"Of course it does." Tess glanced beyond the pair, and her lips tightened. Benton Conway stood in the doorway, Linette pale and lovely by his side.

Jo grimaced. "Him! I was hoping he wouldn't have the nerve to show up tonight."

"Don't be naive," Tess replied, scorn for the man permeating her voice. "He's hoping throwing this party will give him entree to the Guild social circle."

"Quick, ask me to dance," she whispered to Gideon. "I don't want to have to talk to him." Nor did she wish to risk exposing Linette's generous involvement in her plan.

"Of course." Gideon took Tess's arm and led her out onto the dance floor. From the grim expression on his face, one would have assumed that he was going to his execution rather than about to dance.

The truth was, Gideon thought he could have faced an execution with more ease. Holding Tess in his arms in public would be a diabolical mixture of intense pleasure and pain. Ever since that night that he had lost control and kissed her, every moment he spent with her was that way. All he had to do was look at her, and he was on fire.

He had thought his desire for her was tremendous before he kissed her, but he hadn't known the half of it. Now that he had tasted her lips, actually felt her pliant body pressed into his, he wanted her much, much more. That hint of the pleasures of intimacy had merely stoked the fires of his passion. Whenever he was around her, all he could think about was taking her into his arms and kissing her again. It didn't matter where they were or what was going on or how innocent the conversation around them was; his mind conjured heated, lustful images of Tess naked in bed with him.

He couldn't stop his fantasies, but he felt like a cad for having them. How could he think of passion when he knew he had disappointed her so? Ever since their kiss, even after he had apologized, every time he looked at Tess, he saw the pain and sadness in her eyes. She did her best to avoid him, always talking to his mother or Maggie whenever the family was together, and when she could not avoid speaking to him, she treated him with painfully correct courtesy. Tess had sealed her inner self away from him, buried the laughter and friendship that had once flourished between them.

No, if he were honest, he would know that it was he who had destroyed the friendship; he had betrayed her trust in him by grabbing her and kissing her. She must despise him, tolerating his presence only because she loved Jo and Maggie.

Gideon held out his arms, and Tess stepped into them, and they joined the other dancers on the floor. Tess was warm and deliciously soft in his arms, but Gideon struggled not to think about it. He breathed in her scent, and heat seared his skin. He looked down at her face, so lovely and white, color high on her cheeks. Her mouth was kissably soft and moist; her lashes cast shadows on her delicate cheeks. Desire coursed through him, and he was afraid he might begin to tremble.

Tess did not dare look up at Gideon. She kept her eyes on his chest and tried to ignore the warm, melting sensation in her abdomen that had started as soon as she stepped into his arms. Why had she been so foolish as to suggest that they dance? Would he think her forward now? Assume that she was inviting his advances? It would have been better if she had just stayed and faced hateful Benton Conway.

When the dance ended, Gideon courteously escorted Tess to where her mother and Mariana Hill sat talking. Then he hurried off to join a knot of men near the stairs.

Miserable, Tess watched him go. He had scarcely been able to wait to get away from her. If she had needed any further demonstration that he did not love her, now she had it.

Rosemary approached Tess, looking flustered. "I'm sorry," she began apologetically. "I'm afraid we haven't enough dishes for all the refreshments. Mrs. Diggs was wondering where her pound cake was, and I hadn't set it out because I didn't have a dish to put it on. I wondered if you . . ." She broke off, looking at Tess entreatingly.

"If I have a plate you could borrow?" Tess supplied pleasantly. "Of course."

"Oh, thank you!" Rosemary looked relieved. "I hated to ask, because truly I don't want you to have to *do* things for the lending library, because, of course, you've already done more than enough. But I didn't want to upset Mrs. Diggs. I should have thought to bring extra bowls and plates, but I didn't."

"Don't worry about it," Tess said as she walked the young woman to the kitchen. "There was no reason you should have known you'd need extras."

Tess opened the butler's pantry and located a small willowware plate that would do well for the pound cake. Rosemary thanked her profusely. They turned to go back to the dining room, and Tess stopped abruptly. Benton Conway was standing in the doorway.

"Ah, Mrs. Tyrrell," he said smoothly. "What a pleasant surprise. I'm afraid I didn't get to greet you when I first arrived."

Tess straightened her shoulders. Given his pointed reference to her swift vanishing act when he arrived, no doubt he had assumed she was afraid to face him. There was something taunting in the tone of his voice and the glint in his eyes. Tess hated for him to think she was afraid; she simply loathed the man too much to engage in polite social chatter with him.

"Good evening, Mr. Conway," she said. She could hardly be impolite to him in front of his daughter, but she wasn't about to be friendly, either.

Conway's eyes flickered to his daughter, and he said brusquely, "Rosemary, take that into the other room. I want to speak to Mrs. Tyrrell alone."

Rosemary took a step toward the door, then stopped and looked back uncertainly at Tess.

Tess thought it spoke volumes about Conway that

his own daughter seemed reluctant to leave her alone with him. She smiled at Rosemary, unwilling to put the sweet girl in an awkward position with her father. "Go ahead. I'll be there in a minute."

"All right." Rosemary still looked troubled, and she cast a glance at her father, then Tess, before she left.

When the door closed behind her, Benton's face lost all trace of its polite mask. Tess involuntarily stepped back at the sight of the naked, ugly fury that twisted the man's features.

"You bitch!" he spat out, striding across the room until he was standing right in front of her.

Tess's eyes widened. No one in her entire life had ever spoken to her like that, and, despite her low opinion of the scalawag, it stunned her that even he did so.

His fingers curled like talons around her wrist, and he jerked her across the kitchen toward the back door. Tess was again so startled that he had pulled her to the door before she began to resist. She pulled back hard, but his grip was too tight to break.

"Mr. Conway! What do you think you're doing!" she hissed in outrage.

He opened the door and gave her such a hard tug that it felt as if he would pull her arm from its socket. Tess stumbled out onto the porch with him. He closed the door firmly behind them and started down the steps to the yard.

"Mr. Conway!" Tess raised her voice. The last thing she wanted was a scene for all the people in the house to witness, but Conway's actions were frightening her. "Let me go! What are you doing?"

"Giving you what you deserve!" he retorted as he marched her across the back yard toward the bushes and trees edging the garden. He cast a swift, angry look at her. "You think you're so high and mighty, don't you? So clever, to keep me from getting that damn house! Well, I'll tell you what, missy, you're not clever at all."

"I never claimed to be." Tess dug in her heels and pulled back with all her strength, but she was no match for Conway, and he dragged her inexorably along. She thought about screaming, but she couldn't believe he would do her any real harm right here in the back yard of her house, with so many people inside. He probably just wanted to vent his anger at her, and she would just as soon that happen where no one could hear.

"I offered you good money for that house," he growled, pulling her into the shadow of a tall spirea bush. "And you sneered at me as if I was scum!" His eyes glittered in the light of the half moon; his face was contorted with fury.

Tess's fear grew. Benton looked wild and out of control. "Let go of me!" She tugged at her arm, trying to pry his fingers loose with her other hand. "This is insane. I didn't *have* to sell you my house. Just because you've become rich and powerful doesn't mean the rest of us are all going to bow down to you. You can't just have anything you want."

"Or anybody?" he asked, quirking an eyebrow. Suddenly he pulled Tess toward him so hard that she lurched forward, almost falling into him, and he twisted her arm up behind her back so painfully she cried out. "You think I can't have you? Right here and now if I want?"

He leered down at her, lust mingling with the rage in his eyes. "You thwarted me about the house," he growled, "but I can have *you*."

"You're mad!" Tess cried. "There's a whole houseful of people in there! All the people you want so badly to impress, to have toady up to you! You think you'd have any stature left if they found out you'd tried to force me?"

"They won't know." He grinned. "Are you going to scream and bring them running out here to see you in the arms of another woman's husband? That is, presuming that they'd hear you. The windows and doors are closed, and you know what a sturdy house that is. With the music and talk, do you think anyone would hear your feeble cries?"

Tess tried to twist away from him, and he pushed her arm up so high she thought she might faint. "Stop! Let me go!"

"And afterward, who would you tell? I'll deny it, and you know which one of us has friends among the Law, don't you? I'd have an alibi; you'd have nothing but a ruined reputation. Everyone in town would talk about you; you'd be a blot on the sainted Tyrrell name. Your daughter would hear the rumors and suffer the stares. No, I don't think you'd reveal anything to anyone."

He bent her backward, his fingers digging into her arm, and his other hand ran crudely over her breasts.

Tess drew a deep breath and screamed as loudly as she could.

Benton slapped her, hard. The blow dazed Tess. She felt blood start where her teeth had cut the inside of her lip. Thinking he'd silenced her with the demonstration of his superior strength, Benton thrust his hand down the front of her gown. He squeezed her breast, his eyes glinting and his mouth going slack with lust.

"Ah, you're a ripe one, aren't you?" he panted softly. "You look delicate, but there's some meat on you after all. Tasty, too, I'll bet."

"Tess?" Gideon's voice came from the back porch, sounding doubtful. "Are you out here?"

Conway's blow had only momentarily befogged her, and at the sound of Gideon's voice, she screamed, "Gideon! Help!"

Quickly Conway clamped his hand over her mouth, effectively silencing her, and when she began to kick and struggle, he tightened her arm behind her back so painfully that a red mist swam before her eyes and she went slack, teetering on the verge of unconsciousness.

But her brief cry had been enough to bring Gideon running. "Tess? Tess! Where are you?"

He spied a telltale movement of the bushes, and he charged straight in. He saw Tess weakly struggling with a man, though in the darkness he didn't recognize her attacker. He lunged, punching the assailant in the most vulnerable area exposed to him, his lower back. With a grunt of pain, the man released Tess, who slid to the ground. Then the man staggered around to face Gideon.

"Conway!" Fury seized Gideon, and he swung hard, punching the other man in the stomach, then again in the jaw. Conway went down like a felled tree.

But Gideon was too enraged to stop. He grabbed the scalawag by the lapels, hauled him upright, and hit him again. Conway fell to his knees, and Gideon made to pull him up once more.

"No! Gideon!" Tess stumbled to her feet, reaching out to him entreatingly. "Don't, please don't. He's through, can't you see? Don't hit him again!"

Gideon stopped, one hand clenching Conway's shirt, the other drawn back to strike again. He swung his head toward Tess. His voice was low and cold with rage. "I'll kill the son-of-a-bitch."

"No! Please!" Desperately Tess grabbed his arm. Gideon might be in danger already for coming to her rescue. There was no telling what Conway might get his government friends to do in revenge. They might lock Gideon up in jail and throw away the key. If Gideon actually killed the man, he'd be facing a murder trial he couldn't hope to survive. But Tess also knew the Tyrrell men well enough to be sure that an appeal to save himself would not dissuade Gideon from avenging a hurt done to one of the family.

"Spare him. For me," Tess pleaded, her mind racing. "Please, do it for me. Think of the scandal. Everyone would know he'd attacked me."

"Everyone should know what cowardly, perverted

scum he is!" Gideon spat, but she could see that reason was returning to his eyes.

"But you know what everyone will wonder— whether you rescued me before or after he'd . . ."

"Dammit, no one would dare say anything about you!" Gideon exploded, but he did let go of Conway, who flopped ignominiously to the ground at his feet.

"You can't fight *everyone* in town," Tess pointed out, faint amusement tinging her voice. If she had thought Gideon completely different from his brother Shelby, she was seeing one of the resemblances now: that same pigheaded insistence on not letting go of an argument until he had won.

"You shouldn't have to be ashamed because that snake tried to hurt you," he insisted.

"Maybe not, but that doesn't change reality. We both know that everyone would gossip. Benton might be humiliated, but I would have to live with the whispers and the stain."

"I can't let him off scot-free! He ought to be hauled down to the jail."

"Do you honestly think they would find him guilty? A military court—with a Confederate soldier and a Confederate widow testifying against their friend?"

Gideon gritted his teeth. "No. You're right, of course."

He glared down in frustration at the man on the ground. Then he sighed, his shoulders relaxing and his fists unknotting, and Tess knew that she'd won. Gideon squatted down beside Conway and lifted his head by the hair until his foe was forced to look up at him.

"I'm going to let you go because of Tess. But if you ever so much as go near her again, if you even talk to her, I'll come after you. And I'll take you out into the woods and I'll kill you—very slowly. You understand?"

Conway's eyes wavered crazily, but he nodded weakly. "Yes," he gasped through bloody, swollen lips.

"Good." Gideon bent closer and whispered in a

voice like ice, "In case you start thinking you'll get me out of the way, just remember: there are more Tyrrells where I came from, and we're a very clannish bunch."

He stood and turned to Tess. "Come on. Let's get you back inside."

Tess nodded and started toward the house. Though she knew it was only a short distance, it seemed an impossibly long walk. Her legs were trembling with the aftermath of fear and anger, and she stumbled. Gideon grasped her arm to keep her from falling, and she winced and cried out.

"What?" He released her arm immediately, guilt flashing across his face. "What did I do? I'm sorry."

She shook her head. "It's not your fault. My arm hurts. He twisted it behind me to keep me from escaping."

In the light streaming from the windows of the house, Gideon saw for the first time what he hadn't noticed in the dimness of the garden: blood on Tess's face.

"My God! You're bleeding." He reached out to touch her face, but stopped for fear it would cause her more pain. "What happened? Did he hit you?"

Tess nodded. "When I screamed. But it was worth it —you heard me."

Gideon stiffened, and his eyes were suddenly cold and furious. "God damn him! I shouldn't have let that sorry son-of-a-bitch go." He half-turned back toward the bushes where Benton lay.

"Gideon, no!" Tess grabbed his arm. "Don't. Leave it alone." She drew in a gulp of air, feeling suddenly dizzy. "I—don't—" Then, without even planning to, she prevented him from going back to take up the fight with Conway in the simplest way possible: she gave a little sigh, her eyes rolled back in her head, and she fainted.

"Tess!" Gideon grabbed her and pulled her to him, all thought of wreaking revenge on Benton Conway fleeing his mind. He swung her up into his arms and carried her onto the porch.

Carefully he opened the door into the kitchen a crack—not an easy process with a woman in his arms—and peered into the room. Tess would never forgive him if he was caught carrying her into her house. Rumors would be flying all over Pine Creek by morning.

Fortunately there was no one in the kitchen, so Gideon pushed open the door and hurried across the room. Once on the back stairs, he breathed easier. No one outside of Tess's family would be using them.

He went up the steps. Now that the danger of meeting someone was past, he was very aware of holding Tess. She was so small and delicate. It made his blood boil to think of Conway hurting her. His lips pulled back from his teeth in a silent snarl as he thought of the bastard hitting her.

Gideon could not help but notice how soft her body was, too; she was small but very womanly. Her head nestled upon his shoulder, and he could feel one of her breasts pressing against his chest. He knew if his hand slid, he would be touching the other as well. Gideon hated himself for even thinking of it.

He had never been above the first floor of Tess's house, and he had no idea which bedroom was hers. So he walked quietly down the hall, peering into each room for signs of its occupant. He found Ginny asleep in one bedroom, curled up on her side, her plaited blond hair flung across her pillow. He smiled, a lump in his throat, at seeing her looking so angelic. Another room was obviously an upstairs sitting room, furnished with a small sofa and chairs. But the third room he peered into was a woman's, with dainty perfume bottles and a brush and mirror set on the dresser. Amanda's? Then he caught a faint lemon verbena scent, familiar to him from Tess herself, and he knew the room was hers. As he stepped inside, a miniature portrait of Shelby on the bedside table confirmed his opinion.

Gently he laid Tess down on her bed. Then he lit a candle on the nightstand, bathing Tess in its warm glow. In the golden light, her face looked even worse. There was dried blood on her lip and smeared across her chin and cheek, and her skin was reddened and beginning to swell where Conway had slapped her. Gideon was torn between pity and fury. If he could have Benton's neck in his hands right now, he'd squeeze with all his strength. But he wanted just as badly to soothe Tess's pain.

He glanced around and found the washstand. He poured some cool water from the pitcher into the basin and dipped a washcloth into it, then gently wiped the blood from Tess's face.

The cool water revived her, and her eyelids fluttered open. She looked confused. "What—"

She started to sit up, but Gideon laid a firm hand on her shoulder. "Shh. Lie still. You fainted."

"I fainted? But—" Memory returned, and she grimaced, then winced at the pain the movement caused her. "I remember now." She glanced about. "Did you bring me here?"

Gideon nodded. "Don't worry. No one saw me." He smiled a little. "Your reputation is intact."

"Thank you. Ow!" She winced as he touched a sore spot with the washcloth.

"Sorry. Just getting you cleaned up."

"How did you know to come looking for me?

Gideon frowned. "Actually, it was Linette."

"Linette? But why—"

"I'm not sure. She came up to me and said you'd gone outside and you would probably need a wrap. Then she handed me a shawl and asked me if I'd look for you in back and take it to you. I thought it was peculiar, but—" Gideon looked at her. "Did she know you were with Benton?"

"I don't know. Rosemary did. She was there when

he came into the kitchen. I guess she could have told Linette. But why would Linette have assumed—"

"Well, she knows his ways better than anyone, I guess."

"Oh, Gideon, how awful! To know that your husband is—" Tess broke off, shuddering.

Without thinking, Gideon clamped his arms around her and held her tightly as she shivered.

She clung to him. "Oh, Gideon, it was so awful! I was so scared! I thought . . . I thought he would . . ."

"I know." He pulled her into his lap and cradled her, seeking to warm her with his body, to wrap himself around her in complete protection. "I'd like to kill that son-of-a-bitch. If I'd known exactly what he'd done to you, I'd—"

"No!" Tess cried, and her arms tightened around him convulsively. "No, Gideon! You mustn't. I beg of you. Please, please don't do anything to him. He's powerful; he could hurt you."

"Hush, now." Gideon smiled indulgently. "You think I can't take care of myself with someone like Benton Conway?"

"It takes more than strength or courage, Gideon. Benton's wicked. Evil! He'd finagle something so that you wound up in prison. I'm just sure of it. Please, promise me you won't try to even the score with him."

Gideon's mouth twisted. "Tess . . ."

"Please! What—what would happen to us if he got you sent to prison? Or if he had someone kill you? He's capable of that, Gideon! And then where would I be? Or Ginny? Or your mother and Maggie?"

Tess pressed home her argument, desperate to keep Gideon from rushing out to seek revenge for the dishonor done to the Tyrrell name. Fear for himself wouldn't suffice, but he would never do something that might endanger his family. "We need you, Gideon. You can't give in to your anger and leave us unprotected.

Then Benton would win. He's be free to do whatever he wanted to any of us."

Tess tipped back her head and looked up at him. Fire sparked in his pale blue eyes, and his jaw was set grimly. "Please, Gideon."

"All right," he said grudgingly. "I won't do anything rash."

"Promise me?"

"Yes, I promise," he grated out.

Tess knew he hated making the vow. But she also knew that, being Gideon, he would not break it. She laid her head back against his chest, smiling to herself. "Thank you," she said softly.

Her breath brushed his neck, and Gideon couldn't hide the tremor that ran through him. He closed his eyes, fighting to control the desire that rushed up in him. It was unbearably sweet to hold Tess in his arms this way, to comfort her, yet it was also highly arousing. He could feel himself hardening and prayed she could not detect it through the layers of skirts and petticoats between them. He knew he should set her back on the bed, or he would soon betray himself. But he couldn't make himself do it. Not just yet. He had to hold her for a few minutes longer.

Tess lay against Gideon's chest, luxuriating in the warmth and strength that had already chased away most of her fears. It was so easy to forget Benton's awful pawing hands when she was in Gideon's arms this way. It felt so safe here, so good. She only wished that she could stay there forever. If only he loved her . . .

She let out a little sigh and rubbed her cheek against his shirt. Gideon made an odd noise, and his arms suddenly tightened around her. Tess glanced up at him. He was looking down at her, his mouth slack, his eyes glittering. Suddenly Tess's heart speeded up and her loins warmed. Gideon wanted her.

Tess swallowed. Tentatively she placed her hand on his chest. She was trembling inside. She remembered

Benton's hands on her breasts, his mouth on hers, and she wanted Gideon to kiss her and touch her, to wipe those memories away and replace them with hot, cleansing desire. What she was thinking must have been reflected in her gaze, for Gideon drew in a sharp breath, and the light in his eyes flamed higher.

"Gideon . . ." She caressed his name. She reached up and traced his lips with her forefinger, delighting in the heat of his skin, the velvet softness of his lips.

"Tess." His voice shook. He took her finger gently between his teeth, his lips kissing it tenderly. Then his mouth moved down to her palm. He murmured her name again.

His breath was hot against her skin, sending shivers up her arm. Tess moved a little on his lap, and he groaned.

"Don't tempt me, Tess." His voice was low and tortured. "I'm only human. I can't keep from—"

Tess arched up and placed her lips against his. His arms were suddenly like iron around her, his lips claiming hers. Then his tongue was in her mouth, plumbing the sweet depths, and he was laying her back on the bed, his hard body sinking into hers.

Gideon moaned. All the passion held back for so long was rushing up in him, overwhelming reason. He was lost in the intoxication of her mouth, the beckoning softness of her body.

Tess was equally enflamed. Forgotten were the ugly events of the evening, Benton's brutal mistreatment. She was filled with desire, knowing only her hunger. She ached for Gideon to touch her; she yearned to feel his fullness inside her.

Finally his hand slid up her body, hot even through her clothing, until he came at last to her breast. His fingers curled around it, driving Tess's desire even higher. She moaned and twisted as his thumb stroked across her nipple, making it tighten and press against her dress. She hated the restrictions of their clothing;

she wanted to feel his bare flesh against hers, and the frustration was driving her wild. She kissed him even harder, her fingers digging into his back. His mouth widened over hers, consuming her. His fingers fumbled at the buttons of her dress until finally—finally!—he could pull down the loosened bodice and slide his hands beneath her chemise.

Desire shot through Gideon like lightning, and he shuddered under its force, feeling as if he might explode. Her breasts were pillowy soft beneath his rough palms; her nipples exquisitely responsive to his touch. It was all too much—and not nearly enough. He wanted to be inside her, *had* to be in her. He began to pull at her dress.

"No, Gideon, wait," Tess panted, reaching behind her to undo the remaining buttons and make it easier for him.

But her words cut into him, chilling him, and he went still. "Oh, God," he groaned. He sat up, plunging his hands into his hair. "Oh, Jesus, Tess, I'm sorry." He twisted away, hating himself. "I'm sorry. I didn't mean to—I'm not—" He cursed suddenly and vividly. "I *am* like him, though, aren't I? Trying to take you just because I wanted you, without any thought to your feelings. I didn't mean it, though, I swear. I—I lost control."

He jumped to his feet, and Tess reached out frantically for him. "No, Gideon, wait! Wait! I didn't mean— Don't go! Don't leave me like this! Please . . ." A sob escaped her throat.

Gideon turned and looked back at her, his eyes bleak and stark with self-disgust.

"Please," she whispered again. "Please don't go. Stay. I know you don't love me, but I don't care. I just want you to stay. Make love to me." Her breath came in hurried, rasping gasps. "Just let me have this night. I promise I'll never throw it back in your face. I won't make any demands."

Gideon stared at her. He felt suddenly as if he had gone mad. "What? What did you say?"

"Stay with me." Tess went up on her knees, holding out her arms to him. "Please. I know you want me."

"Of course I want you! God, Tess, that's the problem," he said, moving to her side. "I want you too much."

She ran her hands up his arms, all the while staring into his eyes. "No. You can't want me too much."

She smiled, and he couldn't take his eyes from her mouth, soft and moist and swollen from his kisses. "Tess," he groaned. "You're killing me. I can't . . . I can't stay here and not take you. And I refuse to be like Conway!"

"You're nothing like Conway." Her hands went to the buttons of his shirt, and she began to undo them. "You could never be like him. You aren't forcing me. I want you, Gideon. I want you to make love to me."

"Tess." He stared at her, unable to take in her words. "You can't mean—you don't know what you're saying."

"Yes, I do." She reached up to place a light kiss on his chin. She continued to plant soft pecks all over his cheeks and throat and chin.

"No. Stop it," he said weakly, thinking he would die if she did.

"I can't. Come to bed." She kissed the hollow of his throat. "I don't expect you to love me. I only want tonight. I can't—"

"Not love you?" He felt thoroughly bewildered, his brain moving slowly through a red haze of passion. "I already love you, Tess! I've loved you for years. How could I not love you?"

Tess stopped and drew back, looking at him. "What?"

"I love you. Don't you know that?"

Mutely Tess shook her head.

"But that day when I kissed you—surely you realized."

"You didn't say you loved me," Tess protested. "You apologized for doing it! You said it was wrong!"

"It was." He passed a hand across his face, trying to rub away the confusion. "Tess, I kissed you without any regard to how you felt, just like tonight. I was . . . was . . ." He gestured toward the bed. "I was just following my own lust, my own desire! That was what was wrong. I wasn't paying any attention to what you wanted, to what you felt."

"I wanted you to kiss me!" Tess shot back. "That's what I wanted. I love you! When you kissed me that day, I knew . . . I realized . . . But you pulled back. You left. You told me it shouldn't have happened."

For a moment the two of them stared at each other in horror. Then Gideon groaned, and suddenly they began to laugh. Gideon grabbed Tess and pulled her to his chest, and they tumbled backward onto the bed together. "Oh, Tess. Tess. Have I gone mad?"

He rained kisses all over her face and throat, still chuckling as they rolled across the bed. Finally, they stopped, and Gideon rose up on his elbows, looking down at her. Their laughter died.

"I love you," he said quietly.

"I love you," she responded.

He bent and kissed her. "Oh, Tess, I've been a fool."

"So have I." She shook her head. Then she smiled a slow, seductive smile and stretched her hands up above her head sinuously. "Well . . . don't you think we ought to make up for lost time?"

Heat flickered through Gideon's loins. His world was suddenly topsy-turvy, yet in a dizzily wonderful way. He was confused and amazed and deliriously happy—and still throbbing with desire for Tess. But he was determined not to hurt her in any way.

"I want to marry you."

"Good." Tess's smile was teasing, and she reached

up to run her fingers through his hair. "I want to marry you."

"But this . . . Tess, I don't want you to regret anything about us. I don't want there to be any scandal to hurt you."

"I don't plan to tell the world what we do tonight. Do you? And we can get married as soon as you want." She sat up, looking serious. "But right now, the only thing I want is to make love with you. I want to be with you, know you. I want you to be mine."

Gideon could hardly think. He felt as if he were on fire, Tess's words stirred him so. "I am yours," he breathed, leaning forward to brush his mouth against hers. He realized that he held Paradise in his hands, and he would be crazy to let go.

He stood quickly and strode to the door, turning the key and locking it. Relief dawned on Tess's face, and she smiled at him as he walked back to the bed.

He began to pull off his clothes, watching her the entire time. Tess gazed back at him just as steadily, her chest beginning to rise and fall rapidly as he exposed his lean, muscled body bit by bit. Tess began to remove her own clothes, but she had far more items to remove, and Gideon, now completely, wonderfully naked, moved to assist her. She slipped off the bed to aid the process, very aware of his heated gaze on her all the while. It was titillating to watch desire flood his face as he looked at her, lingering over her delicate garments.

At last her breasts were exposed, and her underdrawers slipped down, and she stood naked before the man she loved. Gideon's eyes moved slowly down her, his lips full and soft with passion, his eyes burning. Tess loved his gaze on her, but she loved even more the feel of his hands on her. She moved into his arms. Gideon spread his hands across her back, then ran them slowly down her until he reached the swell of her hips. His fingertips dug into her buttocks, and he pulled her up and into him. Tess gasped at the touch of his hard, insistent manhood against her abdomen. Her eyes fluttered closed, and she rubbed herself against him.

Gideon lifted her up and laid her back on the bed, coming down beside her. He caressed her with great care and tenderness, exploring her body as he had wanted to for years. His lips followed the path of his hands, stoking her desire with slow, lingering kisses, until Tess was writhing and panting.

"Please," she murmured. "Please."

And then he came into her, easing the glorious ache within both of them. Slowly he began to thrust in and pull back, bringing them to the throbbing heights of desire, until finally Tess cried out, tumbling over into the dark, sweet oblivion of passion, and Gideon, with a groan, followed her.

19

The winter months were long and difficult for Maggie. She tried to enter into Tess's happiness over her wedding plans, but she found it hard. She was thinner and more wan. She thought about Will, and she thought about Reid, and few of her thoughts were happy. Will had been a part of her life for so many years—as long as she could remember, really—and it was as if a major part of her world had suddenly disappeared. She had loved him, first as a husband and later as a child, and she missed him desperately. But she was also riddled with guilt. For with her sorrow was mixed a certain sense of relief, a freedom from worry and shame.

She was, she thought, a wicked person even to think of Will's death in such terms. Worse, she had betrayed him before he died. She had forsaken her wedding vows, given her love to another man.

And she still longed for Reid. Even after all these months and with her husband cold in the ground, her love for Reid burned as strong and fiery as ever. There were times when she thought of their lovemaking and felt urgent desire stir in her again, and at those times she was bitterly ashamed of herself, certain that she was wanton and wicked.

The thought that she was free now also crept into her mind; she could marry Reid, could love him without censure. She contemplated writing to him at the return address on the letters he sent Ty. But she quickly pushed such notions away. It was horrible to think that way, as if she were glad Will had died, as if she had been waiting for something to happen to him so that she could marry Reid.

Besides, the idea of contacting Reid was scary. What if he didn't write back? What if he didn't care that she was now free to marry? What if during the last few months he had gotten over her, had discovered their passion was only a momentary thing?

Maggie and Ty didn't lack for visitors. Tess came often, and several ladies from the church called. Jo and Gideon visited, too, for now was their least busy time on the farm. But still Maggie was lonely.

One evening late in January, a knock on the front door awakened her. She sat up, glancing groggily around her. Then she realized that she had dozed off on the parlor sofa, where she had been sitting after supper darning. In her lap was one of Ty's socks, the darning egg in its toe, a needle stuck through it.

She wasn't sure what had roused her until the knock sounded again. "Coming!" she called and stood up, straightening her dress and patting her hair into place.

As she approached the front door, she saw that Ty had come down the stairs and was standing in the hallway uncertainly. He was frowning, but there was a faint spark of hope in his eyes, too. Maggie knew how her son felt. It was awfully late for someone to be calling—it could be dangerous to open the door—and yet . . . Her heart leapt at the thought that maybe it was Reid, coming back to them.

She reached for the doorknob, then hesitated, calling, "Who is it?"

"Maggie? It's me. Hunter."

"Hunter?" Maggie's face lit up, and she hastily unlocked the door and yanked it open.

It was indeed her brother. He stood on the doorstep, his figure dark and vague in the faint light of the quarter moon, but Maggie would have recognized him anywhere, in any light.

"Hunter!" She launched herself at him, wrapping her arms around his neck. Tears filled her eyes and spilled down her cheeks. "Oh, Hunter! Hunter! You're home!"

He hugged her a little awkwardly until Maggie released him and stepped back, taking his hands and pulling him into the hallway with her. "Let me look at you. Come inside where I can see you better."

Hunter pulled off his hat. He was as handsome as ever, with those high, jutting cheekbones and piercing green eyes. His hair was black as night, and his skin was deeply tanned; he was long and lean and muscled. None of those things had changed in the past few years. But now there were lines around his mouth and at the edges of his eyes, and there was a coldness in his gaze, a hard, brittle quality that had not been in the Hunter Maggie had once known. She had nursed the hope that during the time he'd been away he would have lost some of the wariness he'd acquired during the War, but she could see that, if anything, it had only gotten worse, more deeply ingrained. Thanks to a Yankee prison and a faithless fiancée, evidently the devilish, laughing Hunter was gone forever.

"Come in, come. Ty, come and see your uncle! Here, let me take your coat."

Hunter shrugged off his baggy overcoat and handed it to her. Maggie's gaze flew to his hips, where a wide gun belt, complete with holster, revolver, and bullets, was strapped.

"Hunter!" she gasped.

"What?" He followed the direction of her eyes, and he chuckled. "Oh, this?" He touched the butt of the revolver. "Don't worry. I didn't come back to shoot anybody."

He looked out of place, even dangerous, there in her rustic hall, with his rough western clothes, his face dark with a day or two's growth of beard, a gun at his side. Suddenly he hardly seemed like her brother at all. She glanced over at Ty, who was staring at them, wide-eyed.

Hunter unbuckled the gun belt, hooking it over one of the prongs of the coat tree and setting his hat atop it. "Sorry. Didn't mean to scare you, Mags."

"What are you doing wearing a gun like that?"

He shrugged. "Things are different out west. You never know what you're going to run into." He looked at Maggie's shocked face and smiled faintly. "Don't worry, I haven't turned into a gunslinger."

"Gunslinger!" Maggie exclaimed. "What's that?"

"You know, a hired gun. A killer. They usually wear their holsters tied down, so they can draw faster."

"What kinds of places have you been living?" Maggie exclaimed. "I've never heard the likes of this. Hunter . . ."

"Come on, Maggie. It's not a bad place, just different from here. You get used to it."

"I don't know that I'd want to," she retorted tartly.

"Same ol' Mags," Hunter murmured, using the nickname only he and Will had ever dared call her. His face softened with affection as he gazed at her, and for the moment he looked like himself again. "I was afraid somebody might have taken the starch out of you."

"Never." Maggie smiled. "Oh, I'm sorry, Hunter. It's just—I guess I expect people to never change. You seem so different, it's almost scary."

Hunter looked rueful. "Sometimes it's even scary to *be* me."

"Oh, you." Maggie gave him a playful push. She

turned toward her son, who was still standing at the foot of the stairs, watching Hunter in awed silence. "Ty, come here and see your uncle."

"Hello, Ty." Hunter gravely extended his hand to the boy to shake. "It's been a few years. Do you remember me?"

Ty nodded. "Yes, sir."

Hunter arched his eyebrows at his sister. "My, my, Mags, you taught him some manners. Better than Ma was able to drum into me."

"Well, not all of us are so difficult to teach," Maggie retorted teasingly. "Are you hungry? I can throw some supper together."

"Are you joking? After a week on the road, do you think I'd turn down the offer of a home-cooked meal?"

"Good, then let's go into the kitchen."

"I'd better put my horse up first. That is, if you'll let me bunk here for the night."

"Of course!" Maggie's eyes flashed with indignation. "As if you even had to ask! You can sleep in—in Will's bed."

A sober look came over Hunter's face, and he said quietly, "Ma wrote me about Will. I'm sorry."

"I know."

"Are you doing all right?"

"I'm getting by. It's been hard," she admitted.

"Ah, Sis, things never seem to come out right, do they?" Hunter reached out and pulled her to him.

Maggie leaned her head against his chest. It was good to feel her brother's strength supporting her, to breathe in his masculine scent of leather, horses, and sweat. Somehow it made her want to cry.

She straightened up and gave him another little push. "Go on. I'll whip you up some supper."

While Hunter went to unsaddle his horse and take it to the barn, Maggie headed for the kitchen and poked the banked coals in the stove back to life. She added kindling and set a pot of beans to heat, sticking the remainder of their supper's cornbread into the oven. Ty brought in milk and butter from the springhouse, and Maggie pulled a jar of canned cherries out of the pantry for dessert. Before long she had a presentable supper on the table.

Hunter came in the back door and crossed to the washstand to clean up. His boots clumped heavily on the wooden floor, and his spurs jingled. Maggie worried what those lethal-looking spurs might do to her furniture, and she was relieved when Hunter took them off before he sat down at the table.

Hunter wolfed down the hastily thrown together meal like a starved man. Maggie sat across the table from him, sipping a cup of coffee. Ty helped himself to a second dessert.

"Ty!" Maggie exclaimed reprovingly, frowning at him.

"But, Ma . . ." His eyes were wide with innocence. "I've got to keep Uncle Hunter company, don't I?"

Hunter chuckled.

Maggie sent him a sharp glance. "Now, don't you encourage him." But she had to smile, too. "Well, as soon as you've finished that, you're going straight upstairs. It's past your bedtime."

"Ah, Ma . . ."

"I mean it."

Before long Maggie managed to hustle Ty off to bed. Then she returned and sat down at the table with Hunter again. For a moment they looked at each other. Then she asked, "Have you been out to the farm yet? Does Mama know you're here?"

Hunter shook his head. "No. It was so late, I was afraid to wake her. I'll go out to see her and Gideon tomorrow."

"Hunter . . ."

"What?"

"Are you home for good?"

He shrugged. "I don't know. I figured I'd try it for a

while. When Ma wrote me about Will, I reckoned you could use some help around the place. I thought I could stay here, maybe run a few horses. I'm not a farmer like Gideon, but I can raise horses. I brought a small string with me. Not many—just three mares and my stallion—but enough to start. I can buy some foals, breed the mares."

"That sounds perfect! There's lots of pasture on the place—we haven't farmed anything more than a vegetable garden the past few years."

"And Gideon would probably let me use the meadow that adjoins Will's—I mean, your—land." He paused. "But I don't know that I'll stay forever, Maggie. I—I'm not the same as I used to be. I can't seem to stay in one place long. Ever since that Yankee prison, I can't stand to be tied down."

"I know." She smiled sadly, tears in her eyes. "But I'm happy you're even considering it. I'm glad you'll be here for however long it is."

"Thanks." Hunter reached out and covered her hand with his. "You're the best, Mags. Whatever happens, I always know you're behind me."

"Of course. I'm your sister."

"Yeah, well, Gideon's my brother, and that never stopped him from arguing with me about every damn thing I did."

Maggie shrugged. "That's just his way, Hunter. You know he loves you. He just worries about us all."

"I know, I know. But I get a little tired of the way he shows it."

A comfortable silence stretched between them. Then Hunter said softly, "You been doing all right?"

Maggie swallowed. "Yes. I guess. It's been hard. I miss Will."

"Of course you do."

"He wasn't the same as when we'd married, but I still loved him. I know people mean well, but sometimes they'll say things like, 'It's better this way.' How could they think it's better that Will is dead? Do they really believe saying such a thing will make me feel any better?"

"Probably makes *them* feel better." Hunter paused, then asked quietly, "Do you believe in Heaven?"

Maggie stared at him. Hunter had never been one to talk much about religion. "Yes. But what a strange thing to ask. What are you getting at?"

"Well, maybe what people are trying to say to you is that it's better this way because Will will be happier in Heaven. You know I'm not one for church-going and all, but . . . well, maybe Will *is* someplace where he doesn't have to feel confused or lost, where nobody makes fun of him or calls him a dummy. What if he can be like himself again? Wouldn't that be better? Wouldn't it make you happy?"

"You're right," Maggie breathed. And for the first time in months, her heart felt a little lighter. "Will *would* be happier that way. You know, it was odd . . . for an instant, right before he died, Will was almost himself again. He had sacrificed himself to save Ty, been a true father, and there was something in his eyes —a pride, a satisfaction that was clearly adult. I think, in a strange way, he was happy." She frowned. "Maybe that's what I should have been thinking about—Will's finding peace and happiness at last, finding himself again—instead of about my sorrow, my loss. I guess I've been selfish."

"Not selfish. Normal. Natural. When you lose someone, that's what you think about—the pain you feel."

Maggie looked into her brother's eyes, and she saw there a weary sort of sadness that said he knew that kind of pain, had experienced it firsthand.

Her heart ached for him, yet for the first time, Maggie felt that here was someone who would understand her secret pain.

She had never felt free to tell her mother or Gideon or Tess about what had happened between her and Reid

Prescott. They were too good, too noble, and they expected the same of others. Hunter, however, was a different story. He had seen many things in his life, and his expectations of people were anything but lofty. He might better understand what it was like to love someone so much that it overcame all one's good sense and strength and virtue.

"That isn't all, though," she said softly.

"What do you mean?" Hunter looked at her, puzzled.

"I . . ." She hesitated. "Everyone always tells me how good I was to Will. I—I feel so guilty when they do."

Hunter cast her a disbelieving glance. "You weren't good to Will? Come on, Maggie. No one could have been more patient or—"

"I wasn't faithful to him!" Maggie blurted out.

Hunter stared at her, dumbstruck.

"I—I was with another man." She looked down at her hands, clenched together on the table, and took a deep breath. Then she proceeded to tell him about what had happened between her and Reid Prescott. Finally she ran down, and for a long moment, there was silence.

Then Hunter said quietly, "Oh, Maggie." He covered her hands with his. "I'm sorry. You must have been going through hell."

Maggie began to cry, tears running down her face, her shoulders shaking silently. Hunter went around the table and pulled her up from her chair, taking her into his arms and holding her.

"I betrayed him!" she sobbed. "I was unfaithful to him, and now he's dead! I can never make it up to him. I can never make it right."

Hunter rocked her a little, making soothing noises. "It's all right, Maggie. It's all right."

"How can it be? Oh, God, I feel so guilty! Nobody knows. They all think I was so good to him, but they just don't know!" She stepped back from his arms, wiping the tears from her cheeks.

"It doesn't matter what other people know. Or what they think, either. You were good to Will, and nothing you did changed that. You took care of him. You helped him. Lord, Maggie, he wouldn't even have been alive if it weren't for you. Don't you know that?"

"Yes, but it doesn't make up for what I did!"

"I don't know that there's anybody keeping score. Your life happened the way it happened. It wasn't fair; it wasn't right what happened to Will. It wasn't right that you had to bear that kind of burden all those years. But it happened, and you did your best. So what if you were weak for once? So what if you gave in to a normal human impulse? You think that's the worst thing that could happen?"

"N-no . . ."

"You could have been cruel to Will, Maggie. You could have ignored him. You could have wept and moaned that he was such a terrible burden. But you didn't. You were kind and loving to him. Nothing can change that. And Will didn't know about Prescott. He wasn't hurt by what you did."

"And that excuses it?" Maggie asked scornfully.

"I reckon a preacher wouldn't say so, but, hell, I don't know, it seems to me you had a pretty good reason for doing what you did. It didn't make you a wicked person. And it sure as hell didn't kill Will!"

"I know that. It's just that . . ."

"You figure you ought to be perfect."

"I never said that."

"You don't have to. I know you. You have to be the best, the strongest, the bravest. You've always been that way. You never knew when to quit. And you never could tolerate making a mistake."

"Oh, you make me sound like a prig."

Hunter chuckled. "Well, you're not. You're the best and strongest woman I know—besides Ma, of course.

But you're human. You're allowed to make mistakes, just like the rest of us. You think God wouldn't forgive you because you slipped?"

"No. You're right."

"Then forgive yourself, too, Mags."

She looked up at him. Then she smiled tentatively and stepped forward to hug him. "Oh, Hunter, you are the best brother a girl ever had!"

Hunter smiled and gave her a squeeze. "Of course I am, and don't you ever forget it."

"I won't." She released him, smiling. "I'm so glad you came back."

"Me, too."

"Come on, I'll show you to your room. I reckon you're pretty tired."

"Yeah. I started out early this morning."

Hunter picked up the saddlebags he had brought in and slung them over his shoulder, then followed Maggie up the stairs. She pointed toward Ty's door and handed him the candle.

"Good night," she said softly and started toward her room.

"Maggie . . ."

She turned.

"Uh . . . do you ever see Linette?"

"Yes. I mean, I see her in the mercantile and such, but I haven't had any conversation with her. She and I don't exactly travel in the same circle anymore."

"How is she?" Hunter looked down at the floor with great interest.

"Still beautiful."

He nodded, his mouth twisting into a bitter line. "She would be. If the only thing you care for is yourself, I guess it's easy to stay young and beautiful."

Maggie's heart ached for her brother. It was obvious he still hadn't gotten Linette out of his mind. And whether he loved her or hated her, how could he ever hope to find another woman, a better woman, when he was still caught up in the one who had betrayed him?

"Oh, Hunter . . ." Maggie took a step toward him, wishing she could help him as he had helped her.

"Don't. I'm fine." And he moved away, avoiding her sympathy, his face devoid of emotion, his eyes like marble.

Gideon had just returned with his mother from the sunrise service at the small community church at the crossroads when he heard the sound of hooves. Curious, he stepped out of the barn, where he had been stabling the mules, and looked down the road.

The morning sun backlit the approaching rider, and it took Gideon a moment to recognize him. His jaw dropped in astonishment, and he let out a whoop and began to run toward the house.

"Ma!" he yelled. "Ma, get out here!"

His mother's excited face appeared at the kitchen window. "What is it?"

"It's Hunter! Hunter's coming!"

"Lord have mercy!" Jo disappeared from the window as she raced for the door.

Gideon loped across the yard to the front of the house.

Hunter reined his horse to a stop and dismounted, a grin splitting his face. "Gideon!"

"Hunter!"

For an instant, they stood awkwardly grinning at each other. Then they both stepped forward into a manly hug, clapping each other on the back.

Jo, for all her years, flew out the front door and down the steps. "Hunter! Hunter!" Her arms were outstretched, and tears streamed down her cheeks.

Hunter pulled away from Gideon and turned, catching her up in his arms and holding her close. "Ma." He closed his eyes, and Gideon saw him swallow hard.

Gideon himself had to turn away and wipe his eyes
with the palm of his hand.

Jo stepped back, her hands still on his arms, and
gazed up searchingly into Hunter's face. "Oh, Hunter,
you're so thin. Don't they feed you out there?"

Hunter's smile was gleaming white against skin
browned by the hot western sun. "Not like you do,
Ma."

"I'll wager that's the truth," Jo replied emphatically,
and she hugged him again. "I can't believe you've finally come home."

"Well, when you wrote me about Will, I figured I
had to."

"You're right." Jo gave him an earnest look. "Maggie needs you right now. She needs all of us, but maybe
you most of all." She smiled and linked one arm
through Hunter's and the other through Gideon's. "It'll
be so good to have all my children home again."

Except Shelby, Gideon thought sadly, *who will never
be coming home.* But he didn't say it out loud. Let his
mother have her happiness.

"Have you seen Maggie?" Jo asked Hunter as they
walked inside.

"Yes. I stayed there last night. She's gone to church,
but she said to tell you that she and Tess'll be out later."

"You, I take it, didn't feel the need of church?" Jo
asked, giving him a stern look.

Hunter, who once would have responded with a
charming smile and a witty remark to turn aside her
disapproval, simply said, "No, I didn't, Ma. I reckon
church doesn't have much need of me, either."

"Now, that's where you're wrong." Jo waved
toward the sitting room. "You men go sit down and
visit. I have to see to my potatoes or they'll burn. And
I can't have that for your homecoming meal, now can
I?"

The brothers walked into the sitting room, and

Hunter glanced around. "Well, doesn't look like much has changed."

Gideon shrugged. Suddenly he couldn't think of anything to say. Now that the initial excitement of Hunter's arrival was past, he realized that his brother was almost a stranger to him. He shoved his hands into his pockets and shifted uncomfortably. "Well," he ventured finally, "you staying this time?"

"For a while."

"Ma assumes you're home to stay."

"I never said that." Hunter looked at him. "It's what she wants to think."

"I should have known." Gideon sighed and sat down in the rocker.

Hunter raised an eyebrow. "What's that supposed to mean?"

"Nothing. I shouldn't have gotten my hopes up. But for a while there I thought maybe you'd acquired a little bit of responsibility while you were out west."

"No need for me to," Hunter shot back. "You've got enough for all the rest of us put together."

"Damn it, Hunter, you're a grown man now." Gideon stood. "You have a mother and sister who could both use some help. And there's this farm. I can't handle it all myself. I had to let almost half the land lie fallow this year because I didn't have the time to cultivate it."

"I'm not a farmer, Gideon," Hunter said implacably. "You should know that better than anybody else— you've told me enough times."

"I did not tell you you weren't a farmer. I said you could *be* a damned good one if—"

" 'If only you'd try,' " Hunter chorused along with Gideon.

The two brothers glared at each other. Then Hunter stepped away, shaking his head. "Ah, hell, Gideon, we've been together maybe five minutes, and here we are, already arguing. I don't know why you'd even want me to stay. We never agree on anything."

"That's not true."

Hunter looked at Gideon speakingly, and they both began to chuckle.

"All right," Gideon said, "I'll admit we don't often see eye to eye." He looked at Hunter wryly. "You're my brother, and I love you, but nobody could ever get my goat the way you could. Shel used to make me mad sometimes, but you—you were the master at it. Remember the time you had Maggie waylay me downstairs with some sad story while you put frogs in my bed?"

A grin flashed across Hunter's face. "How could I forget? I thought you were going to chase me clean out of the county."

"I probably would have if I hadn't thought Ma would kill me for it."

Both men fell silent. Hunter crossed to the window and stood looking out. Gideon sat back down, watching him, wondering what drove his brother, what made him tick. Hunter had never been much like him. He'd been more like Shelby, but with an added passion for devilment. Despairing of Hunter's careless ways, Gideon had tried to bring him to order, but Hunter had merely resented his attempts. Yet, despite it all, they loved each other with a deep, unspoken devotion, their ties strong and sure in a way neither ever questioned.

"Sometimes," Hunter mused in a low voice, "I miss this place. I remember how it looks, how it smells, how the air feels in the morning when you get up. I've thought about coming back to stay, living at Maggie's place and raising horses. I'm just not sure I can."

"Horses? Really?"

"You know how I've always liked them. I'm good with them, Gid, not like I am with farming."

Gideon looked at him consideringly. "Sounds like a good idea. Hell, Hunter, I don't want to make you farm the rest of your life if you hate it. Surely you know that. I just want you here with us. I want you to be . . . content."

Hunter made a face. "I'm not sure I'll ever be that."

"You want to use the pasture by Will's land? You're welcome to it—you know that. This land is as much yours as mine."

"Thanks. Maybe I will if my spread gets big enough. I only brought a small string of mares with me. I'll have to build better corrals at Maggie's."

Gideon nodded. "You know I'll help you."

"I know."

Gideon hesitated. "I think you could be happy here. I hope you'll give it a chance."

"I don't like being tied down . . ."

"Tied down? Or in the same place as Linette Conway?"

Hunter scowled. "That's all in the past."

"Is it? I'm not sure. Everybody says she's the reason you stay away."

Hunter's eyes flashed. "I'd never run away from a woman."

"I know you're no coward, Hunter. But women can make a man do strange things."

Hunter shrugged, his face hard, his mouth a thin, bitter line. "Linette's nothing to me."

"I'm glad." Gideon didn't add that he didn't believe him. Whatever Hunter felt for Linette Conway, it certainly wasn't indifference.

There was a moment of awkward silence before Hunter forced a smile onto his face and said, "Speaking of women making a man do strange things, Maggie tells me you're finally getting married."

"Yes. In two weeks." A wide grin split Gideon's face. "I can hardly believe it."

"I figured you were a confirmed bachelor."

Gideon shrugged. "I reckon Tess could change any confirmed bachelor's mind."

With studied casualness, Hunter asked, "What was it that happened with her and Benton Conway? Maggie wasn't real explicit about it."

"She told you about that? She knew?" Gideon's eyebrows went up in surprise. "Tess told her?"

Hunter looked puzzled. "I guess so."

"Well, it's true, Benton tried to—" Gideon stopped, his eyes darkening with remembered anger. "Tried to force himself on her. I—"

"What?" Hunter stared. "Maggie didn't say anything about that. She was talking about Benton trying to take Tess's house away or something. And that Linette came up with some idea to save it."

"Oh." Gideon looked guilty. "Oh, Lord, I guess that what Conway did has been so much on my mind, I just figured that was what you were talking about. I should have known Tess wouldn't have told anyone. She's too private." He looked away, decidedly uncomfortable.

"I won't say anything about it," Hunter promised. "To Maggie or anybody."

"Thanks. Tess wouldn't want it known." He sighed. "That's one reason I can't do anything about Conway. But it makes me sick to let him get away with hitting her and—"

"He hit her?" Hunter exploded, his eyes flashing with outraged Tyrrell pride.

Gideon doubled his fists. "He was trying to rape her. She fought him. I wanted to kill the bastard, but Tess was afraid that if I did anything to him, everyone would speculate about why. There'd be gossip about how far things had gone between them. And she was scared that if I even threatened him again, he'd get his cronies in the government to have me thrown into jail."

"It wouldn't surprise me."

"She was so upset, I gave in and promised not to go near him." He shook his head regretfully.

Hunter's eyebrows quirked up, and he grinned wickedly. "That may be, big brother. But *I* didn't make any promise, now did I?"

Gideon looked up at him, surprised. Then his features, too, eased into a grin. "Why, that's right, Hunter. You certainly didn't."

20

It was late at night when Hunter left Maggie's farm and rode into town. He wore his gun belt strapped to his hips and a knife scabbard tucked beneath it.

Maggie had seen him before he stepped out the front door, and her eyes had widened in alarm.

"Hunter! What are you doing?"

"I didn't realize you were still up," he'd said.

"Were you sneaking out?"

"Mags, I'm not Ty, you know. I don't have to sneak out to leave."

"But why are you wearing that?" Her eyes had slipped down to the holster.

"I always like to be safe when I'm riding into a strange town."

"Pine Creek?" she asked incredulously. "You've lived here all your life!"

"It's strange to me now." He winked at her. "Trust me, Maggie, I haven't any plans to shoot anyone."

"Where in town are you going?"

He sighed. "If you must know, I'm paying Benton Conway a visit."

"Hunter! No! Why?"

His smile was thin and anything but pleasant. "I'm just going to have a little talk with the man."

"About what?"

"My family. His manners."

"Hunter . . ."

"Don't worry so—you'll get frown lines."

"Will you stop joking? How can I help but worry when you're going to Benton Conway's house with a gun? I have no idea whether you'll be in Ty's room tomorrow morning or in jail!"

"I'll be right here. You can count on it." He reached out and tapped her lightly on the nose. "Now just go to bed and forget about it, all right?"

"That will be impossible," Maggie muttered grumpily.

Hunter had smiled and walked out the door.

Now he was nearing his destination. When he reached the Conway mansion, he tied his horse, then quietly slipped through the front gate and across the yard to the house. The place was dark except for a light in one upstairs window and another in a corner room on the ground floor.

Hunter quietly mounted the front steps onto the wraparound porch and made his way to the lit corner window. A faint smile touched his lips when he saw Benton Conway at his desk bent over a ledger.

The long windows were closed but not locked, and Hunter simply opened one and stepped into the room. "Hello, Conway."

Benton dropped his pen, startled, and swung around to see who had spoken. He went pale when he saw Hunter Tyrrell standing in the room. His mouth opened, but nothing came out.

"If I were you, I'd be a mite more careful about leaving my windows unlocked like that. There's no telling who might sneak in that way. And a man like you must have plenty of enemies, I'd reckon."

"What the devil are you doing here?" Benton snapped, recovering his voice and some of his color. His eyes slid toward a drawer in his desk.

"If you've got a gun in there, forget it." Hunter's voice was cool and emotionless. "I could draw and shoot you three times over before you got it out. That's one place where I've got the advantage over you, Conway: while you've been back here cheating folks out of their money the last few years, I've learned a few things about killing."

"Don't be absurd," Benton responded, leaning back in his chair. "Why would I try to shoot you? I have nothing against you. The winner doesn't hold anything against the loser, isn't that right?"

One corner of Hunter's mouth curled up. "If you call marrying Linette winning. Personally, I reckon you saved me a lot of misery."

Conway smiled derisively. "I'm not stupid, Tyrrell. All of Pine Creek knows you ran away because you couldn't bear to live in the same town with her. Hardly the picture of a man who didn't care."

"I did care. Once. Linette's a beautiful woman. But, of course, you already know that. Why else would you have been so hot to marry her? But that was all a long time ago, Conway."

"And you're trying to tell me she's not in your blood anymore?"

"Not in my blood or my mind or anywhere else."

"You're lying."

Hunter shrugged. "Believe what you want." He walked around Benton's desk and leaned his hips against it, his legs stretched out in front of him. He was less than a foot away from Conway, and his nearness emphasized the contrast between the two men. Where Benton was soft and pale, fleshy from years of living off the fat of the land, Hunter was whipcord lean and wiry, browned by the sun, toughened by the elements. In his western clothes and with a gun on his hip, he looked fierce and out of place in a rich man's study.

"You know, though," he said softly, gazing unswervingly into Conway's eyes, "I reckon a woman like Linette must be getting pretty tired of being married to a slug like you. I don't imagine it'd take much to persuade her to try another man's bed. She always was hot-blooded," he said with a knowing, taunting smile. "What do you think, Conway? Is Linette satisfied in your bed? Or you think she misses those evenings she and I used to spend down by the creek?"

"What the hell do you want?" the man growled.

"I'm just wondering what you'd look like wearing horns."

"Damn you! You stay away from my wife!" Benton's face was suffused with blood, and he jumped to his feet.

"Oh, I will, Conway. I will. As long as you stay away from Tess."

"What?"

"I heard about what happened in the garden behind the Caldwell house. Now personally, I was all for Gideon and me paying you a little visit, just to show you the error of your ways." He paused, then went on conversationally, "You know, once at a ranch where I was working, one of the hands made the mistake of raping the rancher's daughter. That rancher tied him buck naked to the corral fence and laid him open with a bullwhip. Then he left him for the flies to feast on for a couple of days. I thought that might be a good lesson for you."

Benton paled, and he sank back into his seat. "I—I didn't rape Tess."

"Only because Gideon came along and stopped you. Anyway, you're in luck, because Gideon didn't like my idea. He figured it would start a lot of gossip about Mrs. Tyrrell. So I told him I'd hold off." Hunter paused, and his eyes bored into Conway's. "For now.

But you try anything like that again, and I'll come looking for you. And, I promise you, I'll find you."

"I have friends in the government. You so much as touch me, and I'll have them down on your head in a minute."

"You won't have anybody down on anybody's head if you're dead." Benton's eyes widened, and Hunter let out a mirthless chuckle. "That's right. You have to remember, Conway, that I'm not anything like my big brother. Gideon's an honorable man. He's the kind who'd call you out, then beat you to a pulp fair and square. But me . . . now I'd just sneak in here some night like I just did, and I'd slit you open, belly to gullet."

He slid the bowie knife from its sheath and held it up to the light. "Nice, isn't it? I bought it in Texas. A real popular item there—quieter than a gun."

Benton's face was white, and sweat popped out on his brow, but he blustered to cover his fear. "If you killed me, they'd have you down at the jail within hours, and they'd hang you."

Hunter shook his head sympathetically. "There you go again, Benton, making the mistake of thinking that I'm like the other Tyrrells. That I'd somehow be loyal to this place. But the fact is, I wouldn't stick around Pine Creek long enough for your friends to hunt me down. I'd cut you and I'd be gone, and nobody'd ever find me."

He grinned. "Don't you get it? I wouldn't lose a minute's sleep over sending you to your Maker, and I'm used to living on the run. So there's absolutely nothing to stop me. See? You remember that the next time you get to thinking about putting your hands on Mrs. Tyrrell or about hurting anybody else in my family."

He sauntered to the door and opened it, turning back to look at Benton. "You have a nice night, now."

Hunter closed the door behind him. He walked down the hall toward the front door, heedless now about the noise his bootheels made on the wooden floor.

He heard a sharp gasp and whirled around. The light in the entryway was dim, a single candle burning in a torchiere on the wall, and it took him a moment to discern the figure standing halfway down the stairway.

Her hand was on the railing. Her satin bedrobe hung open, revealing a swath of white nightgown decorated with delicate pink ribbons. Her auburn hair tumbled loosely down her shoulders. Her features were not clear in the feeble light, but Hunter knew them well enough to imagine them exactly: the wide, honey-sweet mouth, the huge, vibrant blue eyes, the perfect complexion and delicate nose and chin.

"Hello, Linette."

"Hunter!" Her voice was barely above a whisper. "What—what are you doing here?"

"I've come back to Pine Creek to live," he said blandly.

"Oh." Linette's eyes were huge in the dim light.

"I was just discussing a few things with your husband."

Linette stared at him. They both knew Benton Conway was the last person Hunter would choose to have a chat with. For a moment they stood looking at each other, neither saying anything. Then Hunter started toward the door.

Before exiting, he turned and looked back up at her. "Tell me something, Linette. Was it worth it?" he asked. "Does money make up for having that lecher's slimy hands on you?"

Linette paled, but she faced him squarely. "Given the same choice, I'd do it again."

Hunter's eyes glittered, but he said nothing, just whirled and walked out the door, slamming it behind him. He strode down the front steps and across the lawn to his horse. Untethering it, he leaped onto its back and dug in his heels. The animal leaped forward, thundering down the street.

Tess's and Gideon's wedding was small and quiet, held at the Caldwell house with only family present. Hunter and Maggie stood up with the couple.

Maggie thought that she had never seen a bride as radiant as Tess, and her heart filled with warmth and hope for the couple. If ever anybody deserved to be happy, it was Tess and Gideon.

Still, looking at them, she couldn't keep from feeling a touch of envy. She couldn't help thinking about it being she standing in front of the preacher, with her hand in Reid's as they pledged their lives and love to each other. She had thought many times about writing to Reid, but still she had held back. Surely Ty had told him about Will's death, and if Reid had wanted to come to her, he would have. Perhaps away from her, he had discovered that he didn't truly love her.

But now, gazing at Tess and Gideon, she chided herself. What if Ty hadn't told Reid? Or if Reid had decided that if she wanted him back, she would have written him? Was she going to let chance keep her from seeking the sort of happiness Tess and Gideon had found?

She had hesitated because of guilt, guilt for breaking her marriage vows, for betraying Will. She had been afraid that her love was wicked and wrong, that her apt punishment for loving Reid was to be separated from him forever.

But, now, looking at Tess's glowing face, she knew that love could never be a sin. What she and Reid had *done* had been a sin, perhaps, but not the emotion behind it. Love was the one true, good thing in life; it was what gave sense to everything else, what gave one hope to go forward.

This very evening she would go home and write Reid

a letter, she decided. She would tell him that Will had died, and she would tell him how she felt, how much she missed him. And then, despite the risk to her pride, she would ask him to come to her.

Maggie looked down as the minister began a prayer for the new couple. When it was over and the preacher was instructing a beaming Gideon to kiss the bride, Maggie's gaze was drawn by a movement in the door-way into the hall.

Her heart seemed to stop. A man was standing there. For a moment she thought she was seeing things, that she had conjured him up out of her very thoughts. But no, there was Reid Prescott, in the flesh, his hat in his hand, his eyes looking straight at her, his features stamped with a strange blend of uncertainty and hope.

"Reid . . ." Maggie breathed. "Reid!" Forgetting all else—her family, the preacher, the new bride and groom—she dropped the flowers she was holding and ran across the room to him.

"Maggie!" He met her halfway, opening his arms to her. She fairly leapt at him, throwing herself into his embrace.

Everyone in the room turned to stare at them in amazement, but for Maggie and Reid nothing and no one existed but each other. They held each other tightly, and Reid rained kisses over Maggie's hair and face, murmuring her name over and over.

"I love you. Oh, Maggie, I've missed you so much."

Maggie could do nothing but laugh and cry, her face as bright as if the sun itself lived within her. Finally they came back to the world enough to realize that they were standing in the middle of a wedding, the cynosure of every eye in the place.

Shakily Maggie stepped back, and Reid reluctantly let her go. Unable to completely separate, they clasped hands and glanced around sheepishly.

"I'm sorry, I'm sorry," Maggie said to the newly-weds, wiping at her tear-stained cheeks. Tess simply smiled and blew her a kiss. Ty strode up to them to give Reid a hearty handshake, then suggested, man to man, "why don't you get her out of her, Reid. I'll see you later, back at the house."

As Maggie glanced around in awe at the startled but smiling faces of her family, Reid swept her outside without another word to anyone. And their hands still clasped, they started walking toward home.

Maggie couldn't stop staring at Reid. She thought she would never get enough of looking at him. Nor was she used to seeing him like this, dressed in a starched white shirt and formal jacket, cufflinks glinting at his wrists. The attire suited him, she thought, perhaps more than the work clothes she had seen him wear before.

"You are even more beautiful than I remembered," he said in a low voice. "I want to kiss you."

Maggie's knees felt weak. "I won't stop you," she said seriously.

He pulled her to a stop and took her into his arms, giving her a long, thorough, dizzying kiss. When at long last he raised his head, Maggie leaned against him, feeling as if her knees had turned to wax.

"Oh, Reid," she murmured. "How did you know? Why did you come back?"

"Ty wrote and told me about Will. I wanted to come to you immediately; I knew that you must be in pain. But I thought you might need some time to yourself, without me here pushing you. And there were a few things I had to clear up." He paused. "I'm sorry about Will."

Maggie nodded, tears in her eyes. "I miss him."

"I've missed him, too."

They joined hands and began strolling again.

"I started practicing medicine again," Reid said after a while.

"Really?" Maggie's eyes lit up. "Oh, Reid, that's wonderful."

He smiled. "I suspected you'd think so. When I got

to my house in Savannah, I wasn't really sure what I was going to do. I began looking through all my old medical books, first to find information about head injuries."

Maggie looked at him, surprised. "Like Will's?"

"Yes. All the time I was here, I kept wishing I knew more, wondering if there was anything that could be done to help him." He shook his head, remembering. "Anyway, once I started reading, I found myself getting more and more involved. And after a while, I thought, What am I doing sitting around being useless? So I opened my office again." He looked down at her and smiled ruefully. "You were right, of course. Whatever mistakes I'd made, that's where I belong. It's what I should be doing. What I want to do."

"Then you're going to go back there?" Fear coiled in Maggie's stomach.

"No. I sold my house and office in Savannah. That was another reason for my delay in getting back here."

"Back here?" Maggie echoed, her heart skittering madly in her chest.

"Yes. I'm planning to set up practice in Pine Creek. I thought the community might welcome a doctor."

"You're going to live here?" Her question came out a squeak.

"Yes, of course. Where else would I live except where you are?" He stopped again and looked down at her intently. "I want to marry you, Maggie. The last few months without you have been hell for me. I've wanted you so badly I thought I'd die from it. I can't tell you how many times I wrote to you and tore up every letter. Nothing I put down could even begin to express how I felt about you. I knew I shouldn't hold on to you; I knew I should let go of you and let you get on with your life. But I couldn't. And *I* can't have a life without you. Marry me, Maggie. Please say you'll marry me."

"Oh, Reid." Maggie gazed at him, tears welling in her eyes. "I love you so much."

"Then say you'll marry me. Tell me we're going to be together for the rest of our lives."

"Yes. Oh, yes, I'll marry you! Anywhere, anytime. I love you."

He took her hand and started them forward again. "Then let's go home, Maggie," he said.

"Yes," she replied, smiling, the love she felt for him shining out of her eyes. "Let's go home."

RAIN LILY by Candace Camp

Maggie Whitcomb's life changed when her shell-shocked husband returned from the Civil War. She nursed him back to physical health, but his mind was shattered. Maggie's marriage vows were forever, but then she met Reid Prescott, a drifter who took refuge on her farm and captured her heart. A heartwarming story of impossible love from bestselling author Candace Camp.

CASTLES IN THE AIR by Christina Dodd

The long-awaited, powerful sequel to the award-winning *Candle in the Window*. Lady Juliana of Moncestus swore that she would never again be forced under a man's power. So when the king promised her in marriage to Raymond of Avrache, Juliana was determined to resist. But had she met her match?

RAVEN IN AMBER by Patricia Simpson

A haunting contemporary love story by the author of *Whisper of Midnight*. Camille Avery arrives at the Nakalt Indian Reservation to visit a friend, only to find her missing. With the aid of handsome Kit Makinna, Camille becomes immersed in Nakalt life and discovers the shocking secret behind her friend's disappearance.

RETURNING by Susan Bowden

A provocative story of love and lies. From the Bohemian '60s to the staid '90s, *Returning* is an emotional roller-coaster ride of a story about a woman whose past comes back to haunt her when she must confront the daughter she gave up for adoption.

JOURNEY HOME by Susan Kay Law

Winner of the 1992 Golden Heart Award. Feisty Jessamyn Johnston was the only woman on the 1853 California wagon train who didn't respond to the charms of Tony Winchester. But as they battled the dangers of their journey, they learned how to trust each other and how to love.

KENTUCKY THUNDER by Clara Wimberly

Amidst the tumult of the Civil War and the rigid confines of a Shaker village, a Southern belle fought her own battle against a dashing Yankee —and against herself as she fell in love with him.

COMING NEXT MONTH

COMING UP ROSES by Catherine Anderson
From the bestselling author of the Comanche trilogy, comes a sensual historical romance. When Zach McGovern was injured in rescuing her daughter from an abandoned well, Kate Blakely nursed him back to health. Kate feared men, but Zach was different, and only buried secrets could prevent their future from coming up roses.

HOMEBODY by Louise Titchener
Bestselling author Louise Titchener pens a romantic thriller about a young woman who must battle the demons of her past, as well as the dangers she finds in her new apartment.

BAND OF GOLD by Zita Christian
The rush for gold in turn-of-the-century Alaska was nothing compared to the rush Aurelia Breighton felt when she met the man of her dreams. But then Aurelia discovered that it was not her he was after but her missing sister.

DANCING IN THE DARK by Susan P. Teklits
A tender and touching tale of two people who were thrown together by treachery and found unexpected love. A historical romance in the tradition of Constance O'Banyon.

CHANCE McCALL by Sharon Sala
Chance McCall knows that he has no right to love Jenny Tyler, the boss's daughter. With only his monthly paycheck and checkered past, he's no good for her, even though she thinks otherwise. But when an accident leaves Chance with no memory, he has no choice but to return to his past and find out why he dare not claim the woman he loves.

SWEET REVENGE by Jean Stribling
There was nothing better than sweet revenge when ex-Union captain Adam McCormick unexpectedly captured his enemy's stepdaughter, Letitia Ramsey. But when Adam found himself falling in love with her, he had to decide if revenge is worth the sacrifice of love.

HIGHLAND LOVE SONG by Constance O'Banyon
Available in trade paperback! From the bestselling author of *Forever My Love*, a sweeping and mesmerizing story continues the DeWinter legacy begun in *Song of the Nightingale*.

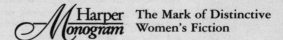

Harper Monogram — The Mark of Distinctive Women's Fiction

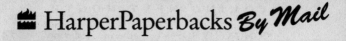

YESTERDAY'S SHADOWS
by Marianne Willman

Bettany Howard was a young orphan traveling west searching for the father who left her years ago. Wolf Star was a Cheyenne brave who longed to know who abandoned him—a white child with a jeweled talisman. Fate decreed they'd meet and try to seize the passion promised. 0-06-104044-4

MIDNIGHT ROSE by Patricia Hagan

From the rolling plantations of Richmond to the underground slave movement of Philadelphia, Erin Sterling and Ryan Youngblood would pursue their wild, breathless passion and finally surrender to the promise of a bold and unexpected love. 0-06-104023-1

WINTER TAPESTRY
by Kathy Lynn Emerson

Cordell vows to revenge the murder of her father. Roger Allington is honor bound to protect his friend's daughter but has no liking for her reckless ways. Yet his heart tells him he must pursue this beauty through a maze of plots to win her love and ignite their smoldering passion. 0-06-100220-8

ANALISE

Analise Caldwell was the reigning belle of New Orleans. Disguised as a Confederate soldier, Union major Mark Schaeffer captured the Rebel beauty's heart as part of his mission. Stunned by his deception, Analise swore never to yield to the caresses of this Yankee spy...until he delivered an ultimatum.

ROSEWOOD

Millicent Hayes had lived all her life amid the lush woodland of Emmetsville, Texas. Bound by her duty to her crippled brother, the dark-haired innocent had never known desire...until a handsome stranger moved in next door.

BONDS OF LOVE

Katherine Devereaux was a willful, defiant beauty who had yet to meet her match in any man—until the winds of war swept the Union innocent into the arms of Confederate Captain Matthew Hampton.

LIGHT AND SHADOW

The day nobleman Jason Somerville broke into her rooms and swept her away to his ancestral estate, Carolyn Mabry began living a dangerous charade. Posing as her twin sister, Jason's wife, Carolyn thought she was helping her gentle twin. Instead she found herself drawn to the man she had so seductively deceived.

CRYSTAL HEART

A seductive beauty, Lady Lettice Kenton swore never to give her heart to any man—until she met the rugged American rebel Charles Murdock. Together on a ship bound for America, they shared a perfect passion, but danger awaited them on the shores of Boston Harbor.

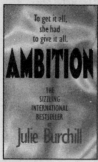